I have edited Clive Gilson's books for over a decade now – he's prolific and can turn his hand to many genres. poetry, short fiction, contemporary novels, folklore, and science fiction – and the common theme is that none of them ever fails to take my breath away. There's something in each story that is either memorably poignant, hauntingly unnerving, or sidesplittingly funny.

Lorna Howarth, *The Write Factor*

Tales From The World's Firesides is a grand project. I've collected "000's of traditional texts as part of other projects, and while many of the original texts are available through channels like Project Gutenberg, some of the narratives can be hard to read by modern readers, & so the Fireside project was born. Put simply, I collect, collate & adapt traditional tales from around the world & publish them as a modern archive. *Part 6* covers a selection of tales from the lands that border the Western Pacific shore and its hinterlands. I'm not laying any claim to insight or specialist knowledge, but these collections are born out of my love of storytelling & I hope that you'll share my affection for traditional tales, myths & legends.

Interior image: Clker-Free-Vector-Images from Pixabay

Cover image by Vilius Kukanauskas from Pixabay

Tales Of The Gùshì Yuán

Traditional tales, fables and sagas from the Chinese tradition.

Compiled, Adapted & Edited by Clive Gilson

Tales from the World's Firesides

Book 1 in Part 6 of the series: The Far East

Tales Of The Gùshì Yuán, edited by Clive Gilson,

Solitude, Bath, UK

www.clivegilson.com

First print edition © 2024, Clive Gilson

All rights reserved. No portion of this book may be reproduced in any form without permission from the publisher, except as permitted by United Kingdom copyright law.

This is a work of fiction. Names, characters, places, and incidents either are the products of the author's imagination or are used fictitiously. Any resemblance to actual persons, living or dead, businesses, companies, events, or locales is entirely coincidental.

Printed by IngramSpark

ISBN: 978-1-915081-06-3

CONTENTS

Preface

The Princess Kwan-Yin

Dschang Liang

The Animals' Peace Party

The Golden Beetle Or Why The Dog Hates The Cat

The Widow Ho

The Bird With Nine Heads

Yang Oerlang

Notscha

The Story Of The Bird Feng

The Lady Of The Moon

The Great Bell

Old Dragonbeard

A Legend Of Confucius

The Beautiful Daughter Of Liu-Kung

Laotsze

The Strange Tale Of Doctor Dog

Kwang-Jui And The God Of The River

The Disowned Princess

Bamboo And The Turtle

The Hen and the Chinese Mountain Turtle

The Eight Immortals

The Story Of Hok Lee And The Dwarfs

The Dragon After His Winter Sleep

In Union Is Strength

The Mysterious Buddhist Robe

The Spirits Of The Yellow River

The Proud Fox and the Crab

The Flower-Elves

The Mad Goose And The Tiger Forest

The Kingdom Of The Ogres

The Nodding Tiger

Yang Gui Fe

The God Of The City – Part 1

The God Of The City – Part 2

The Phantom Vessel

Rose Of Evening

The Mule and the Lion

The Herd Boy And The Weaving Maiden

The Tragedy Of The Yin Family

Lu-San, Daughter Of Heaven

Sam-Chung And The Water Demon

The Proud Chicken

Historical Notes

About The Editor

Preface

I've been collecting and telling stories for a couple of decades now, having had several of my own fictional works published in recent years. My particular focus is on short story writing in the realms of magical realities and science fiction fantasies.

I've always drawn heavily on traditional folk and fairy tales, and in so doing have amassed a digital collection of many thousands of these tales from around the world. It has been one of my long-standing ambitions to gather these stories together and to create a library of tales that tell the stories of places and peoples from all corners of our world.

One of the main motivations for me in undertaking the project is to collect and tell stories that otherwise might be lost or, at best, be forgotten by predominantly English-speaking readers. Given that a lot of my sources are from early collectors, particularly covering works produced in the late eighteenth century, throughout the nineteenth century, and in the early years of the twentieth century, I do make every effort to adapt stories for a modern reader. Early collectors had a different world view to many of us today, and often expressed views about race and gender, for example, that we find difficult to reconcile in the early years of the twenty-first century. I try, although with varying degrees of success, to update these stories with sensitivity while trying to stay as true to the original spirit of each story as I can.

I also want to assure readers that I try not to comment on or appropriate originating cultures. It is almost certainly true that the early collectors of these tales, with their then world views, made assumptions about the originating cultures that have given us these tales. I hope that you'll accept my mission to preserve these tales, however and wherever I find them, as just that. I have, therefore, made sure that every story has a full attribution, covering both the original collector / writer and the collection title that this version has been adapted from, as well as having notes about publishers and other relevant and, I hope, interesting source data. Wherever possible I have added a cultural or indigenous attribution as well, although for some of the titles, the country-based theme is obvious.

This volume, *Tales Told By The Gùshì Yuán*, is the first in a set of collections covering indigenous tales from what we in Europe know now as The Far East. These tales cover a wide range of sources and tales emerging from the wider Chinese diaspora. Many of these tales hark back to older times, well before the significant changes that have taken place in China during the twentieth and twenty-first centuries, but they do, I believe, still hold relevance as a channel through which we can glimpse the cultural splendour of peoples and cultures with a such a distinct and long history.

In Chinese mythology, the character associated with storytelling is often depicted as the "Sage of Stories," who is known as *Shuō Hào* in Mandarin Chinese. The Sage of Stories is often portrayed as a wise and elderly figure who possesses vast knowledge of history, folklore, and legends. He is revered for his ability to captivate audiences with his storytelling skills, imparting wisdom and moral lessons through his tales. While not as prominent as some other mythological figures, the Sage of Stories plays a significant role in Chinese folklore and cultural traditions, symbolizing the importance of oral tradition and storytelling in Chinese society.

The term used in this book's title is *The Gùshì Yuán* (故事圓). This is often referred to as the "Story Circle" or "Circle of Stories," and is a traditional form of Chinese narrative art. It involves storytelling that combines spoken word, performance, and sometimes music to entertain and educate audiences. This art form has roots in ancient China and has evolved over centuries.

The storyteller, known as a *shuoshuren* (說書人), uses vivid descriptions, expressive gestures, and vocal modulation to bring stories to life. The stories themselves can range from historical events, folk tales, myths, legends, and moral parables. These stories often carry cultural and ethical lessons. Traditionally performed in teahouses, marketplaces, and during festivals, Gùshì Yuán serves as both entertainment and a means of preserving cultural heritage. Audience interaction is a crucial aspect, with storytellers often engaging with listeners, responding to their reactions, and sometimes incorporating audience suggestions into the narrative. Gùshì Yuán is, therefore, an important cultural practice that reflects the richness of Chinese oral traditions and continues to be cherished in various forms today.

Overall Chinese legends, folk tales, and fairy tales are revered for several reasons. As with all cultural groups, Chinese folklore reflects the rich cultural heritage of China, spanning thousands of years of history. These tales often contain elements of traditional Chinese values, beliefs, customs, and mythology, providing insight into the cultural and social fabric of the Chinese people.

In parallel with other mainstream cultural groups, many Chinese legends and folk tales convey moral lessons and teachings, often in the form of allegory. These tales often explore themes such as filial piety, loyalty, honesty, humility, and the importance of living in harmony with nature. Through these stories, listeners learn valuable lessons about ethics, virtues, and the consequences of one's actions.

One of the things that I love about these tales is the simple fact that Chinese folklore encompasses some spectacular themes and characters such as legendary heroes and mythical creatures, as well as everyday people facing extraordinary challenges. Stories may feature legendary figures from Chinese history, such as emperors, scholars, and warriors, as well as supernatural beings like dragons, phoenixes, and spirits. Many of these stories are woven with themes that resonate across cultures and time. They explore themes like filial piety, respect for elders, perseverance in the face of adversity, and the importance of compassion and honesty. These messages remain relevant and valuable to readers of all ages.

Another significant factor in their popularity is that Chinese legends and folk tales have endured for centuries and continue to captivate audiences of all ages around the world. The timeless nature of these stories, combined with their universal themes and compelling narratives, ensures their enduring appeal across generations.

Chinese folklore has, by the nature of its breadth and longevity, had a significant influence on Chinese literature, art, music, theatre, and other forms of cultural expression. These tales have inspired countless works of literature, poetry, opera, and visual art, shaping the cultural identity of China and its people.

In summary, Chinese legends, folk tales, and fairy tales hold a special place in the hearts of people worldwide, offering a glimpse into the rich tapestry of Chinese culture, traditions, and values. Their enduring popularity continues to underscore their importance, and through sharing these tales I hope that we can take one small step in building greater understanding between peoples in our often troubled world.

Clive

Bath 2024

Tales Of The Gùshì Yuán

The Princess Kwan-Yin

This story has been adapted from Norman Hinsdale Pitman's version that originally appeared in A Chinese Wonder Book, published in 1919 by E. P. Dutton And Company, New York. A Chinese Wonder Book contains a selection of stories that capture the essence of traditional Chinese culture and storytelling. The book includes tales of magic, dragons, heroes, and supernatural creatures, all woven together with elements of Chinese mythology and folklore.

Once upon a time in China there lived a certain king who had three daughters. The fairest and best of these was Kwan-yin, the youngest. The old king was justly proud of this daughter, for of all the women who had ever lived in the palace she was by far the most attractive. It did not take him long, therefore, to decide that she should be the heir to his throne, and her husband ruler of his kingdom. But, strange to say, Kwan-yin was not pleased at this good fortune. She cared little for the pomp and splendour of court life. She foresaw no pleasure for herself in ruling as a queen, but even feared that in so high a station she might feel out of place and unhappy.

Every day she went to her room to read and study. As a result of this daily labour she soon went far beyond her sisters along the paths of knowledge, and her name was known in the farthest corner of the kingdom as "Kwan-yin, the wise princess." Besides being very fond of books, Kwan-yin was thoughtful of her friends. She was careful about her behaviour both in public and in private. Her warm heart was open at all times to the cries of those in trouble. She was kind to the poor and suffering. She won the love of the lower classes, and was to them a sort of goddess to whom they could appeal whenever they were hungry and in need. Some people even believed that she was a fairy who had come to earth from her home within the Western Heaven, while others said that once, long years before, she had lived in the world as a prince instead of a princess. However this may be, one thing is certain. Kwan-yin was pure and good, and well deserved the praises that were showered upon her.

One day the king called this favourite daughter to the royal bedside, for he felt that the hour of death was drawing near. Kwan-yin kowtowed before her royal father, kneeling and touching her forehead on the floor in sign of deepest reverence. The old man bade her rise and come closer. Taking her hand tenderly in his own, he said, "Daughter, you know well how I love you. Your modesty and virtue, your talent and your love of knowledge, have made you first in my heart. As you know already, I chose you as heir to my kingdom long ago. I promised that your husband should be made ruler in my stead. The time is almost ripe for me to ascend upon the dragon and become a guest on high. It is necessary that you be given at once in marriage."

"But, most exalted father," faltered the princess, "I am not ready to be married."

"Not ready, child! Why, are you not eighteen? Are not the daughters of our nation often wedded long before they reach that age? Because of your desire for learning I have spared you thus far from any thought of a husband, but now we can wait no longer."

"Royal father, hear your child, and do not compel her to give up her dearest pleasures. Let her go into a quiet convent where she may lead a life of study!"

The king sighed deeply at hearing these words. He loved his daughter and did not wish to wound her. "Kwan-yin," he continued, "do you wish to pass by the green spring of youth, to give up this mighty kingdom? Do you wish to enter the doors of a convent where women say farewell to life and all its pleasures? No! Your father will not permit this. It grieves me sorely to disappoint you, but one month from this very day you shall be married. I have chosen for your royal partner a man of many noble parts. You know him by name already, although you have not seen him. Remember that of the hundred virtues filial conduct is the chief, and that you owe more to me than to all else on earth."

Kwan-yin turned pale. Trembling, she would have sunk to the floor, but her mother and sisters supported her, and by their tender care brought her back to consciousness.

Every day of the month that followed, Kwan-yin's relatives begged her to give up what they called her foolish notion. Her sisters had long since given up hope of becoming queen. They were amazed at her stupidity. The very thought of anyone's choosing a convent instead of a throne was to them a sure sign of madness. Over and over again they asked her reason for making so strange a choice. To every question, she shook her head, replying, "A voice from the heavens speaks to me, and I must obey it."

On the eve of the wedding day Kwan-yin slipped out of the palace, and, after a weary journey, arrived at a convent called, "The Cloister of the White Sparrow." She was dressed as a poor maiden. She said that she wished to become a nun. The abbess, not knowing who she was, did not receive her kindly. Indeed, she told Kwan-yin that they could not receive her into the sisterhood, that the building was full. Finally, after Kwan-yin had shed many tears, the abbess let her enter, but only as a sort of servant, who might be cast out for the slightest fault.

Now that Kwan-yin found herself in the life which she had long dreamt of leading, she tried to be satisfied. But the nuns seemed to wish to make her stay among them most miserable. They gave her the hardest tasks to do, and it was seldom that she had a minute to rest. All day long she was busy, carrying water from a well at the foot of the convent hill or gathering wood from a neighbouring forest. At night when her back was almost breaking, she was given many extra tasks, enough to have crushed the spirit of any other woman than this brave daughter of a king. Forgetting her grief, and trying to hide the lines of pain that sometimes wrinkled her fair forehead, she tried to make these hard-hearted women love her. In return for their rough words, she spoke to them kindly, and never did she give way to anger.

One day while poor Kwan-yin was picking up brushwood in the forest she heard a tiger making his way through the bushes. Having no means of defending herself, she breathed a silent prayer to the gods for help, and calmly awaited the coming of the great beast. To her surprise, when the bloodthirsty animal appeared, instead of bounding up to tear her in pieces, he began to make a soft purring noise. He did not try to hurt Kwan-yin, but rubbed against her in a friendly manner, and let her pat him on the head.

The next day the princess went back to the same spot. There she found no fewer than a dozen savage beasts working under the command of the friendly tiger, gathering wood for her. In a short time enough brush and firewood had been piled up to last the convent for six months. Thus, even the wild animals of the forest were better able to judge of her goodness than the women of the sisterhood.

At another time when Kwan-yin was toiling up the hill for the twentieth time, carrying two great pails of water on a pole, an enormous dragon faced her in the road. Now, in China, the dragon is sacred, and Kwan-yin was not at all frightened, for she knew that she had done no wrong.

The animal looked at her for a moment, switched its horrid tail, and shot out fire from its nostrils. Then, dashing the burden from the startled maiden's shoulder, it vanished. Full of fear, Kwan-yin hurried up the hill to the nunnery. As she drew near the inner court, she was amazed to see in the centre of the open space a new building of solid stone. It had sprung up by magic since her last journey down the hill. On going forward, she saw that there were four arched doorways to the fairy house. Above the door facing west was a tablet with these words written on it, "In honour of Kwan-yin, the faithful princess." Inside was a well of the purest water, while, for drawing this water, there a strange machine, the like of which neither Kwan-yin nor the nuns had ever seen.

The sisters knew that this magic well was a monument to Kwan-yin's goodness. For a few days they treated her much better. "Since the gods have dug a well at our very gate," they said, "this girl will no longer need to bear water from the foot of the hill. For what strange reason, however, did the gods write this beggar's name on the stone?"

Kwan-yin heard their unkind remarks in silence. She could have explained the meaning of the dragon's gift, but she chose to let her companions remain in ignorance. Eventually the selfish nuns began to grow careless again, and treated her even worse than before. They could not bear to see the poor girl enjoy a moment's idleness.

"This is a place for work," they told her. "All of us have laboured hard to win our present station. You must do likewise." So they robbed her of every chance for study and prayer, and gave her no credit for the magic well.

One night the sisters were awakened from their sleep by strange noises, and soon they heard outside the walls of the compound the blare of a trumpet. A great army had been sent by Kwan-yin's father to attack the convent, for his spies had eventually been able to trace the runaway princess to this holy retreat.

"Oh, who has brought this woe upon us?" exclaimed all the women, looking at each other in great fear. "Who has done this great evil? There is one among us who has sinned most terribly, and now the gods are about to destroy us."

They gazed at one another, but no one thought of Kwan-yin, for they did not believe her of enough importance to attract the anger of heaven, even though she might have done the most shocking of deeds. Then, too, she had been so meek and lowly while in their holy order that they did not once dream of charging her with any crime.

The threatening sounds outside grew louder and louder. All at once a fearful cry arose among the women, "They are about to burn our sacred dwelling." Smoke was rising just beyond the enclosure where the soldiers were kindling a great fire, the heat of which would soon be great enough to make the convent walls crumble into dust.

Suddenly a voice was heard above the tumult of the weeping sisters, "Alas! I am the cause of all this trouble."

The nuns, turning in amazement, saw that it was Kwan-yin who was speaking. "You?" they exclaimed, astounded.

"Yes, I, for I am indeed the daughter of a king. My father did not wish me to take the vows of this holy order. I fled from the palace. He has sent his army here to burn these buildings and to drag me back a prisoner."

"Then, see what you have brought upon us, miserable girl!" exclaimed the abbess. "See how you have repaid our kindness! Our buildings will be burned above our heads! How wretched you have made us! May heaven's curses rest upon you!"

"No, no!" exclaimed Kwan-yin, springing up, and trying to keep the abbess from speaking these frightful words. "You have no right to say that, for I am innocent of evil. But, wait! You shall soon see whose prayers the gods will answer, yours or mine!" So saying, she pressed her forehead to the floor, praying the almighty powers to save the convent and the sisters.

Outside the crackling of the greedy flames could already be heard. The fire king would soon destroy every building on that hill-top. Mad with terror, the sisters prepared to leave the compound and give up all their belongings to the cruel flames and still more cruel soldiers. Kwan-yin alone remained in the room, praying earnestly for help.

Suddenly a soft breeze sprang up from the neighbouring forest, dark clouds gathered overhead, and, although it was the dry season a drenching shower descended on the flames. Within five minutes the fire was put out and the convent was saved. Just as the shivering nuns were thanking Kwan-yin for the divine help she had brought them, two soldiers who had scaled the outer wall of the compound came in and roughly asked for the princess.

The trembling girl, knowing that these men were obeying her father's orders, poured out a prayer to the gods, and straightway made herself known. They dragged her from the presence of the nuns who had just begun to love her. Thus disgraced before her father's army, she was taken to the capital.

On the morrow, she was led before the old king. The father gazed sadly at his daughter, and then the stern look of a judge hardened his face as he beckoned the guards to bring her forward.

From a neighbouring room came the sounds of sweet music. A feast was being served there amid great splendour. The loud laughter of the guests reached the ears of the young girl as she bowed in disgrace before her father's throne. She knew that this feast had been prepared for her, and that her father was willing to give her one more chance.

"Girl," said the king, eventually regaining his voice, "in leaving the royal palace on the eve of your wedding day, not only did you insult your father, but your king. For this act you deserve to die. However, because of the excellent record you had made for yourself before you ran away, I have decided to give you one more chance to redeem yourself. Refuse me, and the penalty is death: obey me, and all may yet be well, and the kingdom that you spurned is still yours for the asking. All that I require is your marriage to the man whom I have chosen."

"And when, most august King, would you have me decide?" asked Kwan-yin earnestly.

"This very day, this very hour, this very moment," he answered sternly. "What! Would you hesitate between love upon a throne and death? Speak, my daughter, tell me that you love me and will do my bidding!"

It was now all that Kwan-yin could do to keep from throwing herself at her father's feet and yielding to his wishes, not because he offered her a kingdom, but because she loved him and would gladly have made him happy. But her strong will kept her from relenting. No power on earth could have stayed her from doing what she thought her duty.

"Beloved father," she answered sadly, and her voice was full of tenderness, "it is not a question of my love for you, for of that there is no question, for all my life I have shown it in every action. Believe me, if I were free to do your bidding, gladly would I make you happy, but a voice from the gods has spoken, has commanded that I remain a virgin, that I devote my life to deeds of mercy. When heaven itself has commanded, what can even a princess do but listen to that power which rules the earth?"

The old king was far from satisfied with Kwan-yin's answer. He grew furious, his thin wrinkled skin turned purple as the hot blood rose to his head. "Then you refuse to do my bidding! Take her, men! Give to her the death that is due to a traitor to the king!" As they bore Kwan-yin away from his presence the white-haired monarch fell, swooning, from his chair.

That night, when Kwan-yin was put to death, she descended into the lower world of torture. No sooner had she set foot in that dark country of the dead than the vast region of endless punishment suddenly blossomed forth and became like the gardens of Paradise. Pure white lilies sprang up on every side, and the odour of a million flowers filled all the rooms and corridors. King Yama, ruler of the dominion, rushed forth to learn the cause of this wonderful change. No sooner did his eyes rest upon the fair young face of Kwan-yin than he saw in her the emblem of a purity which deserved no home but heaven.

"Beautiful virgin, doer of many mercies," he began, after addressing her by her title, "I beg you in the name of justice to depart from this bloody kingdom. It is not right that the fairest flower of heaven should enter and shed her fragrance in these halls. Guilt must suffer here, and sin find no reward. Depart then, from my dominion. The peach of immortal life shall be bestowed upon you, and heaven alone shall be your dwelling place."

Thus Kwan-yin became the Goddess of Mercy, thus she entered into that glad abode, surpassing all earthly kings and queens. And ever since that time, on account of her exceeding goodness, thousands of poor people breathe out to her each year their prayers for mercy. There is no fear in their gaze as they look at her beautiful image, for their eyes are filled with tears of love.

Tales Of The Gùshì Yuán

Dschang Liang

This story has been adapted from Dr. Richard Wilhelm's version that originally appeared in The Chinese Fairy Book, published in 1921 by Frederick A. Stokes Company, New York. Wilhelm's translations aimed to capture the essence of the original Chinese texts while making them accessible to English-speaking audiences. His deep understanding of Chinese language and culture shone through in his translations, allowing readers to appreciate the beauty and depth of these timeless tales.

Dschang Liang was a native of one of those states which had been destroyed by the Emperor Tsin Schi Huang. And Dschang Liang determined to do a deed for his dead king's sake, and to that end gathered followers with whom to slay Tsin Schi Huang.

One day Tsin Schi Huang was making a progress through the country. When he came to the plain of Bo Lang, Dschang Liang armed his people with iron maces in order to kill him. But Tsin Schi Huang always had two traveling coaches which were exactly alike in appearance. In one of them he sat himself, while in the other was seated another person. Dschang Liang and his followers unfortunately met the decoy wagon, and Dschang Liang was forced to flee from the Emperor's rage. He came to a ruined bridge. An icy wind was blowing, and the snowflakes were whirling through the air. There he met an old, old man wearing a black turban and a yellow gown. The old man let one of his shoes fall into the water, looked at Dschang Liang and said, "Fetch it out, little one!"

Dschang Liang controlled himself, fetched out the shoe and brought it to the old man. The latter stretched out his foot to allow Dschang Liang to put it on, which he did in a respectful manner. This pleased the old man and he said, "Little one, something may be made of you! Come here tomorrow morning early, and I will have something for you."

The following morning at break of dawn, Dschang Liang appeared. But the old man was already there and reproached him, "You are too late. Today I will tell you nothing. Tomorrow you must come earlier."

So it went on for three days, and Dschang Liang's patience was not exhausted. When the old man was satisfied, he brought forth the *Book of Hidden Complements*, and gave it to him. "You must read it," he said, "and then you will be able to rule a great emperor. When your task is completed, seek me at the foot of the Gu Tschong Mountain. There you will find a yellow stone, and I will be by that yellow stone."

Dschang Liang took the book and with its teachings he helped the ancestor of the Han dynasty to conquer the empire. The new emperor made him a count. From that time forward Dschang Liang ate no human food and concentrated in spirit. He kept company with the four whitebeards of the Shang Mountain, and with them shared the sunset roses in the clouds.

Once he met two boys who were singing and dancing:

"Green the garments you should wear,
If to heaven's gate you'd fare;
There the Golden Mother greet,
Bow before the Wood Lord's feet!"

When Dschang Liang heard this, he bowed before the youths, and said to his friends, "Those are angel children of the King Father of the East. The Golden Mother is the Queen of the West. The Lord of Wood is the King Father of the East. They are the two primal powers, the parents of all that is male and female, the root and fountain of heaven and earth, to whom all that has life is indebted for its creation and nourishment. The Lord of Wood is the master of all the male saints, the Golden Mother is the mistress of all the female saints. Whoever would gain immortality, must first greet the Golden Mother and then bow before the King Father. Then he may rise up to the three Pure Ones and stand in the presence of the Highest. The song of the angel children shows the manner in which the hidden knowledge may be acquired."

At about that time the emperor was induced to have some of his faithful servants slain. Then Dschang Liang left his service and went to the Gu Tschong Mountain. There he found the old man by the yellow stone, gained the hidden knowledge, returned home, and feigning illness loosed his soul from his body and disappeared.

Later, when the rebellion of the 'Red Eyebrows' broke out, his tomb was opened, but all that was found within it was a yellow stone, for Dschang Liang was wandering with Laotsze in the invisible world.

Once his grandson Dschang Dau Ling went to Kunlun Mountain, in order to visit the Queen Mother of the West. There he met Dschang Liang. Dschang Dau Ling gained power over demons and spirits, and became the first Taoist pope. And the secret of his power has been handed down in his family from generation to generation.

Tales Of The Gùshì Yuán

The Animals' Peace Party

This story has been adapted from a tale originally told by Kate Douglas Wiggin and Nora Archibald Smith in The Talking Beasts, published in 1911 by Houghton Mifflin Company. The fables in The Talking Beasts are engaging and entertaining, with whimsical characters and imaginative settings. Through these tales, Wiggin and Smith aimed to stimulate the imagination of children while also instilling important values that promote character development and moral growth.

Once upon a time the Horses and Cattle gave a party. Although the Pigs were very greedy, the Horses said, "Let us invite them, and it may be we can settle our quarrels in this way and become better friends. We will call this a Peace Party.

"Generations and generations of pigs have broken through our fences, taken our food, drunk our water, and rooted up our clean green grass, but it is also true that the cattle children have hurt many young pigs.

"All this trouble and fighting is not right, and we know the Master wishes we should live at peace with one another. Do you not think it a good plan to give a Peace Party and settle this trouble?"

The Cattle said, "Who will be the leader of our party and do the inviting? We should have a leader, both gentle and kind, to go to the Pig's home and invite them."

The next day a small and very gentle Cow was sent to invite the Pigs. As she went across to the pigs' yard, all the young ones jumped up and grunted, "What are you coming here for? Do you want to fight?"

"No, I do not want to fight," said the Cow. "I was sent here to invite you to our party. I should like to know if you will come, so that I may tell our leader."

The young Pigs and the old ones talked together and the old ones said, "The New Year feast will soon be here. Maybe they will have some good things for us to eat at the party. I think we should go."

Then the old Pigs found the best talker in all the family, and sent word by him that they would attend the party.

The day came, and the Pigs all went to the party. There were about three hundred all together.

When they arrived they saw that the leader of the cows was the most beautiful of all the herd and very kind and gentle to her guests.

After a while the leader spoke to them in a gentle voice and said to the oldest Pigs, "We think it would be a good and pleasant thing if there were no more quarrels in this pasture.

"Will you tell your people not to break down the fences and spoil the place and eat our food? We will then agree that the oxen and horses shall not hurt your children and all the old troubles shall be forgotten from this day."

Then one young Pig stood up to talk. "All this big pasture belongs to the Master, and not to you," he said. "We cannot go to other places for food. The Master sends a servant to feed us, and sometimes he sends us to your yard to eat the corn and potatoes. The servants clean our pen every day. When summer comes, they fill the ponds with fresh water for us to bathe in. Now, friends, can you not see that this place and this food all belong to the Master? We eat the food and go wherever we like. We take your food only after you have finished. It would spoil on the ground if we did not do this.

So, answer this question… Do our people ever hurt your people? No, even though every year some of our children are killed by bad oxen and cows."

The young pig then continued, "What is our food? It is nothing, but our lives are worth much to us. Our Master never sends our people to work as he does the horses and oxen. He sends us food and allows us to play a year and a year the same, because he likes us best. You see the Horses and Oxen are always at work. Some pull wagons, others plough land for rice, and they must work, sick or well. But our people never work.

Smiling from ear to ear the young pig then said, "Every day at happy time we play, and do you see how fat we are? You never see our bones. Look at the old Horses and the old Oxen. Twenty years' work and no rest! I tell you the Master does not honour the Horses and Oxen as he does the Pigs. Friends, that is all I have to say. Have you any questions to ask? Is what I have said not the truth?"

The old Cow said, "Moo, Moo," and shook her head sadly. The tired old Horses groaned, "Huh, Huh," and never spoke a word.

The cow leader said, "My friends, it is best not to worry about things we cannot know. We do not seem to understand our Master. It will soon be time for the New Year feast day, so, good night. And may the Pig people live in the world as long and happily as the Horses and the Oxen, although our Peace Party did not succeed."

On their way home the little Pigs made a big noise, and everyone said, "We, win! We win, we win!"

Then the old Horses and Oxen talked among themselves. "We are stronger, wiser, and more useful than the Pigs," they said. "Why does the Master treat us so?"

Tales Of The Gùshì Yuán

The Golden Beetle Or Why The Dog Hates The Cat

This story has been adapted from Norman Hinsdale Pitman's version that originally appeared in A Chinese Wonder Book, published in 1919 by E. P. Dutton And Company, New York. A Chinese Wonder Book contains a selection of stories that capture the essence of traditional Chinese culture and storytelling. The book includes tales of magic, dragons, heroes, and supernatural creatures, all woven together with elements of Chinese mythology and folklore.

"What we shall eat tomorrow, I haven't the slightest idea!" said Widow Wang to her eldest son, as he started out one morning in search of work.

"Oh, the gods will provide. I'll find a few coppers somewhere," replied the boy, trying to speak cheerfully, although in his heart he also had not the slightest idea in which direction to turn.

The winter had been a hard one, excessive with extreme cold, deep snow, and violent winds. The Wang house had suffered greatly. The roof had fallen in, weighed down by heavy snow. Then a hurricane had blown a wall over, and Ming-li, the son, up all night and exposed to a bitter cold wind, had caught pneumonia. Long days of illness followed, with the spending of extra money for medicine. All their scant savings had soon melted away, and at the shop where Ming-li had been employed his place was filled by another. When eventually he arose from his sick-bed he was too weak for hard labour and there seemed to be no work in the neighbouring villages for him to do.

Night after night he came home, trying not to be discouraged, but in his heart feeling the deep pangs of sorrow that come to the good son who sees his mother suffering for want of food and clothing.

"Bless his good heart!" said the poor widow after he had gone. "No mother ever had a better boy. I hope he is right in saying the gods will provide. It has been getting so much worse these past few weeks that it seems now as if my stomach were as empty as a rich man's brain. Why, even the rats have deserted our cottage, and there's nothing left for poor Tabby, while old Blackfoot is nearly dead from starvation."

When the old woman referred to the sorrows of her pets, her remarks were answered by a pitiful mewing and woebegone barking from the corner where the two unfed creatures were curled up together trying to keep warm.

Just then there was a loud knocking at the gate. When the widow Wang called out, "Come in!" she was surprised to see an old bald-headed priest standing in the doorway. "Sorry, but we have nothing," she went on, feeling sure the visitor had come in search of food. "We have fed on scraps these two weeks, on scraps and scrapings, and now we are living on the memories of what we used to have when my son's father was living. Our cat was so fat she couldn't climb to the roof. Now look at her. You can hardly see her, she's so thin. No, I'm sorry we can't help you, friend priest, but you see how it is."

"I didn't come for alms," cried the clean-shaven one, looking at her kindly, "but only to see what I could do to help you. The gods have listened long to the prayers of your devoted son. They honour him because he has not waited till you die to do sacrifice for you. They have seen how faithfully he has served you ever since his illness, and now, when he is worn out and unable to work, they are resolved to reward him for his virtue. You likewise have been a good mother and shall receive the gift I am now bringing."

"What do you mean?" faltered Mrs. Wang, hardly believing her ears at hearing a priest speak of bestowing mercies. "Have you come here to laugh at our misfortunes?"

"By no means. Here in my hand I hold a tiny golden beetle which you will find has a magic power greater than any you ever dreamed of. I will leave this precious thing with you, a present from the god of filial conduct."

"Yes, it will sell for a good sum," murmured the other, looking closely at the trinket, "and will give us millet for several days. Thanks, good priest, for your kindness."

"But you must by no means sell this golden beetle, for it has the power to fill your stomachs as long as you live."

The widow stared in open-mouthed wonder at the priest's surprising words.

"Yes, you must not doubt me, but listen carefully to what I tell you. Whenever you wish food, you have only to place this ornament in a kettle of boiling water, saying over and over again the names of what you want to eat. In three minutes take off the lid, and there will be your dinner, smoking hot, and cooked more perfectly than any food you have ever eaten."

"May I try it now?" she asked eagerly.

"As soon as I am gone."

When the door was shut, the old woman hurriedly kindled a fire, boiled some water, and then dropped in the golden beetle, repeating these words again and again:

"Dumplings, dumplings, come to me,
I am thin as thin can be.
Dumplings, dumplings, smoking hot,
Dumplings, dumplings, fill the pot."

Would those three minutes never pass? Could the priest have told the truth? Her old head was nearly wild with excitement as clouds of steam rose from the kettle.

Off came the lid! She could wait no longer.

Wonder of wonders! There before her unbelieving eyes was a pot, full to the brim of pork dumplings, dancing up and down in the bubbling water, the best, the most delicious dumplings she had ever tasted. She ate and ate till there was no room left in her greedy stomach, and then she feasted the cat and the dog until they were ready to burst.

"Good fortune has come at last," whispered Blackfoot, the dog, to Whitehead, the cat, as they lay down to sun themselves outside. "I fear I couldn't have held out another week without running away to look for food. I don't know what's just happened, but there's no use questioning the gods."

Mrs. Wang fairly danced for joy at the thought of her son's return and of how she would feast him.

"Poor boy, how surprised he will be at our fortune, and it's all on account of his goodness to his old mother."

When Ming-li came, with a dark cloud overhanging his brow, the widow saw plainly that disappointment was written there.

"Come, come, lad!" she cried cheerily, "Clear up your face and smile, for the gods have been good to us and I shall soon show you how richly your devotion has been rewarded." So saying, she dropped the golden beetle into the boiling water and stirred up the fire.

Thinking his mother had gone stark mad for want of food, Ming-li stared solemnly at her. Anything was preferable to this misery. Should he sell his last outer garment for a few pennies and buy millet for her? Blackfoot licked his hand comfortingly, as if to say, "Cheer up, master, fortune has turned in our favour." Whitehead leaped upon a bench, purring like a sawmill.

Ming-li did not have long to wait. Almost in the twinkling of an eye he heard his mother crying out, "Sit down at the table, son, and eat these dumplings while they are smoking hot."

Could he have heard correctly? Did his ears deceive him? No, there on the table was a huge platter full of the delicious pork dumplings he liked better than anything else in all the world, except, of course, his mother.

"Eat and ask no questions," counselled the Widow Wang. "When you are satisfied I will tell you everything."

Wise advice! Very soon the young man's chopsticks were twinkling like a little star in the verses. He ate long and happily, while his good mother watched him, her heart overflowing with joy at seeing him eventually able to satisfy his hunger. But still the old woman could hardly wait for him to finish, she was so anxious to tell him her wonderful secret.

"Here, son!" she cried eventually, as he began to pause between mouthfuls, "Look at my treasure!" And she held out to him the golden beetle.

"First tell me what good fairy of a rich man has been filling our hands with silver?"

"That's just what I am trying to tell you," she laughed, "for there was a fairy here this afternoon sure enough, only he was dressed like a bald priest. That golden beetle is all he gave me, but with it comes a secret worth thousands of cash to us."

The youth fingered the trinket idly, still doubting his senses, and waiting impatiently for the secret of his delicious dinner. "But, mother, what has this brass bauble to do with the dumplings, these wonderful pork dumplings, the finest I ever ate?"

"Baubles indeed! Brass! Fie, fie, my boy! You little know what you are saying. Only listen and you shall hear a tale that will open your eyes."

She then told him what had happened, and ended by setting all of the leftover dumplings upon the floor for Blackfoot and Whitehead, a thing her son had never seen her do before, for they had been miserably poor and had had to save every scrap for the next meal.

Now began a long period of perfect happiness. Mother, son, dog and cat, all enjoyed themselves to their hearts' content. All manner of new foods such as they had never tasted were called forth from the pot by the wonderful little beetle. Bird-nest soup, shark's fins, and a hundred other delicacies were theirs for the asking, and soon Ming-li regained all his strength, but, I fear, at the same time grew somewhat lazy, for it was no longer necessary for him to work. As for the two animals, they became fat and sleek and their hair grew long and glossy.

But alas! according to a Chinese proverb, pride invites sorrow. The little family became so proud of their good fortune that they began to ask friends and relatives to dinner that they might show off their good meals. One day a Mr. and Mrs. Chu came from a distant village. They were much astonished at seeing the high style in which the Wangs lived. They had expected a beggar's meal, but went away with full stomachs.

"It's the best stuff I ever ate," said Mr. Chu, as they entered their own tumble-down house.

"Yes, and I know where it came from," exclaimed his wife. "I saw Widow Wang take a little gold ornament out of the pot and hide it in a cupboard. It must be some sort of charm, for I heard her mumbling to herself about pork and dumplings just as she was stirring up the fire."

"A charm, eh? Why is it that other people have all the luck? It looks as if we were doomed forever to be poor."

"Why not borrow Mrs. Wang's charm for a few days until we can pick up a little flesh to keep our bones from clattering? It's fair enough play. Of course, we'll return it sooner or later."

"Doubtless they keep very close watch over it. When would you find them away from home now that they don't have to work anymore? As their house only contains one room, and that no bigger than ours, it would be difficult to borrow this golden trinket. It is harder, for more reasons than one, to steal from a beggar than from a king."

"Luck is surely with us," cried Mrs. Chu, clapping her hands. "They are going this very day to the Temple fair. I overheard Mrs. Wang tell her son that he must not forget he was to take her about the middle of the afternoon.

I will slip back then and borrow the little charm from the box in which she hid it."

"Aren't you afraid of Blackfoot?"

"Pooh! He's so fat he can do nothing but roll. If the widow comes back suddenly, I'll tell her I came to look for my big hair-pin, that I lost it while I was at dinner."

"All right, go ahead, only of course we must remember we're borrowing the thing, not stealing it, for the Wangs have always been good friends to us, and then, too, we have just dined with them."

So skilfully did this crafty woman carry out her plans that within an hour she was back in her own house, gleefully showing the priest's charm to her husband. Not a soul had seen her enter the Wang house. The dog had made no noise, and the cat had only blinked her surprise at seeing a stranger and had gone to sleep again on the floor.

Great was the clamour and weeping when, on returning from the fair in expectation of a hot supper, the widow found her treasure missing. It was long before she could grasp the truth. She went back to the little box in the cupboard ten times before she could believe it was empty, and the room looked as if a cyclone had struck it, so long and carefully did the two unfortunates hunt for the lost beetle.

Then came days of hunger which were all the harder to bear since the recent period of good food and plenty. Oh, if they had only not got used to such dainties! How hard it was to go back to scraps and scrapings!

But if the widow and her son were sad over the loss of the good meals, the two pets were even more so. They were reduced to beggary and had to go forth daily upon the streets in search of stray bones and refuse that decent dogs and cats turned up their noses at.

One day, after this period of starvation had been going on for some time, Whitehead began suddenly to frisk about in great excitement.

"Whatever is the matter with you?" growled Blackfoot. "Are you mad from hunger, or have you caught another flea?"

"I was just thinking over our affairs, and now I know the cause of all our trouble."

"Do you indeed?" sneered Blackfoot.

"Yes, I do indeed, and you'd better think twice before you mock me, for I hold your future in my paw, as you will very soon see."

"Well, you needn't get angry about nothing. What wonderful discovery have you made? Is it that every rat has one tail?"

"First of all, are you willing to help me bring good fortune back to our family?"

"Of course I am. Don't be silly," barked the dog, wagging his tail joyfully at the thought of another good dinner. "Surely! Surely! I will do anything you like if it will bring Dame Fortune back again."

"All right. Here is the plan. There has been a thief in the house who has stolen our mistress's golden beetle. You remember all our big dinners that came from the pot? Well, every day I saw our mistress take a little golden beetle out of the black box and put it into the pot. One day she held it up before me, saying, 'Look, puss, there is the cause of all our happiness. Don't you wish it was yours?' Then she laughed and put it back into the box that stays in the cupboard."

"Is that true?" questioned Blackfoot. "Why didn't you say something about it before?"

"You remember the day Mr. and Mrs. Chu were here, and how Mrs. Chu returned in the afternoon after master and mistress had gone to the fair? I saw her, out of the tail of my eye, go to that very black box and take out the golden beetle. I thought it curious, but never dreamed she was a thief. Alas! I was wrong! She took the beetle, and if I am not mistaken, she and her husband are now enjoying the feasts that belong to us."

"Let's claw them," growled Blackfoot, gnashing his teeth.

"That would do no good," counselled the other, "for they would be sure to come out best in the end. We want the beetle back, that's the main thing. We'll leave revenge to human beings, for that is none of our business."

"What do you suggest?" said Blackfoot. "I am with you through thick and thin."

"Let's go to the Chu house and make off with the beetle."

"Alas, that I am not a cat!" moaned Blackfoot. "If we go there I couldn't get inside, for robbers always keep their gates well locked. If I were like you I could scale the wall. It is the first time in all my life I ever envied a cat."

"We will go together," continued Whitehead. "I will ride on your back when we are fording the river, and you can protect me from strange animals. When we get to the Chu house, I will climb over the wall and manage the rest of the business myself. Only you must wait outside to help me to get home with the prize."

No sooner arranged than done. The companions set out that very night on their adventure. They crossed the river as the cat had suggested, and Blackfoot really enjoyed the swim, for, as he said, it took him back to his puppyhood, while the cat did not get a single drop of water on her face. It was midnight when they reached the Chu house.

"Just wait till I return," purred Whitehead in Blackfoot's ear.

With a mighty spring she reached the top of the mud wall, and then jumped down to the inside court. While she was resting in the shadow, trying to decide just how to go about her work, a slight rustling attracted her attention, and pop, one giant spring, one stretch-out of the claws, and she had caught a rat that had just come out of his hole for a drink and a midnight walk.

Now, Whitehead was so hungry that she would have made short work of this tempting prey if the rat had not opened its mouth and, to her amazement, begun to talk in good cat dialect.

"Pray, good puss, not so fast with your sharp teeth! Kindly be careful with your claws! Don't you know it is the custom now to put prisoners on their honour? I will promise not to run away."

"Pooh! What honour has a rat?"

"Most of us haven't much, I grant you, but my family was brought up under the roof of Confucius, and there we picked up so many crumbs of wisdom that we are exceptions to the rule. If you spare me, I will obey you for life, in fact, will be your humble slave." Then, with a quick jerk, freeing itself, "See, I am loose now, but honour holds me as if I were tied, and so I make no further attempt to get away."

"Much good it would do you," purred Whitehead, her fur crackling noisily, and her mouth watering for a taste of rat steak. "However, I am quite willing to put you to the test. First, answer a few polite questions and I will see if you're a truthful fellow. What kind of food is your master eating now, that you should be so round and plump when I am thin and scrawny?"

"Oh, we have been in luck lately, I can tell you. Master and mistress feed on the fat of the land, and of course we hangers-on get the crumbs."

"But this is a poor tumble-down house. How can they afford such eating?"

"That is a great secret, but as I am in honour bound to tell you, here goes. My mistress has just obtained in some manner or other, a fairy's charm…"

"She stole it from our place," hissed the cat, "I will claw her eyes out if I get the chance. Why, we've been fairly starving for want of that beetle. She stole it from us just after she had been an invited guest! What do you think of that for honour, Sir Rat? Were your mistress's ancestors followers of the sage?"

"Oh, oh, oh! Why, that explains everything!" wailed the rat. "I have often wondered how they got the golden beetle, and yet of course I dared not ask any questions."

"No, certainly not! But listen, friend rat, you get that golden trinket back for me, and I will set you free at once of all obligations. Do you know where she hides it?"

"Yes, in a crevice where the wall is broken. I will bring it to you in a jiffy, but how shall we exist when our charm is gone? There will be a season of scanty food, I fear. Beggars' fare for all of us."

"Live on the memory of your good deed," purred the cat. "It is splendid, you know, to be an honest beggar. Now scoot! I trust you completely since your people lived in the home of Confucius. I will wait here for your return. Ah!" laughed Whitehead to herself, "luck seems to be coming our way again!"

Five minutes later the rat appeared, bearing the trinket in its mouth. It passed the beetle over to the cat, and then with a whisk was off for ever. Its honour was safe, but it was afraid of Whitehead. It had seen the gleam of desire in her green eyes, and the cat might have broken her word if she had not been so anxious to get back home where her mistress could command the wonderful kettle once more to bring forth food.

The two adventurers reached the river just as the sun was rising above the eastern hills.

"Be careful," cautioned Blackfoot, as the cat leaped upon his back for her ride across the stream, "be careful not to forget the treasure. In short, remember that even though you are a female, it is necessary to keep your mouth closed till we reach the other side."

"Thanks, but I don't think I need your advice," replied Whitehead, picking up the beetle and leaping on to the dog's back.

But alas, just as they were nearing the farther shore, the excited cat forgot her wisdom for a moment. A fish suddenly leaped out of the water directly under her nose. It was too great a temptation. Snap went her jaws in a vain effort to land the scaly treasure, and the golden beetle sank to the bottom of the river.

"There!" said the dog angrily, "What did I tell you? Now all our trouble has been in vain, all on account of your stupidity."

For a time there was a bitter dispute, and the companions called each other some very bad names, such as turtle and rabbit. Just as they were starting away from the river, disappointed and discouraged, a friendly frog who had by chance heard their conversation offered to fetch the treasure from the bottom of the stream. No sooner said than done, and after thanking this accommodating animal profusely, they turned homeward once more.

When they reached the cottage the door was shut, and, bark as he would, Blackfoot could not persuade his master to open it. There was the sound of loud wailing inside.

"Mistress is broken-hearted," whispered the cat, "I will go to her and make her happy."

So saying, she sprang lightly through a hole in the paper window, which, alas, was too small and too far from the ground for the faithful dog to enter.

A sad sight greeted the gaze of Whitehead. The son was lying on the bed unconscious, almost dead for want of food, while his mother, in despair, was rocking backwards and forwards wringing her wrinkled hands and crying at the top of her voice for someone to come and save them.

"Here I am, mistress," cried Whitehead, "and here is the treasure you are weeping for. I have rescued it and brought it back to you."

The widow, wild with joy at sight of the beetle, seized the cat in her scrawny arms and hugged the pet tightly to her bosom.

"Breakfast, son, breakfast! Wake up from your swoon! Fortune has come again. We are saved from starvation!"

Soon a steaming hot meal was ready, and you may well imagine how the old woman and her son, heaping praises upon Whitehead, filled the beast's platter with good things, but never a word did they say of the faithful dog, who remained outside sniffing the fragrant odours and waiting in sad wonder, for all this time the artful cat had said nothing of Blackfoot's part in the rescue of the golden beetle.

At last, when breakfast was over, slipping away from the others, Whitehead jumped out through the hole in the window.

"Oh, my dear Blackfoot," she began laughingly, "you should have been inside to see what a feast they gave me! Mistress was so delighted at my bringing back her treasure that she could not give me enough to eat, nor say enough kind things about me. Too bad, old fellow, that you are hungry. You'd better run out into the street and hunt up a bone."

Maddened by the shameful treachery of his companion, the enraged dog sprang upon the cat and in a few seconds had shaken her to death.

"So dies the one who forgets a friend and who loses honour," he cried sadly, as he stood over the body of his companion.

Rushing out into the street, he proclaimed the treachery of Whitehead to the members of his tribe, at the same time advising that all self-respecting dogs should from that time onwards make war upon the feline race.

And that is why the descendants of old Blackfoot, whether in China or in the countries of the West, have waged continual war upon the children and grandchildren of Whitehead, for a thousand generations of dogs have fought them and hated them with a great and lasting hatred.

Tales Of The Gùshì Yuán

The Widow Ho

This story has been adapted from Rev. John MacGowan's version that originally appeared in Chinese Folk-Lore Tales, published in 1910 by MacMillan and Company, London. Chinese Folk-Lore Tales features a variety of stories that cover a wide range of themes, including mythology, morality, adventure, and romance. These tales often incorporate elements of Chinese folklore, legends, and superstitions, providing readers with a glimpse into the beliefs and values of traditional Chinese society.

One day in the early dawn, a distinguished mandarin was leaving the temple of the City God. It was his duty to visit this temple on the first and fifteenth of the moon, whilst the city was still asleep, to offer incense and adoration to the stern-looking figure enshrined within.

This mandarin was Shih-Kung, and a more just or more upright official did not exist in all the fair provinces of the Empire. Wherever his name was mentioned it was received with the profoundest reverence and respect, for the Chinese people have never lost their ideal of Tien-Li, or Divine Righteousness. This ideal is still deeply embedded in the hearts of high and low, rich and poor, and the homage of all classes, even of the most depraved is gladly offered to any man who conspicuously displays this heavenly virtue.

As Shih-Kung was being carried along in his sedan chair, with his numerous retinue following closely behind him, he happened to notice a young woman walking in the road in front of him, and began to wonder what it was that had brought her out at such an unusually early hour. She was dressed in the very deepest mourning, and so after a little more thought he concluded that she was a widow who was on her way to the grave of her late husband to make the usual offerings to his spirit.

All at once a sudden, furious whirlwind screamed about the woman and seemed determined to spend its force upon her, but beyond her nothing was touched by it. Not a leaf on the trees nearby was moved, and not a particle of dust on the road, except just where she stood, was in the least agitated by the fierce tempest that for the moment raged around her.

As Shih-Kung gazed at this strange occurrence, the woman's outer skirt was blown up in the air, and he saw that underneath was another garment of a rich crimson hue. He then knew at once that there was something radically wrong, for no woman of ordinary virtuous character would ever dare to wear such a glaring colour, while she pretended to be in deep mourning. There was something suspicious, too, in the sudden tornado that blew with such terrific violence round the woman only. It was not an accident that brought it there. It was clearly the angry protest of some spirit who had been foully misused, and who was determined that the wrong-doer should not escape the penalty for the evil she had committed.

Calling two of his runners to him, Shih-Kung ordered them to follow the woman and to see where she was going and what she did there, and then to report to him immediately, for he suspected that she might be complicit in her husband's death.

When he received a report of a troubling nature, he at once issued a warrant for the arrest of the widow, and at the same time sent officers to bring the coffin that contained the body of her husband from its burying-place.

When the widow appeared before the mandarin, she denied that she knew anything of the cause of her husband's death. He had come home drunk one night, she declared, and had fallen senseless on the ground. After a great deal of difficulty, she had managed to lift him up on to the bed, where he lay in a drunken slumber, just as men under the influence of liquor often do, so that she was not in the least anxious or disturbed about him. During the night she fell asleep as she watched by his side, and when she woke up she found to her horror that he was dead.

"That is all that can be said about the case," she concluded, "and if you now order an examination of the body, it simply means that you have suspicions about me, for no other person was with him but myself when he died. I protest therefore against the body being examined. If, however, you are determined to do so, I warn you that if you find no signs of violence on it, you expose yourself according to the laws of China to the punishment of death."

"I am quite prepared to take the responsibility," replied the mandarin, "and I have already ordered the Coroner to open the coffin and to make a careful examination of the body."

This was accordingly done, but no trace of injury, not even the slightest bruise, could be discovered on any part of the dead man's body.

The county magistrate was greatly distressed at this result of the enquiry, and hastened to Shih-Kung in order to obtain his advice as to what steps he should now take to escape the punishment of death which he had incurred by his action. The Viceroy agreed that the matter had indeed assumed a most serious aspect. "But you need not be anxious," he added, "about what you have done. You have only acted by my orders, and therefore I assume all responsibility for the proceedings which you have adopted to discover the murderer."

Late in the afternoon, as the sun began to disappear behind the mountains of the west, Shih-Kung slipped out by a side door of his yamen, dressed as a peddler of cloth, and with pieces of various kinds of material resting on his shoulders. His disguise was so perfect that no one, as he passed down the street, dreamed of suspecting that instead of being a wandering draper, he was in reality the Governor-General of the Province, who was trying to obtain evidence of a murder that had recently been committed in his own capital.

Travelling on down one street after another, Shih-Kung came eventually to the outskirts of the town, where the dwellings were more scattered and the population was less dense. By this time it was growing dark, so when he came to a house that stood quite apart by itself, he knocked at the door. An elderly woman with a pleasant face and a motherly look about her asked him in a kind and gentle voice what he wanted.

"I have taken the liberty," he replied, "of coming to your house to see whether you would not kindly allow me to lodge with you for the night. I am a stranger in this region," he continued, "and have travelled far from my home to sell my cloth. The night is fast falling, and I know not where to spend it, and so I beg of you to take me in. I do not want charity, for I am quite able to pay you liberally for any trouble I may cause you, and tomorrow morning, as early as you may desire, I shall proceed on my wanderings, and you will be relieved of me."

"My good man," she replied, "I am perfectly willing that you should lodge here for the night, only I am afraid you may have to endure some annoyance from the conduct of my son when he returns home later in the evening."

"My business leads me into all kinds of company," he assured her, "and I meet people with a great variety of dispositions, but I generally manage to get on with them all. It may be so with your son."

With a good-natured smile, the old lady then showed him into a little room just off the one which was used as a sitting room. Shih-Kung was very tired, so he threw himself down, just as he was, on a trestle bed that stood in the corner, and began to think over his plans for solving the mystery of the murder. By-and-by he fell fast asleep.

About midnight he woke up at the sound of voices in the next room, and heard the mother saying, "I want you to be very careful how you treat the peddler, and not to use any of your coarse language to him. Although he looks only a common man, I am sure he is a gentleman, for he has a refined way with him that shows he must have come from no mean family. I did not really want to take him in, as I knew you might object, but the poor man was very tired, and it was getting dark, and he declared he had no place to go to, so that eventually I consented to let him stay. It is only for the night, and tomorrow at break of day he says he must be on his travels again."

"I do most strongly dislike having a strange man in the house," replied a voice which Shih-Kung concluded was the son's, "and I shall go and have a look at him in order to satisfy myself about him."

Taking a lantern in his hand, he came close up to where Shih-Kung was lying, and flashing the light upon his face, looked down anxiously at him for a few moments. Apparently he was satisfied, for he cried out in a voice that could easily be heard in the other room, "All right, mother, I am content. The man has a good face, and I do not think I have anything to fear from him. Let him remain."

Shih-Kung now considered that it was time for him to act. He stretched himself and yawned as though he were just waking out of sleep, and then, sitting up on the edge of the bed, he looked into the young man's face and asked him who he was.

"Oh!" he replied in a friendly way, "I am the son of the old lady who gave you permission to stay here for the night. For certain reasons, I am not at all anxious to have strangers about the house, and at first I very much objected to have you here. But now that I have had a good look at you, my objections have all vanished. I pride myself upon being a good judge of character, and I may tell you that I have taken a fancy to you. But come away with me into the next room, for I am going to have a little supper, and as my mother tells me that you fell asleep without having had anything to eat, I have no doubt you will be glad to join me."

As they sat talking over the meal, they became very friendly and confidential with each other, and the sam-shu that the son kept drinking from a tiny cup, into which it was poured from a steaming kettle, had the effect of loosening his tongue and causing him to speak more freely than he would otherwise have done.

From his long experience of the shady classes of society, Shih-Kung very soon discovered what kind of a man his companion was, and felt that here was a mine from which he might draw valuable information to help him in reaching the facts he wished to discover.

Looking across the table at the son, whose face was by this time flushed with the spirit he had been drinking, and with a hasty glance around the room, as though he were afraid that someone might overhear him, he said in a low voice, "I want to tell you a great secret. You have opened your heart a good deal to me, and now I am going to do the same with you. I am not really a peddler of cloth, as I have pretended to be. I have been simply using that business to disguise my real occupation, which I do not want anyone to know."

"And what, may I ask, may be the trade in which you are engaged, and of which you seem to be so ashamed that you dare not openly confess it?" asked the son.

"Well, I am what I call a benevolent thief," replied Shih-Kung.

"A benevolent thief!" exclaimed the other in astonishment. "I have never heard of such a thing before, and I should very much like to know what is meant by it."

"I must tell you," explained the guest, "that I am not a common thief who takes the property of others for his own benefit. I never steal for myself. My practice is to find out where men have made money unjustly, and then by certain means at my command I deprive them of some of their unlawful gains and distribute them amongst the people they have wronged. In this way I have been the means of bringing suitable punishment on the heads of the guilty, and at the same time of relieving the necessities of those who have suffered at their hands."

"I am astonished at what you tell me," replied the son, "though I do not believe all you say about not taking a share in the plunder you get. But now that you have opened your heart to me, I shall repay your confidence by telling you what I am. I am a real thief, and I support my mother, who does not suspect the truth, and keep the home together, simply by what I steal from others."

He then proceeded to give an account of some of the adventures he had met with in the course of his expeditions by night to rooms and houses which, as he always found out beforehand by careful spying, contained valuables that could be easily carried away.

While he was relating these stories, Shih-Kung's eyes gleamed with delight, for he saw that the man had fallen into the trap which had been laid for him, and felt confident that before the night was over he would be in possession of some clue to the mystery he was endeavouring to solve. He was disgusted with the sordid details of the criminal life of which the man before him seemed to be proud, yet with wonderful patience this mandarin, with his large powers of mind, and with a genius for statesmanship which had made him famous throughout the Empire, sat for hours enduring the wretched talk of this common thief. But his reward came in due time.

"By the way," exclaimed this man whose business it was to break into homes when the small hours of the morning found their inmates wrapped in slumber, "some time ago I had a most remarkable experience, and as you have shown yourself such a good fellow, I will tell you about it, if you do not think it too late to do so."

"I shall be most delighted to hear you relate it," said his guest. "I have been greatly entertained by your vivid way of describing the adventures through which you have passed. You deserve to be classed amongst the great heroes of old, who have made their names famous by their deeds of daring. Go on, I pray you, and tell me the particulars of this unusual experience."

"Well," proceeded the man, "I had very carefully planned to pay a visit to a certain house just outside the walls of the city. It was an easy one to get in to without any danger of being observed, for it was in a quiet street, where passers-by are very few after dark. It was a gloomy place after sunset, for the high walls that looked down upon it threw deep and heavy shadows, which faint-hearted people declare are really unhappy and restless ghosts prowling about to harass and distress the unwary.

"It was a little after midnight, when with stealthy footsteps I crept along the narrow streets, keeping as much as I could under cover of the houses, where the darkness lay deepest. Every home was hushed in slumber. The only things that really troubled me were the dogs, which, with an intelligence far greater than that of their masters, suspected me of some evil purpose, and barked at me and made wild snaps at my legs. I managed, however, to evade them and finally to arrive at the house I intended to rob.

"When I got close up to it, I was surprised to find a light burning inside. There was another thing, too, that I could not understand, and this was that a little side door by which I had planned to enter had not been bolted, but had been left ajar so that any prowling robber could easily gain admittance through it. Taking off my shoes, I walked on tiptoe along the stone-paved courtyard in the direction of the room where the light was burning, and that is when I saw the result of a man lost to the world in the deepest despair. It cut against my usual sense of what is what, but I wish I could have helped him to lighten the load that had clearly weighed down his heart. Oh, sir, if I could only have had the opportunity of whispering a single sentence into his ear."

"It is your duty," interposed his guest, "to proceed tomorrow morning to the mandarin's yamen, and tell your story to the county magistrate, so that a great wrong may not go unpunished."

"That I can never do," promptly replied the man. "What do you think would happen were I to do what you suggest? I am a thief. I get my living by thieving. I was in the house on the night of the murder for the purpose of robbery. That would all come out when I give my evidence. After I had proved the murder, what would become of me? I should be cast into prison, and I might have to lie there for years, for who would ever bail out a thief? And then my poor mother would starve, for she has to depend on me entirely for her living, and she would be compelled to go on the streets and beg for charity from door to door. No, it is impossible for me ever to interfere in this case."

Shih-Kung recognized the difficulty in which the man was placed, and yet without his evidence it would be impossible to convict the woman of the crime she had committed. He accordingly thought out a plan which he felt would remove the obstacles that stood in the way of securing him as a witness.

Turning to the man, he said, "I have had a very pleasant evening with you, and I thank you for your courtesy and hospitality. I feel my heart moved with a desire for a deeper friendship than mere words can ever express, and so I propose that you and I become sworn brothers, so that whatever may befall us in the future we shall stand by each other to the very death."

The young man looked up with astonishment at this unexpected proposal, but the sudden flash in his eyes and the smile that overspread his countenance showed that it was very pleasing to him.

"I shall be delighted to agree," he quickly replied, "but when shall we have an opportunity of appearing in the temple, and of registering our vow in the presence of the god?"

"There is no need to go to any temple," Shih-Kung replied. "Your family idol, which sits over there enshrined before us, will be quite sufficient for our purpose. Give me a pen and paper, and I will write out the articles of our brotherhood and present them to the god."

In a few minutes the document was written out according to the minute rules laid down by the law which binds two men in a sworn brotherhood. By the most solemn oaths Shih-Kung and this thief agreed to assist each other in any extremity in which either might be placed in the future. Any call from one to the other must be instantly responded to. No danger and no peril to life or limb must be allowed to deter either of them when the cry for help or deliverance was heard. Each was to regard the interests of the other as identical with his own, and as long as life lasted, the obligation to succour in every time of need could never be relaxed or annulled.

To prove that this solemn engagement was no mere passing whim of the moment, it had to be read in the hearing of the household god, who happened to be the Goddess of Mercy. She would then be an everlasting witness of the transaction, and with the invisible forces at her command would visit pains and penalties on the one who broke his oath. Standing in front of her shrine, Shih-Kung read out the articles of agreement, word by word, in a slow and measured tone suited to the solemnity of the occasion. He then lighted the paper at the lamp, and both men gazed at it until nothing was left but ashes, when each of them knew that the Goddess had received the document and had placed it in her archives in the far-off Western Heaven as a record of the vows made in her presence in those early hours of the morning.

When they sat down again, Shih-Kung looked with a strong and masterful gaze at his newly-created brother and said to him, "You and I are now sworn brothers, and of course we must be frank with each other. I do not wish to deceive you any longer, so I must tell you that I am neither a peddler of cloth, nor a benevolent thief in the sense in which you understood the term. I am in fact Shih-Kung, the Viceroy of this Province."

No sooner did the man hear the name of this great mandarin, who was a profound source of terror to the evil-doers within his jurisdiction, than he fell on his knees before him in the most abject fright, and repeatedly knocking his head on the ground, besought him to have mercy on him.

Raising him up gently with his hand, Shih-Kung told him to lay aside all his fears. "You are my brother now," he said, "and we have just sworn in the presence of the Goddess to defend each other with our lives. I shall certainly perform my part of the oath. From this moment your fortune is made, and as for your mother, who received me with such gracious courtesy, it shall be my privilege to provide for her as long as she lives."

Emboldened by these words of the great statesman, the young man appeared at the second inquest, which Shih-Kung ordered to be held, and gave such testimony that the guilt of the wretched wife was clearly established, and due punishment meted out to her.

Tales Of The Gùshì Yuán

The Bird With Nine Heads

This story has been adapted from Dr. Richard Wilhelm's version that originally appeared in The Chinese Fairy Book, published in 1921 by Frederick A. Stokes Company, New York. Wilhelm's translations aimed to capture the essence of the original Chinese texts while making them accessible to English-speaking audiences. His deep understanding of Chinese language and culture shone through in his translations, allowing readers to appreciate the beauty and depth of these timeless tales.

Long, long ago, there once lived a king and a queen who had a daughter. One day, when the daughter went walking in the garden, a tremendous storm suddenly came up and carried her away with it. Now the storm had come from the bird with nine heads, who had robbed the princess, and brought her to his cave. The king did not know where his daughter had disappeared, so he had proclaimed throughout the land, "Whoever brings back the princess may have her for his bride!"

Now a youth had seen the bird as he was carrying the princess to his cave. This cave, though, was in the middle of a sheer wall of rock. One could not climb up to it from below, nor could one climb down to it from above. And as the youth was walking around the rock, another youth came along and asked him what he was doing there. So the first youth told him that the bird with nine heads had carried off the king's daughter, and had brought her up to his cave. The other chap knew what he had to do. He called together his friends, and they lowered the youth to the cave in a basket. And when he went into the cave, he saw the king's daughter sitting there, and washing the wound of the bird with nine heads, for the hound of heaven had bitten off his tenth head, and his wound was still bleeding. The princess, however, motioned to the youth to hide, and he did so. When the king's daughter had washed his wound and bandaged it, the bird with nine heads felt so comfortable, that one after another, all his nine heads fell asleep. Then the youth stepped forth from his hiding-place, and cut off his nine heads with a sword.

But the king's daughter said, "It would be best if you were hauled up first, and I came after."

"No," said the youth. "I will wait below here, until you are safe."

At first the king's daughter was not willing, yet eventually she allowed herself to be persuaded, and climbed into the basket. But before she did so, she took a long pin from her hair, broke it into two halves and gave him one and kept the other. She also divided her silken kerchief with him, and told him to take good care of both her gifts. But when the other man had drawn up the king's daughter, he took her along with him, and left the youth in the cave, in spite of all his calling and pleading.

The youth now took a walk about the cave. There he saw a number of maidens, all of whom had been carried off by the bird with nine heads, and who had perished there of hunger. And on the wall hung a fish, nailed against it with four nails. When he touched the fish, the latter turned into a handsome youth, who thanked him for delivering him, and they agreed to regard each other as brothers. Soon the first youth grew very hungry. He stepped out in front of the cave to search for food, but only stones were lying there. Then, suddenly, he saw a great dragon, who was licking a stone. The youth imitated him, and before long his hunger had disappeared.

He next asked the dragon how he could get away from the cave, and the dragon nodded his head in the direction of his tail, as much as to say he should seat himself upon it. So he climbed up, and in the twinkling of an eye he was down on the ground, and the dragon had disappeared. He then went on until he found a tortoise-shell full of beautiful pearls. But they were magic pearls, for if you flung them into the fire, the fire ceased to burn and if you flung them into the water, the water divided and you could walk through the midst of it. The youth took the pearls out of the tortoise-shell, and put them in his pocket. Not long after he reached the sea-shore. Here he flung a pearl into the sea, and at once the waters divided and he could see the sea-dragon.

The sea-dragon cried, "Who is disturbing me here in my own kingdom?"

The youth answered, "I found pearls in a tortoise-shell, and have flung one into the sea, and now the waters have divided for me."

"If that is the case," said the dragon, "then come into the sea with me and we will live there together."

Then the youth recognized him for the same dragon whom he had seen in the cave. And with him was the youth with whom he had formed a bond of brotherhood: He was the dragon's son.

"Since you have saved my son and become his brother, I am your father," said the old dragon. And he entertained him hospitably with food and wine.

One day his friend said to him, "My father is sure to want to reward you. But accept no money, nor any jewels from him, but only the little gourd flask over yonder. With it you can conjure up whatever you wish."

And, sure enough, the old dragon asked him what he wanted by way of a reward, and the youth answered, "I want no money, nor any jewels. All I want is the little gourd flask over yonder."

At first the dragon did not wish to give it up, but eventually he did let him have it, after all. And then the youth left the dragon's castle.

When he set his foot on dry land again he felt hungry. At once a table stood before him, covered with a fine and plenteous meal. He ate and drank. After he had gone on a while, he felt weary. And there stood an ass, waiting for him, on which he mounted. After he had ridden for a while, the ass's gait seemed too uneven, and along came a wagon, into which he climbed. But the wagon shook him up too, greatly, and he thought, "If I only had a litter! That would suit me better." No more had he thought so, than the litter came along, and he seated himself in it. And the bearers carried him to the city in which dwelt the king, the queen and their daughter.

When the other youth had brought back the king's daughter, it was decided to hold the wedding. But the king's daughter was not willing, and said, "He is not the right man. My deliverer will come and bring with him half of the long pin for my hair, and half my silken kerchief as a token."

But when the youth did not appear for so long a time, and the other one pressed the king, the king grew impatient and said, "The wedding shall take place tomorrow!"

Then the king's daughter went sadly through the streets of the city, and searched and searched in the hope of finding her deliverer. And this was on the very day that the litter arrived. The king's daughter saw the half of her silken handkerchief in the youth's hand, and filled with joy, she led him to her father. There he had to show his half of the long pin, which fitted the other exactly, and then the king was convinced that he was the right, true deliverer. The false bridegroom was now punished, the wedding celebrated, and they lived in peace and happiness till the end of their days.

Tales Of The Gùshì Yuán

Yang Oerlang

This story has been adapted from Dr. Richard Wilhelm's version that originally appeared in The Chinese Fairy Book, published in 1921 by Frederick A. Stokes Company, New York. Wilhelm's translations aimed to capture the essence of the original Chinese texts while making them accessible to English-speaking audiences. His deep understanding of Chinese language and culture shone through in his translations, allowing readers to appreciate the beauty and depth of these timeless tales.

The second daughter of the Ruler of Heaven once came down upon the earth and secretly became the wife of a mortal man named Yang. And when she returned to Heaven she was blessed with a son. But the Ruler of Heaven was very angry at this desecration of the heavenly halls. He banished her to earth and covered her with the Wu-I hills. Her son, however, Oerlang by name, the nephew of the Ruler of Heaven, was extraordinarily gifted by nature.

By the time he was full grown he had learned the magic art of being able to control eight times nine transformations. He could make himself invisible, or could assume the shape of birds and beasts, grasses, flowers, snakes and fishes, as he chose. He also knew how to empty out seas and remove mountains from one place to another. So he went to the Wu-I hills and rescued his mother, whom he took on his back and carried away.

They stopped to rest on a flat ledge of rock. Then the mother said, "I am very thirsty!"

Oerlang climbed down into the valley in order to fetch her water, and some time passed before he returned. When he did his mother was no longer there. He searched eagerly, but on the rock lay only her skin and bones, and a few blood-stains. Now you must know that at that time there were still ten suns in the heavens, glowing and burning like fire. The Daughter of Heaven, it is true, was divine by nature, yet because she had incurred the anger of her father and had been banished to earth, her magic powers had failed her. Then, too, she had been imprisoned so long beneath the hills in the dark that, coming out suddenly into the sunlight, she had been devoured by its blinding radiance.

When Oerlang thought of his mother's sad end, his heart ached. He took two mountains on his shoulders, pursued the suns and crushed them to death between the mountains. And whenever he had crushed another sun-disk, he picked up a fresh mountain. In this way he had already slain nine of the ten suns, and there was but one left. And as Oerlang pursued him relentlessly, he hid himself in his distress beneath the leaves of the portulacca plant. But there was a rainworm close by who betrayed his hiding-place, and kept repeating, "There he is! There he is!"

Oerlang was about to seize him, when a messenger from the Ruler of the Heaven suddenly descended from the skies with a command, "Sky, air and earth need the sunshine. You must allow this one sun to live, so that all created beings may live. Yet, because you rescued your mother, and showed yourself to be a good son, you shall be a god, and be my bodyguard in Highest Heaven, and shall rule over good and evil in the mortal world, and have power over devils and demons." Oerlang received this command he ascended to Heaven.

Then the sun-disk came out again from beneath the portulacca leaves, and out of gratitude, since the plant had saved him, he bestowed upon it the gift of a free-blooming nature, and ordained that it never need fear the sunshine. To this very day one may see on the lower side of the portulacca leaves quite delicate little white pearls. They are the sunshine that remained hanging to the leaves when the sun hid under them. But the sun pursues the rainworm, when he ventures forth out of the ground, and dries him up as a punishment for his treachery.

Since that time Yang Oerlang has been honoured as a god. He has oblique, sharply marked eyebrows, and holds a double-bladed, three-pointed sword. Two servants stand beside him, with a falcon and a hound, for Yang Oerlang is a great hunter. The falcon is the falcon of the gods, and the hound is the hound of the gods. When brute creatures gain possession of magic powers or demons oppress men, he subdues them by means of the falcon and hound.

Tales Of The Gùshì Yuán

Notscha

This story has been adapted from Dr. Richard Wilhelm's version that originally appeared in The Chinese Fairy Book, published in 1921 by Frederick A. Stokes Company, New York. Wilhelm's translations aimed to capture the essence of the original Chinese texts while making them accessible to English-speaking audiences. His deep understanding of Chinese language and culture shone through in his translations, allowing readers to appreciate the beauty and depth of these timeless tales.

The oldest daughter of the Ruler of Heaven had married the great general Li Dsing. Her sons were named Gintscha, Mutscha and Notscha. But when Notscha was given her, she dreamed at night that a Taoist priest came into her chamber and said, "Swiftly receive the Heavenly Son!" And straightway a radiant pearl glowed within her. And she was so frightened at her dream that she awoke. And when Notscha came into the world, it seemed as though a ball of flesh were turning in circles like a wheel, and the whole room was filled with strange fragrances and a crimson light.

Li Dsing was much frightened, and thought it was an apparition. He clove the circling ball with his sword, and out of it leaped a small boy whose whole body glowed with a crimson radiance. But his face was delicately shaped and white as snow. About his right arm he wore a golden armlet and around his thighs was wound a length of crimson silk, whose glittering shine dazzled the eyes. When Li Dsing saw the child he took pity on him and did not slay him, while his wife began to love the boy dearly.

When three days had passed, all his friends came to wish him joy. They were just sitting at the festival meal when a Taoist priest entered and said, "I am the Great One. This boy is the bright Pearl of the Beginning of Things, bestowed upon you as your son. Yet the boy is wild and unruly, and will kill many men. Therefore I will take him as my pupil to gentle his savage ways." Li Dsing bowed his thanks and the Great One disappeared.

When Notscha was seven years old he once ran away from home. He came to the river of nine bends, whose green waters flowed along between two rows of weeping-willows. The day was hot, and Notscha entered the water to cool himself. He unbound his crimson silk cloth and whisked it about in the water to wash it. But while Notscha sat there and whisked his scarf about in the water, it shook the castle of the Dragon-King of the Eastern Sea to its very foundations. So the Dragon-King sent out a Triton, terrible to look upon, who was to find out what was the matter. When the Triton saw the boy he began to scold him, but the boy merely looked up and said, "What a strange-looking beast you are, and you can actually talk!" Then the Triton grew enraged, leaped up and struck at Notscha with his axe. But the latter avoided the blow, and threw his golden armlet at him. The armlet struck the Triton on the head and he sank down dead.

Notscha laughed and said, "And there he has gone and made my armlet bloody!" And he once more sat down on a stone, in order to wash his armlet. Then the crystal castle of the dragon began to tremble as though it were about to fall apart. And a watchman also came and reported that the Triton had been slain by a boy. So the Dragon-King sent out his son to capture the boy. And the son seated himself on the water-cleaving beast, and came up with a thunder of great waves of water.

Notscha straightened up and said, "That is a big wave!" Suddenly he saw a creature rise out of the waves, on whose back sat an armed man who cried in a loud voice, "Who has slain my Triton?"

Notscha answered, "The Triton wanted to slay me so I killed him. What difference does it make?" Then the dragon assailed him with his halberd. But Notscha said, "Tell me who you are before we fight."

"I am the son of the Dragon-King," was the reply.

"And I am Notscha, the son of General Li Dsing. You must not rouse my anger with your violence, or I will skin you, together with that old mud-fish, your father!"

Then the dragon grew wild with rage, and came storming along furiously. But Notscha cast his crimson cloth into the air, so that it flashed like a ball of fire, and cast the dragon-youth from his breast. Then Notscha took his golden armlet and struck him on the forehead with it, so that he had to reveal himself in his true form as a golden dragon, and fall down dead.

Notscha laughed and said, "I have heard tell that dragon-sinews make good cords. I will draw one out and bring it to my father, and he can tie his armour together with it." And with that he drew out the dragon's back sinew and took it home.

In the meantime the Dragon-King, full of fury, had hastened to Notscha's father, Li Dsing, and demanded that Notscha be delivered up to him. But Li Dsing replied, "You must be mistaken, for my boy is only seven years old and incapable of committing such misdeeds."

While they were still quarrelling Notscha came running up and cried, "Father, I'm bringing along a dragon's sinew for you, so that you may bind your armour with it!"

Now the dragon broke out into tears and furious scolding. He threatened to report Li Dsing to the Ruler of the Heaven, and took himself off, snorting with rage. Li Dsing grew very much excited, told his wife what had happened, and both began to weep.

Notscha, however, came to them and said, "Why do you weep? I will just go to my master, the Great One, and he will know what is to be done."

And no sooner had he said the words than he had disappeared. He came into his master's presence and told him the whole tale. The latter said, "You must get ahead of the dragon, and prevent him from accusing you in Heaven!" Then he did some magic, and Notscha found himself set down by the gate of Heaven, where he waited for the dragon.

It was still early in the morning, the gate of Heaven had not yet been opened, nor was the watchman at his post. But the dragon was already climbing up. Notscha, whom his master's magic had rendered invisible, threw the dragon to the ground with his armlet, and began to pitch into him. The dragon scolded and screamed.

"There the old worm flounders about," said Notscha, "and does not care how hard he is beaten! I will scratch off some of his scales."

And with these words he began to tear open the dragon's festal garments, and rip off some of the scales beneath his left arm, so that the red blood dripped out. Then the dragon could no longer stand the pain and begged for mercy. But first he had to promise Notscha that he would not complain of him before the latter would let him go. And then the dragon had to turn himself into a little green snake, which Notscha put into his sleeve and took back home with him. But no sooner had he drawn the little snake from his sleeve than it assumed human shape. The dragon then swore that he would punish Li Dsing in a terrible manner, and disappeared in a flash of lightning.

Li Dsing was now angry with his son in earnest. Therefore Notscha's mother sent him to the rear of the house to keep out of his father's sight. Notscha disappeared and went to his master, in order to ask him what he should do when the dragon returned. His master advised him and Notscha went back home. And all the Dragon Kings of the four seas were assembled, and had bound his parents, with cries and tumult, in order to punish them.

Notscha ran up and cried with a loud voice, "I will take the punishment for whatever I have done! My parents are blameless! What is the punishment you wish to lay upon me?"

"Life for life!" said the dragon.

"Very well then, I will destroy myself!" And so he did and the dragons went off satisfied, while Notscha's mother buried him with many tears.

But the spiritual part of Notscha, his soul, fluttered about in the air, and was driven by the wind to the cave of the Great One. He took it in and said to it, "You must appear to your mother! Forty miles distant from your home rises a green mountain cliff. On this cliff she must build a shrine for you. And after you have enjoyed the incense of human adoration for three years, you shall once more have a human body."

Notscha appeared to his mother in a dream, and gave her the whole message, and she awoke in tears. But Li Dsing grew angry when she told him about it. "It serves the accursed boy right that he is dead! It is because you are always thinking of him that he appears to you in dreams. You must pay no attention to him."

The woman said no more, but thenceforward he appeared to her daily, as soon as she closed her eyes, and grew more and more urgent in his demand. Finally all that was left for her to do was to erect a temple for Notscha without Li Dsing's knowledge.

And Notscha performed great miracles in his temple. All prayers made in it were granted. And from far away people streamed to it to burn incense in his honour.

Thus half a year passed. Then Li Dsing, on the occasion of a great military drill, once came by the cliff in question, and saw the people crowding thickly about the hill like a swarm of ants. Li Dsing inquired what there were to see upon the hill.

"It is a new god, who performs so many miracles that people come from far and near to honour him."

"What sort of a god is he?" asked Li Dsing. They did not dare conceal from him who the god was. Then Li Dsing grew angry. He spurred his horse up the hill and, sure enough, over the door of the temple was written, "Notscha's Shrine." And within it was the likeness of Notscha, just as he had appeared while living.

Li Dsing said, "While you were alive you brought misfortune to your parents. Now that you are dead you deceive the people. It is disgusting!" With these words he drew forth his whip, beat Notscha's idolatrous likeness to pieces with it, had the temple burned down, and the worshipers mildly reproved. Then he returned home.

Now Notscha had been absent in the spirit upon that day. When he returned he found his temple destroyed, and the spirit of the hill gave him the details. Notscha hurried to his master and related with tears what had befallen him.

The latter was roused and said, "It is Li Dsing's fault. After you had given back your body to your parents, you were no further concern of his. Why should he withdraw from you the enjoyment of the incense?"

Then the Great One made a body of lotus-plants, gave it the gift of life, and enclosed the soul of Notscha within it. This done he called out in a loud voice, "Arise!" A drawing of breath was heard, and Notscha leaped up once more in the shape of a small boy. He flung himself down before his master and thanked him. The latter bestowed upon him the magic of the fiery lance, and Notscha thenceforward had two whirling wheels beneath his feet: The wheel of the wind and the wheel of fire. With these he could rise up and down in the air. The master also gave him a bag of panther-skin in which to keep his armlet and his silken cloth.

Now Notscha had determined to punish Li Dsing. Taking advantage of a moment when he was not watched, he went away, thundering along on his rolling wheels to Li Dsing's dwelling. The latter was unable to withstand him and fled. He was almost exhausted when his second son, Mutscha, the disciple of the holy Pu Hain, came to his aid from the Cave of the White Crane. A violent quarrel took place between the brothers, they began to fight, and Mutscha was overcome, while Notscha once more rushed in pursuit of Li Dsing. At the height of his extremity, however, the holy Wen Dschu of the Hill of the Five Dragons, the master of Gintscha, Li Dsing's oldest son, stepped forth and hid Li Dsing in his cave. Notscha, in a rage, insisted that he be delivered up to him, but Wen Dschu said, "Elsewhere you may indulge your wild nature to your heart's content, but not in this place."

And when Notscha in the excess of his rage turned his fiery lance upon him, Wen Dschu stepped back a pace, shook the seven-petaled lotus from his sleeve, and threw it into the air. A whirlwind arose, clouds and mists obscured the sight, and sand and earth were flung up from the ground. Then the whirlwind collapsed with a great crash.

Notscha fainted, and when he regained consciousness found himself bound to a golden column with three thongs of gold, so that he could no longer move. Wen Dschu now called Gintscha to him and ordered him to give his unruly brother a good thrashing. And this he did, while Notscha, obliged to stand it, stood grinding his teeth.

In his extremity he saw the Great One floating by, and called out to him, "Save me, O Master!" But the latter did not notice him, instead he entered the cave and thanked Wen Dschu for the severe lesson which he had given Notscha. Finally they called Notscha to them and ordered him to be reconciled to his father. Then they dismissed them both and seated themselves to play chess.

But no sooner was Notscha free than he again fell into a rage, and renewed his pursuit of his father. He had again overtaken Li Dsing when still another saint came forward to defend the latter. This time it was the old Buddha of the Radiance of the Light. When Notscha attempted to battle with him he raised his arm, and a pagoda shaped itself out of red, whirling clouds and closed around Notscha. Then Radiance of Light placed both his hands on the pagoda and a fire arose within it which burned Notscha so that he cried loudly for mercy. Then he had to promise to beg his father's forgiveness and always to obey him in the future. Not till he had promised all this did the Buddha let him out of the pagoda again. And he gave the pagoda to Li Dsing, and taught him a magic saying which would give him mastery over Notscha. It is for this reason that Li Dsing is called the Pagoda-bearing King of Heaven.

Later on Li Dsing and his three sons, Gintscha, Mutscha and Notscha, aided King Wu of the Dschou dynasty to destroy the tyrant Dschou-Sin.

None could withstand their might. Only once did a sorcerer succeed in wounding Notscha in the left arm. Any other would have died of the wound. But the Great One carried him into his cave, healed his wound and gave him three goblets of the wine of the gods to drink, and three fire-dates to eat. When Notscha had eaten and drunk he suddenly heard a crash at his left side and another arm grew out from it. He could not speak and his eyes stood out from their sockets with horror. But it went on as it had begun. Six more arms grew out of his body and two more heads, so that finally he had three heads and eight arms.

He called out to his Master, "What does all this mean?"

But the latter only laughed and said, "All is as it should be. Thus equipped you will really be strong!"

Then he taught him a magic incantation by means of which he could make his arms and heads visible or invisible as he chose. When the tyrant Dschou-Sin had been destroyed, Li Dsing and his three sons, while still on earth, were taken up into heaven and seated among the gods.

Tales Of The Gùshì Yuán

The Story Of The Bird Feng

This story has been adapted from Edmund Dulac's version that originally appeared in Edmund Dulac's Fairy-Book, published in 1916 by George H. Doran and Company, New York. What sets Edmund Dulac's Fairy Book apart is the exquisite artwork by Dulac himself. His illustrations are highly detailed and evocative, often depicting scenes from the stories with a dreamlike quality. Dulac's use of colour and composition adds depth and emotion to the tales, enhancing the reader's experience and bringing the narratives to life in a visually stunning way.

In the Book of the Ten Thousand Wonders there are three hundred and thirty-three stories about the bird called Feng, and this is one of them.

Ta-Khai, Prince of Tartary, dreamt one night that he saw in a place where he had never been before an enchantingly beautiful young maiden who could only be a princess. He fell desperately in love with her, but before he could either move or speak, she had vanished. When he awoke he called for his ink and brushes, and, in the most accomplished willow-leaf style, he drew her image on a piece of precious silk, and in one corner he wrote these lines:

The flowers of the pæony

Will they ever bloom?

A day without her

Is like a hundred years.

He then summoned his ministers, and, showing them the portrait, asked if anyone could tell him the name of the beautiful maiden, but they all shook their heads and stroked their beards They did not know who she was.

So displeased was the prince that he sent them away in disgrace to the most remote provinces of his kingdom. All the courtiers, the generals, the officers, and every man and woman, high and low, who lived in the palace came in turn to look at the picture. But they all had to confess their ignorance. Ta-Khai then called upon the magicians of the kingdom to find out by their art the name of the princess of his dreams, but their answers were so widely different that the prince, suspecting their ability, condemned them all to have their noses cut off. The portrait was shown in the outer court of the palace from sunrise till sunset, and exalted travellers came in every day, gazed upon the beautiful face, and came out again. None could tell who she was.

Meanwhile the days were weighing heavily upon the shoulders of Ta-Khai, and his sufferings cannot be described, he ate no more, he drank no more, and ended by forgetting which was day and which was night, what was in and what was out, what was left and what was right. He spent his time roaming over the mountains and through the woods crying aloud to the gods to end his life and his sorrow.

It was thus, one day, that he came to the edge of a precipice. The valley below was strewn with rocks, and the thought came to his mind that he had been led to this place to put a term to his misery. He was about to throw himself into the depths below when suddenly the bird Feng flew across the valley and appeared before him, saying, "Why is Ta-Khai, the mighty Prince of Tartary, standing in this place of desolation with a shadow on his brow?"

Ta-Khai replied, "The pine tree finds its nourishment where it stands, the tiger can run after the deer in the forests, the eagle can fly over the mountains and the plains, but how can I find the one for whom my heart is thirsting?"

And he told the bird his story.

The Feng, which in reality was a Feng-Hwang, that is, a female Feng, rejoined, "Without the help of Supreme Heaven it is not easy to acquire wisdom, but it is a sign of the benevolence of the spiritual beings that I should have come between you and destruction. I can make myself large enough to carry the largest town upon my back, or small enough to pass through the smallest keyhole, and I know all the princesses in all the palaces of the earth. I have taught them the six intonations of my voice, and I am their friend. Therefore show me the picture, O Ta-Khai, and I will tell you the name of her whom you saw in your dream."

Then the wonderful bird, like a fire of many colours came down from heaven, alighted before the Prince, who dropped the portrait at her feet. They went to the palace, and, when the portrait was shown once more, the bird became as large as an elephant, and exclaimed, "Sit on my back, O Ta-Khai, and I will carry you to the place of your dream. There you will find her of the transparent face with the drooping eyelids under the crown of dark hair such as you have depicted, for these are the features of Sai-Jen, the daughter of the King of China, and alone can be likened to the full moon rising under a black cloud."

At nightfall they were flying over the palace of the king just above a magnificent garden. And in the garden sat Sai-Jen, singing and playing upon the lute. The Feng-Hwang deposited the prince outside the wall near a place where bamboos were growing and showed him how to cut twelve bamboos between the knots to make the flute which is called Pai-Siao and has a sound sweeter than the evening breeze on the forest stream.

And as he blew gently across the pipes, they echoed the sound of the princess's voice so harmoniously that she cried, "I hear the distant notes of the song that comes from my own lips, and I can see nothing but the flowers and the trees, it is the melody the heart alone can sing that has suffered sorrow on sorrow, and to which alone the heart can listen that is full of longing."

At that moment the wonderful bird, like a fire of many colours come down from heaven, alighted before the princess, dropping at her feet the portrait.

She opened her eyes in utter astonishment at the sight of her own image. And when she had read the lines inscribed in the corner, she asked, trembling, "Tell me, O Feng-Hwang, who is he, so near, but whom I cannot see, that knows the sound of my voice and has never heard me, and can remember my face and has never seen me?"

Then the bird spoke and told her the story of Ta-Khai's dream, adding, "I come from him with this message, for I brought him here on my wings. For many days he has longed for this hour, let him now behold the image of his dream and heal the wound in his heart."

Swift and overpowering is the rush of the waves on the pebbles of the shore, and Sai-Jen felt like a little pebble when Ta-Khai stood before her....

The Feng-Hwang illuminated the garden sumptuously, and a breath of love was stirring the flowers under the stars.

It was in the palace of the King of China that were celebrated in the most ancient and magnificent style the nuptials of Sai-Jen and Ta-Khai, Prince of Tartary.

And this is one of the three hundred and thirty-three stories about the bird Feng as it is told in the Book of the Ten Thousand Wonders.

Tales Of The Gùshì Yuán

The Lady Of The Moon

This story has been adapted from Dr. Richard Wilhelm's version that originally appeared in The Chinese Fairy Book, published in 1921 by Frederick A. Stokes Company, New York. Wilhelm's translations aimed to capture the essence of the original Chinese texts while making them accessible to English-speaking audiences. His deep understanding of Chinese language and culture shone through in his translations, allowing readers to appreciate the beauty and depth of these timeless tales.

In the days of the Emperor Yau there lived a prince by the name of Hou I, who was a mighty hero and a good archer. Once ten suns rose together in the sky, and shone so brightly and burned so fiercely that the people on earth could not endure them. So the Emperor ordered Hou I to shoot at them. And Hou I shot nine of them down from the sky. Besides his bow, Hou I also had a horse which ran so swiftly that even the wind could not catch up with it. He mounted it to go hunting, and the horse ran away and could not be stopped.

Hou I eventually came to Kunlun Mountain and met the Queen-Mother of the Jasper Sea. And she gave him the herb of immortality. He took it home with him and hid it in his room. But his wife who was named Tschang O, once ate some of it on the sly when he was not at home, and she immediately floated up to the clouds. When she reached the moon, she ran into the castle there, and has lived there ever since as the Lady of the Moon.

Tales Of The Gùshì Yuán

On a night in mid-autumn, an emperor of the Tang dynasty once sat at wine with two sorcerers. And one of them took his bamboo staff and cast it into the air, where it turned into a heavenly bridge, on which the three climbed up to the moon together. There they saw a great castle on which was inscribed, 'The Spreading Halls of Crystal Cold.' Beside it stood a cassia tree which blossomed and gave forth a fragrance filling all the air. And in the tree sat a man who was chopping off the smaller boughs with an axe.

One of the sorcerers said, "That is the man in the moon. The cassia tree grows so luxuriantly that in the course of time it would overshadow all the moon's radiance. Therefore it has to be cut down once in every thousand years."

Then they entered the spreading halls. The silver stories of the castle towered one above the other, and its walls and columns were all formed of liquid crystal. In the walls were cages and ponds, where fishes and birds moved as though alive. The whole moon-world seemed made of glass. While they were still looking about them on all sides the Lady of the Moon stepped up to them, clad in a white mantle and a rainbow-colored gown. She smiled and said to the emperor, "You are a prince of the mundane world of dust. Great is your fortune since you have been able to find your way here!"

And she called for her attendants, who came flying up on white birds, and sang and danced beneath the cassia tree. A pure clear music floated through the air. Beside the tree stood a mortar made of white marble, in which a jasper rabbit ground up herbs. That was the dark half of the moon. When the dance had ended, the emperor returned to earth again with the sorcerers. And he had the songs which he had heard on the moon written down and sung to the accompaniment of flutes of jasper in his pear-tree garden.

Note: This fairy-tale is traditional. The archer Hou I is placed by legend in different epochs. He also occurs in connection with other myths regarding the moon, for one tale recounts how he saved the moon during an eclipse by means of his arrows. The goddess of the ice also has her habitation in the moon. The hare in the moon is a favourite figure. He grinds the grains of maturity or the herbs that make the elixir of life. The rain-toad Tschan, who has three legs, is also placed on the moon. According to one version of the story, Tschang O took the shape of this toad.

Tales Of The Gùshì Yuán

The Great Bell

This story has been adapted from Norman Hinsdale Pitman's version that originally appeared in A Chinese Wonder Book, published in 1919 by E. P. Dutton And Company, New York. A Chinese Wonder Book contains a selection of stories that capture the essence of traditional Chinese culture and storytelling. The book includes tales of magic, dragons, heroes, and supernatural creatures, all woven together with elements of Chinese mythology and folklore.

The mighty Yung-lo sat on the great throne surrounded by a hundred attendants. He was sad, for he could think of no wonderful thing to do for his country. He fidgeted with his silken fan nervously and snapped his long finger-nails in the impatience of despair.

"Woe is me!" he cried eventually, his sorrow getting the better of his usual calmness. "I have picked up the great capital and moved it from the South to Beijing and have built here a mighty city. I have surrounded my city with a wall, even thicker and greater than the famous wall of China. I have constructed in this city scores of temples and palaces. I have had the wise men and scholars compile a great book of wisdom, made up of 23,000 volumes, the largest and most wonderful collection of learning ever gathered together by the hands of men. I have built watch-towers, bridges, and giant monuments, and now, alas, as I approach the end of my days as ruler of the Middle Kingdom there is nothing more to be done for my people. Better far that I should even now close my tired eyes for ever and mount up on high to be the guest of the dragon, than live on in idleness, giving to my children an example of uselessness and sloth."

"But, your Majesty," began one of Yung-lo's most faithful courtiers, named Ming-lin, falling upon his knees and knocking his head three times on the ground, "if you would only deign to listen to your humble slave, I would dare to suggest a great gift for which the many people of Beijing, your children, would rise up and bless you both now and in future generations."

"Only tell me of such a gift and I will not only grant it to the imperial city, but as a sign of thanksgiving to you for your sage counsel I will bestow upon you the royal peacock feather."

"It is not for one of my small virtues," replied the delighted official, "to wear the feather when others so much wiser are denied it, but if it please your Majesty, remember that in the northern district of the city there has been erected a bell-tower which as yet remains empty. The people of the city need a giant bell to sound out the fleeting hours of the day, that they may be urged on to perform their labours and not be idle. The water-clock already marks the hours, but there is no bell to proclaim them to the populace."

"A good suggestion," answered the Emperor, smiling, "and yet who is there among us that has skill enough in bell-craft to do the task you propose? I am told that to cast a bell worthy of our imperial city requires the genius of a poet and the skill of an astronomer."

"True, most mighty one, and yet permit me to say that Kwan-yu, who so skilfully moulded the imperial cannon, can also cast a giant bell. He alone of all your subjects is worthy of the task, for he alone can do it justice."

Now, the official who proposed the name of Kwan-yu to the Emperor had two objects in so doing. He wished to quiet the grief of Yung-lo, who was mourning because he had nothing left to do for his people, and, at the same time, to raise Kwan-yu to high rank, for Kwan-yu's only daughter had for several years been betrothed to Ming-lin's only son, and it would be a great stroke of luck for Ming-lin if his daughter-in-law's father should come under direct favour of the Emperor.

"Depend upon it, Kwan-yu can do the work better than any other man within the length and breadth of your empire," continued Ming-lin, again bowing low three times.

"Then summon Kwan-yu at once to my presence, that I may confer with him about this important business."

In great glee Ming-lin arose and backed himself away from the golden throne, for it would have been very improper for him to turn his coat-tails on the Son of Heaven.

But it was with no little fear that Kwan-yu undertook the casting of the great bell.

"Can a carpenter make shoes?" he had protested when Ming-lin had broken the Emperor's message to him.

"Yes," replied the other quickly, "if they be like those worn by the little island dwarfs, and, therefore, made of wood. Bells and cannon are cast from similar material. You ought easily to adapt yourself to this new work."

Now when Kwan-yu's daughter found out what he was about to undertake, she was filled with a great fear.

"Oh, honoured father," she cried, "think well before you give this promise. As a cannon-maker you are successful, but who can say about the other task? And if you fail, the Great One's wrath will fall heavily upon you."

"Just hear the girl," interrupted the ambitious mother. "What do you know about success and failure? You'd better stick to the subject of cooking and baby-clothes, for you will soon be married. As for your father, pray let him attend to his own business. It is unseemly for a girl to meddle in her father's affairs."

And so poor Ko-ai, for that was the maiden's name, was silenced, and went back to her fancy-work with a big tear stealing down her fair cheek, for she loved her father dearly and there had come into her heart a strange terror at thought of his possible danger.

Meanwhile, Kwan-yu was summoned to the Forbidden City, which is in the centre of Beijing, and in which stands the Imperial palace. There he received his instructions from the Son of Heaven.

"And remember," said Yung-lo in conclusion, "this bell must be so great that the sound of it will ring out to a distance of thirty-three miles on every hand. To this end, you should add gold and brass in proper proportions, for they give depth and strength to everything with which they mingle. Furthermore, in order that this giant may not be lacking in the quality of sweetness, you must add silver in due proportion, while the sayings of the sages must be engraved on its sides."

Now when Kwan-yu had really received his commission from the Emperor he searched the bookstalls of the city to find if possible some ancient descriptions of the best methods used in bell-casting. Also he offered generous wages to all who had ever had experience in the great work for which he was preparing. Soon his great foundry was alive with labourers, huge fires were burning, great piles of gold, silver and other metals were lying here and there, ready to be weighed.

Whenever Kwan-yu went out to a public tea-house all of his friends plied him with questions about the great bell.

"Will it be the largest in the world?"

"Oh, no," he would reply, "that is not necessary, but it must be the sweetest-toned, for we Chinese strive not for size, but for purity, not for greatness, but for virtue."

"When will it be finished?"

"Only the gods can tell, for I have had little experience, and perhaps I shall fail to mix the metals properly."

Every few days the Son of Heaven himself would send an imperial messenger to ask similar questions, for a king is likely to be just as curious as his subjects, but Kwan-yu would always modestly reply that he could not be certain, it was very doubtful when the bell would be ready.

At last, however, after consulting an astrologer, Kwan-yu appointed a day for the casting, and then there came another courtier robed in splendid garments, saying that at the proper hour the Great One himself would for the first time cross Kwan-yu's threshold, for he wanted to see the casting of the bell he had ordered for his people. On hearing this, Kwan-yu was sore afraid, for he felt that somehow, in spite of all his reading, in spite of all the advice he had received from well-wishers, there was something lacking in the mixture of the boiling metals that would soon be poured into the giant mould. In short, Kwan-yu was about to discover an important truth that this great world has been thousands of years in learning, namely, that mere reading and advice cannot produce skill, that true skill can come only from years of experience and practice. On the brink of despair, he sent a servant with money to the temple, to pray to the gods for success in his venture. Truly, despair and prayer rhyme in every language.

Ko-ai, his daughter, was also afraid when she saw the cloud on her father's brow, for she it was, you remember, who had tried to prevent him from undertaking the Emperor's commission. She also went to the temple, in company with a faithful old servant, and prayed to heaven.

The great day dawned. The Emperor and his courtiers were assembled, the former sitting on a platform built for the occasion. Three attendants waved beautiful hand-painted fans about his imperial brow, for the room was very warm, and a huge block of ice lay melting in a bowl of carved brass, cooling the hot air before it should blow upon the head of the Son of Heaven.

Kwan-yu's wife and daughter stood in a corner at the back of the room, peering anxiously towards the cauldron of molten liquid, for well they knew that Kwan-yu's future rank and power depended on the success of this enterprise. Around the walls stood Kwan-yu's friends, and at the windows groups of excited servants strained their necks, trying to catch a glimpse of royalty, and for once afraid to chatter. Kwan-yu himself was hurrying here and there, now giving a final order, now gazing anxiously at the empty

Tales Of The Gùshì Yuán

mould, and again glancing towards the throne to see if his imperial master was showing signs of impatience.

Eventually all was ready, everyone was waiting breathlessly for the sign from Yung-lo which should start the flowing of the metal. A slight bow of the head, a lifting of the finger! The glowing liquid, hissing with delight at being freed even for a moment from its prison, ran forward faster and faster along the channel that led into the great earthen bed.

The bell-maker covered his eyes with his fan, afraid to look at the swiftly-flowing stream. Were all his hopes to be suddenly dashed by the failure of the metals to mix and harden properly? A heavy sigh escaped him as eventually he looked up at the thing he had created. Something had indeed gone wrong, he knew in the flash of an eye that misfortune had overtaken him.

Yes, sure enough, when eventually the earthen casting had been broken, even the smallest child could see that the giant bell, instead of being a thing of beauty was a sorry mass of metals that would not blend.

"Alas!" said Yung-lo, "here is indeed a mighty failure, but even in this disappointment I see an object lesson well worthy of consideration, for behold, in yonder elements are all the materials of which this country is made up. There are gold and silver and the baser metals. United in the proper manner they would make a bell so wonderfully beautiful and so pure of tone that the very spirits of the Western heavens would pause to look and listen. But divided they form a thing that is hideous to eye and ear. Oh, my China, how many wars are there from time to time among the different sections, weakening the country and making it poor! If only all these peoples, great and small, the gold and silver and the baser elements, would unite, then would this land be really worthy of the name of the Middle Kingdom!"

The courtiers all applauded this speech of the great Yung-lo, but Kwan-yu remained on the ground where he had thrown himself at the feet of his sovereign. Still bowing his head and moaning, he cried out, "Ah, your

Tales Of The Gùshì Yuán

Majesty! I urged you not to appoint me, and now indeed you see my unfitness. Take my life, I beg you, as a punishment for my failure."

"Rise, Kwan-yu," said the great Prince. "I would be a mean master indeed if I did not grant you another trial. Rise up and see that your next casting profits by the lesson of this failure."

So Kwan-yu arose, for when the King speaks, all men must listen. The next day he began his task once more, but still his heart was heavy, for he did not know the reason of his failure and was therefore unable to correct his error. For many months he laboured night and day. Hardly a word would he speak to his wife, and when his daughter tried to tempt him with a dish of sunflower seed that she had parched herself, he would reward her with a sad smile, but would by no means laugh with her and joke as had formerly been his custom. On the first and fifteenth day of every moon he went himself to the temple and implored the gods to grant him their friendly assistance, while Ko-ai added her prayers to his, burning incense and weeping before the grinning idols.

Again the great Yung-lo was seated on the platform in Kwan-yu's foundry, and again his courtiers hovered round him, but this time, as it was winter, they did not flirt the silken fans. The Great One was certain that this casting would be successful. He had been lenient with Kwan-yu on the first occasion, and now eventually he and the great city were to profit by that mercy.

Again he gave the signal, and once more every neck was craned to see the flowing of the metal. But, alas, when the casing was removed it was seen that the new bell was no better than the first. It was, in fact, a dreadful failure, cracked and ugly, for the gold and silver and the baser elements had again refused to blend into a united whole.

With a bitter cry which touched the hearts of all those present, the unhappy Kwan-yu fell upon the floor. This time he did not bow before his master, for at the sight of the miserable conglomeration of useless metals his courage failed him, and he fainted. When eventually he came to, the first sight that met his eyes was the scowling face of Yung-lo.

Then he heard, as in a dream, the stern voice of the Son of Heaven, "Unhappy Kwan-yu, can it be that you, upon whom I have ever heaped my favours, have twice betrayed the trust? The first time, I was sorry for you and willing to forget, but now that sorrow has turned into anger. Yes, the anger of heaven itself is upon you. Now, I bid you mark well my words. A third chance you shall have to cast the bell, but if on that third attempt you fail, then by order of the Vermilion Pencil both you and Ming-lin, who recommended you, shall pay the penalty."

For a long time after the Emperor had departed, Kwan-yu lay on the floor surrounded by his attendants, but chief of all those who tried to restore him was his faithful daughter. For a whole week he wavered between life and death, and then eventually there came a turn in his favour. Once more he regained his health, once more he began his preparations.

Yet all the time he was about his work his heart was heavy, for he felt that he would soon journey into the dark forest, the region of the great yellow spring, the place from which no pilgrim ever returns. Ko-ai, too, felt more than ever that her father was in the presence of a great danger.

"Surely," she said one day to her mother, "a raven must have flown over his head. He is like the proverb of the blind man on the blind horse coming at midnight to a deep ditch. Oh, how can he cross over?"

Willingly would this dutiful daughter have done anything to save her loved one. Night and day she racked her brains for some plan, but all to no avail.

On the day before the third casting, as Ko-ai was sitting in front of her brass mirror braiding her long black hair, suddenly a little bird flew in at the window and perched upon her head. Immediately the startled maiden seemed to hear a voice as if some good fairy were whispering in her ear, "Do not hesitate. You must go and consult the famous juggler who even now is visiting the city. Sell your jade-stones and other jewels, for this man of wisdom will not listen unless his attention is attracted by huge sums of money."

The feathered messenger flew out of her room, but Ko-ai had heard enough to make her happy. She despatched a trusted servant to sell her jade and her jewels, charging him on no account to tell her mother. Then, with a great sum of money in her possession she sought out the magician who was said to be wiser than the sages in knowledge of life and death.

"Tell me," she implored, as the greybeard summoned her to his presence, "tell me how I can save my father, for the Emperor has ordered his death if he fails a third time in the casting of the bell."

The astrologer, after plying her with questions, put on his tortoise-shell glasses and searched long in his book of knowledge. He also examined closely the signs of the heavens, consulting the mystic tables over and over again. Finally, he turned toward Ko-ai, who all the time had been awaiting his answer with impatience.

"Nothing could be plainer than the reason of your father's failure, for when a man seeks to do the impossible, he can expect Fate to give him no other answer. Gold cannot unite with silver, nor brass with iron, unless the blood of a maiden is mingled with the molten metals, but the girl who gives up her life to bring about the fusion must be pure and good."

With a sigh of despair Ko-ai heard the astrologer's answer. She loved the world and all its beauties, she loved her birds, her companions, her father, she had expected to marry soon, and then there would have been children to love and cherish. But now all these dreams of happiness must be forgotten. There was no other maiden to give up her life for Kwan-yu. She, Ko-ai, loved her father and must make the sacrifice for his sake.

And so the day arrived for the third trial, and a third time Yung-lo took his place in Kwan-yu's factory, surrounded by his courtiers. There was a look of stern expectancy on his face. Twice he had excused his underling for failure. Now there could be no thought of mercy. If the bell did not come from its cast perfect in tone and fair to look upon, Kwan-yu must be punished with the severest punishment that could be meted out to man. That was why there was a look of stern expectancy on Yung-lo's face, for he really loved Kwan-yu and did not wish to send him to his death.

As for Kwan-yu himself, he had long ago given up all thought of success, for nothing had happened since his second failure to make him any surer this time of success. He had settled up his business affairs, arranging for a goodly sum to go to his beloved daughter, he had bought the coffin in which his own body would be laid away and had stored it in one of the principal rooms of his dwelling, he had even engaged the priests and musicians who should chant his funeral dirge, and, last but not least, he had arranged with the man who would have charge of chopping off his head, that one fold of skin should be left uncut, as this would bring him better luck on his entry into the spiritual world than if the head were severed entirely from the body.

And so we may say that Kwan-yu was prepared to die. In fact, on the night before the final casting he had a dream in which he saw himself kneeling before the headsman and cautioning him not to forget the binding agreement the latter had entered into.

Of all those present in the great foundry, perhaps the devoted Ko-ai was the least excited. Unnoticed, she had slipped along the wall from the spot where she had been standing with her mother and had planted herself directly opposite the huge tank in which the molten, seething liquid bubbled, awaiting the signal when it should be set free. Ko-ai gazed at the Emperor, watching intently for the well-known signal. When eventually she saw his head move forward she sprang with a wild leap into the boiling liquid, at the same time crying in her clear, sweet voice, "For you, dear father! It is the only way!"

The molten white metal received the lovely girl into its ardent embrace, received her, and swallowed her up completely, as in a tomb of liquid fire.

Mad with grief at the sight of his loved one giving up her life, a sacrifice to save him, Kwan-yu had sprung forward to hold her back from her terrible death, but had succeeded only in catching one of her tiny, jewelled slippers as she sank out of sight for ever, a dainty, silken slipper, to remind him always of her wonderful sacrifice. In his wild grief, as he clasped this pitiful little memento to his heart, he would himself have leaped in and followed her to her death if his servants had not restrained him until the Emperor had repeated his signal and the liquid had been poured into the cast. As the sad eyes of all those present peered into the molten river of metals rushing to its earthen bed, they saw not a single sign remaining of the departed Ko-ai.

This, then, my children, is the time-worn legend of the great bell of Beijing, a tale that has been repeated a million times by poets, story-tellers and devoted mothers, for you must know that on this third casting, when the earthen mould was removed, there stood revealed the most beautiful bell that eye had ever looked upon, and when it was swung up into the bell-tower there was immense rejoicing among the people. The silver and the gold and the iron and the brass, held together by the blood of the virgin, had blended perfectly, and the clear voice of the monster bell rang out over the great city, sounding a deeper, richer melody than that of any other bell within the limits of the Middle Kingdom, or, for that matter, of all the world.

And, strange to say, even yet the deep-voiced colossus seems to cry out the name of the maiden who gave herself a living sacrifice, "Ko-ai! Ko-ai! Ko-ai!" so that all the people may remember her deed of virtue ten thousand years ago. And between the mellow peals of music there often seems to come a plaintive whisper that may be heard only by those standing near, "Hsieh! Hsieh", the Chinese word for slipper. "Alas!" say all who hear it, "Ko-ai is crying for her slipper. Poor little Ko-ai!"

And now, my dear children, this tale is almost finished, but there is still one thing you must by no means fail to remember. By order of the Emperor, the face of the great bell was engraved with precious sayings from the classics, so that even in its moments of silence the bell might teach lessons of virtue to the people.

"Behold," said Yung-lo, as he stood beside the grief-stricken father, "amongst all yonder texts of wisdom, the priceless sayings of our honoured sages, there is none that can teach to my children so sweet a lesson of filial love and devotion as that one last act of your devoted daughter. For though she died to save you, her deed will still be sung and extolled by my people when you are passed away, yes, even when the bell itself has crumbled into ruins."

Old Dragonbeard

This story has been adapted from Dr. Richard Wilhelm's version that originally appeared in The Chinese Fairy Book, published in 1921 by Frederick A. Stokes Company, New York. Wilhelm's translations aimed to capture the essence of the original Chinese texts while making them accessible to English-speaking audiences. His deep understanding of Chinese language and culture shone through in his translations, allowing readers to appreciate the beauty and depth of these timeless tales.

At the time of the last emperor of the Sui dynasty, the power was in the hands of the emperor's uncle, Yang Su. He was proud and extravagant. In his halls stood choruses of singers and bands of dancing girls, and serving-maids stood ready to obey his least sign. When the great lords of the empire came to visit him he remained comfortably seated on his couch while he received them.

In those days there lived a bold hero named Li Dsing. He came to see Yang Su in humble clothes in order to bring him a plan for the quieting of the empire.

He made a low bow to which Yang Su did not reply, and then he said, "The empire is about to be troubled by dissension and heroes are everywhere taking up arms. You are the highest servant of the imperial house. It should be your duty to gather the bravest around the throne. And you should not rebuff people by your haughtiness!"

When Yang Su heard him speak in this fashion he collected himself, rose from his place, and spoke to him in a friendly manner.

Li Dsing handed him a memorial, and Yang Su entered into talk with him concerning all sorts of things. A serving-maid of extraordinary beauty stood beside them. She held a red fan in her hand, and kept her eyes fixed on Li Dsing. The latter at length took his leave and returned to his inn.

Later in the day someone knocked at his door. He looked out, and there, before the door, stood a person turbaned and gowned in purple, and carrying a bag slung from a stick across his shoulder.

Li Dsing asked who it was and received the answer, "I am the fan-bearer of Yang Su!"

With that she entered the room, threw back her mantle and took off her turban. Li Dsing saw that she was a maiden of eighteen or nineteen.

She bowed to him, and when he had replied to her greeting she began, "I have dwelt in the house of Yang Su for a long time and have seen many famous people, but none who could equal you. I will serve you wherever you go!"

Li Dsing answered, "The minister is powerful. I am afraid that we will plunge ourselves into misfortune."

"He is a living corpse, in whom the breath of life grows scant," said the fan-bearer, "and we need not fear him."

He asked her name, and she said it was Dschang, and that she was the oldest among her brothers and sisters.

And when he looked at her, and considered her courageous behaviour and her sensible words, he realized that she was a girl of heroic cast, and they agreed to marry and make their escape from the city in secret. The fan-bearer put on men's clothes, and they mounted horses and rode away. They had determined to go to Taiyuanfu.

On the following day they stopped at an inn. They had their room put in order and made a fire on the hearth to cook their meal. The fan-bearer was combing her hair. It was so long that it swept the ground, and so shining that you could see your face in it. Li Dsing had just left the room to groom the horses.

Suddenly a man who had a long curling moustache like a dragon made his appearance. He came along riding on a lame mule, threw his leather bag on the ground in front of the hearth, took a pillow, made himself comfortable on a couch, and watched the fan-bearer as she combed her hair. Li Dsing saw him and grew angry, but the fan-bearer had at once seen through the stranger. She motioned Li Dsing to control himself, quickly finished combing her hair and tied it in a knot.

Then she greeted the guest and asked his name.

He told her that he was named Dschang.

"Why, my name is also Dschang," she said, "so we must be relatives!" Thereupon she bowed to him as her elder brother.

"How many are there of you brothers?" she then inquired.

"I am the third," he answered, "and you?"

"I am the oldest sister."

"How fortunate that I should have found a sister today," said the stranger, highly pleased.

Then the fan-bearer called to Li Dsing through the door and said, "Come in! I wish to present my third brother to you!"

Then Li Dsing came in and greeted him.

They sat down beside each other and the stranger asked, "What have you to eat?"

"A leg of mutton," was the answer.

"I am quite hungry," said the stranger.

So Li Dsing went to the market and brought bread and wine. The stranger drew out his dagger, cut the meat, and they all ate in company. When they had finished the stranger fed the rest of the meat to his mule.

Then he said, "Sir Li, you seem to be a moneyless knight. How did you happen to meet my sister?"

Li Dsing told him how it had occurred.

"And where do you wish to go now?"

"To Taiyuanfu," was the answer.

The stranger said, "You do not seem to be an ordinary fellow. Have you heard anything regarding a hero who is supposed to be in this neighbourhood?"

Li Dsing answered, "Yes, indeed, I know of one, whom heaven seems destined to rule."

"And who might he be?" inquired the other.

"He is the son of Duke Li Yuan of Tang, and he is no more than twenty years of age."

"Could you present him to me some time?" asked the stranger.

And when Li Dsing assured him that he could, he continued, "The astrologers say that a special sign has been noticed in the air above Taiyuanfu. Perhaps it is caused by the very man. Tomorrow you may await me at the Fenyang Bridge!"

With these words he mounted his mule and rode away, and he rode so swiftly that he seemed to be flying.

The fan-bearer said to Li Dsing, "He is not a pleasant customer to deal with. I noticed that at first he had no good intentions. That is why I united him to us by bonds of relationship."

Then they set out together for Taiyuanfu, and at the appointed place, sure enough, they met Dragonbeard. Li Dsing had an old friend, a companion of the Prince of Tang.

He presented the stranger to this friend, named Liu Wendsing, saying, "This stranger is able to foretell the future from the lines of the face, and would like to see the prince."

Thereupon Liu Wendsing took him to the prince. The prince was clothed in a simple indoor robe, but there was something impressive about him, which made him remarked among all others. When the stranger saw him, he fell into a profound silence, and his face turned grey. After he had drunk a few flagons of wine he took his leave.

"That man is a true ruler," he told Li Dsing. "I am almost certain of the fact, but to be sure my friend must also see him."

Then he arranged to meet Li Dsing on a certain day at a certain inn.

"When you see this mule before the door, together with a very lean jackass, then you may be certain I am there with my friend."

On the day set Li Dsing went there and, sure enough he saw the mule and the jackass before the door. He gathered up his robe and descended to the upper story of the inn. There sat old Dragonbeard and a Taoist priest over their wine. When the former saw Li Dsing he was much pleased, bade him sit down and offered him wine. After they had pledged each other, all three returned to Liu Wendsing. He was engaged in a game of chess with the prince. The prince rose with respect and asked them to be seated.

As soon as the Taoist priest saw his radiant and heroic countenance he was disconcerted, and greeted him with a low bow, saying, "The game is up!"

When they took their leave Dragonbeard said to Li Dsing, "Go on to Sianfu, and when the time has come, ask for me at such and such a place."

And with that he went away snorting.

Tales Of The Gùshì Yuán

Li Dsing and the fan-bearer packed up their belongings, left Taiyuanfu and travelled on toward the West. At that time Yang Su died, and great disturbance arose throughout the empire.

In the course of a few days Li Dsing and his wife reached the meeting-place appointed by Dragonbeard. They knocked at a little wooden door, and out came a servant, who led them through long passages. When they emerged magnificent buildings arose before them, in front of which stood a crowd of slave girls. Then they entered a hall in which the most valuable dowry that could be imagined had been piled up. There were mirrors, clothes, jewellery, all more beautiful than earth is wont to show. Handsome slave girls led them to the bath, and when they had changed their garments their friend was announced. He stepped in clad in silks and fox-pelts, and looking almost like a dragon or a tiger. He greeted his guests with pleasure and also called in his wife, who was of exceptional loveliness. A festive banquet was served, and all four sat down to it. The table was covered with the most expensive viands, so rare that they did not even know their names. Flagons and dishes and all the utensils were made of gold and jade, and ornamented with pearls and precious stones. Two companies of girl musicians alternately blew flutes and chalameaus. They sang and danced, and it seemed to the visitors that they had been transported to the palace of the Lady of the Moon. The rainbow garments fluttered, and the dancing girls were beautiful beyond all the beauty of earth.

After they had banqueted, Dragonbeard commanded his servitors to bring in couches upon which embroidered silken covers had been spread. And after they had seen everything worth seeing, he presented them with a book and a key.

Then he said, "In this book are listed the valuables and the riches which I possess. I make you a wedding-present of them. Nothing great may be undertaken without wealth, and it is my duty to endow my sister properly. My original intention had been to take the Middle Kingdom in hand and do something with it. But since a ruler has already arisen to reign over it, what is there to keep me in this country? For Prince Tang of Taiyuanfu is a real hero, and will have restored order within a few years' time. You must both of you aid him, and you will be certain to rise to high honours. You, my sister, are not alone beautiful, but you have also the right way of looking at things. None other than yourself would have been able to recognize the true worth of Li Dsing, and none other than Li Dsing would have had the good fortune to encounter you. You will share the honours which will be your husband's portion, and your name will be recorded in history. The treasures which I bestow upon you, you are to use to help the true ruler. Bear this in mind! And in ten years' time a glow will rise far away to the South-east, and it shall be a sign that I have reached my goal. Then you may pour a libation of wine in the direction of the South-east, to wish me good fortune!"

Then, one after another, his servitors and slave-girls greeted Li Dsing and the fan-bearer, and said to them, "This is your master and mistress!" When he had spoken these words, he took his wife's hand, they mounted three steeds which were held ready, and rode away.

Li Dsing and his wife now established themselves in the house, and found themselves possessed of countless wealth. They followed Prince Tang, who restored order to the empire, and aided him with their money. Thus the great work was accomplished, and after peace had been restored throughout the empire, Li Dsing was made Duke of We, and the fan-bearer became a duchess.

Ten years later the duke was informed that in the empire beyond the sea a thousand ships had landed an army of a hundred thousand armoured soldiers, who had conquered the country, killed its prince, and set up their leader as king. And order now reigned in that empire.

Then the duke knew that Dragonbeard had accomplished his aim. He told his wife, and they robed themselves in robes of ceremony and offered wine to wish him good fortune. And they saw a radiant crimson ray flash up on the South-eastern horizon. No doubt Dragonbeard had answered, and both of them were very happy.

Tales Of The Gùshì Yuán

Note: Yang Su died in the year 606 A.D. Li Dsing was a historical person, 571-649 A.D. Li Yuan was the founder of the Tang dynasty, 565-635 A.D. His famous son, to whom he owed the throne, the "Prince of Tang," was named Li Schi Min. His father abdicated in 618 in his favour.

A Legend Of Confucius

This story has been adapted from Dr. Richard Wilhelm's version that originally appeared in The Chinese Fairy Book, published in 1921 by Frederick A. Stokes Company, New York. Wilhelm's translations aimed to capture the essence of the original Chinese texts while making them accessible to English-speaking audiences. His deep understanding of Chinese language and culture shone through in his translations, allowing readers to appreciate the beauty and depth of these timeless tales.

When Confucius came to the earth, the Kilin, that strange beast which is the prince of all four-footed animals, and only appears when there is a great man on earth, sought the child and spat out a jade whereon was written, 'Son of the Watercrystal you are destined to become an uncrowned king!' And Confucius grew up, studied diligently, learned wisdom and came to be a saint. He did much good on earth, and ever since his death has been revenced as the greatest of teachers and masters. He had foreknowledge of many things. And even after he had died he gave evidence of this.

Once, when the wicked Emperor Tsin Schi Huang had conquered all the other kingdoms, and was traveling through the entire empire, he came to the homeland of Confucius. And he found his grave. And, finding his grave, he wished to have it opened and see what was in it. All his officials advised him not to do so, but he would not listen to them. So a passage was dug into the grave, and in its main chamber they found a coffin, whose wood appeared to be quite fresh. When struck it sounded like metal. To the left of the coffin was a door, which led into an inner chamber. In this chamber stood a bed, and a table with books and clothing, all as though meant for the use of a living person. Tsin Schi Huang seated himself on the bed and looked down. And there on the floor stood two shoes of red silk, whose tips were adorned with a woven pattern of clouds. A bamboo staff leaned against the wall. The Emperor, in jest, put on the shoes, took the staff and left the grave. But as he did so a tablet suddenly appeared before his eyes on which stood the following lines:

O'er kingdoms six Tsin Schi Huang his army led,

To open my grave and find my humble bed;

He steals my shoes and takes my staff away

To reach Schakiu, and his last earthly day!

Tsin Schi Huang was much alarmed, and had the grave closed again. But when he reached Schakiu he fell ill of a hasty fever of which he died.

Note: The Kilin is an okapi-like legendary beast of the most perfected kindness, prince of all the four-footed animals. The "Watercrystal" is the dark Lord of the North, whose element is water and wisdom, for which last reason Confucius is termed his son. Tsin Schi Huang (BCE. 200) is the burner of books and reorganizer of China famed in history.

Tales Of The Gùshì Yuán

The Beautiful Daughter Of Liu-Kung

This story has been adapted from Rev. John MacGowan's version that originally appeared in Chinese Folk-Lore Tales, published in 1910 by MacMillan and Company, London. Chinese Folk-Lore Tales features a variety of stories that cover a wide range of themes, including mythology, morality, adventure, and romance. These tales often incorporate elements of Chinese folklore, legends, and superstitions, providing readers with a glimpse into the beliefs and values of traditional Chinese society.

In one of the central provinces of this long-lived Empire of China, there lived in very early times a man of the name of Chan. He was a person of a bright, active nature which made him enjoy life, and caused him to be popular amongst his companions and a favourite with everyone who knew him. But he was also a scholar, well-versed in the literature of his country, and he spent every moment that he could spare in the study of the great writings of the famous men of former days.

In order that he might be interrupted as little as possible in his pursuit of learning, he engaged a room in a famous monastery some miles away from his own home. The only inhabitants of this monastery were a dozen or so Buddhist priests, who, except when they were engaged in the daily services of the temple, lived a quiet, humdrum, lazy kind of existence which harmonized well with the solitude and the majestic stillness of the mountain scenery by which they were surrounded.

This monastery was indeed one of the most beautiful in China. It was situated on the slope of a hill, looking down upon a lovely valley, where the natural solitude was as complete as the most devoted hermit could desire. The only means of getting to it were the narrow hill footpaths along which the worshippers from the great city and the scattered villages wound in and out on festal days, when they came trooping to the temple to make their offerings to the famous God enshrined within.

Chan was a diligent student, and rarely indulged in recreation of any kind. Occasionally, when his mind became oppressed with excessive study he would go for a quiet walk along the hillside, but these occasions were few and far between, for he made up for every hour he spent away from his beloved books by still closer application to them in the hours that followed.

One day he was strolling in an aimless kind of way on the hillside, when suddenly a party of hunters from the neighbouring city of Eternal Spring came dashing into view. They were a merry group and full of excitement, for they had just sighted a fox which Chan had seen a moment before flying away at its highest speed in mortal dread of its pursuers.

Prominent amongst the hunters was a young girl, who was mounted on a fiery little steed, so full of spirit and so eager to follow in the mad chase after the prey, that its rider seemed to have some difficulty in restraining it. The girl herself was a perfect picture. Her face was the loveliest that Chan had ever looked upon, and her figure, which her trim hunting dress showed off to the utmost advantage, was graceful in the extreme. As she swept by him with her face flushed with excitement and her features all aglow with health, Chan felt at once that he had lost his heart and that he was deeply and profoundly in love with her.

On making enquiries, he found that she was named Willow, that she was the daughter of the chief mandarin of the town in which she lived, and that she was intensely fond of the chase and delighted in galloping over the hills and valleys in the pursuit of the wild animals to be found there. So powerfully had Chan's mind been affected by what he had seen of Willow, that he had already begun to entertain serious thoughts of making her his wife, but while his mind was full of this delightful prospect he was plunged into the deepest grief by hearing that she had suddenly died. For some days he was so stricken with sorrow that he lost all interest in life, and could do nothing but dwell on the memory of her whom he had come to love with all the devotion of his heart.

A few weeks after the news of her death, the quiet of the retreat was one day broken by a huge procession which wound its way along the mountain path leading to the monastery doors. On looking out, Chan saw that many of the men in this procession were dressed in sackcloth, and that in front of it was a band of musicians producing weird, shrill notes on their various instruments.

By these signs Chan knew that what he saw was a funeral, and he expected to see the long line of mourners pass on to some spot on the hillside where the dead would be buried. Instead of that, however, they entered through the great gates of the monastery, and the coffin, the red pall of which told him that it contained the body of a woman, was carried into an inner room of the building and laid on trestles that had been made ready for it.

After the mourners had dispersed, Chan asked one of the priests the name of the woman who had died, and how it was that the coffin was laid within the precincts of the temple instead of in the house of the deceased, where it could be looked after by her relatives and where the customary sacrifices to the spirit of the dead could be offered more conveniently than in the monastery.

The bonze replied that this was a peculiar case, calling for special treatment. "The father of the poor young girl who died so suddenly," he said, "was the mandarin of the neighbouring city of Eternal Spring. Just after the death of his daughter an order came from the Emperor transferring him to another district, a thousand miles from here.

"The command was very urgent that he should proceed without delay to take up his post in the far-off province, and that he was to allow nothing to hinder him from doing so. He could not carry his daughter's body with him on so long a journey, and no time was permitted to take the coffin to his home, where she might be buried amongst her own kindred. It was equally impossible to deposit the coffin in the yamen he was about to leave, for the new mandarin who was soon to arrive would certainly object to have the body of a stranger in such close proximity to his family. It might bring him bad luck, and his career as an official might end in disaster.

"Permission was therefore asked from our abbot to allow the coffin to be placed in one of our vacant rooms, until the father some day in the future can come and bear the body of his beloved daughter to the home of his ancestors, there to be laid at rest amongst his own people.

"This request was readily granted, for whilst he was in office the mandarin showed us many favours, and his daughter was a beautiful girl who was beloved by everyone, and so we were only too glad to do anything in our power to help in this unhappy matter."

Chan was profoundly moved when he realized that the woman whom he had loved as his own life lay dead within a chamber only a few steps away from his own. His passion, instead of being crushed out of his heart by the thought that she was utterly beyond his reach, and by no possibility could ever be more to him than a memory, seemed to grow in intensity as he became conscious that it was an absolutely hopeless one.

On that very same evening, about midnight, when silence rested on the monastery, and the priests were all wrapped in slumber, Chan, with a lighted taper in his hand, stole with noiseless footsteps along the dark passages into the chamber of death where his beloved lay. Kneeling beside the coffin with a heart full of emotion, in trembling accents he called upon Willow to listen to the story of his passion.

He spoke to her just as though she were standing face to face with him, and he told her how he had fallen in love with her on the day on which he had caught a glimpse of her as she galloped in pursuit of the fox that had fled through the valley from the hunters. He had planned, he told her, to make her his wife, and he described, in tones through which the tears could be heard to run, how heart-broken he was when he heard of her death.

"I want to see you," he continued, "for I feel that I cannot live without you. You are near to me, and yet oh, how far away. Can you not come from the Land of Shadows, where you are now, and comfort me by one vision of your fair face, and one sound of the voice that would fill my soul with the sweetest music?"

For many months the comfort of Chan's life was this nightly visit to the chamber where his dead love lay. Not a single night passed without his going to tell her of the unalterable and undying affection that filled his heart, and whilst the temple lay shrouded in darkness, and the only sounds that broke the stillness were those inexplicable ones in which nature seems to indulge when man is removed by sleep from the scene, Chan was uttering those love notes which had lain deeply hidden within his soul, but which now in the utter desolation of his heart burst forth to ease his pain by their mere expression.

One night as he was sitting poring over his books, he happened to turn round, and was startled to see the figure of a young girl standing just inside the door of his room. It seemed perfectly human, and yet it was so ethereal that it had the appearance of a spirit of the other world. As he looked at the girl with a wondering gaze, a smile lit up her beautiful features, and he then discovered to his great joy that she was none other than Willow, his lost love whom he had despaired of ever seeing again.

With her face wreathed in smiles, she sat down beside him and said in a timid, modest way, "I am here tonight in response to the great love which has never faltered since the day I died. That is the magnet which has had the power of drawing me from the Land of Shadows. I felt it there, and many speak about it in that sunless country. Even Yam-lo, the lord of the spirits of that dreary world, has been moved by your unchanging devotion, so much so that he has given me permission to come and see you, in order that I might tell you how deeply my heart is moved by the profound affection that you have exhibited for me all these months during which you never had any expectation of its being returned."

For many months this sweet intercourse between Chan and his beloved Willow was carried on, and no one in the whole monastery knew anything of it. The interviews always took place about midnight, and Willow, who seemed to pass with freedom through closed doors or the stoutest walls, invariably vanished during the small hours of the morning.

One evening whilst they were conversing on topics agreeable to them both, Willow unburdened her heart to Chan, and told him how unhappy she was in the world of spirits.

"You know," she said, "that before I died I was not married, and so I am only a wandering spirit with no place where I can rest, and no friends to whom I can take myself. I travel here and there and everywhere, feeling that no one cares for me, and that there are no ties to bind me to any particular place or thing. For a young girl like me, this is a very sad and sorrowful state of things."

"There is another thing that adds to my sorrow in the Land of Shadows," she went on to say, with a mournful look on her lovely countenance. "I was very fond of hunting when I was in my father's home, and many a wild animal was slain in the hunting expeditions in which I took an active part. This has all told against me in the world in which I am now living, and for the share I took in destroying life I have to suffer by many pains and penalties which are hard for me to endure."

"My sin has been great," she said, "and so I wish to make special offerings in this temple to the Goddess of Mercy and implore her to send down to the other world a good report of me to Yam-lo, and intercede with him to forgive the sins of which I have been guilty. If you will do this for me, I promise that after I have been born again into the world I will never forget you, and if you like to wait for me I shall willingly become your wife and serve you with the deepest devotion of which my heart is capable, as long as Heaven will permit you and me to live together as husband and wife."

From this time, much to the astonishment of the priests in the monastery, Chan began to show unwonted enthusiasm for the service of the Goddess, and would sometimes spend hours before her image and repeat long prayers to her. This was all the more remarkable, as the scholar had rarely if ever shown any desire to have anything to do with the numerous gods which were enshrined in various parts of the temple.

After some months of this daily appeal to the Goddess of Mercy, Willow informed him that his prayers had been so far successful that the misery of her lot in the Land of Shadows had been greatly mitigated. The pleadings of the Goddess with Yam-lo had so influenced his heart towards Willow that she believed her great sin in the destruction of animal life had been forgiven, and there were signs that the dread ruler of the Underworld was looking upon her with kindness.

Chan was delighted with this news, and his prayers and offerings became still more frequent and more fervent. He little dreamed that his devotion to the Goddess would be the means of his speedy separation from Willow, but so it was. One evening she came as usual to see him, but instead of entering with smiling face and laughter in her eyes, she was weeping bitterly as though she were in the direst sorrow. Chan was in the greatest distress when he saw this and asked her to explain the reason for her grief.

"The reason for my tears," she said, "is because after this evening I shall not see you again. Your petitions to the Goddess have had such a powerful effect upon her mind that she has used all her influence with Yam-lo to induce him to set me free from the misery of the Land of Shadows, and so I am to leave that sunless country and to be born again into life in this upper world."

As she uttered these words her tears began to flow once more and her whole frame was convulsed with sobbing.

"I am glad," she said, "that I am to be born once more and live amongst men, but I cannot bear the thought of having to be separated for so long from you. Let us not grieve too much, however. It is our fate, and we may not rebel against it. Yam-lo has been kinder to me than he has ever been to anyone in the past, for he has revealed to me the family into which I am to be born and the place where they live, so if you come to me in eighteen years you will find me waiting for you. Your love has been so great that it has entered into my very soul, and there is nothing that can ever efface it from my heart. A thousand re-births may take place, but never shall I love any one as I love you."

Chan professed that he was greatly comforted by this confession of her love, but all the same he felt in despair when he thought of the future. "When next I see you," he said with a sigh, "I shall be getting so old that you, a young girl in the first flush of womanhood, will not care to look at me. My hair will have turned grey and my face will be marked with wrinkles, and in the re-birth you will have forgotten all that took place in the Land of Shadows, and the memory of me will have vanished from your heart for ever."

Willow looked with loving but sorrowful eyes upon her lover as he was expressing his concern about the future, but quickly assured him that nothing in the world would ever cause her to cease to remember him with the tenderest affection.

"In order to comfort you," she said, "let me tell you of two things that the dread Yam-lo, out of consideration for your love for me, has granted me, two things which he has never bestowed upon any other mortal who has come within the region of his rule. The first is, he has allowed me to inspect the book of Life and Death, in which is recorded the history of every human being, with the times of their re-births and the places in which they are to be born. I want you this very minute to write down the secret which has been revealed to me as to my new name and family and the place where I shall reside, so that you will have no difficulty in finding me, when eighteen years hence you shall come to claim me as your wife.

"The next is a gift so precious that I have no words in which to express my gratitude for its having been bestowed upon me. It is this. I am given the privilege of not forgetting what has taken place during my stay in the Land of Shadows, and so when I am re-born into another part of China, with a new father and mother, I shall hold within my memory my recollection of you. The years will pass quickly, for I shall be looking for you, and this day eighteen years hence will be the happiest in my life, for it will bring you to me never more to be separated from me."

"But I must hasten on," she hurriedly exclaimed, "for the footsteps of fate are moving steadily towards me. In a few minutes the gates of Hades will have closed against me, and Willow will have vanished, and I shall be a babe once more with my new life before me. See, but a minute more is left to me, and I seem to have so much to say. Farewell! Never forget me! I shall ever remember you, but my time is come!"

As she uttered these words, a smile of ineffable sweetness flashed across, her beautiful face, and she was gone.

Chan was inexpressibly sad at the loss he had sustained by the re-birth of Willow, and in order to drive away his sorrow he threw his heart and soul into his studies. His books became his constant companions, and he tried to find in them a solace for the loneliness which had come upon him since the visits of Willow had ceased. He also became a diligent worshipper of the idols, and especially of the Goddess of Mercy, who had played such an important part in the history of his beloved Willow.

The years went slowly by, and Chan began to feel that he was growing old. His hair became dashed with silver threads, and wrinkles appeared in his forehead and under his eyes. The strain of waiting for the one woman who had taken complete possession of his heart had been too much for him. As the time drew near, too, when he should go to meet her, a great and nervous dread began to fill him with anxiety. Would she recognize him? And would she, a young girl of eighteen, be content to accept as a husband a man so advanced in years as he now was? These questions were constantly flashing through his brain.

Eventually only a few months remained before he was to set out on his journey to the distant province where Yam-lo had decided that Willow was to begin her new life on earth.

He was sitting one evening in his study, brooding over the great problem that would be solved before long, when a man dressed in black silently entered the room. Looking on Chan with a kindly smile which seemed to find its way instantly to his heart, he informed him that he was a fairy from the Western Heaven and that he had been specially deputed by the rulers there to render him all the assistance in his power at this particular crisis, when they knew his heart was so full of anxiety.

"We have all heard in that far-off fairyland," he continued, "of the devotion you have shown to Willow, and how during all the years which have intervened since you saw her last you have never faltered in your love for her. Such affection is rare among mortals, and the dwellers in fairyland would like to help in bringing together two such loving hearts, for let me assure you that however strong your feeling for the one whom you are so anxious to see again, she on her part is just as deeply in love with you, and is now counting the days until she will be able to see you and until you need never again be parted from each other. In order to assist in this happy consummation, I want you to take a short trip with me. It will only take a few hours, and you will then find that something has happened to remove all your fears as to how you will be received by Willow."

The fairy man then led Chan to the door, and gave a wave of his hand in the direction of the sky. Instantly the sound of the fluttering and swish of wings was heard, and in a moment a splendid eagle landed gracefully at their feet. Taking their seats upon its back, they found themselves flashing at lightning speed away through the darkness of the night. Higher and higher they rose, till they had pierced the heavy masses of clouds which hung hovering in the sky. Swift as an arrow the eagle still cleft its way upward until the clouds had vanished to an infinite distance below them, and still onward they were borne in the mighty stillness of an expanse where no human being had ever travelled before.

Chan felt his heart throb with a nervousness which he could not control. What if the bird should tire, he thought, and he should be dropped into the fathomless abyss below? Life's journey would then come to a tragic end. Where, too, was he being carried and how should he be ever able to return to his far-off home on the earth? He was becoming more and more agitated, when the fairy took hold of his hand and in a voice which at once stilled his fears, assured him that there was not the least danger in this journey through the air.

"We are as safe here," he assured him, "as though we were standing upon a mountain whose roots lie miles below the surface of the earth. And see," he continued, pointing to something in the distance, "we shall arrive at our destination in the course of a few seconds."

True enough, he had hardly finished speaking when a land, fairer than Chan had ever seen on earth or pictured in imagination, loomed up suddenly in front of them, and before he could gather together his astonished thoughts, the eagle had landed them on its shores, and with outspread wings was soaring into the mystery of the unknown beyond.

The fairy now led Chan along a road surrounded by the most bewildering beauty. Rare flowers, graceful trees, and birds which made the groves resound with the sweetest music, were objects that kept his mind in one continual state of delight. Before long they arrived in front of a magnificent palace, so grand and vast that Chan felt afraid to enter within its portals, or even tread the avenue leading up to it.

Once more his companion relieved Chan's anxiety by assuring him that he was an expected guest, and that the Queen of this fairy country had sent him to earth specially to invite him to come and visit her, in order that she might bestow upon him a blessing which would enrich the whole of his life and would enable him to spend many happy years with her whom he had loved with such devotion.

Chan was ushered into a large reception hall, where he was met by a very stately lady, with a face full of benevolence, whom he at once recognized, from the images he had often worshipped, as the Goddess of Mercy. He was startled when he discovered in what august presence he was standing, and began to tremble with excitement as he realized that here in actual life was the famous personage whose image was worshipped by the millions of China, and whose influence spread even into the Land of Shadows.

Seeing Chan's humility and evident terror of her, the Goddess spoke to him in a gentle, loving voice, and told him to have no fear, for she had summoned him to her presence not to rebuke but to comfort him.

"I know your story," she said, "and I think it is a beautiful one. Before I was raised to the high position I now occupy I was at one time a woman like Willow, and I can sympathize with her in her devotion to you because of the wonderful love you have shown her from the first moment that you saw her.

"I know, too, your anxiety about your age, and your fear that when Willow sees you with the marks of advancing years upon you, her love may die out and you will be left with your heart broken and in despair. I have foreseen this difficulty, and I am going to have it removed.

"The fairy who brought you here," she continued, "will now take you round the palace grounds, and if you will carry out my wishes, the fears which have been troubling you for years shall entirely vanish. You will then meet Willow with a heart as light as that of any man in the flush of youth, who awaits the coming of the bridal chair which bears his future wife to his home."

Chan at once, without any hesitation, followed his guide through the spacious grounds which surrounded the palace, and was finally led to the edge of a beautiful little lake embowered amongst trees and ferns, and rare and fragrant flowers. It was the most exquisite scene on which his vision had ever rested.

With a kindly look at his companion, the fairy said, "This beautiful piece of water goes by the name of the 'Fountain of Eternal Youth,' and it is the Queen's express desire that you should bathe in it."

Quickly undressing, Chan plunged into the pool and for a moment sank beneath the surface of the waters. Emerging quickly from them, a delightful feeling of new-born strength seemed to be creeping in at every pore of his body. The sense of advancing age passed away, and the years of youth appeared to come back to him again. He felt as though he were a young man once more, for the weary doubts, which for some years past had made his footsteps lag, had gone with his first plunge into those fragrant waters.

By-and-by he came out of this 'Fountain of Eternal Youth' with the visions and ambitions of his young manhood rushing through his brain. His powers, which seemed of late to have become dull and sluggish, had recovered the impetus which in earlier years had carried him so successfully through many a severe examination. His thoughts, too, about Willow had so completely changed that instead of dreading the day when he should stand before her, his one passionate desire now was to start upon his journey to keep his appointment with her.

Chan and the fairy then proceeded to the edge of the vast and boundless expanse which bordered the palace of the Goddess, and found a magnificent dragon waiting to convey them back to earth. No sooner had they taken their seats on its back than it fled with the swiftness of the wind through the untrodden spaces of the air, until at length the mountains came looming out of the dim and shadowy distance, and with a rush Chan found himself safely landed at the door of the temple from which he had taken his departure for his amazing journey to the Western Heaven.

Whilst these wonderful things were taking place, Willow, or rather Precious Pearl, as she had been named by her new parents, who of course had no knowledge of her previous history, had grown up to be a most beautiful and fascinating woman.

During all these years she had never ceased to look forward with an anxious heart to the day when she would once more meet the man to whom she had betrothed herself eighteen years ago. Latterly she had begun to count the days that must still elapse before she could see him again. She never forgot the night in the temple when she bade him "Good-bye" just before she was reborn into this world. The day and the hour had been stamped upon her memory, and since then the years had seemed to travel with halting, leaden feet, as though they were loath to move on. But now only a few months remained, and no doubt ever entered her brain that Chan would fail her.

Just about this time her mother had an offer of marriage for her from a very wealthy and distinguished family, and contrary to the usual custom of mothers in China she asked her daughter what she thought of the proposal. Pearl was distressed beyond measure, and prayed and entreated her mother on no account to broach the subject to her again, as she could never entertain any proposition of the kind.

Amazed at such a statement, her mother begged her to explain her reason for such strange views. "Girls at your age," she said, "are usually betrothed and are thinking of having homes of their own. This is the universal custom throughout the Empire, and therefore there must be some serious reason why you will not allow me to make arrangements for your being allied to some respectable family."

Pearl had been feeling that the time was drawing near when she would have to divulge the secret of her love affair, and she considered that now was the best opportunity for doing so. To the astonishment therefore of her mother, who believed that she was romancing, she told her the whole story of the past, how Chan had fallen in love with her, and how after she had died and had come under the control of Yam-lo in the Land of Shadows, that dread lord had permitted her spirit to visit her lover in the temple where her body had been laid until a lucky resting-place could be found for it on the hillside. She also explained how it had been agreed between them that she was to wait for him until after the lapse of eighteen years, when she would be old enough to become his wife. "In a few months the time will be up," she concluded, "and so I beseech you not to speak of my being betrothed to anyone else, for I feel that if I am compelled to marry any other than Chan I shall die."

The mother was thunderstruck at this wonderful story which her daughter told her. She could only imagine that Pearl had in some way or another been bewitched, and was under a fatal delusion that she was in love with some hero of romance, to whom she believed she was betrothed. Still, her daughter had always been most loving and devoted to her, and had shown more brightness and ability than Chinese girls of her age usually possessed. Her mother did not like, therefore, to reprove her for what she considered her ridiculous ideas, so she determined to try another plan to cure her of her folly.

"What age was this man Chan," she asked, "when you entered into this engagement with him?"

"He was just thirty," Pearl replied. "He was of very good family and a scholar, and had distinguished himself for his proficiency in the ancient literature of China."

"Oh, then he must be nearly fifty now. A fine mate he would make for you, a young girl of only eighteen! But who knows how he may have changed since last you saw him? His hair must be turning grey, and his teeth may have fallen out, and for anything you know he may have been dead and buried so long ago that by this time they have taken up his bones, and nothing is left of him but his ashes."

"Oh, I do pray that nothing of that kind has happened to him," cried Pearl, in a tone of voice which showed the anguish she was suffering. "Let us leave the question for a few months, and then when he comes for me, as I know he will, you will find by personal knowledge what a splendid man he is, and how entirely worthy he is of being your son-in-law."

On the day which had been appointed under such romantic circumstances eighteen years before, Chan arrived in the town, and after taking a room in an inn and making certain enquiries, he made his way to the home where he believed that Willow resided. On his arrival, however, he was roughly told by the servant that no such person as Willow lived there, and that they did not like strangers coming about the house. Indeed he was given plainly to understand that the sooner he left, the better everyone would be pleased. This treatment was of course part of a scheme devised by Pearl's parents to frustrate any plans that Chan might have formed for seeing her. They were determined not to give their daughter to a man so old as he must be, and therefore they decided that an interview between the two must be prevented at all hazards.

Chan was greatly distressed at the rebuff which he had received. Had Willow after all made a mistake eighteen years ago when she gave him the name of this town as the place where her new home was to be? He had carefully written it down at her dictation, and it had been burned into his brain all the years since. No, there could be no mistake on that point. If there were any, then it was one that had been made purposely by Yam-lo in order to deceive them both. That idea, however, was unthinkable, and so there must be something else to account for his not finding Willow as he had expected. He at once made enquiries at the inn at which he was staying, and found that there was a daughter at the very house to which he had gone, and that in almost every particular the description he was given of her corresponded with his beloved Willow.

In the meantime, poor Pearl was in a state of the greatest anxiety. The eventful day on which she was to meet her lover had opened for her with keen expectation of meeting him after their long and romantic separation. She had never for one moment doubted that he would keep his engagement with her. An instinct which she could not explain made her feel certain that he was still alive, and that nothing in the world would prevent him from meeting her, as had been agreed upon between them at that eventful parting in the temple eighteen years before.

As the day wore on, however, and there were no signs of Chan, Pearl's distress became exceedingly pitiful, and when night came and her mother declared that nothing had been seen of him, she was so stricken with despair that she lost all consciousness, and had to be carried to bed, where she lay in a kind of trance from which, for some time, it seemed impossible to arouse her.

When eventually she did regain consciousness, her mother tried to comfort her by saying that perhaps Chan was dead, or that he had forgotten her in the long course of years, and that therefore she must not grieve too much. "You are a young girl," she said, "and you have a long life before you. Chan is an old man by this time, no doubt he has long ago married, and the home ties which he has formed have caused him to forget you. But you need not be broken-hearted on that account. There are many other men who will be more suitable for you than he could possibly be. By-and-by we shall arrange a marriage for you, and then life will appear to you very different from what it does now."

Instead of being comforted, however, Pearl was only the more distressed by her mother's words. Her love, which had begun in the Land of Shadows, and which had been growing in her heart for the last eighteen years, was not one to be easily put aside by such plausible arguments as those she had just listened to. The result was that she had a relapse, and for several days her life was in great danger.

The father and mother, fearing now that their daughter would die, determined, as there seemed no other remedy, to bring Chan to their home, and see whether his presence would not deliver Pearl from the danger in which the doctor declared she undoubtedly was.

The father accordingly went to the inn where he knew Chan was staying, and to his immense surprise he found him to be a young man of about twenty-five, highly polished in manner, and possessed of unusual intelligence. For some time he utterly refused to believe that this handsome young fellow was really the man with whom Pearl was so deeply in love, and it was not until Chan had told him the romantic story of his life that he could at all believe that he was not being imposed upon. Eventually, however, he was so taken with Chan that he became determined to do all in his power to bring about his marriage with his daughter.

"Come with me at once," he said, "and see if your presence will not do more than the cleverest doctors in the town have been able to accomplish. Pearl has been so distressed at not seeing you that she is now seriously ill, and we have been afraid that she would die of a broken heart."

When they arrived at the house Chan was taken into the sick-room, and the girl gazed into his face with a look of wonderment. "I do not seem to recognize you," she said in a feeble voice. "You are much younger than Chan, and although there is something about you that reminds me of him, I cannot realize that you are the same person with whom my spirit eighteen years ago held fellowship in the monastery where my body lay unburied."

Chan proceeded to explain the mystery. "For years," he said, "my mind was troubled about the difference between our ages. I was afraid that when you saw me with grey hairs and with wrinkles on my face, your love would receive a shock, and you might regret that you had ever pledged yourself to me. Although you had vanished from my sight, my prayers still continued to be offered to the Goddess of Mercy. She had heard them for you, you remember, when you were in the Land of Shadows, and through her intercession Yam-lo had forgiven your sins, and had made life easier for you in that gloomy country.

"I still continued to pray to her, hoping in some vague way that she would intervene to bring about the desire of my heart, and that when in due time I should meet you again, every obstacle to our mutual love would be forever removed.

"One day a fairy came into the very room where your spirit had often conversed with me. He carried me away with him to the Western Heaven and brought me into the very presence of the Goddess of Mercy. She gave directions for me to bathe in the 'Fountain of Eternal Youth,' and I became young again. That is why you see me now with a young face and a young nature, but my heart in its love for you has never changed, and never will as long as life lasts."

As he was telling this entrancing story, a look of devoted love spread over the beautiful countenance of Pearl. She gradually became instinct with life, and before he had finished speaking, the lassitude and exhaustion which had seemed to threaten her very life entirely disappeared. A rosy look came over her face, and her coal-black eyes flashed with hidden fires.

"Now I know," she cried, "that you are Chan. You are so changed that when I first caught sight of you my heart sank, for I had pictured an older man, and I could not at once realize that you were the same Chan who showed such unbounded love for me in the years gone by.

"It was not that I should have loved you less even though you had been older. My heart would never have changed. It was only my doubt as to your reality that made me hesitate, but now my happiness is great, for since through the goodness of the Goddess you have recovered your youth, I need not fear that the difference between our years may in the near future bring to us an eternal separation."

In a few days Pearl was once more herself again. Her parents, delighted with the romantic turn that things had taken and highly pleased with Chan himself, arranged for the betrothal of their daughter to him, and in the course of a few months, the loving couple were united in marriage. And so, after years of waiting, the happy consummation was accomplished, which Heaven and the Goddess of Mercy and even the dread Ruler of the Land of Shadows had each taken a share in bringing about, and for many and many a long year the story of Chan and his wife was spread abroad throughout the region in which they lived.

Tales Of The Gùshì Yuán

Laotsze

This story has been adapted from Dr. Richard Wilhelm's version that originally appeared in The Chinese Fairy Book, published in 1921 by Frederick A. Stokes Company, New York. Wilhelm's translations aimed to capture the essence of the original Chinese texts while making them accessible to English-speaking audiences. His deep understanding of Chinese language and culture shone through in his translations, allowing readers to appreciate the beauty and depth of these timeless tales.

Laotsze is really older than heaven and earth put together. He is the Yellow Lord or Ancient, who created this world together with the other four. At various times he has appeared on earth, under various names. His most celebrated incarnation, however, is that of Laotsze, 'The Old Child,' which name he was given because he made his appearance on earth with white hair.

He acquired all sorts of magic powers by means of which he extended his life-span. Once he hired a servant to do his bidding. He agreed to give him a hundred pieces of copper daily, yet he did not pay him, and finally he owed him seven million, two hundred thousand pieces of copper. Then he mounted a black steer and rode to the West. He wanted to take his servant along. But when they reached the Han-Gu pass, the servant refused to go further, and insisted on being paid. Yet Laotsze gave him nothing.

When they came to the house of the guardian of the pass, red clouds appeared in the sky. The guardian understood this sign and knew that a holy man was drawing near. So he went out to meet him and took him into his house. He questioned him with regard to hidden knowledge, but Laotsze only stuck out his tongue at him and would not say a word. Nevertheless, the guardian of the pass treated him with the greatest respect in his home.

Laotsze's servant told the servant of the guardian that his master owed him a great deal of money, and begged the latter to put in a good word for him. When the guardian's servant heard how large a sum it was, he was tempted to win so wealthy a man for a son-in-law, and he married him to his daughter. Finally the guardian heard of the matter and came to Laotsze together with the servant.

Then Laotsze said to his servant, "You rascally servant. You really should have been dead long ago. I hired you, and since I was poor and could give you no money, I gave you a life-giving talisman to eat. That is how you still happen to be alive. I said to you, 'If you will follow me into the West, the land of Blessed Repose, I will pay you your wages in yellow gold.' But you did not wish to do this."

And with that he patted his servant's neck. Thereupon the latter opened his mouth, and spat out the life-giving talisman. The magic signs written on it with cinnabar, quite fresh and well-preserved, might still be seen. But the servant suddenly collapsed and turned into a heap of dry bones. Then the guardian of the pass cast himself to earth and pleaded for him. He promised to pay the servant for Laotsze and begged the latter to restore him to life. So Laotsze placed the talisman among the bones and at once the servant came to life again. The guardian of the pass paid him his wages and dismissed him.

Then he adored Laotsze as his master, and the latter taught him the art of eternal life, and left him his teachings, in five thousand words, which the guardian wrote down. The book which thus came into being is the *Tao Teh King, The Book of the Way and Life*. Laotsze then disappeared from the eyes of men. The guardian of the pass however, followed his teachings, and was given a place among the immortals.

Tales Of The Gùshì Yuán

Note: The Taoists like to assert that Laotsze's journey to the West was undertaken before the birth of Buddha, who, according to many, is only a reincarnation of Laotsze.

The Strange Tale Of Doctor Dog

This story has been adapted from Norman Hinsdale Pitman's version that originally appeared in A Chinese Wonder Book, published in 1919 by E. P. Dutton And Company, New York. A Chinese Wonder Book contains a selection of stories that capture the essence of traditional Chinese culture and storytelling. The book includes tales of magic, dragons, heroes, and supernatural creatures, all woven together with elements of Chinese mythology and folklore.

Far up in the mountains of the Province of Hunan in the central part of China, there once lived in a small village a rich gentleman who had only one child. This girl, like the daughter of Kwan-yu in the story of the Great Bell, was the very joy of her father's life.

Now Mr. Min, for that was this gentleman's name, was famous throughout the whole district for his learning, and, as he was also the owner of much property, he spared no effort to teach Honeysuckle the wisdom of the sages, and to give her everything she craved. Of course this was enough to spoil most children, but Honeysuckle was not at all like other children. As sweet as the flower from which she took her name, she listened to her father's slightest command, and obeyed without ever waiting to be told a second time.

Her father often bought kites for her, of every kind and shape. There were fish, birds, butterflies, lizards and huge dragons, one of which had a tail more than thirty feet long. Mr. Min was very skilful in flying these kites for little Honeysuckle, and so naturally did his birds and butterflies circle round and hover about in the air that almost any child would have been deceived and said, "Why, there is a real bird, and not a kite at all!"

Then again, he would fasten a queer little instrument to the string, which made a kind of humming noise, as he waved his hand from side to side. "It is the wind singing, Daddy," cried Honeysuckle, clapping her hands with joy, "singing a kite-song to both of us."

Sometimes, to teach his little darling a lesson if she had been the least naughty, Mr. Min would fasten queerly twisted scraps of paper, on which were written many Chinese words, to the string of her favourite kite.

"What are you doing, Daddy?" Honeysuckle would ask. "What can those queer-looking papers be?"

"On every piece is written a sin that we have done."

"What is a sin, Daddy?"

"Oh, when Honeysuckle has been naughty, that is a sin!" he answered gently. "Your old nurse is afraid to scold you, and if you are to grow up to be a good woman, Daddy must teach you what is right."

Then Mr. Min would send the kite up high, high over the house-tops, even higher than the tall Pagoda on the hillside. When all his cord was let out, he would pick up two sharp stones, and, handing them to Honeysuckle, would say, "Now, daughter, cut the string, and the wind will carry away the sins that are written down on the scraps of paper."

"But, Daddy, the kite is so pretty. Mayn't we keep our sins a little longer?" she would innocently ask.

"No, child, it is dangerous to hold on to one's sins. Virtue is the foundation of happiness," he would reply sternly, choking back his laughter at her question. "Make haste and cut the cord."

So Honeysuckle, always obedient, at least with her father, would saw the string in two between the sharp stones, and with a childish cry of despair would watch her favourite kite, blown by the wind, sail farther and farther away, until eventually, straining her eyes, she could see it sink slowly to the earth in some far-distant meadow.

"Now laugh and be happy," Mr. Min would say, "for your sins are all gone. See that you don't get a new supply of them."

Honeysuckle was also fond of seeing the Punch and Judy show, for, you must know, this old-fashioned amusement for children was enjoyed by little folks in China, perhaps three thousand years before your great-grandfather was born. It is even said that the great Emperor, Mu, when he saw these little dancing images for the first time, was greatly enraged at seeing one of them making eyes at his favourite wife. He ordered the showman to be put to death, and it was with difficulty the poor fellow persuaded his Majesty that the dancing puppets were not really alive at all, but only images of cloth and clay.

No wonder then that Honeysuckle liked to see Punch and Judy if the Son of Heaven himself had been deceived by their queer antics into thinking them real people of flesh and blood.

But we must hurry on with our story, or some of our readers will be asking, "But where is Dr. Dog? Are you never coming to the hero of this tale?"

One day when Honeysuckle was sitting inside a shady pavilion that overlooked a tiny fish-pond, she was suddenly seized with a violent attack of colic. Frantic with pain, she told a servant to summon her father, and then without further ado, she fell over in a faint upon the ground.

When Mr. Min reached his daughter's side, she was still unconscious. After sending for the family physician to come post haste, he got his daughter to bed, but although she recovered from her fainting fit, the extreme pain continued until the poor girl was almost dead from exhaustion.

Now, when the learned doctor arrived and peered at her from under his gigantic spectacles, he could not discover the cause of her trouble. However he did not confess his ignorance, but proceeded to prescribe a huge dose of boiling water, to be followed a little later by a compound of pulverized deer's horn and dried toad skin.

Poor Honeysuckle lay in agony for three days, all the time growing weaker and weaker from loss of sleep. Every great doctor in the district had been summoned for consultation, and two had come from Changsha, the chief city of the province, but all to no avail. It was one of those cases that seem to be beyond the power of even the most learned physicians. In the hope of receiving the great reward offered by the desperate father, these wise men searched from cover to cover in the great Chinese Cyclopaedia of Medicine, trying in vain to find a method of treating the unhappy maiden.

Mr. Min sent out a proclamation in every direction, describing his daughter's illness, and offering to bestow on her a handsome dowry and give her in marriage to whoever should be the means of bringing her back to health and happiness. He then sat at her bedside and waited, feeling that he had done all that was in his power. There were many answers to his invitation. Physicians, old and young, came from every part of the Empire to try their skill, and when they had seen poor Honeysuckle and also the huge pile of silver shoes her father offered as a wedding gift, they all fought with might and main for her life, some having been attracted by her great beauty and excellent reputation, others by the tremendous reward.

But, alas for poor Honeysuckle! Not one of all those wise men could cure her! One day, when she was feeling a slight change for the better, she called her father, and, clasping his hand with her tiny one said, "Were it not for your love I would give up this hard fight and pass over into the dark wood, or, as my old grandmother says, fly up into the Western Heavens. For your sake, because I am your only child, and especially because you have no son, I have struggled hard to live, but now I feel that the next attack of that dreadful pain will carry me away. And oh, I do not want to die!"

Here Honeysuckle wept as if her heart would break, and her old father wept too, for the more she suffered the more he loved her.

Just then her face began to turn pale. "It is coming! The pain is coming, father! Very soon I shall be no more. Good-bye, father! Good-bye, good…"

Here her voice broke and a great sob almost broke her father's heart. He turned away from her bedside, for he could not bear to see her suffer. He walked outside and sat down on a rustic bench, his head fell upon his bosom, and the great salt tears trickled down his long grey beard.

As Mr. Min sat there overcome with grief, he was startled at hearing a low whine. Looking up he saw, to his astonishment, a shaggy mountain dog about the size of a Newfoundland. The huge beast looked into the old man's eyes with so intelligent and human an expression, with such a sad and wistful gaze, that the greybeard addressed him, saying, "Why have you come? To cure my daughter?"

The dog replied with three short barks, wagging his tail vigorously and turning toward the half-opened door that led into the room where the girl lay.

By this time, willing to try any chance whatever of reviving his daughter, Mr. Min bade the animal follow him into Honeysuckle's apartment. Placing his forepaws upon the side of her bed, the dog looked long and steadily at the wasted form before him and held his ear intently for a moment over the maiden's heart. Then, with a slight cough he deposited from his mouth into her outstretched hand, a tiny stone. Touching her wrist with his right paw, he motioned to her to swallow the stone.

"Yes, my dear, obey him," counselled her father, as she turned to him inquiringly, "for good Dr. Dog has been sent to your bedside by the mountain fairies, who have heard of your illness and who wish to invite you back to life again."

Without further delay the sick girl, who was by this time almost burned away by the fever, raised her hand to her lips and swallowed the tiny charm. Wonder of wonders! No sooner had it passed her lips than a miracle occurred. The red flush passed away from her face, the pulse resumed its normal beat, the pains departed from her body, and she arose from the bed well and smiling.

Flinging her arms about her father's neck, she cried out in joy, "Oh, I am well again, well and happy, thanks to the medicine of the good physician."

The noble dog barked three times, wild with delight at hearing these tearful words of gratitude, bowed low, and put his nose in Honeysuckle's outstretched hand.

Mr. Min, greatly moved by his daughter's magical recovery, turned to the strange physician, saying, "Noble Sir, were it not for the form you have taken, for some unknown reason, I would willingly give four times the sum in silver that I promised for the cure of the girl, into your possession. As it is, I suppose you have no use for silver, but remember that so long as we live, whatever we have is yours for the asking, and I beg of you to prolong your visit, to make this the home of your old age. In short, remain here for ever as my guest, nay, as a member of my family."

The dog barked thrice, as if in assent. From that day he was treated as an equal by father and daughter. The many servants were commanded to obey his slightest whim, to serve him with the most expensive food on the market, to spare no expense in making him the happiest and best-fed dog in all the world. Day after day he ran at Honeysuckle's side as she gathered flowers in her garden, lay down before her door when she was resting, and guarded her Sedan chair when she was carried by servants into the city. In short, they were constant companions, and a stranger would have thought they had been friends from childhood.

One day, however, just as they were returning from a journey outside her father's compound, at the very instant when Honeysuckle was alighting from her chair, without a moment's warning, the huge animal dashed past the attendants, seized his beautiful mistress in his mouth, and before anyone could stop him, bore her off to the mountains. By the time the alarm was sounded, darkness had fallen over the valley and as the night was cloudy no trace could be found of the dog and his fair burden.

Once more the frantic father left no stone unturned to save his daughter. Huge rewards were offered, bands of woodmen scoured the mountains high and low, but, alas, no sign of the girl could be found! The unfortunate father gave up the search and began to prepare himself for the grave. There was nothing now left in life that he cared for, nothing but thoughts of his departed daughter. Honeysuckle was gone for ever.

"Alas!" he said, quoting the lines of a famous poet who had fallen into despair:

"My whiting hair would make an endless rope,
Yet would not measure all my depth of woe."

Several long years passed by. These were years of sorrow for the ageing man, pining for his departed daughter. One beautiful October day he was sitting in the very same pavilion where he had so often sat with his darling. His head was bowed forward on his breast, and his forehead was lined with grief. A rustling of leaves attracted his attention. He looked up. Standing directly in front of him was Dr. Dog, and there, riding on his back, clinging to the animal's shaggy hair, was Honeysuckle, his long-lost daughter, while standing nearby were three of the handsomest boys he had ever set eyes upon!

"Ah, my daughter! My darling daughter, where have you been all these years?" cried the delighted father, pressing the girl to his aching breast. "Have you suffered many a cruel pain since you were snatched away so suddenly? Has your life been filled with sorrow?"

"Only at the thought of your grief," she replied, tenderly, stroking his forehead with her slender fingers, "only at the thought of your suffering, only at the thought of how I should like to see you every day and tell you that my husband was kind and good to me. For you must know, dear father, this is no mere animal that stands beside you. This Dr. Dog, who cured me and claimed me as his bride because of your promise, is a great magician. He can change himself at will into a thousand shapes. He chooses to come here in the form of a mountain beast so that no one may penetrate the secret of his distant palace."

"Then he is your husband?" faltered the old man, gazing at the animal with a new expression on his wrinkled face.

"Yes, my kind and noble husband, the father of my three sons, your grandchildren, whom we have brought to pay you a visit."

"And where do you live?"

"In a wonderful cave in the heart of the great mountains, a beautiful cave whose walls and floors are covered with crystals, and encrusted with sparkling gems. The chairs and tables are set with jewels, the rooms are lighted by a thousand glittering diamonds. Oh, it is lovelier than the palace of the Son of Heaven himself! We feed on the flesh of wild deer and mountain goats, and fish from the clearest mountain stream. We drink cold water out of golden goblets, without first boiling it, for it is purity itself. We breathe fragrant air that blows through forests of pine and hemlock. We live only to love each other and our children, and oh, we are so happy! And you, father, you must come back with us to the great mountains and live there with us the rest of your days, which, the gods grant, may be very many."

The old man pressed his daughter once more to his breast and embraced the children, who clambered over him rejoicing at the discovery of a grandfather they had never seen before.

From Dr. Dog and his fair Honeysuckle are sprung, it is said, the well-known race of people called the Yus, who even now inhabit the mountainous regions of the Canton and Hunan provinces. It is not for this reason, however, that we have told the story here, but because we felt sure every reader would like to learn the secret of the dog that cured a sick girl and won her for his bride.

Kwang-Jui And The God Of The River

This story has been adapted from Rev. John MacGowan's version that originally appeared in Chinese Folk-Lore Tales, published in 1910 by MacMillan and Company, London. Chinese Folk-Lore Tales features a variety of stories that cover a wide range of themes, including mythology, morality, adventure, and romance. These tales often incorporate elements of Chinese folklore, legends, and superstitions, providing readers with a glimpse into the beliefs and values of traditional Chinese society.

Kwang-Jui lived with his widowed mother in a retired part of the country. His father had been dead for some time, and Kwang-Jui was now the only one upon whom the fortunes of the home could be built. He was a very studious lad, and was possessed of remarkable abilities, the result being that he successfully passed the various Imperial Examinations, even the final one in the capital, where the Sovereign himself presided as examiner.

After this last examination, as the men were waiting outside the Hall for the names of those who had satisfied the Emperor to be read out a considerable crowd had collected. Most of these people had come from mere curiosity to see the Imperial Edict, and to discover who the scholar was that stood first on the list. The excitement was intense, and speculation ran rife as to which of the candidates, who had come from almost every province in the Empire, was going to obtain the place of honour which was the dream and the ambition of every scholar in the land.

Eventually every breath was hushed, and every voice stilled in silence, as one of the high officials of the Palace, attended by an imposing retinue, came out of the great central doors, which had been flung wide open at his approach. In a clear voice he began to read the list. It was headed by the name of Kwang-Jui.

At this precise moment occurred an incident which was destined to change the whole current of Kwang-Jui's career. As he was standing overcome with emotion in consequence of the supreme honour which had been conferred upon him by the Emperor's Edict, a small round ball, beautifully embroidered, was thrown from an upper window of a house across the way, and struck him on the shoulder.

It may here be explained that it was a custom in the early days of the history of China to allow any young maiden who was reluctant to have her husband chosen for her by her parents, to make use of what was called 'The throwing of the embroidered ball' in order to discover the man whom the gods intended her to marry. This ball was made of some soft material, wrapped round with a piece of red silk which was covered with variegated figures, worked by the damsel's own hands and emblematic of the love by which the hearts of husband and wife are bound indissolubly to each other. It was firmly believed by every maiden of this romantic type that the man who was struck by the ball from her fair hands was the one whom Heaven had selected as her husband, and no parent would ever dream of refusing to accept a choice made in this way.

Whilst Kwang-Jui was gazing in amused wonder at the symbol which he understood so well, a messenger from the house from which it had been thrown requested him in respectful tones to accompany him to his master, who desired to discuss with him a most important subject.

As Kwang-Jui entered the house, he discovered to his astonishment that it belonged to the Prime Minister, who received him with the utmost cordiality, and after a long conversation declared that he was prepared to submit to the will of the gods, and to accept him as his son-in-law. Kwang-Jui was of course in raptures at the brilliant prospects which were suddenly opening up before him. The day, indeed, was a red-letter one, an omen, he hoped, that fate was preparing to pour down upon him good fortune in the future. In one brief day he had been hailed as the most distinguished scholar in the Empire, and he had also been acknowledged as the son-in-law of the Empire's greatest official, who had the power of placing him in high positions where he could secure not only honours but also wealth sufficient to drive poverty away for ever from his home.

As there was no reason for delay, the hand of the beautiful daughter who had thrown the embroidered ball, and who was delighted that Heaven had chosen for her such a brilliant husband, was bestowed upon him by her parents. Times of great rejoicing succeeded, and when Kwang-Jui thought of the quiet and uninteresting days when he was still unknown to fame, and contrasted them with his present life, it seemed to him as though he were living in fairy-land. His wildest dreams in the past had never conjured up anything so grand as the life he was now leading. In one bound he had leaped from comparative poverty to fame and riches.

After a time, through the influence of his father-in-law, and with the hearty consent of the Emperor, who remembered what a brilliant student he had been, Kwang-Jui was appointed to be Prefect of an important district in the centre of China.

Taking his bride with him, he first of all proceeded to his old home, where his mother was waiting with great anxiety to welcome her now famous son. The old lady felt rather nervous at meeting her new daughter-in-law, seeing that the latter came from a family which was far higher in rank and far more distinguished than any in her own clan. As it was very necessary that Kwang-Jui should take up his office as Prefect without any undue delay, he and his mother and his bride set out in the course of a few days on the long journey to the distant Prefecture, where their lives were destined to be marred by sorrow and disaster.

They had travelled the greater part of the way, and had reached a country market-town that lay on their route, when Kwang-Jui's mother, worn out with the toilsome journey, fell suddenly ill. The doctor who was called in shook his head and pronounced that she was suffering from a very serious complaint, which, whilst not necessarily fatal, would necessitate a complete rest for at least two or three months. Any further travelling must therefore be abandoned for the present, as it might be attended with the most serious consequences to the old lady.

Both husband and wife were greatly distressed at the unlucky accident which placed them in such an awkward position at this wayside inn. They were truly grieved at the serious sickness of their mother, but they were still more puzzled as to what course they should pursue in these most trying circumstances. The Imperial Rescript appointing Kwang-Jui to his office as Prefect commanded him to take up his post on a certain definite date. To delay until his mother would again be able to endure the fatigues of travel was out of the question, as disobedience to the Emperor's orders would be attended by his grave displeasure. Eventually his mother suggested that he and his wife should go on ahead, and that after taking up the duties of his office he should then delegate them for a time to his subordinates and return to take her home.

This advice Kwang-Jui decided to carry out, though with great reluctance, as he was most unwilling to abandon his mother to the care of strangers. He accordingly made all the arrangements he possibly could for her comfort whilst they were parted from each other, he had servants engaged to attend upon her, and he left sufficient money with her to meet all her expenses during his absence.

With a mind full of consideration for his mother, and wishing to show how anxious he was to give her pleasure, he went out into the market of the town to see if he could buy a certain kind of fish of which she was passionately fond. He had hardly got outside the courtyard of the inn, when he met a fisherman with a very fine specimen of the very fish that he wished to purchase.

As he was discussing the price with the man, a certain something about the fish arrested his attention. There was a peculiar look in its eyes that seemed full of pathos and entreaty. Its gaze was concentrated upon him, so human-like and with such intensity, that he instinctively felt it was pleading with him to do something to deliver it from a great disaster. This made him look at it more carefully, and to his astonishment the liquid eyes of the fish were still fixed upon him with a passionate regard that made him quiver with excitement.

"Fisherman," he said, "I want to buy this fish, and here is the price that you ask for it. I have but one stipulation to make, and that is that you take it to the river from which you caught it, and set it free to swim away wherever it pleases. Remember that if you fail to carry out this part of the bargain, great sorrow will come upon you and your home."

Little did either of them dream that the fish was the presiding God of the River, who for purposes of his own had transformed himself into this form, and who, while swimming up and down the stream had been caught in the net of the fisherman.

After travelling for some hours Kwang-Jui and his wife came to the bank of a considerable river, where they hired a large boat to convey them to their destination.

The boatman they engaged was a man of very low character. He had originally been a scholar and of good family, but, utterly depraved and immoral, he had gradually sunk lower and lower in society, until eventually he had been compelled to fly from his home to a distant province, and there to engage in his present occupation in order to earn his living. The large amount of property which Kwang-Jui had with him seemed to arouse the worst passions in this man, and while the boat was being carried along by a fair wind and a flowing tide, he planned in his mind how he was to become the possessor of it. By the time that they reached the place where they were to anchor for the night, he had already decided what measures he should adopt.

A little after midnight, accordingly, he crept stealthily towards the place where Kwang-Jui was sleeping, stabbed him to the heart and threw his body into the fast-flowing river. He next threatened the wife that if she dared to utter a sound, he would murder her also and send her to join her husband in the Land of Shadows. Paralyzed with terror, she remained speechless, and only a stifled sob and groan now and again breaking from her agonized heart. Her first serious idea was to commit suicide, and she was preparing to fling herself into the water that gurgled along the sides of the boat, when she was restrained by the thought that if she destroyed herself, she would never be able to avenge her husband's death or bring punishment upon the villain who had just murdered him.

It was not mere robbery, however, that was in the mind of the man who had committed this great crime. He had bigger ideas than that. He had noticed that in personal appearance he very much resembled his victim, so he determined to carry out the daring project of passing himself off as Kwang-Jui, the mandarin whom the Emperor had despatched to take up the appointment of Prefect.

Having threatened the widow that instant death would be her portion if she breathed a word to anyone about the true state of the case, and having arrayed himself in the official robes of the man whom he had stabbed to death, the boatman appeared at the yamen, where he presented the Imperial credentials and was duly installed in his office. It never entered his mind that it was not cowardice which kept the widow silent, but the stern resolve of a brave and high-minded woman that she would do her part to see that vengeance should in time fall upon the man who had robbed her of a husband whom she looked upon as the direct gift of Heaven.

Now, immediately after the body of Kwang-Jui had been cast into the water, the customary patrol sent by the God of the River to see that order was kept within his dominions, came upon it, and conveyed it with all speed into the presence of the god himself.

The latter looked at it intently for a moment, and then exclaimed in great excitement, "Why, this is the very person who only yesterday saved my life, when I was in danger of being delivered over to a cruel death! I shall now be able to show my gratitude by using all the power I possess to serve his interests. Bring him to the Crystal Grotto," he continued, "where only those who have distinguished themselves in the service of the State have ever been allowed to lie. This man has a claim upon me such as no one before him ever possessed. He is the saviour of my life, and I will tenderly care for him until the web of fate has been spun, and, the vengeance of Heaven having been wreaked upon his murderer, he shall once more re-join the wife from whom he has been so ruthlessly torn."

With the passing of the months, the widow of Kwang-Jui gave birth to a son, the very image of his father. It was night-time when he was born, and not long after his birth, a mysterious voice, which could not be traced, was heard distinctly saying, "Let the child be removed without delay from the yamen, before the return of the Prefect, as otherwise its life will not be safe."

Accordingly, on the morrow, the babe, about whose destiny even Heaven itself seemed concerned, was carefully wrapped round with many coverings to protect it against the weather. Inside the inmost dress, there was enclosed a small document, telling the child's tragic story and describing the danger from a powerful foe which threatened its life. In order to be able to identify her son, it might be after the lapse of many years, the mother cut off the last joint of the little finger of his left hand, and then, with tears and sighs, and with her heart full of unspoken agony, she took a last, lingering look upon the face of the little one.

A confidential slave woman carried him out of her room, and by devious ways and secret paths finally laid him on the river's bank. Casting a final glance at the precious bundle to see that no danger threatened it, she hurried back in the direction of the city, with the faint cries of the abandoned infant still sounding in her ears.

And now the child was in the hands of Heaven. This was evident from the fact that in a few minutes the abbot of the monastery, which could be seen crowning the top of a neighbouring hill, passed along the narrow pathway by the side of the river. Hearing a baby's cry, he hastened towards the place from which the sounds came, and picking up the little bundle, and realizing that the infant had been deserted, he carried it up to the monastery and made every arrangement for its care and comfort. Fortunately he was a man of a deeply benevolent nature, and no more suitable person could have been found to take charge of the child.

We must now allow eighteen years to pass by. The child that had been left on the margin of the river had grown up to be a fine, handsome lad. The abbot had been his friend ever since the day when his heart had been touched by his cries, and his love for the little foundling had grown with the years. The boy had become a kind of son to him, and in order not to be parted from him he had taught him the temple duties, so that he was now a qualified priest in the service of the gods.

One morning the young man, whose name was Sam-Choang, came to the abbot with a restless, dissatisfied look on his face, and begged to be told who his father was, and who his mother. The old priest, who had long been aware of the tragic story of Kwang-Jui's murder, felt that the time had come when the lad ought to know what he had hereto concealed from him. Taking out the document which he had found upon him as a baby, he read it to him, and then the great secret was out. After this a long and serious discussion took place between the two as to the wisest methods to be adopted for bringing the Prefect to justice and delivering the lad's mother from the humiliating position which she had so heroically borne for all these eighteen years.

The next day a young priest, with shaven head and dressed in the usual slate-coloured gown, appeared at the yamen of the Prefect to solicit subscriptions for the neighbouring monastery. As the Prefect was absent on some public business, he was ushered into the reception-room, where he was received by his mother, who had always been a generous supporter of the Goddess of Mercy.

At the first sight of this striking-looking young bonze, she found her heart agitated in a strange and powerful way, such as she had not experienced for many a long year, and when she noticed that the little finger on his left hand was without the last joint, she trembled with the utmost excitement.

After a few words about the object for which he had come, the young priest slipped into her hand the very paper which she had written eighteen years ago, and as she looked at her own handwriting and then gazed into his face and saw the striking likeness to the man at whom she had thrown the embroidered ball, the mother-instinct within her flashed suddenly out, and she recognized that this handsome lad was her own son. The joy of the mother as she looked upon the face of Sam-Choang was reflected in the sparkling eyes and glowing look of pleasure that lit up his whole countenance.

Retiring for a short time his mother returned with a letter which she handed to him. In a low voice she told him that it was to her father, who still lived in the capital, and to whom he was to take it without any delay. In order to prevent suspicion on the part of the Prefect, he was to travel as a priest, who was endeavouring to obtain subscriptions for his monastery. He was to be sure, also, to visit the place where his grandmother had been left, and to try and find out what had become of her. In order to defray his expenses she gave him a few bars of gold, which he could exchange for the current money at the banks on the way.

When Sam-Choang arrived at the inn where his father had parted with his grandmother, he could find no trace of her. A new landlord was in possession, who had never even heard her name, but on enquiring amongst the shopkeepers in the neighbourhood, he found to his horror that she was now a member of the beggars' camp, and that her name was enrolled amongst that degraded fraternity.

On reaching the wretched hovel where she was living, he discovered that when her money was exhausted and no remittance came to her from her son, she had been driven out on to the street by the innkeeper, and from that time had tramped the country, living on the scraps and bits which were bestowed upon her by the benevolent. Great was her joy when her grandson led her away to the best inn in the place, and on his departure gave her an ample supply of money for all her needs until they should meet again.

When Sam-Choang reached the capital and handed his mother's letter to his grandfather, the most profound excitement ensued. As soon as the Emperor was officially informed of the case, he determined that the severest punishment should be inflicted upon the man who had not only committed a cruel murder, but through it had dared to usurp a position which could only be held at the Sovereign's command. An Imperial Edict was accordingly issued ordering the Prime Minister to take a considerable body of troops and proceed with all possible speed to the district where such an unheard-of crime had been committed, and there to hand over the offender to immediate execution.

By forced marches, so as to outstrip any private intelligence that might have been sent from the capital, the avenging force reached the city a little before the break of day. Here they waited in silence outside the city gates, anxiously listening for the boom of the early gun which announces the dawn, and at the same time causes the gates to be flung wide open for the traffic of the day to commence.

As soon as the warders had admitted the waiting crowd outside, the soldiers, advancing at a run, quickly reached the yamen, and arrested the Prefect. Without form of trial but simply with a curt announcement from the Prime Minister that he was acting upon instructions from the Emperor, the mandarin was dragged unceremoniously through the gaping crowds that rushed from their doors to see the amazing spectacle.

The feet of Fate had marched slowly but with unerring certainty, and had eventually reached the wretched criminal.

But where was he being taken? This road did not lead to the execution ground, where malefactors were doomed to end their careers in shame. Street after street was passed, and still the stern-faced soldiers forced the mandarin down the main thoroughfares, whose sides had often been lined with respectful crowds as he swept by with his haughty retinue. Eventually they reached the city gate, through which they marched, and then on towards the river, which could be seen gleaming like a silver thread in the distance.

Arrived at its bank, the troops formed into a square with the prisoner in the centre. Addressing him, the Prime Minister said, "I have selected this spot rather than the public execution ground where criminals are put to death. Your crime has been no common one, and so today, in the face of high Heaven whose righteousness you have dared to violate, and within sound of the flowing waters of the stream that witnessed the murder, you shall die."

Half a dozen soldiers then threw him violently to the ground, and in a few minutes the executioner had torn his bleeding heart from his bosom. Then, standing with it still in his hand, he waited by the side of the Prime Minister, who read out to the great multitude the indictment which had been drawn up against the Prefect. In this he described his crimes, and at the same time appealed to Heaven and to the God of the River to take measures to satisfy and appease the spirit of him who had been cut off in the prime of life by the man who had just been executed.

As soon as the reading of the document had been concluded, it was set fire to and allowed to burn until only the blackened ashes remained. These, together with the criminal's heart, were then cast into the river. They were thus formally handed over to the god, who would see that in the Land of Shadows there should come a further retribution on the murderer for the crimes he had committed on earth.

The water patrol happened to pass by soon after the ashes and heart had been flung into the river, and picking them up most carefully, they carried them to the official residence of the god. The indictment was at once formally entered amongst the archives of the office, to be used as evidence when the case was in due time brought before the notice of Yam-lo, and after looking at the heart with intense scrutiny for some little time, the god exclaimed, "And so the murderer has eventually received some part of the punishment he so richly deserved. It is now time for me to awake the sleeping husband, so that he may be restored to the wife from whom he has been separated for eighteen years."

Passing into the Crystal Grotto, where the unconscious form of Kwang-Jui had reposed for so many years, the god touched the body gently with his hand, and said, "Friend, arise! Your wife awaits you, with loving ones who have long mourned you. Many years of happiness are still before you, and the honours that your Sovereign will bestow upon you shall place you amongst the famous men of the State. Arise, and take your place once more amongst the living!"

The Prime Minister was sitting with his daughter, listening to the sad story of the years of suffering through which she had passed, when the door was silently opened, and the figure of her long-lost husband glided in. Both started up in fear and amazement, for they believed that what they saw was only a restless spirit which had wandered from the Land of Shadows and would speedily vanish again from their sight. In this, however, they were delightfully disappointed. Kwang-Jui and his wife were once more reunited, and for many a long year their hearts were so full of gladness and contentment, that the sorrows which they had endured gradually became effaced from their memories. They always thought with the deepest gratitude of the God of the River, who for eighteen years had kept the unconscious husband alive and had finally restored him to his heart-broken wife.

Tales Of The Gùshì Yuán

The Disowned Princess

This story has been adapted from Dr. Richard Wilhelm's version that originally appeared in The Chinese Fairy Book, published in 1921 by Frederick A. Stokes Company, New York. Wilhelm's translations aimed to capture the essence of the original Chinese texts while making them accessible to English-speaking audiences. His deep understanding of Chinese language and culture shone through in his translations, allowing readers to appreciate the beauty and depth of these timeless tales.

At the time that the Tang dynasty was reigning there lived a man named Liu I, who had failed to pass his examinations for the doctorate. So he travelled home again. He had gone six or seven miles when a bird flew up in a field, and his horse shied and ran ten miles before he could stop him. There he saw a woman who was herding sheep on a hillside. He looked at her and she was lovely to look upon, yet her face bore traces of hidden grief. Astonished, he asked her what the matter was.

The woman began to sob and said, "Fortune has forsaken me, and I am in need and ashamed. Since you are kind enough to ask I will tell you all. I am the youngest daughter of the Dragon-King of the Sea of Dungting, and was married to the second son of the Dragon-King of Ging Dschou. Yet my husband ill-treated and disowned me. I complained to my step-parents, but they loved their son blindly and did nothing. And when I grew insistent they both became angry, and I was sent out here to herd sheep."

When she had done, the woman burst into tears and lost all control of herself. Then she continued, "The Sea of Dungting is far from here, yet I know that you will have to pass it on your homeward journey. I should like to give you a letter to my father, but I do not know whether you would take it."

Liu I answered, "Your words have moved my heart. Would that I had wings and could fly away with you. I will be glad to deliver the letter to your father. Yet the Sea of Dungting is long and broad, and how am I to find him?"

"On the southern shore of the Sea stands an orange-tree," answered the woman, "which people call the tree of sacrifice. When you get there you must loosen your girdle and strike the tree with it three times in succession. Then someone will appear whom you must follow. When you see my father, tell him in what need you found me, and that I long greatly for his help."

Then she fetched out a letter from her breast and gave it to Liu I. She bowed to him, looked toward the east and sighed, and, unexpectedly, tears suddenly rolled from the eyes of Liu I as well. He took the letter and thrust it in his bag.

Then he asked her, "I cannot understand why you have to herd sheep. Do the gods slaughter cattle like men?"

"These are not ordinary sheep," answered the woman, "these are rain-sheep."

"But what are rain-sheep?"

"They are the thunder-rams," replied the woman.

And when he looked more closely he noticed that these sheep walked around in proud, savage fashion, quite different from ordinary sheep.

Liu I added, "But if I deliver the letter for you, and you succeed in getting back to the Sea of Dungting in safety, then you must not use me like a stranger."

The woman answered, "How could I use you as a stranger? You shall be my dearest friend."

And with these words they parted.

In course of a month Liu I reached the Sea of Dungting, asked for the orange-tree and, sure enough, found it. He loosened his girdle, and struck the tree with it three times. At once a warrior emerged from the waves of the sea, and asked, "Where do you come from, honoured guest?"

Liu I said, "I have come on an important mission and want to see the King."

The warrior made a gesture in the direction of the water, and the waves turned into a solid street along which he led Liu I. The dragon-castle rose before them with its thousand gates, and magic flowers and rare grasses bloomed in luxurious profusion. The warrior bade him wait at the side of a great hall.

Liu I asked, "What is this place called?"

"It is the Hall of the Spirits," was the reply.

Liu I looked about him. All the jewels known to earth were there in abundance. The columns were of white quartz, inlaid with green jade, the seats were made of coral, the curtains of mountain crystal as clear as water, the windows of burnished glass, adorned with rich lattice-work. The beams of the ceiling, ornamented with amber, rose in wide arches. An exotic fragrance filled the hall, whose outlines were lost in darkness.

Liu I had waited for the king a long time. To all his questions the warrior replied, "Our master is pleased at this moment to talk with the priest of the sun up there on the coral-tower about the sacred book of the fire. He will, no doubt, soon be through."

Liu I went on to ask, "Why is he interested in the sacred book of the fire?"

The reply was, "Our master is a dragon. The dragons are powerful through the power of water. They can cover hill and dale with a single wave. The priest is a human being. Human beings are powerful through fire. They can burn the greatest palaces by means of a torch. Fire and water fight each other, being different in their nature. For that reason our master is now talking with the priest, in order to find a way in which fire and water may complete each other."

Before they had quite finished there appeared a man in a purple robe, bearing a sceptre of jade in his hand. The warrior said, "This is my master!"

Liu I bowed before him.

The king asked, "Are you not a living human being? What has brought you here?"

Liu I gave his name and explained, "I have been to the capital and there failed to pass my examination. When I was passing by the Ging Dschou River, I saw your daughter, whom you love, herding sheep in the wilderness. The winds tousled her hair, and the rain drenched her. I could not bear to see her trouble and spoke to her. She complained that her husband had cast her out and wept bitterly. Then she gave me a letter for you. And that is why I have come to visit you, O King!"

With these words he fetched out his letter and handed it to the king. When the latter had read it, he hid his face in his sleeve and said with a sigh, "It is my own fault. I picked out a worthless husband for her. Instead of securing her happiness I have brought her to shame in a distant land. You are a stranger and yet you have been willing to help her in her distress, for which I am very grateful to you."

Then he once more began to sob, and all those about him shed tears. Thereupon the monarch gave the letter to a servant who took it into the interior of the palace, and soon the sound of loud lamentations rose from the inner rooms.

The king was alarmed and turned to an official, "Go and tell them within not to weep so loudly! I am afraid that Tsian Tang may hear them."

"Who is Tsian Tang?" asked Liu I.

"He is my beloved brother," answered the king. "Formerly he was the ruler of the Tsian-Tang River, but now he has been deposed."

Liu I asked, "Why should the matter be kept from him?"

"He is so wild and uncontrollable," was the reply, "that I fear he would cause great damage. The deluge which covered the earth for nine long years in the time of the Emperor Yau was the work of his anger. Because he fell out with one of the kings of heaven, he caused a great deluge that rose and covered the tops of five high mountains. Then the king of heaven grew angry with him, and gave him to me to guard. I had to chain him to a column in my palace."

Before he had finished speaking a tremendous turmoil arose, which split the skies and made the earth tremble, so that the whole palace began to rock, and smoke and clouds rose hissing and puffing. A red dragon, a thousand feet long, with flashing eyes, blood-red tongue, scarlet scales and a fiery beard came surging up. He was dragging along through the air the column to which he had been bound, together with its chain. Thunders and lightnings roared and darted around his body, while sleet and snow, and rain, and hail-stones whirled about him in confusion. There was a crash of thunder, and he flew up to the skies and disappeared.

Liu I fell to earth in terror. The king helped him up with his own hand and said, "Do not be afraid! That is my brother, who is hastening to Ging Dschou in his rage. We will soon have good news!"

Then he had food and drink brought in for his guest. When the goblet had thrice made the rounds, a gentle breeze began to murmur and a fine rain fell. A youth clad in a purple gown and wearing a lofty hat entered. A sword hung at his side. His appearance was manly and heroic. Behind him walked a girl radiantly beautiful, wearing a robe of misty fragrance. And when Liu I looked at her it was the dragon-princess whom he had met on his way! A throng of maidens in rosy garments received her, laughing and giggling, and led her into the interior of the palace. The king, however, presented Liu I to the youth and said, "This is Tsian Tang, my brother!"

Tsian Tang thanked him for having brought the message. Then he turned to his brother and said, "I have fought against the accursed dragons and have utterly defeated them!"

"How many did you slay?"

"Six hundred thousand."

"Were any fields damaged?"

"The fields were damaged for eight hundred miles around."

"And where is the heartless husband?"

"I ate him alive!"

Then the king was alarmed and said, "What the fickle boy did was not to be endured, it is true. But still you were a little too rough with him. In future you must not do anything of the sort again." And Tsian Tang promised not to.

That evening Liu I was feasted at the castle. Music and dancing lent charm to the banquet, and a thousand warriors with banners and spears in their hands stood at attention. Trombones and trumpets resounded, and drums and kettledrums thundered and rattled as the warriors danced a war-dance. The music expressed how Tsian Tang had broken through the ranks of the enemy, and the hair of the guest who listened to it rose on his head in terror.

Then, again, there was heard the music of strings, flutes and little golden bells. A thousand maidens in crimson and green silk danced around. The return of the princess was also told in tones. The music sounded like a song of sadness and plaining, and all who heard it were moved to tears.

The King of the Sea of Dungting was filled with joy. He raised his goblet and drank to the health of his guest, and all sorrow departed from them. Both rulers thanked Liu I in verses, and Liu I answered them in a rimed toast. The crowd of courtiers in the palace-hall applauded. Then the King of the Sea of Dungting drew forth a blue cloud-casket in which was the horn of a rhinoceros, which divides the water. Tsian Tang brought out a platter of red amber on which lay a carbuncle. These they presented to their guest, and the other inmates of the palace also heaped up embroideries, brocades and pearls by his side. Surrounded by shimmer and light Liu I sat there, smiling, and bowed his thanks to all sides. When the banquet was ended he slept in the Palace of Frozen Radiance.

On the following day another banquet was held. Tsian Tang, who was not quite himself, sat carelessly on his seat and said, "The Princess of the Dungting Sea is handsome and delicately fashioned. She has had the misfortune to be disowned by her husband, and today her marriage is annulled. I should like to find another husband for her. If you were agreeable it would be to your advantage. But if you were not willing to marry her, you may go your way, and should we ever meet again we will not know each other."

Liu I was angered by the careless way in which Tsian Tang spoke to him. The blood rose to his head and he replied, "I served as a messenger, because I felt sorry for the princess, but not in order to gain an advantage for myself. To kill a husband and carry off a wife is something an honest man does not do. And since I am only an ordinary man, I prefer to die rather than do as you say."

Tsian Tang rose, apologized and said, "My words were over-hasty. I hope you will not take them ill!" And the King of the Dungting Sea also spoke kindly to him, and censured Tsian Tang because of his rude speech. So there was no more said about marriage.

On the following day Liu I took his leave, and the Queen of the Dungting Sea gave a farewell banquet in his honour.

With tears the queen said to Liu I, "My daughter owes you a great debt of gratitude, and we have not had an opportunity to make it up to you. Now you are going away and we see you go with heavy hearts!"

Then she ordered the princess to thank Liu I.

The princess stood there, blushing, bowed to him and said, "We will probably never see each other again!" Then tears choked her voice.

It is true that Liu I had resisted the stormy urging of her uncle, but when he saw the princess standing before him in all the charm of her loveliness, he felt sad at heart, yet he controlled himself and went his way. The treasures which he took with him were incalculable. The king and his brother themselves escorted him as far as the river.

When, on his return home, he sold no more than a hundredth part of what he had received, his fortune already ran into the millions, and he was wealthier than all his neighbours. He decided to take a wife, and heard of a widow who lived in the North with her daughter. Her father had become a Taoist in his later years and had vanished in the clouds without ever returning. The mother lived in poverty with the daughter, yet since the girl was beautiful beyond measure she was seeking a distinguished husband for her.

Liu I was content to take her, and the day of the wedding was set. And when he saw his bride unveiled on the evening of her wedding day, she looked just like the dragon-princess. He asked her about it, but she merely smiled and said nothing.

After a time heaven sent them a son. Then she told her husband, "Today I will confess to you that I am truly the Princess of Dungting Sea. When you had rejected my uncle's proposal and gone away, I fell ill of longing, and was near death. My parents wanted to send for you, but they feared you might take exception to my family. And so it was that I married you disguised as a human maiden. I had not ventured to tell you until now, but since heaven has sent us a son, I hope that you will love his mother as well."

Then Liu I awoke as though from a deep sleep, and from that time on both were very fond of each other.

One day his wife said, "If you wish to stay with me eternally, then we cannot continue to dwell in the world of men. We dragons live ten thousand years, and you shall share our longevity. Come back with me to the Sea of Dungting!"

Ten years passed and no one knew where Liu I, who had disappeared, might be. Then, by accident, a relative went sailing across the Sea of Dungting. Suddenly a blue mountain rose up out of the water.

The seamen cried in alarm, "There is no mountain on this spot! It must be a water-demon!"

While they were still pointing to it and talking, the mountain drew near the ship, and a gaily-coloured boat slid from its summit into the water. A man sat in the middle, and fairies stood at either side of him. The man was Liu I. He beckoned to his cousin, and the latter drew up his garments and stepped into the boat with him. But when he had entered the boat it turned into a mountain. On the mountain stood a splendid castle, and in the castle stood Liu I, surrounded with radiance, and with the music of stringed instruments floating about him.

They greeted each other, and Liu I said to his cousin, "We have been parted no more than a moment, and your hair is already grey!"

His cousin answered, "You are a god and blessed. I have only a mortal body. Thus fate has decreed."

Then Liu I gave him fifty pills and said, "Each pill will extend your life for the space of a year. When you have lived the tale of these years, come to me and dwell no longer in the earthly world of dust, where there is nothing but toil and trouble."

Then he took him back across the sea and disappeared.

His cousin, however, retired from the world, and fifty years later, and when he had taken all the pills, he disappeared and was never seen again.

Note: The outcast princess is represented as "herding sheep." In Chinese the word sheep is often used as an image for clouds. Tsian Tang is the name of a place used for the name of the god of that place. The deluge is the flood which the great Yu regulated as minister of the Emperor Yau.

Tales Of The Gùshì Yuán

Bamboo And The Turtle

This story has been adapted from Norman Hinsdale Pitman's version that originally appeared in A Chinese Wonder Book, published in 1919 by E. P. Dutton And Company, New York. A Chinese Wonder Book contains a selection of stories that capture the essence of traditional Chinese culture and storytelling. The book includes tales of magic, dragons, heroes, and supernatural creatures, all woven together with elements of Chinese mythology and folklore.

A party of visitors had been seeing the sights at Hsi Ling. They had just passed down the Holy Way between the huge stone animals when Bamboo, a little boy of twelve, son of a keeper, rushed out from his father's house to see the mandarins go by. Such a parade of great men he had never seen before, even on the feast days. There were ten sedan chairs, with bearers dressed in flaming colours, ten long-handled, red umbrellas, each carried far in front of its proud owner, and a long line of horsemen.

When this grand procession had filed past, Bamboo was almost ready to cry because he could not run after the sightseers as they went from temple to temple and from tomb to tomb. But, alas, his father had ordered him never to follow tourists. "If you do, they will take you for a beggar, Bamboo," he had said shrewdly, "and if you're a beggar, then your daddy's one too. Now they don't want any beggars around the royal tombs." So Bamboo had never known the pleasure of pursuing the rich. Many times he had turned back to the little mud house, almost broken-hearted at seeing his playmates running, full of glee, after the great men's chairs.

On the day when this story opens, just as the last horseman had passed out of sight among the cedars, Bamboo chanced to look up toward one of the smaller temple buildings of which his father was the keeper. It was the house through which the visitors had just been shown. Could his eyes be deceiving him? No, the great iron doors had been forgotten in the hurry of the moment, and there they stood wide open, as if inviting him to enter.

In great excitement he scurried toward the temple. How often he had pressed his head against the bars and looked into the dark room, wishing and hoping that someday he might go in. And yet, not once had he been granted this favour. Almost every day since babyhood he had gazed at the high stone shaft, or tablet, covered with Chinese writing, that stood in the centre of the lofty room, reaching almost to the roof. But with still greater surprise his eyes had feasted on the giant turtle underneath, on whose back the column rested. There are many such tablets to be seen in China, many such turtles patiently bearing their loads of stone, but this was the only sight of the kind that Bamboo had seen. He had never been outside the Hsi Ling forest, and, of course, knew very little of the great world beyond.

It is no wonder then that the turtle and the tablet had always astonished him. He had asked his father to explain the mystery. "Why do they have a turtle? Why not a lion or an elephant?" For he had seen stone figures of these animals in the park and had thought them much better able than his friend, the turtle, to carry loads on their backs.

"Why it's just the custom," his father had replied, the answer always given when Bamboo asked a question, "just the custom." The boy had tried to imagine it all for himself, but had never been quite sure that he was right, and now, joy of all joys, he was about to enter the very turtle-room itself. Surely, once inside, he could find some answer to this puzzle of his childhood.

Breathless, he dashed through the doorway, fearing every minute that someone would notice the open gates and close them before he could enter. Just in front of the giant turtle he fell in a little heap on the floor, which was covered inch-deep with dust. His face was streaked, his clothes were a sight to behold, but Bamboo cared nothing for such trifles. He lay there for a few moments, not daring to move. Then, hearing a noise outside, he crawled under the ugly stone beast and crouched in his narrow hiding-place, as still as a mouse.

"There, there!" said a deep voice. "See what you are doing, stirring up such a dust! Why, you will strangle me if you are not careful."

It was the turtle speaking, and yet Bamboo's father had often told him that it was not alive. The boy lay trembling for a minute, too much frightened to get up and run.

"No use in shaking so, my lad," the voice continued, a little kindlier. "I suppose all boys are alike, good for nothing but kicking up a dust." He finished this sentence with a hoarse chuckle, and the boy, seeing that he was laughing, looked up with wonder at the strange creature.

"I meant no harm in coming," said the child finally. "I only wanted to look at you more closely."

"Oh, that was it, hey? Well, that is strange. All the others come and stare at the tablet on my back. Sometimes they read aloud the nonsense written there about dead emperors and their titles, but they never so much as look at me, at *me* whose father was one of the great four who made the world."

Bamboo's eyes shone with wonder. "What! *Your* father helped make the world?" he gasped.

"Well, not my father exactly, but one of my grandfathers, and it amounts to the same thing, doesn't it. But, listen, I hear a voice. The keeper is coming back. Run up and close those doors, so he won't notice that they have not been locked. Then you may hide in the corner there until he has passed. I have something more to tell you."

Bamboo did as he was told. It took all his strength to swing the heavy doors into place. He felt very important to think that he was doing something for the grandson of a maker of the world, and it would have broken his heart if this visit had been ended just as it was beginning.

Sure enough, his father and the other keepers passed on, never dreaming that the heavy locks were not fastened as usual. They were talking about the great men who had just gone. They seemed very happy and were jingling some coins in their hands.

"Now, my boy," said the stone turtle when the sound of voices had died away and Bamboo had come out from his corner, "maybe you think I'm proud of my job. Here I've been holding up this chunk for a hundred years, I who am fond of travel. During all this time night and day, I have been trying to think of some way to give up my position. Perhaps it's honourable, but, you may well imagine, it's not very pleasant."

"I should think you would have the backache," ventured Bamboo timidly.

"Backache! Well, I think so, back, neck, legs, eyes, everything I have is aching, aching for freedom. But, you see, even if I had kicked up my heels and overthrown this monument, I had no way of getting through those iron bars," and he nodded toward the gate.

"Yes, I understand," agreed Bamboo, beginning to feel sorry for his old friend.

"But, now that you are here, I have a plan, and a good one it is, too, I think. The watchmen have forgotten to lock the gate. What is to prevent my getting my freedom this very night? You open the gate, I walk out, and no one the wiser."

"But my father will lose his head if they find that he has failed to do his duty and you have escaped."

"Oh, no, not at all. You can slip his keys tonight, lock the gates after I am gone, and no one will know just what has happened. Why it will make this building famous. It won't hurt your father, but will do him good. So many travellers will be anxious to see the spot from which I vanished. I am too heavy for a thief to carry off, and they will be sure that it is another miracle of the gods. Oh, I shall have a good time out in the big world."

Just here Bamboo began to cry.

"Now what is the silly boy blubbering about?" sneered the turtle. "Is he nothing but a cry-baby?"

"No, but I don't want you to go."

"Don't want me to go, eh? Just like all the others. You're a fine fellow! What reason have you for wanting to see me weighed down here all the rest of my life with a mountain on my back? Why, I thought you were sorry for me, and it turns out that you are as mean as anybody else."

"It is so lonely here, and I have no playmates. You are the only friend I have."

The tortoise laughed loudly. "Ho, ho! So it's because I make you a good playmate, eh? Now, if that's your reason, that's another story altogether. What do you say to going with me then? I, too, need a friend, and if you help me to escape, why, you are the very friend for me."

"But how shall you get the tablet off your back?" questioned Bamboo doubtfully. "It's very heavy."

"That's easy, just walk out of the door. The tablet is too tall to go through. It will slide off and sit on the floor instead of on my shell."

Bamboo, wild with delight at the thought of going on a journey with the turtle, promised to obey the other's commands. After supper, when all were asleep in the little house of the keeper, he slipped from his bed, took down the heavy key from its peg, and ran pell-mell to the temple.

"Well, you didn't forget me, did you?" asked the turtle when Bamboo swung the iron gates open.

"Oh, no, I would not break a promise. Are you ready?"

"Yes, quite ready." So saying, the turtle took a step. The tablet swayed backward and forward, but did not fall. On walked the turtle until finally he stuck his ugly head through the doorway. "Oh, how good it looks outside," he said. "How pleasant the fresh air feels! Is that the moon rising over yonder? It's the first time I've seen it for an age. My word! just look at the trees! How they have grown since they set that tombstone on my back! There's a regular forest outside now."

Bamboo was delighted when he saw the turtle's glee at escaping. "Be careful," he cried, "not to let the tablet fall hard enough to break it."

Even as he spoke, the awkward beast waddled through the door. The upper end of the monument struck against the wall, toppled off, and fell with a great crash to the floor. Bamboo shivered with fear. Would his father come and find out what had happened?

"Don't be afraid, my boy. No one will come at this hour of the night to spy on us."

Bamboo quickly locked the gates, ran back to the house, and hung the key on its peg. He took a long look at his sleeping parents, and then returned to his friend. After all, he would not be gone long and his father would surely forgive him.

Soon the comrades were walking down the broad road, very slowly, for the tortoise is not swift of foot and Bamboo's legs were none too long.

"Where are you going?" said the boy eventually, after he had begun to feel more at home with the turtle.

"Going? Where should you think I would want to go after my century in prison? Why, back to the first home of my father, back to the very spot where the great god, P'anku, and his three helpers hewed out the world."

"And is it far?" faltered the boy, beginning to feel just the least bit tired.

"At this rate, yes, but, bless my life, you didn't think we could travel all the way at this snail's pace, I hope. Jump on my back, and I'll show you how to go. Before morning we shall be at the end of the world, or rather, the beginning."

"Where is the beginning of the world?" asked Bamboo. "I have never studied geography."

"We must cross China, then Tibet, and eventually in the mountains just beyond we shall reach the spot which P'anku made the centre of his labour."

At that moment Bamboo felt himself being lifted from the ground. At first he thought he would slip off the turtle's rounded shell, and he cried out in fright.

"Never fear," said his friend. "Only sit quietly, and there will be no danger."

They had now risen far into the air, and Bamboo could look down over the great forest of Hsi Ling all bathed in moonlight. There were the broad white roads leading up to the royal tombs, the beautiful temples, the buildings where oxen and sheep were prepared for sacrifice, the lofty towers, and the high tree-covered hills under which the emperors were buried. Until that night Bamboo had not known the size of this royal graveyard. Could it be that the turtle would carry him beyond the forest? Even as he asked himself this question he saw that they had reached a mountain, and the turtle was ascending higher, still higher, to cross the mighty wall of stone.

Bamboo grew dizzy as the turtle rose farther into the sky. He felt as he sometimes did when he played whirling games with his little friends, and got so dizzy that he tumbled over upon the ground. However, this time he knew that he must keep his head and not fall, for it must have been almost a mile to the ground below him. eventually they had passed over the mountain and were flying above a great plain. Far below Bamboo could see sleeping villages and little streams of water that looked like silver in the moonlight. Now, directly beneath them was a city. A few feeble lights could be seen in the dark narrow streets, and Bamboo thought he could hear the faint cries of peddlers crying their midnight wares.

"That's the capital of Shan-shi just below us," said the turtle, breaking his long silence. "It is almost two hundred miles from here to your father's house, and we have taken less than half an hour. Beyond that is the Province of the Western Valleys. In one hour we shall be above Tibet."

On they whizzed at lightning speed. If it had not been hot summertime Bamboo would have been almost frozen. As it was, his hands and feet were cold and stiff. The turtle, as if knowing how chilly he was, flew nearer to the ground where it was warmer. How pleasant for Bamboo! He was so tired that he could keep his eyes open no longer and he was soon soaring in the land of dreams.

When he woke up it was morning. He was lying on the ground in a wild, rocky region. Not far away burned a great wood fire, and the turtle was watching some food that was cooking in a pot.

"Ho, ho, my lad! So you have eventually woken up after your long ride. You see we are a little early. No matter if the dragon does think he can fly faster, I beat him, didn't I? Why, even the phoenix laughs at me and says I am slow, but the phoenix has not come yet either. Yes, I have clearly broken the record for speed, and I had a load to carry too, which neither of the others had, I am sure."

"Where are we?" questioned Bamboo.

"In the land of the beginning," said the other wisely. "We flew over Tibet, and then went northwest for two hours. If you haven't studied geography you won't know the name of the country. But, here we are, and that is enough, isn't it, enough for anyone? And today is the yearly feast-day in honour of the making of the world. It was very fortunate for me that the gates were left open yesterday. I am afraid my old friends, the dragon and the phoenix, have almost forgotten what I look like. It is so long since they saw me. Lucky beasts they are, not to be loaded down under an emperor's tablet. Hello! I hear the dragon coming now if I am not mistaken. Yes, here he is. How glad I am to see him!"

Bamboo heard a great noise like the whirr of enormous wings, and then, looking up, saw a huge dragon just in front of him. He knew it was a dragon from the pictures he had seen and the carvings in the temples.

The dragon and the turtle had no sooner greeted each other, both very happy at the meeting, than they were joined by a queer-looking bird, unlike any that Bamboo had ever seen, but which he knew was the phoenix. This phoenix looked somewhat like a wild swan, but it had the bill of a cock, the neck of a snake, the tail of a fish and the stripes of a dragon. Its feathers were of five colours.

When the three friends had chatted merrily for a few minutes, the turtle told them how Bamboo had helped him to escape from the temple.

"A clever boy," said the dragon, patting Bamboo gently on the back.

"Yes, yes, a clever boy indeed," echoed the phoenix.

"Ah," sighed the turtle, "if only the good god, P'anku, were here, shouldn't we be happy! But, I fear he will never come to this meeting-place. No doubt he is off in some distant spot, cutting out another world. If I could only see him once more, I feel that I should die in peace."

"Just listen!" laughed the dragon. "As if one of us could die! Why, you talk like a mere mortal."

All day long the three friends chatted, feasted, and had a good time looking round at the places where they had lived so happily when P'anku had been cutting out the world. They were good to Bamboo also and showed him many wonderful things of which he had never dreamed.

"You are not half so mean-looking and so fierce as they paint you on the flags," said Bamboo in a friendly voice to the dragon just as they were about to separate.

The three friends laughed heartily.

"Oh, no, he's a very decent sort of fellow, even if he is covered with fish-scales," joked the phoenix.

Just before they bade each other good-bye, the phoenix gave Bamboo a long scarlet tail-feather for a keepsake, and the dragon gave him a large scale which turned to gold as soon as the boy took it into his hand.

"Come, come, we must hurry," said the turtle. "I am afraid your father will think you are lost." So Bamboo, after having spent the happiest day of his life, mounted the turtle's back, and they rose once more above the clouds. Back they flew even faster than they had come. Bamboo had so many things to talk about that he did not once think of going to sleep, for he had really seen the dragon and the phoenix, and if he never were to see anything else in his life, he would always be happy.

Suddenly the turtle stopped short in his swift flight, and Bamboo felt himself slipping. Too late he screamed for help, too late he tried to save himself. Down, down from that dizzy height he tumbled, turning, twisting, thinking of the awful death that was surely coming. Swish! He shot through the treetops trying vainly to clutch the friendly branches. Then with a loud scream he struck the ground, and his long journey was ended.

"Come out from under that turtle, boy! What are you doing inside the temple in the dirt? Don't you know this is not the proper place for you?"

Bamboo rubbed his eyes. Though only half awake, he knew it was his father's voice.

"But didn't it kill me?" he said as his father pulled him out by the heel from under the great stone turtle.

"What killed you, foolish boy? What can you be talking about? But I'll half-kill you if you don't hurry out of this and come to your supper. Really I believe you are getting too lazy to eat. The idea of sleeping the whole afternoon under that turtle's belly!"

Bamboo, not yet fully awake, stumbled out of the tablet room, and his father locked the iron doors.

Tales Of The Gùshì Yuán

The Hen and the Chinese Mountain Turtle

This story has been adapted from a tale originally told by Kate Douglas Wiggin and Nora Archibald Smith in The Talking Beasts, published in 1911 by Houghton Mifflin Company. The fables in The Talking Beasts are engaging and entertaining, with whimsical characters and imaginative settings. Through these tales, Wiggin and Smith aimed to stimulate the imagination of children while also instilling important values that promote character development and moral growth.

Four hundred and fifty years ago in Lze-Cheung Province, Western China, there lived an old farmer named Ah-Po.

The young farmers all said Ah-Po knew everything. If they wanted to know when it would rain, they asked Ah-Po, and when he said, "It will not rain tomorrow," or, "You will need your bamboo-hat this time tomorrow," it was as he said. He knew all about the things of nature and how to make the earth yield best her fruits and seeds, and some said he was a prophet.

One day Ah-Po caught a fine Mountain Turtle. It was so large that it took both of Ah-Po's sons to carry it home. They tied its legs together and hung it on a strong stick, and each son put an end of the stick on his shoulder.

Ah-Po said, "We will not kill the Turtle. He is too old to eat, and I think we will keep him and watch the rings grow around his legs each year." So they gave him a corner in the barnyard and fed him rice and water.

Ah-Po had many Chickens, and for three months the Turtle and Chickens lived in peace with each other. But one day all the young Chickens came together and laughed at the Turtle. Then they said to him, "Why do you live here so long? Why do you not go back to your own place? This small barnyard corner is not so good as your cave in the wilderness. You have only a little sand and grass to live on here. The servant feeds you, but she never gives you any wilderness fruits. You are very large, and you take up too much room. We need all the room there is here. You foolish old thing, do you think our fathers and mothers want you? No. There is not one of our people who likes you. Besides, you are not clean. You make too much dirt. The servant girl gave you this water to drink, and your water bowl is even now upside down. You scatter rice on our floor. Too many flies come here to see you, and we do not like flies."

The Turtle waited until they had all finished scolding. Then he said, "Do you think I came here myself? Who put me here, do you know? Do you suppose I like to be in jail? You need not be jealous. I never ate any rice that belonged to you or your family. I am not living in your house. What are you complaining about? If our master should take your whole family and sell it, he would only get one piece of silver. Who and what are you to talk so much? Wait and see, someday I may have the honoured place."

Some of the Chickens went home and told their mother, "We had an argument with the Turtle today and he had the last word. Tomorrow we want you to go with us and show him that a Chicken can argue as well as a Turtle."

The next day all the Chickens of the barnyard went to see the Turtle. And the old Hen said, "My children came here to play yesterday, and you scolded them and drove them away. You said all my family was not worth one piece of silver. You think you are worth many pieces of gold, I suppose. No one likes you. Your own master would not eat you. And the market people would never buy a thing so old and tough as you are. But I suppose you will have to stay here in our yard a thousand years or so, until you die. Then they will carry you to the wilderness and throw you into the Nobody-Knows Lake."

Then the Turtle answered and said, "I am a Mountain Turtle. I come from a wise family, and it is not easy for even man to catch me. Educated men, doctors, know that I am useful for sickness, but if all the people knew the many ways they could use me, I think there would soon be no more turtles in the world. Many Chinese know that my skin is good for skin disease, and my forefeet are good for the devil-sickness in children, as they drive the devil away, and then my shells are good for sore throat, and my stomach is good for stomach-ache, and my bones are good for tooth-ache. Do you remember that not long ago our master brought three turtle eggs to feed your children? I heard him say: 'Those little Chickens caught cold in that damp place, and so I must give them some turtle eggs.' I saw your children eat those three eggs, and in two or three days they were well.

"So you see the Turtle is a useful creature in the world, even to Chickens. Why do you not leave me in peace? As I must stay here against my will, it is not right that your children should trouble me. Sometimes they take all my rice and I go hungry, for our master will not allow me to go outside of this fence to hunt food for myself. I never come to your house and bother you, but your children will not even let me live in peace in the little corner our master gave me. If I had a few of my own people here with me, as you have, I think you would not trouble me. But I have only myself, while you are many.

"Yesterday your children scolded me and disturbed my peace. To-day you come again, and tomorrow and many tomorrows will see generations and still more unhatched generations of Chickens coming here to scold me, I fear, for the length of life of a cackling hen is as a day to me, a Mountain Turtle. I know the heaven is large, I know the earth is large and made for all creatures alike. But you think the heavens and the earth were both made for you and your Chickens only. If you could drive me away today you would try tomorrow to drive the dog away, and in time you would think the master himself ought not to have enough of your earth and air to live in. This barnyard is large enough for birds, chickens, ducks, geese, and pigs. It makes our master happy to have us all here."

The Chickens went away ashamed. Talking to each other about it, they said, "The Turtle is right. It is foolish to want everything. We barnyard creatures must live at peace with each other until we die. The barnyard is not ours, we use it only a little while."

Tales Of The Gùshì Yuán

The Eight Immortals

This story has been adapted from Dr. Richard Wilhelm's version that originally appeared in The Chinese Fairy Book, published in 1921 by Frederick A. Stokes Company, New York. Wilhelm's translations aimed to capture the essence of the original Chinese texts while making them accessible to English-speaking audiences. His deep understanding of Chinese language and culture shone through in his translations, allowing readers to appreciate the beauty and depth of these timeless tales.

There is a legend which declares that Eight Immortals dwell in the heavens. The first is named Dschung Li Kuan. He lived in the time of the Han dynasty, and discovered the wonderful magic of golden cinnabar, the philosopher's stone. He could melt quicksilver and burn lead and turn them into yellow gold and white silver. And he could fly through the air in his human form. He is the chief of the Eight Immortals.

The second is named Dschang Go. In primal times he gained hidden knowledge. It is said that he was really a white bat, who turned into a man. In the first days of the Tang dynasty an ancient with a white beard and a bamboo drum on his back, was seen riding backward on a black ass in the town of Tschang An. He beat the drum and sang, and called himself old Dschang Go. Another legend says that he always had a white mule with him which could cover a thousand miles in a single day. When he had reached his destination he would fold up the animal and put it in his trunk. When he needed it again, he would sprinkle water on it with his mouth, and the beast would regain its first shape.

The third is named Lu Yuan or Lu Dung Bin (The Mountain Guest). His real name was Li, and he belonged to the ruling Tang dynasty. But when the Empress Wu seized the throne and destroyed the Li family to almost the last man, he fled with his wife into the heart of the mountains. They changed their names to Lu, and, since they lived in hiding in the caverns in the rocks, he called himself the Mountain Guest or the Guest of the Rocks. He lived on air and ate no bread. Yet he was fond of flowers. And in the course of time he acquired the hidden wisdom.

In Lo Yang, the capital city, the peonies bloomed with special luxuriance. And there dwelt a flower fairy, who changed herself into a lovely maiden with whom Guest of the Rocks, when he came to Lo Yang, was wont to converse. Suddenly along came the Yellow Dragon, who had taken the form of a handsome youth. He mocked the flower fairy. Guest of the Rocks grew furious and cast his flying sword at him, cutting off his head. From that time onward he fell back again into the world of mundane pleasure and death. He sank down into the dust of the diurnal, and was no longer able to wing his way to the upper regions. Later he met Dschung Li Kuan, who delivered him, and then he was taken up in the ranks of the Immortals.

Willowelf was his disciple. This was an old willow-tree which had drawn into itself the most ethereal powers of the sunrays and the moonbeams, and had thus been able to assume the shape of a human being. His face is blue and he has red hair. Guest of the Rocks received him as a disciple. Emperors and kings of future times honour Guest of the Rocks as the ancestor and master of the pure sun. The people call him Grandfather Lu. He is very wise and powerful. And therefore the people still stream into Grandfather Lu's temples to obtain oracles and pray for good luck. If you want to know whether you will be successful or not in an undertaking, go to the temple, light incense and bow your head to earth. On the altar is a bamboo goblet, in which are some dozens of little lottery sticks. You must shake them while kneeling, until one of the sticks flies out. On the lottery-stick is inscribed a number. This number must then be looked up in the Book of Oracles, where it is accompanied by a four-line stanza. It is said that fortune and misfortune, strange to think, occur to one just as foretold by the oracle.

The fourth Immortal is Tsau Guo Gui (Tsau the Uncle of the State). He was the younger brother of the Empress Tsau, who for a time ruled the land. For this reason he was called the Uncle of the State. From his earliest youth he had been a lover of the hidden wisdom. Riches and honours were no more to him than dust. It was Dschung Li Kuan who aided him to become immortal.

The fifth is called Lan Tsai Ho. Nothing is known of his true name, his time nor his family. He was often seen in the market-place, clad in a torn blue robe and wearing only a single shoe, beating a block of wood and singing the nothingness of life.

The sixth Immortal is known as Li Tia Guai (Li with the iron crutch). He lost his parents in early youth and was brought up in his older brother's home. His sister-in-law treated him badly and never gave him enough to eat. Because of this he fled into the hills, and there learned the hidden wisdom.

Once he returned in order to see his brother, and said to his sister-in-law, "Give me something to eat!"

She answered, "There is no kindling wood on hand!"

He replied, "You need only to prepare the rice. I can use my leg for kindling wood, only you must not say that the fire might injure me, and if you do not no harm will be done."

His sister-in-law wished to see his art, so she poured the rice into the pot. Li stretched one of his legs out under it and lit it. The flames leaped high and the leg burned like coal.

When the rice was nearly boiled his sister-in-law said, "Won't your leg be injured?"

And Li replied angrily, "Did I not warn you not to say anything! Then no harm would have been done. Now one of my legs is lamed."

With these words he took an iron poker and fashioned it into a crutch for himself. Then he hung a bottle-gourd on his back, and went into the hills to gather medicinal herbs. And that is why he is known as Li with the Iron Crutch.

It is also told of him that he was often in the habit of ascending into the heavens in the spirit to visit his master Laotsze. Before he left he would order a disciple to watch his body and soul within it, so that the latter did not escape. Should seven days have gone by without his spirit returning, then he would allow his soul to leave the empty tenement. Unfortunately, after six days had passed, the disciple was called to the death-bed of his mother, and when the master's spirit returned on the evening of the seventh day, the life had gone out of its body. Since there was no place for his spirit in his own body, in his despair he seized upon the first handy body from which the vital essence had not yet dispersed. It was the body of a neighbour, a lame cripple, who had just died, so that from that time on the master appeared in his form.

The seventh Immortal is called Hang Siang Dsi. He was the nephew of the famous Confucian scholar Han Yu, of the Tang dynasty. From his earliest youth he cultivated the arts of the deathless gods, left his home and became a Taoist. Grandfather Lu awakened him and raised him to the heavenly world. Once he saved his uncle's life. The latter had been driven from court because he had objected when the emperor sent for a bone of Buddha with great pomp. When he reached the Blue Pass in his flight, a deep snowfall had made the road impassable. His horse had floundered in a snow-drift, and he himself was well-nigh frozen. Then Hang Siang Dsi suddenly appeared, helped him and his horse out of the drift, and brought them safely to the nearest inn along the Blue Pass. Han Yu sang a verse, in which these lines occurred:

Tsin Ling Hill 'mid clouds doth lie,

And home is far, beyond my sight!

Round the Blue Pass snow towers high,

And who will lead the horse aright?

Suddenly it occurred to him that several years before, Hang Siang Dsi had come to his house to congratulate him on his birthday. Before he had left, he had written these words on a slip of paper, and his uncle had read them, without grasping their meaning. And now he was unconsciously singing the very lines of that song that his nephew had written. So he said to Hang Siang Dsi, with a sigh, "You must be one of the Immortals, since you were able thus to foretell the future!"

And three times Hang Siang Dsi sought to deliver his wife from the bonds of earth. For when he left his home to seek the hidden wisdom, she sat all day long yearning for his presence. Hang Siang Dsi wished to release her into immortality, but he feared she was not capable of translation. So he appeared to her in various forms, in order to try her, once as a beggar, another time as a wandering monk. But his wife did not grasp her opportunities. Eventually he took the shape of a lame Taoist, who sat on a mat, beat a block of wood and read sutras before the house.

His wife said, "My husband is not at home. I can give you nothing."

The Taoist answered, "I do not want your gold and silver, I want you. Sit down beside me on the mat, and we will fly up into the air and you shall find your husband again!"

Hereupon the woman grew angry and struck at him with a cudgel.

Then Hang Siang Dsi changed himself into his true form, stepped on a shining cloud and was carried aloft. His wife looked after him and wept loudly, but he had disappeared and was not seen again.

The eighth Immortal is a girl and was called Ho Sian Gu. She was a peasant's daughter, and though her step-mother treated her harshly she remained respectful and industrious. She loved to give alms, though her step-mother tried to prevent her. Yet she was never angry, even when her step-mother beat her. She had sworn not to marry, and eventually her step-mother did not know what to do with her.

One day, while she was cooking rice, Grandfather Du came and delivered her. She was still holding the rice-spoon in her hand as she ascended into the air. In the heavens she was appointed to sweep up the fallen flowers at the Southern Gate of Heaven.

Note: The legends of the Eight Immortals, regarded as one group, do not go back further than the Manchu dynasty, though individual ones among them were known before. Some of the Immortals, like Han Siang Dsi, are historic personages, others purely mythical.

Tales Of The Gùshì Yuán

The Story Of Hok Lee And The Dwarfs

This story has been adapted from Andrew Lang's version that originally appeared in The Green Fairy Book, published in 1902 by Longmans, Green And Co., London And New York. Each volume in the coloured fairy book series features a diverse selection of fairy tales and folklore, gathered from various cultures and regions. While many of the stories are well-known European fairy tales, such as those by the Brothers Grimm and Hans Christian Andersen, Lang also included lesser-known tales from countries like Russia, India, Japan, and Africa. This diversity introduced readers to a wide range of cultural traditions and storytelling styles.

There once lived in a small town in China a man named Hok Lee. He was a steady industrious man, who not only worked hard at his trade, but did all his own house-work as well, for he had no wife to do it for him. "What an excellent industrious man is this Hok Lee!" said his neighbours. "How hard he works. He never leaves his house to amuse himself or to take a holiday as others do!"

But Hok Lee was by no means the virtuous person his neighbours thought him. True, he worked hard enough by day, but at night, when all respectable folk were fast asleep, he used to steal out and join a dangerous band of robbers, who broke into rich people's houses and carried off all they could lay hands on.

This state of things went on for some time, and, though a thief was caught now and then and punished, no suspicion ever fell on Hok Lee, he was such a very respectable, hard-working man.

Hok Lee had already amassed a good store of money as his share of the proceeds of these robberies when it happened one morning on going to market that a neighbour said to him, "Why, Hok Lee, what is the matter with your face? One side of it is all swelled up."

True enough, Hok Lee's right cheek was twice the size of his left, and it soon began to feel very uncomfortable.

"I will bind up my face," said Hok Lee. "Doubtless the warmth will cure the swelling." But no such thing. Next day it was worse, and day by day it grew bigger and bigger till it was nearly as large as his head and became very painful.

Hok Lee was at his wits' ends about what to do. Not only was his cheek unsightly and painful, but his neighbours began to jeer and make fun of him, which hurt his feelings very much indeed.

One day, as luck would have it, a travelling doctor came to the town. He sold not only all kinds of medicine, but also dealt in many strange charms against witches and evil spirits Hok Lee determined to consult him, and asked him into his house.

After the doctor had examined him carefully, he said, "This, O Hok Lee, is no ordinary swelled face. I strongly suspect you have been doing some wrong deed which has called down the anger of the spirits on you. None of my drugs will avail to cure you, but, if you are willing to pay me handsomely, I can tell you how you may be cured."

Then Hok Lee and the doctor began to bargain together, and it was a long time before they could come to terms. However, the doctor got the better of it in the end, for he was determined not to part with his secret under a certain price, and Hok Lee had no mind to carry his huge cheek about with him to the end of his days. So he was obliged to part with the greater portion of his ill-gotten gains.

When the Doctor had pocketed the money, he told Hok Lee to go on the first night of the full moon to a certain wood and there to watch by a particular tree. After a time he would see the dwarfs and little sprites who live underground come out to dance. When they saw him they would be sure to make him dance too. "And mind you dance your very best," added the doctor. "If you dance well and please them they will grant you a petition and you can then beg to be cured, but if you dance badly they will most likely do you some mischief out of spite." With that he took leave and departed.

Happily the first night of the full moon was near, and at the proper time Hok Lee set out for the wood. With a little trouble he found the tree the doctor had described, and, feeling nervous, he climbed up into it.

He had hardly settled himself on a branch when he saw the little dwarfs assembling in the moonlight. They came from all sides, till at length there appeared to be hundreds of them. They seemed in high glee, and danced and skipped and capered about, whilst Hok Lee grew so eager watching them that he crept further and further along his branch till at length it gave a loud crack. All the dwarfs stood still, and Hok Lee felt as if his heart stood still also.

Then one of the dwarfs called out, "Someone is up in that tree. Come down at once, whoever you are, or we must come and fetch you."

In great terror, Hok Lee proceeded to come down, but he was so nervous that he tripped near the ground and came rolling down in the most absurd manner. When he had picked himself up, he came forward with a low bow, and the dwarf who had first spoken and who appeared to be the leader, said, "Now, then, who are you, and what brings you here?"

So Hok Lee told him the sad story of his swelled cheek, and how he had been advised to come to the forest and beg the dwarfs to cure him.

"It is well," replied the dwarf. "We will see about that. First, however, you must dance before us. Should your dancing please us, perhaps we may be able to do something, but should you dance badly, we shall assuredly punish you, so now take warning and dance away.'

With that, he and all the other dwarfs sat down in a large ring, leaving Hok Lee to dance alone in the middle. He felt half frightened to death, and besides was a good deal shaken by his fall from the tree and did not feel at all inclined to dance. But the dwarfs were not to be trifled with.

"Begin!" cried their leader, and "Begin!" shouted the rest in chorus.

So in despair Hok Lee began. First he hopped on one foot and then on the other, but he was so stiff and so nervous that he made but a poor attempt, and after a time sank down on the ground and vowed he could dance no more.

The dwarfs were very angry. They crowded round Hok Lee and abused him. 'You came here to be cured, indeed!" they cried, "You have brought one big cheek with you, but you shall take away two." And with that they ran off and disappeared, leaving Hok Lee to find his way home as best he might.

He hobbled away, weary and depressed, and not a little anxious on account of the dwarfs' threat.

Nor were his fears unfounded, for when he rose next morning his left cheek was swelled up as big as his right, and he could hardly see out of his eyes. Hok Lee felt in despair, and his neighbours jeered at him more than ever. The doctor, too, had disappeared, so there was nothing for it but to try the dwarfs once more

He waited a month till the first night of the full moon came round again, and then he trudged back to the forest, and sat down under the tree from which he had fallen. He had not long to wait. Before long the dwarfs came trooping out till all were assembled.

"I don't feel quite easy," said one; "I feel as if some horrid human being were near us."

When Hok Lee heard this he came forward and bent down to the ground before the dwarfs, who came crowding round, and laughed heartily at his comical appearance with his two big cheeks.

"What do you want?' they asked, and Hok Lee told them of his fresh misfortunes, and begged to be allowed one more trial at dancing that the dwarfs consented, for there is nothing they love so much as being amused.

Now, Hok Lee knew how much depended on his dancing well, so he plucked up a good spirit and began, first quite slowly, and faster by degrees, and he danced so well and gracefully, and made such new and wonderful steps, that the dwarfs were quite delighted with him.

They clapped their tiny hands, and shouted, "Well done, Hok Lee, well done, go on, dance more, for we are pleased."

And Hok Lee danced on and on, till he really could dance no more, and was obliged to stop.

Then the leader of the dwarfs said, "We are well pleased, Hok Lee, and as a recompense for your dancing your face shall be cured. Farewell."

With these words he and the other dwarfs vanished, and Hok Lee, putting his hands to his face, found to his great joy that his cheeks were reduced to their natural size. The way home seemed short and easy to him, and he went to bed happy, and resolved never to go out robbing again.

Next day the whole town was full of the news of Hok's sudden cure. His neighbours questioned him, but could get nothing from him, except the fact that he had discovered a wonderful cure for all kinds of diseases.

After a time a rich neighbour, who had been ill for some years, came, and offered to give Hok Lee a large sum of money if he would tell him how he might get cured. Hok Lee consented on condition that he swore to keep the secret. He did so, and Hok Lee told him of the dwarfs and their dances.

The neighbour went off, carefully obeyed Hok Lee's directions, and was duly cured by the dwarfs. Then another and another came to Hok Lee to beg his secret, and from each he extracted a vow of secrecy and a large sum of money. This went on for some years, so that at length Hok Lee became a very wealthy man, and ended his days in peace and prosperity.

Tales Of The Gùshì Yuán

The Dragon After His Winter Sleep

This story has been adapted from Dr. Richard Wilhelm's version that originally appeared in The Chinese Fairy Book, published in 1921 by Frederick A. Stokes Company, New York. Wilhelm's translations aimed to capture the essence of the original Chinese texts while making them accessible to English-speaking audiences. His deep understanding of Chinese language and culture shone through in his translations, allowing readers to appreciate the beauty and depth of these timeless tales.

Once there was a scholar who was reading in the upper story of his house. It was a rainy, cloudy day and the weather was gloomy. Suddenly he saw a little thing which shone like a fire-fly. It crawled upon the table, and wherever it went it left traces of burns, curved like the tracks of a rainworm. Gradually it wound itself about the scholar's book and the book, too, grew black. Then it occurred to him that it might be a dragon. So he carried it out of doors on the book. There he stood for quite some time, but it sat uncurled, without moving in the least.

Then the scholar said, "It shall not be said of me that I was lacking in respect." With these words he carried back the book and once more laid it on the table. Then he put on his robes of ceremony, made a deep bow and escorted the dragon out on it again.

No sooner had he left the door, than he noticed that the dragon raised his head and stretched himself. Then he flew up from the book with a hissing sound, like a radiant streak. Once more he turned around toward the scholar, and his head had already grown to the size of a barrel, while his body must have been a full fathom in length. He gave one more snaky twist, and then there was a terrible crash of thunder and the dragon went sailing through the air.

The scholar then returned and looked to see which way the little creature had come. And he could follow his tracks here and there, to his chest of books.

Note: The dragon, head of all scaled creatures and insects, hibernates during the winter according to the Chinese belief. At the time he is quite small. When the first spring storm comes he flies up to the clouds on the lightning.

In Union Is Strength

This story has been adapted from a tale originally told by Penrhyn Wingfield Coussens in The Jade Story Book, stories From The Orient, published in 1922 by Duffield And Company, New York. One of the notable aspects of The Jade Story Book is Coussens' engaging narrative style, which brings the characters and settings to life while staying true to the spirit of the original tales.

A lion was wandering over the desert, seeking water. It was very hot, and the sun had dried so many pools that it was a long time before he found a well where he could assuage his thirst. But this he did eventually, although the water in it was not at all fresh. However, he was too thirsty to care much whether it was stale or not.

He reached down to drink, and then his ears were assailed with the buzzing of mosquitoes, who said to him, "Lion, leave us in peace. We did not ask you to come here and drink up our home, and you are not welcome."

This surprised the Lion, who was not used to being spoken to in such an impertinent manner. He roared and said, "Do you know whom you are speaking to? I am the Lion, the King of all beasts. What affair of yours is it what I do? Leave me at once, or I will kill you all."

But the Mosquitoes said, "You are one, and we are many. For generations this old well has been our home, and it is not for you to say that we must go. Take our advice and seek another well, or trouble will visit you."

"You insignificant little creatures, how dare you address me in such manner," roared the Lion. "Why, in one minute I can swallow you all and you will make only the very smallest part of a mouthful for me. Know that when I speak all beasts of the forest and the wilderness bow before me, and tremble. Now fly away, all of you, for I am going to drink."

"We know how great your renown is," said the Mosquitoes, "but we do not fear you. If you wish to fight us we are very willing to have it so, but we will not allow you to destroy our home."

The Lion was now enraged more than he had ever been before. Such language to him, the King, meant that destruction must be meted out to those who dared to use it. He roared again, and made ready to kill the foolish Mosquitoes.

But he found that he had undertaken no easy task. The Mosquitoes flew into his ears, his eyes, his nose and his mouth. They stung him all over his body, and soon he knew that he was conquered. He shook himself, he rolled over and over on the ground, but he could not drive them away.

Then he jumped high into the air, and when he came down his head and fore feet went into the well, and he was unable to release himself.

And so he died, thus teaching a lesson to those who are so proud of their own might that they all think all others must bow down to them. The water in the well was the home of the Mosquitoes, and he had no right to deprive them of it. Had he made a request for water with gentle words, it would without doubt have been given to him, but in the foolishness of his pride and anger he demanded that which was not his. Gentleness, and consideration for others will bring their reward.

The Mysterious Buddhist Robe

This story has been adapted from Rev. John MacGowan's version that originally appeared in Chinese Folk-Lore Tales, published in 1910 by MacMillan and Company, London. Chinese Folk-Lore Tales features a variety of stories that cover a wide range of themes, including mythology, morality, adventure, and romance. These tales often incorporate elements of Chinese folklore, legends, and superstitions, providing readers with a glimpse into the beliefs and values of traditional Chinese society.

The short visit which the Emperor Li Shih-ming paid to the Land of Shadows had produced a profound impression on his mind. The pain and misery that men had to endure there, because of the evils they had committed in this life by their own voluntary action, had been brought before him in a most vivid manner. He had seen with his own eyes what he had always been unwilling to believe, namely, that wrong-doing is in every case followed by penalties, which have to be paid either in this world or the next.

He was now convinced that the doctrine of the sages on this point was true, for he had witnessed the horrors that criminals who had practically escaped punishment in this life had to suffer when they came under the jurisdiction of Yam-lo.

What distressed him most of all, however, was the grim thought which clung to him and refused to be silenced, that a large number of those in the Land of Shadows who were suffering from hunger and nakedness, were there as the result of his own cruelty and injustice, and that the cries of these men and women would reach to Heaven, and in due time bring down vengeance on himself.

With this fear of coming judgment there was at the same time mingled in his mind an element of compassion, for he was really sorry for the poor wretches whom he had seen in the "City of the Wronged Ones," and whose reproaches and threats of divine vengeance had entered into his very soul.

He therefore determined to institute a magnificent service for those spirits of the dead, who through the injustice of rulers, or the impotence of law, or private revenge, had lost their lives and were suffering untold hardships in the other world. He would have prayers said for their souls, that would flood their lives with plenty, and in course of time would open up the way for their being reborn into the world of men.

In this way he would propitiate those whom he had injured, and at the same time accumulate such an amount of merit for his benevolence, that the gods would make it easy for him when his time of reckoning came, and the accounts of his life were made up and balanced.

As this ceremony was to be one such as had never before been held at any period of Chinese history, he was anxious that the man who should be the leader and conductor of it should not be one of the men of indifferent lives who are usually found in the Buddhist temples and monasteries. He must be a man of sterling character, and of a life so pure and holy that no stain could be found upon it to detract from the saintly reputation he had acquired.

His Majesty accordingly sent out edicts to all the Viceroys in the Empire, commanding them to issue proclamations throughout the length and breadth of the country, telling the people of the great religious service which he was going to hold in the capital for the unhappy spirits in the Land of Shadows. In these edicts he ordered that search should be made for a priest of unblemished character, one who had proved his love for his fellow-men by great acts of sympathy for them. This man was to be invited to present himself before the Emperor, to take charge of the high and splendid service which had been designed by the Sovereign himself.

The tidings of this noble conception of Li Shih-ming spread with wonderful rapidity throughout his dominions, and even reached the far-off Western Heaven, where the mysterious beings who inhabit that happy land are ever on the alert to welcome any movement for the relief of human suffering. The Goddess of Mercy considered the occasion of such importance that she determined to take her share of responsibility for this distinguished service, by providing suitable vestments in which the leader of the great ceremony should be attired.

So it came to pass that while men's minds were excited about the proposed celebration for the dead, two priests suddenly appeared in the streets of the capital. No one had ever seen such old-fashioned and weird-looking specimens of manhood before. They were mean and insignificant in appearance, and the distinctive robes in which they were dressed were so travel-stained and unclean that it was evident they had not been washed for many a long day.

Men looked at them with astonishment as they passed along the road, for there was something so strange about them that they seemed to have come down from a far-off distant age, and to have suddenly burst into a civilization which had long out-grown the type from which they were descended. But by-and-by their curious old-world appearance was forgotten in amazement at the articles they carried with them. These were carefully wrapped in several folds of cloth to keep them from being soiled, though the two priests were perfectly willing to unfold the wrappers, and exhibit them to anyone who wished to examine them.

The precious things which were preserved with such jealous care were a hat and robe such as an abbot might wear on some great occasion when the Buddhist faith was using its most elaborate ceremonial to perform some function of unusual dignity and importance. There was also a crosier, beautifully wrought with precious stones, which was well worthy of being held in the hand of the highest functionary of the Church in any of its most sacred and solemn services. The remarkable thing about the hat and robe was their exquisite beauty. The richness of the embroidered work, the quaint designs, the harmonious blending of colours, and the subtle exhibition of the genius of the mind which had fashioned and perfected them, arrested the attention of even the lowest class in the crowds of people who gathered round the two priests to gaze upon the hat and robe, with awe and admiration in their faces.

Some instinct that flashed through the minds of the wondering spectators told them that these rare and fairy-like vestments were no ordinary products manufactured in any of the looms throughout the wide domains of the Empire. No human mind or hand had ever designed or worked out the various hues and shades of such marvellous colours as those which flashed before their eyes, and which possessed a delicacy and beauty such as none of the great artists of the past had ever been able to produce.

The priests from the various temples and monasteries of the capital soon heard the reports that spread through the city about the marvellous hat and robe, and flocked in large numbers to see these wonderful things, which the two curious-looking men were displaying to all who cared to gaze upon them.

"Do you wish to dispose of these things?" asked one of the city priests.

"If anyone can pay the price at which we are prepared to sell, we shall be willing to part with them to him," was the reply.

"And what may the price be?" anxiously enquired the priest.

"The hat and robe will cost four thousand taels, and the crosier, which is of the rarest materials and manufacture, will be sold for the same amount."

At this a great laugh resounded through the crowd. In those days eight thousand taels was a huge fortune which only one or two of the wealthiest men of the State could have afforded to give. The boisterous mirth, however, which convulsed the crowd when they heard the fabulous sums asked by these strangers for their articles, soon became hushed when the latter proceeded to explain that the sums demanded were purposely prohibitive, in order that the sacred vestments should not fall into the hands of anyone who was unworthy to possess them.

"You are all aware," said one of the strangers, "that His Majesty the Emperor, recognizing that the service for the dead which he is about to hold is one of momentous importance, not only to the spirits suffering in the Land of Shadows, but also to the prosperity and welfare of the Chinese Empire, has already issued edicts to secure the presence of some saintly and godly priest, who shall be worthy to superintend the prayers that will be said for the men and women who are leading dreary lives in the land over which Yam-lo rules."

The story of these two men spread with great rapidity throughout the homes of all classes in the metropolis, and when it was understood that they had no desire to make money by the rare and beautiful articles which they readily displayed to the crowds that followed them whenever they appeared on the streets, they began to be surrounded with a kind of halo of romance. Men whispered to each other that these were no common denizens of the earth, but fairies in disguise, who had come as messengers from the Goddess of Mercy. The garments which they had with them were such as no mortal eyes had ever beheld, and were clearly intended for use only at some special ceremony of exceptional importance such as that which the Emperor was planning to have carried out.

At length rumours reached the palace of the strange scenes which were daily taking place in the streets of the capital, and Li Shih-ming sent officers to command the two strange priests to appear in his presence.

When they were brought before him, and he saw the wonderful robe embroidered in delicate hues and colours such as no workman had ever been known to design before, and grasped the crosier which sparkled and flashed with the brilliancy of the precious stones adorning it, the Emperor felt that the invisible gods had approved of his design for the solemn service for the dead and had prepared vestments for the High Priest which would be worthy of the exalted position he would occupy in the great ceremony.

"I hear that you want eight thousand taels for these articles," said the Emperor to the two men, who stood respectfully before him.

"We are not anxious, your Majesty," replied one of the strangers, "about the price. That is to us of very little importance. We have mentioned this large sum simply to prevent any man of unworthy mind from becoming their possessor.

"There is a peculiarity about that robe," he continued. "Any person of pure and upright heart who wears it will be preserved from every kind of disaster that can possibly assail him in this world. No sorrow can touch him, and the schemes of the most malignant of evil spirits will have no influence upon him. On the other hand, any man who is under the dominion of any base passion, if he dares to put on that mystic robe, will find himself involved in all kinds of calamities and sorrows, which will never leave him until he has put it off and laid it aside for ever.

"What we are really here for," he concluded, "is to endeavour to assist your Majesty in the discovery of a priest of noble and blameless life who will be worthy of presiding at the service you are about to hold for the unhappy spirits in the Land of Shadows. When we have found him we shall consider that our mission has been fulfilled, and we can then return and report the success we have achieved."

At this moment despatches from high officials throughout the country were presented to the Emperor, all recommending Sam-Chaong as the only man in the dominions who was fit to act as High Priest in the proposed great service. As Sam-Chaong happened to be then in the capital, he was sent for and, being approved of by His Majesty, was at once appointed to the sacred office, which he alone of the myriads of priests in China seemed to be worthy of occupying.

The two strangers, who had been noting the proceedings with anxious and watchful eyes, expressed their delight at the decision that had been arrived at. Stepping up to Sam-Chaong with the most reverential attitude, they presented him with the costly vestments which had excited the wonder and admiration of everyone who had seen them. Refusing to receive any remuneration for them, they bowed gracefully to the Emperor and retired. As the door of the audience-chamber closed upon them they vanished from human sight, and no trace of them could anywhere be found.

On the great day appointed by the Emperor, such a gathering was assembled as China in all the long history of the past had never before witnessed. Abbots from far-off distant monasteries were there, dressed in their finest vestments. Aged priests, with faces wrinkled by the passage of years, and young bonzes in their slate-coloured gowns, had travelled over the hills and mountains of the North to be present, and took up their positions in the great building. Men of note, too, who had made themselves famous by their devoted zeal for the ceremonies of the Buddhist faith and by their munificent gifts to the temples and shrines, had come with great retinues of their clansmen to add to the splendour and dignity of the occasion.

But the chief glory and attraction of the day to the assembled crowds was the Emperor, Li Shih-Ming. Never had he been seen in such pomp and circumstance as on this occasion. Close round him stood the princes of the royal family, the great officers of state and the members of the Cabinet in their rich and picturesque dresses. Immediately beyond were earls and dukes, viceroys of provinces and great captains and commanders, whose fame for mighty deeds of valour in the border warfare had spread through every city and town and hamlet in the Empire.

There were also present some of the most famous scholars of China, who, though not members of the Buddhist faith, yet felt that they could not refuse the invitation which the Emperor had extended to them.

In short, the very flower of the Empire was gathered together to carry out the benevolent purpose of rescuing the spirits of the dead from an intolerable state of misery which only the living had the power of alleviating.

The supreme moment, however, was when Sam-Chaong and more than a hundred of the priests most distinguished for learning and piety in the whole of the church, marched in solemn procession, chanting a litany, and took their places on the raised platform from which they were to conduct the service for the dead.

During the ceremony, much to his amazement, Li Shih-Ming saw the two men who had bestowed the fairy vestments on Sam-Chaong, standing one on each side of him, but though they joined heartily in the proceedings, he could not help noticing that a look of dissatisfaction and occasionally of something which seemed like contempt, rested like a shadow on their faces.

At the close of the service he commanded them to appear before him, and expressed his surprise at their conduct, when they explained that the discontent they had shown was entirely due to a feeling that the ritual which had been used that day was one entirely inadequate to the occasion. It was so wanting in dignity and loftiness of conception, they said, that though some ease might be brought to the spirits suffering in the Land of Shadows from the service which had been performed, it would utterly fail in the most important particular of all, namely, their deliverance from Hades, and their rebirth into the land of the living.

That this was also a matter which had given the Goddess of Mercy a vast amount of concern was soon made evident to the Emperor, for in the midst of this conversation there suddenly sounded, throughout the great hall in which the vast congregation still lingered, a voice saying, "Send Sam-Chaong to the Western Heaven to obtain the ritual which shall there be given him and which shall be worthy of being chanted by a nation."

This command from the invisible Goddess produced such an impression upon the Emperor that he made immediate preparations for the departure of Sam-Chaong on his momentous journey, and in a few days, supplied with everything necessary for so toilsome an undertaking, the famous priest started on what seemed a wild and visionary enterprise in pursuit of an object which anyone with less faith than himself would have deemed beyond the power of any human being to accomplish.

In order to afford him protection by the way and to act as his body-servants, the Emperor appointed two men to accompany Sam-Chaong on the long journey which he had undertaken at the command of the Goddess of Mercy. His Majesty would indeed have given him a whole regiment of soldiers, if he had been willing to accept them, but he absolutely refused to take more than just two men. He relied chiefly on the fairy robe which he had received, for that secured him from all danger from any foes whom he might meet on the road. Moreover, his mission, as he assured the Emperor, was one of peace and good-will, and it would not harmonize either with his own wishes or with those of the Goddess for him to be in a position to avenge his wrongs by the destruction of human life.

Before many days had elapsed Sam-Chaong began to realize the perilous nature of the service he had been called upon to perform. One afternoon, the travellers were jogging leisurely along in a wild and unsettled district, when suddenly two fierce-looking hobgoblins swooped down upon them, and almost before a word could be said had swallowed up both his poor followers. They were proceeding to do the same with Sam-Chaong when a fairy appeared upon the scene, and sent them flying with screams of terror to the caverns in the neighbouring hills where their homes seemed to be.

For a moment or two, Sam-Chaong was in extreme distress. He had just escaped an imminent peril, he was absolutely alone in an apparently uninhabited region, and the shadows of night were already darkening everything around. He was wondering where he would spend the night, when a man appeared upon the scene and invited him to come home with him to a mountain village on the spur of the hills which rose abruptly some distance away in front of them.

Although an entire stranger, who had never even heard Sam-Chaong's name, this man treated his guest right royally and gave him the very best that his house contained. Deeply impressed with the generous treatment he had received, Sam-Chaong determined that he would repay his host's generosity by performing an act which would be highly gratifying both to him and to all the members of his household.

Arranging a temporary altar in front of the image of the household god, who happened to be the Goddess of Mercy, he chanted the service for the dead before it with such acceptance that the spirit of the father of his host, who had been confined in the Land of Shadows, was released from that sunless land and was allowed to be reborn and take his place amongst the living. Moreover, that very night, the father appeared before his son in a vision, and told him that in consequence of the intercession of Sam-Chaong, whose reputation for piety was widely known in the dominions of Yam-lo, he had been allowed to leave that dismal country and had just been born into a family in the province of Shensi.

The son was rejoiced beyond measure at this wonderful news, and in order to show his gratitude for this generous action, he volunteered to accompany Sam-Chaong right to the very frontiers of China and to share with him any dangers and hardships he might have to endure by the way.

After many weary days of travelling this part of the journey was eventually accomplished, and they were about to separate at the foot of a considerable hill which lay on the border line between China and the country of the barbarians beyond, when a loud and striking voice was heard exclaiming, "The priest has come! The priest has come!"

Sam-Chaong asked his companion the meaning of these words and to what priest they referred.

"There is a tradition in this region," replied the man, "that five hundred years ago, a certain fairy, inflamed with pride, dared to raise himself in rebellion against the Goddess of Mercy in the Western Heaven. To punish him she turned him into a monkey, and confined him in a cave near the top of this hill. There she condemned him to remain until Sam-Chaong should pass this way, when he could earn forgiveness by leading the priest into the presence of the Goddess who had commanded him to appear before her."

Ascending the hill in the direction of the spot from where the cry "The priest has come!" kept ringing through the air, they came upon a natural cavern, the mouth of which was covered by a huge boulder, nicely poised in such a position that all exit from it was rendered an impossibility. Peering through the crevices at the side, they could distinctly see the figure of a monkey raising its face with an eager look of expectation in the direction of Sam-Chaong and his companion.

"Let me out," it cried, "and I will faithfully lead you to the Western Heaven, and never leave you until you find yourself standing in the presence of the Goddess of Mercy."

"But how am I to get you out?" asked Sam-Chaong. "The boulder that shuts you in is too large for human hands to move, and so, though I pity you in your misfortune and greatly desire your help to guide me along the unknown paths that lie before me, I fear that the task of setting you free must fall to other hands than mine."

"Deliverance is easier than you imagine," replied the monkey. "Cast your eye along the edge of this vast rock, which the Goddess with but a simple touch of one of her fingers moved into its place five hundred years ago, as though it had been the airiest down that ever floated in a summer's breeze, and you will see something yellow standing out in marked contrast to the black lichen-covered stone. That is the sign-manual of the Goddess. She printed it on the rock when she condemned me centuries ago to be enclosed within this narrow cell until you should come and release me. Your hand alone can remove that mystic symbol and save me from the penalty of a living death."

Following the directions of the monkey, Sam-Chaong carefully scraped away the yellow-coloured tracings which he tried in vain to decipher, and when the last faint scrap had been finally removed, the huge, gigantic boulder silently moved aside with a gentle, easy motion and tilted itself to one side until the prisoner had emerged, when once more it slid gracefully back into its old position.

Under the guidance of the monkey, who had assumed the appearance of a strong and vigorous young athlete, Sam-Chaong proceeded on his journey, over mountains so high that they seemed to touch the very heavens, and through valleys which lay at their foot in perpetual shadow, except only at noon-tide when the sun stood directly overhead. Then again they travelled across deserts whose restless, storm-tossed, sandy billows left no traces of human footsteps, and where death seemed, like some cunning foe, to be lying in wait to destroy their lives.

It was here that Sam-Chaong realized the protecting care of the Goddess in providing such a valuable companion as the monkey proved himself to be. He might have been born in these sandy wastes, so familiar was he with their moods. There was something in the air, and in the colours of the sky at dawn and at sunset, that told him what was going to happen, and he could say almost to a certainty whether any storm was coming to turn these silent deserts into storm-tossed oceans of sand, which more ruthless even than the sea, would engulf all living things within their pitiless depths. He knew, moreover, where the hidden springs of water lay concealed beneath the glare and glitter that pained the eyes simply to look upon them, and without a solitary landmark in the boundless expanse, by unerring instinct, he would travel straight to the very spot where the spring bubbled up from the great fountains below.

Having crossed these howling wildernesses, where Sam-Chaong must have perished had he travelled alone, they came to a region inhabited by a pastoral people, but abounding in bands of robbers. Monkey was a daring fellow and was never afraid to meet any foe in fair fight, yet for the sake of Sam-Chaong, whose loving disposition had been insensibly taming his wild and fiery nature, he tried as far as possible to avoid a collision with any evil characters, whether men or spirits, who might be inclined to have a passage of arms with them.

One day they had passed over a great plain, where herds of sheep could be seen in all directions browsing under the watchful care of their shepherds, and they had come to the base of the foot-hills leading to a mountainous country beyond, when the profound meditation in which Sam-Chaong was usually absorbed was suddenly interrupted by a startled cry from Monkey.

Drawing close up to him, he said in a low voice, "Do you see those six men who are descending the hill and coming in our direction? They look like simple-minded farmers, and yet they are all devils who have put on the guise of men in order to be able to take us unawares. Their real object is to kill you, and thus frustrate the gracious purpose of the Goddess, who wishes to deliver the souls in the Land of Shadows from the torments they are enduring there.

"I know them well," he went on, "they are fierce and malignant spirits and very bold, for rarely have they ever been put to flight in any conflict in which they have been engaged. They little dream, however, who it is you have by your side. If they did they would come on more warily, for though I am single-handed they would be chary of coming to issues with me.

"But I am glad," he continued, "that they have not yet discovered who I am, for my soul has long desired just such a day as this, when in a battle that shall be worthy of the gods, my fame shall spread throughout the Western Heaven and even into the wide domains of the Land of Shadows."

With a cry of gladness, as though some wondrous good-fortune had befallen him, he bounded along the road to meet the coming foe, and in contemptuous tones challenged them to mortal combat.

No sooner did they discover who it was that dared to champion Sam-Chaong with such bold and haughty front, than with hideous yells and screams they rushed tumultuously upon him, hoping by a combined attack to confuse him and to make him fly in terror before them.

In this however they had reckoned without their host. With a daring quite as great as theirs, but with a skill far superior to that of the six infuriated demons, Monkey seized a javelin which came gleaming through the air just at the precise moment that he needed it, and hurled it at one of his opponents with such fatal effect that he lay sprawling on the ground, and with a cry that might have come from a lost spirit breathed his last.

And now the battle became a mighty one indeed. Arrows shot from invisible bows flew quicker than flashes of light against this single mighty fighter, but they glanced off a magic shield which fairy arts had interposed in front of him. Weapons such as mortal hands had never wielded in any of the great battles of the world were now brought into play, but never for a moment did

Monkey lose his head. With marvellous intrepidity he warded them off, and striking back with one tremendous lunge, he laid another of the demons dead at his feet.

Dismay began to raise the coward in the minds of those who were left, and losing heart they turned to those subtle and cunning devices that had never before failed in their attacks on mankind. Their great endeavour now was to inveigle Monkey into a position where certain destruction would be sure to follow. Three-pronged spears were hurled against him with deadly precision, and had he not at that precise moment leaped high into the air no power on earth could have saved him.

It was at this tremendous crisis in the fight that Monkey won his greatest success. Leaping lightly to the ground whilst the backs of his foes were still turned towards him, he was able with the double-edged sword which he held in each of his hands to despatch three more of his enemies. The last remaining foe was so utterly cowed when he beheld his comrades lying dead upon the road that he took to flight, and soon all that was to be seen of him was a black speck slowly vanishing on the distant horizon.

Thus ended the great battle in which Monkey secured such a signal victory over the wild demons of the frozen North, and Sam-Chaong drew near to gaze upon the mangled bodies of the fierce spirits who but a moment ago were fighting so desperately for their very lives.

Now, Sam-Chaong was a man who naturally had the tenderest heart for every living thing, and so, as he looked, a cloud of sadness spread over his countenance and he sighed as he thought of the destruction of life which he had just witnessed. It was true that the demons had come with the one settled purpose of killing him, and there was no reason therefore why he should regret their death. But life to him was always precious, no matter in what form it might be enshrined. Life was the special gift of Heaven, and could not be wilfully destroyed without committing a crime against the gods.

So absorbed did Sam-Chaong become in this thought, and so sombre were the feelings filling his heart, that he entirely forgot to thank the hero by his side who had risked his life for him, and but for whose prowess he would have fallen a victim to the deadly hatred of these enemies of mankind. Feelings of resentment began to spring up in the mind of Monkey as he saw that Sam-Chaong seemed to feel more pity for the dead demons than gratitude for the heroic efforts which had saved him from a cruel death.

"Are you dissatisfied with the services I have rendered to you today?" he asked him abruptly.

"My heart is deeply moved by what you have done for me," replied Sam-Chaong. "My only regret is that you could not have delivered me without causing the death of these poor wretched demons, and thus depriving them of the gift of life, a thing as dear to them as it is to you or me."

Now Monkey, who was of a fierce and hasty temper, could not brook such meagre praise as this, and so in passionate and indignant language he declared that no longer would he be content to serve so craven a master, who, though beloved of the Goddess, was not a man for whom he would care to risk his life again.

With these words he vaulted into the air, and soared away into the distance, on and on through countless leagues of never-ending sky, until he came to the verge of a wide-spreading ocean. Plunging into this as though it had been the home in which he had always lived, he made his way by paths with which he seemed familiar, until he reached the palace of the Dragon Prince of the Sea, who received him with the utmost cordiality and gave him an invitation to remain with him as his guest as long as he pleased.

For some time he entertained himself with the many marvellous sights which are hidden away beneath the waters of the great ocean and which have a life and imagery of their own, stranger and more mysterious perhaps than those on which men are accustomed to look. But in time he became restless and dissatisfied with himself. The unpleasant thought crept slowly into his heart that in a moment of passion he had basely deserted Sam-Chaong and had left him helpless in a strange and unknown region, and worse still that he had been unfaithful to the trust which the Goddess had committed to him.

He became uncomfortably conscious, too, that though he had fled to the depths of the ocean he could never get beyond the reach of her power, and that whenever she wished to imprison him in the mountain cavern where he had eaten out his heart for five hundred years, she could do so with one imperious word of command.

In this mood of repentance for his past errors, he happened to cast his eye upon a scroll which hung in one of the rooms of the palace. As he read the story on it his heart smote him, and from that moment he determined to hasten back to the post from which he had fled.

The words on the scroll were written in letters of gold and told how on a certain occasion in the history of the past the fairies determined to assist the fortunes of a young man named Chang-lung, who had gained their admiration because of the nobility of character which he had exhibited in his ordinary conduct in life. He belonged to an extremely poor family, and so without some such aid as they could give him, he could never attain that eminence in the State which would enable him to be of service to his country. But he must first be tested to see whether he had the force of character necessary to bear the strain which greatness would put upon him. Accordingly one of the most experienced amongst their number was despatched to make the trial.

Assuming the guise of an old countryman in poor and worn-out clothing, the fairy sat down on a bridge over a stream close to the village where the favourite of the gods lived. By-and-by Chang-lung came walking briskly along. Just as he came up to the disguised fairy, the latter let one of his shoes drop into the water below. With an air of apparent distress, he begged the young man to wade into the stream and pick it up for him.

Cheerfully smiling, Chang-lung at once jumped into the water. In a moment he had returned with the shoe and was handing it to the old man, when the latter requested him to put it on his foot for him. This was asking him to do a most menial act, which most men would have scornfully resented, but Chang-lung, pitying the decrepit-looking old stranger, immediately knelt on the ground and carefully fastened the dripping shoe on to his foot.

Whilst he was in the act of doing this, the fairy, as if by accident, skilfully managed to let the other shoe slip from his foot over the edge of the bridge into the running stream. Apologizing for his stupidity, and excusing himself on the ground that he was an old man and that his fingers were not as nimble as they used to be, he begged Chang-lung to repeat his kindness and do him the favour of picking up the second shoe and restoring it to him.

With the same cheery manner, as though he were not being asked to perform a servile task, Chang-lung once more stepped into the shallow brook and bringing back the shoe, proceeded without any hesitation to repeat the process of putting it on the old man's foot.

The fairy was now perfectly satisfied. Thanking Chang-lung for his kindness, he presented him with a book, which he took out of one of the sleeves of his jacket, and urging him to study it with all diligence, vanished out of his sight. The meeting that day on the country bridge had an important influence on the destiny of Chang-lung, who in time rose to great eminence and finally became Prime Minister of China.

As Monkey studied the golden words before him, he contrasted his own conduct with that of Chang-lung, and, pricked to the heart by a consciousness of his wrong, he started at once, without even bidding farewell to the Dragon Prince of the Sea, to return to the service of Sam-Chaong.

He was just emerging from the ocean, when who should be standing waiting for him on the yellow sands of the shore but the Goddess of Mercy herself, who had come all the way from her distant home to warn him of the consequences that would happen to him were he ever again to fail in the duty she had assigned him of leading Sam-Chaong to the Western Heaven.

Terrified beyond measure at the awful doom which threatened him, and at the same time truly repentant for the wrong he had committed, Monkey bounded up far above the highest mountains which rear their peaks to the sky, and fled with incredible speed until he stood once more by the side of Sam-Chaong.

No reproof fell from the latter's lips as the truant returned to his post. A tender gracious smile was the only sign of displeasure that he evinced.

"I am truly glad to have you come back to me," he said, "for I was lost without your guidance in this unknown world in which I am travelling. I may tell you, however, that since you left me the Goddess appeared to me and comforted me with the assurance that you would before long resume your duties and be my friend, as you have so nobly been in the past. She was very distressed at my forlorn condition and was so determined that nothing of the kind should happen again in the future, that she graciously presented me with a mystic cap wrought and embroidered by the fairy hands of the maidens in her own palace.

"'Guard this well,' she said, 'and treasure it as your very life, for it will secure you the services of one who for five hundred years was kept in confinement in order that he might be ready to escort you on the way to the Western Heaven. He is the one man who has the daring and the courage to meet the foes who will endeavour to destroy you on your journey, but he is as full of passion as the storm when it is blowing in its fury. Should he ever desert you again, you have but to place this cap on your head, and he will be wrung with such awful and intolerable agonies that though he were a thousand miles away he would hurry back with all the speed he could command to have you take it off again, so that he might be relieved from the fearful pains racking his body.'"

After numerous adventures too long to relate, Sam-Chaong reached the borders of an immense lake, many miles in extent, spanned by a bridge of only a single foot in width. With fear and trembling, as men tremble on the brink of eternity, and often with terror in his eyes and a quivering in his heart as he looked at the narrow foothold on which he was treading, he finally crossed in safety, when he found to his astonishment that the pulsations of a new life had already begun to beat strongly within him. Beyond a narrow strip of land, which bounded the great expanse of water over which he had just passed, was a wide flowing river, and on its bank was a boat with a ferryman in it ready to row him over.

When they had reached the middle of the stream, Sam-Chaong saw a man struggling in the water as if for dear life. Moved with pity he urged upon the boatman to go to his rescue and deliver him from drowning. He was sternly told, however, to keep silence.

"The figure you see there," said the boatman, "is yourself, or rather, it is but the shell of your old self, in which you worked out your redemption in the world beyond, and which you could never use in the new life upon which you have entered."

On the opposite bank of the river stood the Goddess of Mercy, who with smiling face welcomed him into the ranks of the fairies.

Since then, it is believed by those whose vision reaches further than the grey and common scenes of earthly life, Sam-Chaong has frequently appeared on earth, in various disguises, when in some great emergency more than human power was required to deliver men from destruction. There is one thing certain at least, these gifted people declare, and that is that in the guise of a priest Sam-Chaong did once more revisit this world and delivered to the Buddhist faith the new ritual which the Goddess of Mercy had prepared for it, and which is used today in its services throughout the East.

Tales Of The Gùshì Yuán

The Spirits Of The Yellow River

This story has been adapted from Dr. Richard Wilhelm's version that originally appeared in The Chinese Fairy Book, published in 1921 by Frederick A. Stokes Company, New York. Wilhelm's translations aimed to capture the essence of the original Chinese texts while making them accessible to English-speaking audiences. His deep understanding of Chinese language and culture shone through in his translations, allowing readers to appreciate the beauty and depth of these timeless tales.

The spirits of the Yellow River are called Dai Wang, or 'Great King'. For many hundreds of years the river inspectors reported that all sorts of monsters showed themselves in the waves of the stream, at times in the shape of dragons, at others in that of cattle and horses, and whenever such a creature made an appearance a great flood followed. That is why temples were built along the riverbanks. The higher spirits of the river were honoured as kings, the lower ones as captains, and hardly a day went by without their being honoured with sacrifices or theatrical performances. Whenever, after a dam had been broken, and the leak was closed again, then the emperor sent officials with sacrifices and ten great bars of Tibetan incense. This incense was burned in a great sacrificial censer in the temple court, and the river inspectors and their subordinates all went to the temple to thank the gods for their aid. These river gods, it is said, were good and faithful servants of former rulers, who died in consequence of their toil in keeping the dams unbroken. After they died their spirits became river-kings, in their physical bodies, however, they appear as lizards, snakes and frogs. The following is a contemporary nineteenth century account of the river-kings and captains.

◆

The mightiest of all the river-kings is the Golden Dragon-King. He frequently appears in the shape of a small golden snake with a square head, low forehead and four red dots over his eyes. He can make himself large or small at will, and cause the waters to rise and fall. He appears and vanishes unexpectedly, and lives in the mouths of the Yellow River and the Imperial Canal. But in addition to the Golden Dragon-King there are dozens of river-kings and captains, each of whom has his own place. The sailors of the Yellow River all have exact lists in which the lives and deeds of the river-spirits are described in detail.

The river-spirits love to see theatrical performances. Opposite every temple is a stage. In the hall stands the little spirit-tablet of the river-king, and on the altar in front of it a small bowl of golden lacquer filled with clean sand. When a little snake appears in it, the river-king has arrived. Then the priests strike the gong and beat the drum and read from the holy books. The official is at once informed and he sends for a company of actors. Before they begin to perform the actors go up to the temple, kneel, and beg the king to let them know which play they are to give. And the river-god picks one out and points to it with his head, or else he writes signs in the sand with his tail. The actors then at once begin to perform the desired play.

The river-god cares naught for the fortunes or misfortunes of human beings. He appears suddenly and disappears in the same way, as best suits him.

Between the outer and the inner dam of the Yellow River are a number of settlements. Now it often happens that the yellow water moves to the very edge of the inner walls. Rising perpendicularly, like a wall, it gradually advances. When people see it coming they hastily burn incense, bow in prayer before the waters, and promise the river-god a theatrical performance. Then the water retires and the word goes round, "The river-god has asked for a play again!"

In a village in that section there once dwelt a wealthy man. He built a stone wall, twenty feet high, around the village, to keep away the water. He did not believe in the spirits of the river, but trusted in his strong wall and was quite unconcerned.

One evening the yellow water suddenly rose and towered in a straight line before the village. The rich man had them shoot cannon at it. Then the water grew stormy, and surrounded the wall to such a height that it reached the openings in the battlements. The water foamed and hissed, and seemed about to pour over the wall. Then everyone in the village was very much frightened. They dragged up the rich man and he had to kneel and beg for pardon. They promised the river-god a theatrical performance, but in vain, but when they promised to build him a temple in the middle of the village and give regular performances, the water sank more and more and gradually returned to its bed. And the village fields suffered no damage, for the earth, fertilized by the yellow slime, yielded a double crop.

Once a scholar was crossing the fields with a friend in order to visit a relative. On their way they passed a temple of the river-god where a new play was just being performed. The friend asked the scholar to go in with him and look on. When they entered the temple court they saw two great snakes upon the front pillars, who had wound themselves about the columns, and were thrusting out their heads as though watching the performance. In the hall of the temple stood the altar with the bowl of sand. In it lay a small snake with a golden body, a green head and red dots above his eyes. His neck was thrust up and his glittering little eyes never left the stage. The friend bowed and the scholar followed his example.

Softly he said to his friend, "What are the three river-gods called?"

"The one in the temple," was the reply, "is the Golden Dragon-King. The two on the columns are two captains. They do not dare to sit in the temple together with the king."

This surprised the scholar, and in his heart he thought, "Such a tiny snake! How can it possess a god's power? It would have to show me its might before I would worship it."

He had not yet expressed these secret thoughts before the little snake suddenly stretched forth his head from the bowl, above the altar. Before the altar burned two enormous candles. They weighed more than ten pounds and were as thick as small trees. Their flame burned like the flare of a torch. The snake now thrust his head into the middle of the candle-flame. The flame must have been at least an inch broad, and was burning red. Suddenly its radiance turned blue, and was split into two tongues. The candle was so enormous and its fire so hot that even copper and iron would have melted in it, but it did not harm the snake.

Then the snake crawled into the censer. The censer was made of iron, and was so large one could not clasp it with both arms. Its cover showed a dragon design in open-work. The snake crawled in and out of the holes in this cover, and wound his way through all of them, so that he looked like an embroidery in threads of gold. Finally all the openings of the cover, large and small, were filled by the snake. In order to do so, he must have made himself several dozen feet long. Then he stretched out his head at the top of the censer and once more watched the play.

Thereupon the scholar was frightened, he bowed twice, and prayed, "Great King, you have taken this trouble on my account! I honour you from my heart!"

No sooner had he spoken these words than, in a moment, the little snake was back in his bowl, and just as small as he had been before.

In Dsiningdschou they were celebrating the river god's birthday in his temple. They were giving him a theatrical performance for a birthday present. The spectators crowded around as thick as a wall, when who should pass but a simple peasant from the country, who said in a loud voice, "Why, that is nothing but a tiny worm! It is a great piece of folly to honour it like a king!"

Before ever he had finished speaking the snake flew out of the temple. He grew and grew, and wound himself three times around the stage. He became as thick around as a small pail, and his head seemed like that of a dragon. His eyes sparkled like golden lamps, and he spat out red flame with his tongue. When he coiled and uncoiled the whole stage trembled and it seemed as though it would break down. The actors stopped their music and fell down on the stage in prayer. The whole multitude was seized with terror and bowed to the ground. Then some of the old men came along, cast the peasant on the ground, and gave him a good thrashing. So he had to cast himself on his knees before the snake and worship him. Then all heard a noise as though a great many firecrackers were being shot off. This lasted for some time, and then the snake disappeared.

East of Shantung lies the city of Dongschou. There rises an observation-tower with a great temple. At its feet lies the water-city, with a sea-gate at the North, through which the flood-tide rises up to the city. A camp of the boundary guard is established at this gate.

Once upon a time there was an officer who had been transferred to this camp as captain. He had formerly belonged to the land forces, and had not yet been long at his new post. He gave some friends a banquet, and before the pavilion in which they feasted lay a great stone shaped somewhat like a table. Suddenly a little snake was seen crawling on this stone. It was spotted with green, and had red dots on its square head. The soldiers were about to kill the little creature when the captain went out to look into the matter.

When he had looked he laughed and said, "You must not harm him! He is the river-king of Dsiningdschou. When I was stationed in Dsiningdschou he sometimes visited me, and then I always gave sacrifices and performances in his honour. Now he has come here expressly in order to wish his old friend luck, and to see him once more."

There was a band in camp, the bandsmen could dance and play like a real theatrical troupe. The captain quickly had them begin a performance, had another banquet with wine and delicate foods prepared, and invited the river-god to sit down to the table.

Tales Of The Gùshì Yuán

Gradually evening came and yet the river-god made no move to go.

So the captain stepped up to him with a bow and said, "Here we are far removed from the Yellow River, and these people have never yet heard your name spoken. Your visit has been a great honour for me. But the women and fools who have crowded together chattering outside, are afraid of hearing about you. Now you have visited your old friend, and I am sure you wish to get back home again."

With these words he had a litter brought up, cymbals were beaten and fireworks set off, and finally a salute of nine guns was fired to escort him on his way. Then the little snake crawled into the litter, and the captain followed after. In this order they reached the port, and just when it was about time to say farewell, the snake was already swimming in the water. He had grown much larger, nodded to the captain with his head, and disappeared.

Then there were doubts and questionings, "But the river-god lives a thousand miles away from here, how does he get to this place?"

Said the captain, "He is so powerful that he can get to any place, and besides, from where he dwells a waterway leads to the sea. To come down that way and swim to sea is something he can do in a moment's time!"

Note, These spirits are thought to have placed many hindrances in the way of the erection of the railroad bridge across the Yellow River. Images of the gods were first introduced in China by the Buddhists. The old custom, which Confucianism and ancestor-worship still follow, holds that the seat of the gods is a small wooden tablet on which the name of the god to be honoured is written. Theatrical performances as religious services were as general in China as they were in ancient Greece. Dsiningdschou was a district capital on the Imperial Canal, near the Yellow River.

Tales Of The Gùshì Yuán

The Proud Fox and the Crab

This story has been adapted from a tale originally told by Kate Douglas Wiggin and Nora Archibald Smith in The Talking Beasts, published in 1911 by Houghton Mifflin Company. The fables in The Talking Beasts are engaging and entertaining, with whimsical characters and imaginative settings. Through these tales, Wiggin and Smith aimed to stimulate the imagination of children while also instilling important values that promote character development and moral growth.

One day a Fox said to a Crab, "Crawling thing, did you ever run in all your life?"

"Yes," said the Crab, "I run very often from the mud to the grass and back to the river."

"Oh, shame!" said the Fox, "That is no distance to run. How many feet and legs do you have? I have only four. Why, if I had as many feet as you have, I would run at least six times as fast as you do. Did you know that you are really a very slow, stupid creature? Though I have only four feet I run ten times as far as you do. I never heard of anyone with so many feet as you have, running so slowly."

The Crab said, "Would you like to run a race with a stupid creature like me? I will try to run as fast as you. I know I am small, so suppose we go to the scales and see how much heavier you are. As you are ten times larger than I, of course you will have to run ten times faster.

"Another reason why you can run so fast is because you have such a fine tail and hold it so high. If you would allow me to put it down, I do not think you would run any faster than I."

"Oh, very well," said the Fox, contemptuously, "do as you like, and still the race will be so easy for me that I will not even need to try. Your many legs and your stupid head do not go very well together. Now, if I had my sense and all of your legs, no creature in the forest could outrun me. As it is, there are none that can outwit me. I am known as the sharp-witted. Even man says, 'Qui-kwat-wui-lai' (sly as a fox). So do what you will, stupid one."

"If you will let me tie your beautiful tail down so it will stay," said the Crab, "I am sure I can win the race."

"Oh, no, you cannot," said the Fox. "But I will prove to even your stupid, slow brain that it will make no difference. Now, how do you wish that I should hold my tail?"

Said the Crab, "If you will allow me to hang something on your tail to hold it down, I am sure you cannot run faster than I."

"Do as you like," said the Fox.

"Allow me to come nearer," said the Crab, "and when I have it fastened to your tail, I will say 'Ready!' Then you are to start."

So the Crab crawled behind and caught the Fox's tail with his pincers and said, "Ready!" The Fox ran and ran until he was tired. And when he stopped, there was the Crab beside him.

"Where are you now?" said the Crab. "I thought you were to run ten times faster than I. You are not even ahead of me with all your boasting."

The Fox, panting for breath, hung his head in shame and went away where he might never see the crab again.

Tales Of The Gùshì Yuán

The Flower-Elves

This story has been adapted from Dr. Richard Wilhelm's version that originally appeared in The Chinese Fairy Book, published in 1921 by Frederick A. Stokes Company, New York. Wilhelm's translations aimed to capture the essence of the original Chinese texts while making them accessible to English-speaking audiences. His deep understanding of Chinese language and culture shone through in his translations, allowing readers to appreciate the beauty and depth of these timeless tales.

Once upon a time there was a scholar who lived retired from the world in order to gain hidden wisdom. He lived alone and in a secret place. And all about the little house in which he dwelt he had planted every kind of flower, and bamboos and other trees. There it lay, quite concealed in its thick grove of flowers. With him he had only a boy servant, who dwelt in a separate hut, and who carried out his orders. He was not allowed to appear before his master unless summoned. The scholar loved his flowers as he did himself. Never did he set his foot beyond the boundaries of his garden.

It chanced that once there came a lovely spring evening. Flowers and trees stood in full bloom, a fresh breeze was blowing, the moon shone clearly. And the scholar sat over his goblet and was grateful for the gift of life.

Suddenly he saw a maiden in dark garments come tripping up in the moonlight. She made a deep courtesy, greeted him and said, "I am your neighbour. We are a company of young maids who are on our way to visit the eighteen aunts. We should like to rest in this court for a while, and therefore ask your permission to do so."

The scholar saw that this was something quite out of the common, and gladly gave his consent. The maiden thanked him and went away.

In a short time she brought back a whole crowd of maids carrying flowers and willow branches. All greeted the scholar. They were charming, with delicate features, and slender, graceful figures. When they moved their sleeves, a delightful fragrance was exhaled. There is no fragrance known to the human world which could be compared with it.

The scholar invited them to sit down for a time in his room. Then he asked them, "Whom have I really the honour of entertaining? Have you come from the castle of the Lady in the Moon, or the Jade Spring of the Queen-Mother of the West?"

"How could we claim such high descent?" said a maiden in a green gown, with a smile. "My name is Salix." Then she presented another, clad in white, and said, "This is Mistress Prunophora", then one in rose, "and this is Persica", and finally one in a dark-red gown, "and this is Punica. We are all sisters and we want to visit the eighteen zephyr-aunts today. The moon shines so beautifully this evening and it is so charming here in the garden. We are most grateful to you for taking pity on us."

"Yes, yes," said the scholar.

Then the sober-clad servant suddenly announced, "The zephyr-aunts have already arrived!"

At once the girls rose and went to the door to meet them.

"We were just about to visit you, aunts," they said, smiling. "This gentleman here had just invited us to sit for a moment. What a pleasant coincidence that you aunts have come here, too. This is such a lovely night that we must drink a goblet of nectar in honour of you aunts!"

Thereon they ordered the servant to bring what was needed.

"May one sit down here?" asked the aunts.

"The master of the house is most kind," replied the maids, "and the spot is quiet and hidden."

And then they presented the aunts to the scholar. He spoke a few kindly words to the eighteen aunts. They had a somewhat irresponsible and airy manner. Their words fairly gushed out, and in their neighbourhood one felt a frosty chill.

Meanwhile the servant had already brought in table and chairs. The eighteen aunts sat at the upper end of the board, the maids followed, and the scholar sat down with them at the lowest place. Soon the entire table was covered with the most delicious foods and most magnificent fruits, and the goblets were filled with a fragrant nectar. They were delights such as the world of men does not know! The moon shone brightly and the flowers exhaled intoxicating odours. After they had partaken of food and drink the maids rose, danced and sung. Sweetly the sound of their singing echoed through the falling gloam, and their dance was like that of butterflies fluttering about the flowers. The scholar was so overpowered with delight that he no longer knew whether he were in heaven or on earth.

When the dance had ended, the girls sat down again at the table, and drank the health of the aunts in flowing nectar. The scholar, too, was remembered with a toast, to which he replied with well-turned phrases.

But the eighteen aunts were somewhat irresponsible in their ways. One of them, raising her goblet, by accident poured some nectar on Punica's dress. Punica, who was young and fiery, and very neat, stood up angrily when she saw the spot on her red dress.

"You are really very careless," she said, in her anger. "My other sisters may be afraid of you, but I am not!"

Then the aunts grew angry as well and said, "How dare this young chit insult us in such a manner!"

And with that they gathered up their garments and rose.

All the maids then crowded about them and said, "Punica is so young and inexperienced! You must not bear her any ill-will! Tomorrow she shall go to you switch in hand, and receive her punishment!"

But the eighteen aunts would not listen to them and went off. Thereupon the maids also said farewell, scattered among the flower-beds and disappeared. The scholar sat for a long time lost in dreamy yearning.

On the following evening the maids all came back again.

"We all live in your garden," they told him. "Every year we are tormented by naughty winds, and therefore we have always asked the eighteen aunts to protect us. But yesterday Punica insulted them, and now we fear they will help us no more. But we know that you have always been well disposed toward us, for which we are heartily grateful. And now we have a great favour to ask, that every New Year's day you make a small scarlet flag, paint the sun, moon and five planets on it, and set it up in the eastern part of the garden. Then we sisters will be left in peace and will be protected from all evil. But since New Year's day has passed for this year, we beg that you will set up the flag on the twenty-first of this month. For the East Wind is coming and the flag will protect us against him!"

The scholar readily promised to do as they wished, and the maids all said with a single voice, "We thank you for your great kindness and will repay it!" Then they departed and a sweet fragrance filled the entire garden.

The scholar, however, made a red flag as described, and when early in the morning of the day in question the East Wind really did begin to blow, he quickly set it up in the garden.

Suddenly a wild storm broke out, one that caused the forests to bend, and broke the trees. The flowers in the garden alone did not move.

Then the scholar noticed that Salix was the willow, Prunophora the plum, Persica the peach, and the saucy Punica the Pomegranate, whose powerful blossoms the wind cannot tear. The eighteen zephyr-aunts, however, were the spirits of the winds.

In the evening the flower-elves all came and brought the scholar radiant flowers as a gift of thanks.

"You have saved us," they said, "and we have nothing else we can give you. If you eat these flowers you will live long and avoid old age. And if you, in turn, will protect us every year, then we sisters, too, will live long."

The scholar did as they told him and ate the flowers. And his figure changed and he grew young again like a youth of twenty. And in the course of time he attained the hidden wisdom and was placed among the Immortals.

Note. Salix: the names of the "Flower Elves" are given in the Chinese as family names, whose sound suggests the flower-names without exactly using them. In the translation the play on words is indicated by the Latin names. "Zephyr-aunts": In Chinese the name given the aunt is "Fong," which in another stylization means "wind."

The Mad Goose And The Tiger Forest

This story has been adapted from Norman Hinsdale Pitman's version that originally appeared in A Chinese Wonder Book, published in 1919 by E. P. Dutton And Company, New York. A Chinese Wonder Book contains a selection of stories that capture the essence of traditional Chinese culture and storytelling. The book includes tales of magic, dragons, heroes, and supernatural creatures, all woven together with elements of Chinese mythology and folklore.

Hu-lin was a little slave girl. She had been sold by her father when she was scarcely more than a baby, and had lived for five years with a number of other children in a wretched houseboat. Her cruel master treated her very badly. He made her go out upon the street, with the other girls he had bought, to beg for a living. This kind of life was especially hard for Hu-lin. She longed to play in the fields, above which the huge kites were sailing in the air like giant birds. She liked to see the crows and magpies flying here and there. It was great fun to watch them build their stick nests in the tall poplars. But if her master ever caught her idling her time away in this manner he beat her most cruelly and gave her nothing to eat for a whole day. In fact he was so wicked and cruel that all the children called him Black Heart.

Early one morning when Hu-lin was feeling very sad about the way she was treated, she resolved to run away, but, she had not gone more than a hundred yards from the houseboat when she saw Black Heart following her. He caught her, scolded her most dreadfully, and gave her such a beating that she felt too faint to stir.

For several hours she lay on the ground without moving a muscle, moaning as if her heart would break. "Ah, if only someone would save me!" she thought, "How good I would be all the rest of my days!"

Now, not far from the river there lived an old man in a tumble-down shanty. The only companion he had was a goose that watched the gate for him at night and screamed out loudly if any stranger dared to prowl about the place. Hu-lin and this goose were close friends, and the slave girl often stopped to chat with the wise fowl as she was passing the old man's cottage. In this way she had learned that the bird's owner was a miser who kept a great deal of money hidden in his yard. Ch'ang, the goose, had an unusually long neck, and was thus able to pry into most of his master's affairs. As the fowl had no member of his own family to talk with, he told all he knew to Hu-lin.

On the very morning when Black Heart gave Hu-lin a beating for trying to run away, Ch'ang made a startling discovery. His lord and master was not really an old miser, but a young man in disguise. Ch'ang, feeling hungry, had slipped into the house at daybreak to see if any scraps had been left from the last evening's meal. The bedroom door had blown open in the night, and there lay a young man sound asleep, instead of the greybeard whom the gander called his master. Then, before his very eyes, the youth changed suddenly into his former shape and was an old man again.

In his excitement, forgetting all about his empty stomach, the terror-stricken goose rushed out into the yard to think over the mystery, but the longer he puzzled, the stranger it all seemed. Then he thought of Hu-lin, and wished that she would come by, that he might ask her opinion. He had a high regard for the slave girl's knowledge and believed that she would understand fully what had taken place.

Ch'ang went to the gate. As usual, it was locked, and there was nothing for him to do but wait for his master to rise. Two hours later the miser walked out into the yard. He seemed in good spirits, and he gave Ch'ang more to eat than usual. After taking his morning smoke on the street in front of the house, he strolled around it leaving the front gate ajar.

This was precisely what the gander had been expecting. Slipping quietly into the road, he turned towards the river where he could see the houseboats lined up at the wharf. On the sand nearby lay a well-known form.

"Hu-lin," he called as he drew near, "wake up, for I have something to tell you."

"I am not asleep," she answered, turning her tear-stained face towards her friend.

"Why, what's the matter? You've been crying again. Has old Black Heart been beating you?"

"Hush! He's taking a nap in the boat. Don't let him hear you."

"It's not likely he would understand goose-talk if he did," replied Ch'ang, smiling. "However, I suppose it's always best to be on the safe side, so I'll whisper what I have to say."

Putting his bill close to her ear, he told Hu-lin of his recent discovery, and ended by asking her to tell him what it all meant.

The child forgot her own misery at hearing his wonderful story. "Are you quite sure there was not some friend of the miser's spending the night with him?" she asked gravely.

"Yes, yes, perfectly sure, for he has no friends," replied the gander. "Besides, I was in the house just before he locked up for the night, and I saw neither hair nor hide of any other person."

"Then he must be a fairy in disguise!" announced Hu-lin wisely.

"A fairy! What's that?" questioned Ch'ang, more and more excited.

"Why, you old goose, don't you know what a fairy is?" And Hu-lin laughed outright. By this time she had forgotten her own troubles and was becoming more and more amused at what she had heard. "Listen!" she said in a low tone, and speaking very slowly, "A fairy is..." Here she lowered her voice to a whisper.

The gander nodded violently as she went on with her explanation, and when she had finished, was speechless with amazement, for a few moments. "Well," he said finally, "if my master is that kind of man, suppose you slip away quietly and come with me, for, if a fairy is what you say he is, he can save you from all your troubles and make me happy for the rest of my days."

"I wonder if I dare?" she answered, looking round fearfully towards the houseboat, from the open scuttle of which came the sound of deep snoring.

"Yes, yes, of course!" coaxed Ch'ang. "He gave you such a beating that he won't be afraid of your taking to your heels again very soon."

Hurriedly they went to the miser's compound. Hu-lin's heart was beating fast as she tried to decide what to say when she should actually stand before the fairy. The gate was still partly open and the two friends entered boldly.

"Come this way," said Ch'ang. "He must be in the back-yard digging in his garden."

But when they reached the vegetable patch there was no one to be seen.

"This is very strange," whispered the gander. "I don't understand it, for I have never known him to grow tired of work so early. Surely he cannot have gone to rest."

Led by her friend, Hu-lin entered the house on tiptoe. The door of the miser's bedroom stood wide open, and they saw that there was no one either in that room or any other room of the miserable cottage.

"Come, let's see what kind of bed he sleeps on," said Hu-lin, filled with curiosity. "I have never been in a fairy's room. It must be different from other people's rooms."

"No, no, just a plain brick bed, like all the rest," answered Ch'ang, as they crossed the threshold.

"Does he have a fire in cold weather?" asked Hu-lin, stooping to examine the small fire hole in the bricks.

"Oh, yes, a hot fire every night, and even in spring when other people have stopped having fires, the brick bed is hot every night."

"Well, that's rather strange for a miser, don't you think?" said the girl. "It costs more to keep a fire going than it does to feed a man."

"Yes, that's true," agreed Ch'ang, pruning his feathers. "I hadn't thought of that. It is very strange. Hu-lin, you're a wise child. Where did you learn so much?"

At that moment the gander turned pale at hearing the gate slam loudly and the bar thrown into place.

"Good gracious! What ever shall we do?" asked Hu-lin. "What will he say if he finds us here?"

"No telling," said the other, trembling, "but, my dear little friend, we are certainly caught, for we can't get away without his seeing us."

"Yes, and I've already had one beating today! And such a hard one that I don't believe I could live through another," sighed the child, as the tears began to flow.

"There, there, little girl, don't worry! Let's hide in this dark corner behind the baskets," suggested the gander, just as the master's step was heard at the front door.

Soon the frightened companions were crouching on the ground, trying to hide. Much to their relief, however, the miser did not go into his bedroom, and they soon heard him hard at work in the garden. All that day the two remained in their hiding place, afraid to show themselves outside the door.

"I can't imagine what he would say if he found out that his watch-goose had brought a stranger into the house," said Ch'ang.

"Perhaps he would think we were trying to steal some of the money he has hidden away," she answered, laughing, for as Hu-lin became used to her cramped quarters she grew less frightened. At any rate she was not nearly so much afraid of the miser as she had thought she was. "Besides," she reflected, "he can't be so bad as old Black Heart."

Thus the day wore on and darkness fell over the land. By this time girl and goose were fast asleep in one corner of the miser's room and knew nothing more of what was happening.

When the first light of a new day filtered through the paper-covered window above the miser's bed, Hu-lin awoke with a start, and at first she could not think where she was. Ch'ang was staring at her with wide-open frightened eyes that seemed to be asking, "What can it all mean? It is more than my goose brain can think out."

For on the bed, instead of the miser, there lay a young man whose hair was a black as a raven's wing. A faint smile lightened up his handsome face, as if he was enjoying some delightful dream. A cry of wonder escaped Hu-lin's lips before she could hold it back. The sleeper's eyes opened instantly and were fixed upon her. The girl was so frightened that she could not move, and the gander trembled violently as he saw the change that had come over his master.

The young man was even more surprised than his guests, and for two minutes he was speechless. "What does this mean?" he asked, finally, looking at Ch'ang. "What are you doing in my bedroom and who is this child who seems so frightened?"

"Forgive me, kind sir, but what have you done to my master?" asked the gander, giving question for question.

"Am I not your master, you mad creature?" said the man, laughing. "You are more stupid than ever this morning."

"My master was old and ugly, but you are still young and handsome," replied Ch'ang in a tone of flattery.

"What," shouted the other, "you say I am still young?"

"Why, yes. Ask Hu-lin, if you don't believe me."

The man turned towards the little girl.

"Yes, indeed you are, sir," she replied in answer to his look. "Never have I seen a man so beautiful."

"At last! At last!" he cried, laughing joyfully, "I am free, free, free from all my troubles, but how it has come about is more than I can say!"

For a few minutes he stood in a deep study, snapping his long fingers as if trying to solve some hard problem. eventually a smile lighted up his face. "Ch'ang," he asked, "what was it you called your guest when you spoke of her a minute ago?"

"I am Hu-lin," said the child simply, "Hu-lin, the slave girl."

He clapped his hands. "That's right! That's right!" he cried. "I see it all now, it is as plain as day." Then, noticing the look of wonder on her face, "It is to you that I owe my freedom from a wicked fairy, and if you like, I'll tell you the story of my misfortune."

"Please do, kind sir," she replied eagerly. "I told Ch'ang that you were a fairy, and I should like to know if I was right."

"Well, you see," he began, "my father is a rich man who lives in a distant county. When I was a boy he gave me everything I wished. I was so humoured and petted from earliest childhood that eventually I began to think there was nothing at all in the world I could not have for the asking, and nothing that I must not do if I wished to.

"My teacher often scolded me for having such notions. He told me there was a proverb: 'Men die for gain, birds perish to get food.' He thought such men were very foolish. He told me that money would go a long way towards making a man happy, but he always ended by saying that the gods were more powerful than men. He said I must always be careful not to make the evil spirits angry. Sometimes I laughed in his face, telling him that I was rich and could buy the favour of gods and fairies. The good man would shake his head, saying, 'Take care, my boy, or you will be sorry for these rash speeches.'"

"One day, after he had been giving me a long lecture of this sort, we were walking in the garden of my father's compound. I was even more daring than usual and told him that I cared nothing for the rules other people followed. 'You say,' said I, 'that this well here in my father's yard is ruled by a spirit, and that if I were to anger him by jumping over it, he would be vexed and give me trouble.' 'Yes,' he said, 'that is exactly what I said, and I repeat it. Beware, young man, beware of idle boasting and of breaking the law.' 'What do I care for a spirit that lives on my father's land?' I answered with a sneer. 'I don't believe there is a spirit in this well. If there is, it is only another of my father's slaves.'

"So saying, and before my tutor could stop me, I leaped across the mouth of the well. No sooner had I touched the ground than I felt a strange shrinking of my body. My strength left me in the twinkling of an eye, my bones shortened, my skin grew yellow and wrinkled. I looked at my pigtail and found that the hair had suddenly grown thin and white. In every way I had been changed completely into an old man.

"My teacher stared at me in amazement, and when I asked him what it all meant my voice was as shrill as that of early childhood. 'Alas, my dear pupil,' he replied, 'now you will believe what I told you. The spirit of the well is angry at your wicked conduct and has punished you. You have been told a hundred times that it is wrong to leap over a well, yet you did this very thing,' 'But is there nothing that can be done,' I cried, 'is there no way of restoring my lost youth?' He looked at me sadly and shook his head.

"When my father learned of my sad condition he was terribly upset. He did everything that could be done to find some way for me to regain my youth. He had incense burned at a dozen temples and he himself offered up prayers to various gods. I was his only son, and he could not be happy without me. Eventually, when everything else had been done, my worthy teacher thought of asking a fortune-teller who had become famous in the city. After inquiring about everything that had led up to my sad plight, the wise man said that the spirit of the well, as a punishment, had changed me into a miser. He said that only when I was sleeping would I be in my natural state, and even then if any one chanced to enter my room or catch a glimpse of my face, I would be at once changed back into a greybeard."

"I saw you yesterday morning," shouted the gander. "You were young and handsome, and then before my very eyes you were changed back into an old man!"

"To continue my story," said the young man, "the fortune-teller eventually announced that there was only one chance for my recovery and that a very small one. If at any time, while I was in my rightful shape, that is, as you see me now, a mad goose should come in, leading a tiger-forest out of slavery, the charm would be broken, and the evil spirit would no longer have control over me. When the fortune-teller's answer was brought to my father, he gave up hope, and so did I, for no one understood the meaning of such a senseless riddle.

"That night I left my native city, resolved not to disgrace my people any longer by living with them. I came to this place, bought this house with some money my father had given me, and at once began living the life of a miser. Nothing satisfied my greed for money. Everything must be turned into cash. For five years I have been storing away money, and, at the same time, starving myself, body and soul.

"Soon after my arrival here, remembering the fortune-teller's riddle, I decided that I would keep a goose to serve as night watch-man instead of a dog. In this way I made a start at working out the riddle."

"But I am not a mad goose," hissed the gander angrily. "If it had not been for me you would still be a wrinkled miser."

"Quite right, dear Ch'ang, quite right," said the young man soothingly, "you were not mad, so I gave you the name *Ch'ang*, which means mad, and thus made a mad goose of you."

"Oh, I see," said Hu-lin and Ch'ang together. "How clever!"

"So, you see, I had part of my cure here in my back-yard all the time, but though I thought as hard as I could, I could think of no way of securing that

Ch'ang should lead a tiger-forest into my room while I was sleeping. The thing seemed absurd, and I soon gave up trying to study it out. Today by accident it has really come to pass."

"So I am the tiger-forest, am I?" laughed Hu-lin.

"Yes, indeed, you are, my dear child, a pretty little tiger-forest, for *Hu* means *tiger*, and *lin* is surely good Chinese for a *grove of trees*. Then, too, you told me you were a slave girl. Hence, Ch'ang led you out of slavery."

"Oh, I am so glad!" said Hu-lin, forgetting her own poverty, "I'm so glad that you don't have to be a horrible old miser any longer."

Just at that moment there was a loud banging on the front gate.

"Who can be knocking in that fashion?" asked the young man in astonishment.

"Alas, it must be Black Heart, my master," said Hu-lin, beginning to cry.

"Don't be frightened," said the youth, soothingly stroking the child's head. "You have saved me, and I shall certainly do as much for you. If this Mr. Black Heart doesn't agree to a fair proposal he shall have a black eye to remember his visit by."

It did not take long for the grateful young man to buy Hu-lin's liberty, especially as he offered as much for her freedom as her master had expected to get when she was fourteen or fifteen years of age.

When Hu-lin was told of the bargain she was wild with delight. She bowed low before her new master and then, kneeling, touched her head nine times on the floor. Rising, she cried out, "Oh, how happy I am, for now I shall be yours for ever and ever and ever, and good old Ch'ang shall be my playmate."

"Yes, indeed," he assured her, "and when you are a little older I shall make you my wife. At present you will go with me to my father's house and become my little betrothed."

"And I shall never again have to beg for crusts on the street?" she asked him, her eyes full of wonder.

"No, never!" he answered, laughing, "And you need never fear another beating."

The Kingdom Of The Ogres

This story has been adapted from Dr. Richard Wilhelm's version that originally appeared in The Chinese Fairy Book, published in 1921 by Frederick A. Stokes Company, New York. Wilhelm's translations aimed to capture the essence of the original Chinese texts while making them accessible to English-speaking audiences. His deep understanding of Chinese language and culture shone through in his translations, allowing readers to appreciate the beauty and depth of these timeless tales.

In the land of Annam there once dwelt a man named Su, who sailed the seas as a merchant. Once his ship was suddenly driven on a distant shore by a great storm. It was a land of hills broken by ravines and green with luxuriant foliage, yet he could see something along the hills which looked like human dwellings. So he took some food with him and went ashore. No sooner had he entered the hills than he could see at either hand the entrances to caves, one close beside the other, like a row of beehives. So he stopped and looked into one of the openings. And in it sat two ogres, with teeth like spears and eyes like fiery lamps. They were just devouring a deer. The merchant was terrified by this sight and turned to flee, but the ogres had already noticed him and they caught him and dragged him into their cave. Then they talked to each other with animal sounds, and were about to tear his clothes from his body and devour him. But the merchant hurriedly took a bag of bread and dried meat out and offered it to them. They divided it, ate it up and it seemed to taste good to them. Then they once more went through the bag, but he gestured with his hand to show them that he had no more.

Then he said, "Let me go, for aboard my ship I have frying-pans and cooking-pots, vinegar and spices. With these I could prepare your food."

The ogres did not understand what he was saying, however, and were still ferocious. So he tried to make them understand in mime, and finally they seemed to get an idea of his meaning. So they went to the ship with him, and he brought his cooking gear to the cave, collected brush-wood, made a fire and cooked the remains of the deer. When it was done to a turn he gave them some of it to eat, and the two creatures devoured it with the greatest satisfaction. Then they left the cave and closed the opening with a great rock. In a short space of time they returned with another deer they had caught. The merchant skinned it, fetched fresh water, washed the meat and cooked several kettles full of it. Suddenly in came a whole herd of ogres, who devoured all he had cooked, and became quite animated over their eating. They all kept pointing to the kettle which seemed too small to them. When three or four days had passed, one of the ogres dragged in an enormous cooking-pot on his back, which was then used exclusively.

Now the ogres crowded about the merchant, bringing him wolves and deer and antelopes, which he had to cook for them, and when the meat was done they would call him to eat it with them.

Thus a few weeks passed and they gradually came to have such confidence in him that they let him run about freely. And the merchant listened to the sounds which they uttered, and learned to understand them. In fact, before very long he was able to speak the language of the ogres himself. This pleased the latter greatly, and they brought him a young ogre girl and made her his wife. She gave him valuables and fruit to win his confidence, and in course of time they grew much attached to each other.

One day the ogres all rose very early, and each one of them hung a string of radiant pearls about his neck. They ordered the merchant to be sure and cook a great quantity of meat. The merchant asked his wife what it all meant.

"This will be a day of high festival," she answered, "we have invited the great king to a banquet."

But to the other ogres she said, "The merchant has no string of pearls!"

Then each of the ogres gave him five pearls and his wife added ten, so that he had fifty pearls in all. These his wife threaded and hung the pearl necklace about his neck, and there was not one of the pearls which was not worth at least several hundred ounces of silver.

Then the merchant cooked the meat, and having done so left the cave with the whole herd in order to receive the great king. They came to a broad cave, in the middle of which stood a huge block of stone, as smooth and even as a table. Round it were stone seats. The place of honour was covered with a leopard-skin, and the rest of the seats with deerskins. Several dozen ogres were sitting around the cave in rank and file.

Suddenly a tremendous storm blew up, whirling around the dust in columns, and a monster appeared who had the figure of an ogre. The ogres all crowded out of the cave in a high state of excitement to receive him. The great king ran into the cave, sat down with his legs outstretched, and glanced about him with eyes as round as an eagle's. The whole herd followed him into the cave, and stood at either side of him, looking up to him and folding their arms across their breasts in the form of a cross in order to do him honour.

The great king nodded, looked around and asked, "Are all the folk of the Wo-Me hills present?"

The entire herd declared that they were.

Then he saw the merchant and asked, "Where does he hail from?"

His wife answered for him, and all spoke with praise of his art as a cook. A couple of ogres brought in the cooked meat and spread it out on the table. Then the great king ate till he could eat no more, praised it with his mouth full, and said that in the future they were always to furnish him with food of this kind.

Then he looked at the merchant and asked, "Why is your necklace so short?"

With these words he took ten pearls from his own necklace, pearls as large and round as the bullets of a blunderbuss. The merchant's wife quickly took them on his behalf and hung them around his neck, and the merchant crossed his arms like the ogres and spoke his thanks. Then the great king went off again, flying away like lightning on the storm.

In the course of time heaven sent the merchant children, two boys and a girl. They all had a human form and did not resemble their mother. Gradually the children learned to speak and their father taught them the language of men. They grew up, and were soon so strong that they could run across the hills as though on level ground.

One day the merchant's wife had gone out with one of the boys and the girl and had been absent for half-a-day. The north wind was blowing briskly, and in the merchant's heart there awoke a longing for his old home. He took his son by the hand and went down to the sea-shore. There his old ship was still lying, so he climbed into it with his boy, and in a day and a night was back in Annam again.

When he reached home he loosened two of his pearls from his chain, and sold them for a great quantity of gold, so that he could keep house in handsome style. He gave his son the name of Panther, and when the boy was fourteen years of age he could lift thirty hundred weight with ease. Yet he was rough by nature and fond of fighting. The general of Annam, astonished at his bravery, appointed him a colonel, and in putting down a revolt his services were so meritorious that he was already a general of the second rank when but eighteen.

At about this time another merchant was also driven ashore by a storm on the island of Wo-Me. When he reached land he saw a youth who asked him with astonishment, "Are you not from the Middle Kingdom?"

The merchant told him how he had come to be driven ashore on the island, and the youth led him to a little cave in a secret valley. Then he brought deer-flesh for him to eat, and talked with him. He told him that his father had also come from Annam, and it turned out that his father was an old acquaintance of the man to whom he was talking.

"We will have to wait until the wind blows from the North," said the youth, "then I will come and escort you. And I will give you a message of greeting to take to my father and brother."

"Why do you not go along yourself and hunt up your father?" asked the merchant.

"My mother does not come from the Middle Kingdom," replied the youth. "She is different in speech and appearance, so it cannot go well for her."

One day the wind blew strongly from the North, and the youth came and escorted the merchant to his ship, and ordered him, at parting, not to forget a single one of his words.

When the merchant returned to Annam, he went to the palace of Panther, the general, and told him all that had happened. When Panther listened to him telling about his brother, he sobbed with bitter grief. Then he secured leave of absence and sailed out to sea with two soldiers. Suddenly a typhoon arose, which lashed the waves until they spurted sky-high. The ship turned turtle, and Panther fell into the sea. He was seized by a creature and flung up on a strand where there seemed to be dwellings. The creature who had seized him looked like an ogre, so Panther addressed him in the ogre tongue. The ogre, surprised, asked him who he was, and Panther told him his whole story.

The ogre was pleased and said, "Wo-Me is my old home, but it lies about eight thousand miles away from here. This is the kingdom of the poison dragons."

Then the ogre fetched a ship and had Panther seat himself in it, while he himself pushed the ship before him through the water so that it clove the waves like an arrow. It took a whole night, but in the morning a shoreline appeared to the North, and there on the strand stood a youth on look-out. Panther recognized his brother. He stepped ashore and they clasped hands and wept. Then Panther turned around to thank the ogre, but the latter had already disappeared.

Panther now asked after his mother and sister and was told that both were well and happy, so he wanted to go to them with his brother. But the latter told him to wait, and went off alone. Not long after he came back with their mother and sister. And when they saw Panther, both wept with emotion. Panther now begged them to return with him to Annam.

But his mother replied, "I fear that if I went, people would mock me because of my figure."

"I am a high officer," replied Panther, "and people would not dare to insult you."

So they all went down to the ship together with him. A favourable wind filled their sails and they sped home as swiftly as an arrow flies. On the third day they reached land. But the people whom they encountered were all seized with terror and ran away. Then Panther took off his mantle and divided it among the three so that they could dress themselves.

When they reached home and the mother saw her husband again, she at once began to scold him violently because he had said not a word to her when he went away. The members of his family, who all came to greet the wife of the master of the house, did so with fear and trembling. But Panther advised his mother to learn the language of the Middle Kingdom, dress in silks, and accustom herself to human food. This she agreed to do, yet she and her daughter had men's clothing made for them. The brother and sister gradually grew fairer of complexion, and looked like the people of the Middle Kingdom. Panther's brother was named Leopard, and his sister Ogrechild. Both possessed great bodily strength.

But Panther was not pleased to think that his brother was so uneducated, so he had him study. Leopard was highly gifted, he understood a book at first reading, yet he felt no inclination to become a man of learning. To shoot and to ride was what he best loved to do. So he rose to high rank as a professional soldier, and finally married the daughter of a distinguished official.

It was long before Ogrechild found a husband because all suitors were afraid of their mother-in-law to be. But Ogrechild finally married one of her brother's subordinates. She could draw the strongest bow, and strike the tiniest bird at a distance of a hundred paces. Her arrow never fell to earth without having scored a hit. When her husband went out to battle she always accompanied him, and that he finally became a general was largely due to her. Leopard was already a field marshal at the age of thirty, and his mother accompanied him on his campaigns. When a dangerous enemy drew near, she buckled on armour, and took a knife in her hand to meet him in place of her son. And among the enemies who encountered her there was not a single one who did not flee from her in terror. Because of her courage the emperor bestowed upon her the title of "The Superwoman."

Tales Of The Gùshì Yuán

The Nodding Tiger

This story has been adapted from Norman Hinsdale Pitman's version that originally appeared in A Chinese Wonder Book, published in 1919 by E. P. Dutton And Company, New York. A Chinese Wonder Book contains a selection of stories that capture the essence of traditional Chinese culture and storytelling. The book includes tales of magic, dragons, heroes, and supernatural creatures, all woven together with elements of Chinese mythology and folklore.

Just outside the walls of a Chinese city there lived a young woodcutter named T'ang and his old mother, a woman of seventy. They were very poor and had a tiny one-room shanty, built of mud and grass, which they rented from a neighbour. Every day young T'ang rose bright and early and went up on the mountain near their house. There he spent the day cutting firewood to sell in the city nearby. In the evening he would return home, take the wood to market, sell it, and bring back food for his mother and himself. Now, though these two people were poor, they were very happy, for the young man loved his mother dearly, and the old woman thought there was no one like her son in all the world. Their friends, however, felt sorry for them and said, "What a pity we have no grasshoppers here, so that the T'angs could have some food from heaven!"

One day young T'ang got up before daylight and started for the hills, carrying his axe on his shoulder. He bade his mother good-bye, telling her that he would be back early with a heavier load of wood than usual, for the morrow would be a holiday and they must eat good food. All day long Widow T'ang waited patiently, saying to herself over and over as she went about her simple work, "The good boy, the good boy, how he loves his old mother!"

In the afternoon she began watching for his return, but in vain. The sun was sinking lower and lower in the west, but still he did not come. Eventually the old woman was frightened.

"My poor son!" she muttered. "Something has happened to him."

Straining her feeble eyes, she looked along the mountain path. Nothing was to be seen there but a flock of sheep following the shepherd.

"Woe is me!" moaned the woman. "My boy! my boy!"

She took her crutch from its corner and limped off to a neighbour's house to tell him of her trouble and beg him to go and look for the missing boy.

Now this neighbour was kind-hearted, and willing to help old Mother T'ang, for he felt very sorry for her. "There are many wild beasts in the mountains," he said, shaking his head as he walked away with her, thinking to prepare the frightened woman for the worst, "and I fear that your son has been carried off by one of them."

Widow T'ang gave a scream of horror and sank upon the ground. Her friend walked slowly up the mountain path, looking carefully for signs of a struggle. Eventually when he had gone halfway up the slope he came to a little pile of torn clothing spattered with blood. The woodman's axe was lying by the side of the path, also his carrying pole and some rope. There could be no mistake. After making a brave fight, the poor youth had been carried off by a tiger.

Gathering up the torn garments, the man went sadly down the hill. He dreaded seeing the poor mother and telling her that her only boy was indeed gone for ever. At the foot of the mountain he found her still lying on the ground. When she looked up and saw what he was carrying, with a cry of despair she fainted away. She did not need to be told what had happened.

Friends bore her into the little house and gave her food, but they could not comfort her. "Alas!" she cried, "What use is it to live? He was my only boy. Who will take care of me in my old age? Why have the gods treated me in this cruel way?"

She wept, tore her hair, and beat her chest, until people she said had gone mad. The longer she mourned, the more violent she became.

The next day, however, much to the surprise of her neighbours, she set out for the city, making her way along slowly by means of her crutch. It was a pitiful sight to see her, so old, so feeble, and so lonely. Everyone was sorry for her and pointed her out, saying, "See! the poor old soul has no one to help her!"

In the city she asked her way to the public hall. When she found the place she knelt at the front gate, calling out loudly and telling of her ill-fortune. Just at this moment the mandarin, or city judge, walked into the court room to try any cases which might be brought before him. He heard the old woman weeping and wailing outside, and bade one of the servants let her enter and tell him of her wrongs.

Now this was just what the Widow T'ang had come for. Calming herself, she hobbled into the great hall of trial.

"What is the matter, old woman? Why do you raise such an uproar in front of my yamen? Speak up quickly and tell me of your trouble."

"I am old and feeble," she began, "lame and almost blind. I have no money and no way of earning money. I have not one relative now in all the empire. I depended on my only son for a living. Every day he climbed the mountain, for he was a woodcutter, and every evening he came back home, bringing enough money for our food. But yesterday he went and did not return. A mountain tiger carried him off and ate him, and now, alas, there seems to be no help for it. I must die of hunger. My bleeding heart cries out for justice. I have come into this hall today, to beg your worship to see that the slayer of my son is punished. Surely the law says that none may shed blood without giving his own blood in payment."

"But, woman, are you mad?" cried the mandarin, laughing loudly. "Did you not say it was a tiger that killed your son? How can a tiger be brought to justice? Of a truth, you must have lost your senses."

The judge's questions were of no avail. The Widow T'ang kept up her clamour. She would not be turned away until she had gained her purpose. The hall echoed with the noise of her howling. The mandarin could stand it no longer. "Hold! woman," he cried, "stop your shrieking. I will do what you ask. Only go home and wait until I summon you to court. The slayer of your son shall be caught and punished."

The judge was, of course, only trying to get rid of the demented mother, thinking that if she were only once out of his sight, he could give orders not to let her into the hall again. The old woman, however, was too sharp for him. She saw through his plan and became more stubborn than ever.

"No, I cannot go," she answered, "until I have seen you sign the order for that tiger to be caught and brought into this judgment hall."

Now, as the judge was not really a bad man, he decided to humour the old woman in her strange plea. Turning to the assistants in the court room he asked which of them would be willing to go in search of the tiger. One of these men, named Li-neng, had been leaning against the wall, half asleep. He had been drinking heavily and so had not heard what had been going on in the room. One of his friends gave him a poke in the ribs just as the judge asked for volunteers.

Thinking the judge had called him by name, he stepped forward, knelt on the floor, saying, "I, Li-neng, can go and do the will of your worship."

"Very well, you will do," answered the judge. "Here is your order. Go forth and do your duty." So saying, he handed the warrant to Li-neng. "Now, old woman, are you satisfied?" he continued.

"Quite satisfied, your worship," she replied.

"Then go home and wait there until I send for you."

Mumbling a few words of thanks, the unhappy mother left the building.

When Li-neng went outside the court room, his friends crowded round him. "Drunken sot!" they laughed, "Do you know what you have done?"

Li-neng shook his head. "Just a little business for the mandarin, isn't it? Quite easy."

"Call it easy, if you like. What, man, arrest a tiger, a man-eating tiger and bring him to the city? Better go and say good-bye to your father and mother. They will never see you again."

Li-neng slept off his drunkenness, and then saw that his friends were right. He had been very foolish. But surely the judge had meant the whole thing only as a joke! No such order had ever been written before. It was plain that the judge had hit on this plan simply to get rid of the wailing old woman. Li-neng took the warrant back to the judgment hall and told the mandarin that the tiger could not be found.

But the judge was in no mood for joking. "Can't be found? And why not? You agreed to arrest this tiger. Why is it that today you try to get out of your promise? I can by no means permit this, for I have given my word to satisfy the old woman in her cry for justice."

Li-neng knelt and knocked his head on the floor. "I was drunk," he cried, "when I gave my promise. I knew not what you were asking. I can catch a man, but not a tiger. I know nothing of such matters. Still, if you wish it, I can go into the hills and hire hunters to help me."

"Very well, it makes no difference how you catch him, as long as you bring him into court. If you fail in your duty, there is nothing left but to beat you until you succeed. I give you five days."

During the next few days Li-neng left no stone unturned in trying to find the guilty tiger. The best hunters in the country were employed. Night and day they searched the hills, hiding in mountain caves, watching and waiting, but finding nothing. It was all very trying for Li-neng, since he now feared the heavy hands of the judge more than the claws of the tiger. On the fifth day he had to report his failure. He received a thorough beating, fifty blows on the back. But that was not the worst of it. During the next six weeks, try as he would, he could find no traces of the missing animal. At the end of each five days, he got another beating for his pains. The poor fellow was in despair. Another month of such treatment would lay him on his deathbed. This he knew very well, and yet he had little hope. His friends shook their heads when they saw him. "He is drawing near the wood," they said to each other, meaning that he would soon be in his coffin. "Why don't you flee the country?" they asked him. "Follow the tiger's example. You see he has escaped completely. The judge would make no effort to catch you if you should go across the border into the next province."

Li-neng shook his head on hearing this advice. He had no desire to leave his family for ever, and he felt sure of being caught and put to death if he should try to run away.

One day after all the hunters had given up the search in disgust and gone back to their homes in the valley, Li-neng entered a mountain temple to pray. The tears rained down his cheeks as he knelt before the great fierce-looking idol. "Alas, I am a dead man!" he moaned between his prayers, "A dead man, for now there is no hope. Would that I had never touched a drop of wine!"

Just then he heard a slight rustling nearby. Looking up, he saw a huge tiger standing at the temple gate. But Li-neng was no longer afraid of tigers. He knew there was only one way to save himself.

"Ah," he said, looking the great cat straight in the eye, "you have come to eat me, have you? Well, I fear you would find my flesh a trifle tough, since I have been beaten with four hundred blows during these six weeks. You are the same fellow that carried off the woodman last month, aren't you? This woodman was an only son, the sole support of an old mother. Now this poor woman has reported you to the mandarin, who, in turn, has had a warrant drawn up for your arrest. I have been sent out to find you and lead you to trial. For some reason or other you have acted the coward, and remained in hiding. This has been the cause of my beating. Now I don't want to suffer any longer as a result of your murder. You must come with me to the city and answer the charge of killing the woodman."

All the time Li-neng was speaking, the tiger listened closely. When the man was silent, the animal made no effort to escape, but, on the contrary, seemed willing and ready to be captured. He bent his head forward and let Li-neng slip a strong chain over it. Then he followed the man quietly down the mountain, through the crowded streets of the city, into the court room. All along the way there was great excitement. "The man-slaying tiger has been caught," shouted the people. "He is being led to trial."

The crowd followed Li-neng into the hall of justice. When the judge walked in, everyone became as quiet as the grave. All were filled with wonder at the strange sight of a tiger being called before a judge.

The great animal did not seem to be afraid of those who were watching so curiously. He sat down in front of the mandarin, for all the world like a huge cat. The judge rapped on the table as a signal that all was ready for the trial.

"Tiger," he said, turning toward the prisoner, "did you eat the woodman whom you are charged with killing?"

The tiger gravely nodded his head.

"Yes, he killed my boy!" screamed the aged mother. "Kill him! Give him the death that he deserves!"

"A life for a life is the law of the land," continued the judge, paying no attention to the forlorn mother, but looking the accused directly in the eye. "Did you not know it? You have robbed a helpless old woman of her only son. There are no relatives to support her. She is crying for vengeance. You must be punished for your crime. The law must be enforced. However, I am not a cruel judge. If you can promise to take the place of this widow's son and support the woman in her old age, I am quite willing to spare you from a disgraceful death. What do you say, will you accept my offer?"

The gaping people craned their necks to see what would happen, and once more they were surprised to see the savage beast nod his head in silent agreement.

"Very well, then, you are free to return to your mountain home, only, of course, you must remember your promise."

The chains were taken from the tiger's neck, and the great animal walked silently out of the yamen, down the street, and through the gate opening towards his beloved mountain cave.

Once more the old woman was very angry. As she hobbled from the room, she cast sour glances at the judge, muttering over and over again, "Who ever heard of a tiger taking the place of a son? A pretty game this is, to catch the brute, and then to set him free." There was nothing for her to do, however, but to return home, for the judge had given strict orders that on no account was she to appear before him again.

Almost broken-hearted she entered her desolate hovel at the foot of the mountain. Her neighbours shook their heads as they saw her. "She cannot live long," they said. "She has the look of death on her wrinkled face. Poor soul, she has nothing to live for, nothing to keep her from starving."

But they were mistaken. Next morning when the old woman went outside to get a breath of fresh air she found a newly killed deer in front of her door. Her tiger-son had begun to keep his promise, for she could see the marks of his claws on the dead animal's body. She took the carcass into the house and dressed it for the market. On the city streets next day she had no trouble in selling the flesh and skin for a handsome sum of money. All had heard of the tiger's first gift, and no one was anxious to drive a close bargain.

Laden with food, the happy woman went home rejoicing, with money enough to keep her for many a day. A week later the tiger came to her door with a roll of cloth and some money in his mouth. He dropped these new gifts at her feet and ran away without even waiting for her thank-you. The Widow T'ang now saw that the judge had acted wisely. She stopped grieving for her dead son and began to love in his stead the handsome animal that had come to take his place so willingly.

The tiger grew much attached to his foster-mother and often purred contentedly outside her door, waiting for her to come and stroke his soft fur.

He no longer had the old desire to kill. The sight of blood was not nearly so tempting as it had been in his younger days. Year after year he brought the weekly offerings to his mistress until she was as well provided for as any other widow in the country.

Eventually in the course of nature the good old soul died. Kind friends laid her away in her last resting place at the foot of the great mountain. There was money enough left out of what she had saved to put up a handsome tombstone, on which this story was written just as you have read it here. The faithful tiger mourned long for his dear mistress. He lay on her grave, wailing like a child that had lost its mother. Long he listened for the voice he had loved so well, long he searched the mountain-slopes, returning each night to the empty cottage, but all in vain. She whom he loved was gone for ever.

One night he vanished from the mountain, and from that day to this no one in that province has ever seen him. Some who know this story say that he died of grief in a secret cave which he had long used as a hiding-place. Others add, with a wise shrug of the shoulders, that, like Shanwang, he was taken to the Western Heaven, there to be rewarded for his deeds of virtue and to live as a fairy for ever afterwards.

Yang Gui Fe

This story has been adapted from Dr. Richard Wilhelm's version that originally appeared in The Chinese Fairy Book, published in 1921 by Frederick A. Stokes Company, New York. Wilhelm's translations aimed to capture the essence of the original Chinese texts while making them accessible to English-speaking audiences. His deep understanding of Chinese language and culture shone through in his translations, allowing readers to appreciate the beauty and depth of these timeless tales.

The favourite wife of the emperor Ming Huang of the Tang dynasty was the celebrated Yang Gui Fe. She so enchanted him by her beauty that he did whatever she wished him to do. But she brought her cousin to the court, a gambler and a drinker, and because of him the people began to murmur against the emperor. Finally a revolt broke out, and the emperor was obliged to flee. He fled with his entire court to the land of the four rivers.

But when they reached a certain pass his own soldiers mutinied. They shouted that Yang Gui Fe's cousin was to blame for all, and that he must die or they would go no further. The emperor did not know what to do. eventually the cousin was delivered up to the soldiers and was slain. But still they were not satisfied.

"As long as Yang Gui Fe is alive she will do all in her power to punish us for the death of her cousin, so she must die as well!"

Sobbing, she fled to the emperor. He wept bitterly and endeavoured to protect her, but the soldiers grew more and more violent. Finally she was hung from a pear-tree by a eunuch.

The emperor longed so greatly for Yang Gui Fe that he ceased to eat, and could no longer sleep. Then one of his eunuchs told him of a man named Yang Shi Wu, who was able to call up the spirits of the departed. The emperor sent for him and Yang Shi Wu appeared.

That very evening he recited his magic incantations, and his soul left its body to go in search of Yang Gui Fe. First he went to the Nether World, where the shades of the departed dwell. Yet no matter how much he looked and asked he could find no trace of her. Then he ascended to the highest heaven, where sun, moon and stars make their rounds, and looked for her in empty space. Yet she was not to be found there, either. So he came back and told the emperor of his experience. The emperor was dissatisfied and said, "Yang Gui Fe's beauty was divine. How can it be possible that she had no soul!"

The magician answered, "Between hill and valley and amid the silent ravines dwell the blessed. I will go back once more and search for her there."

So he wandered about on the five holy hills, by the four great rivers and through the islands of the sea. He went everywhere, and finally came to fairyland.

The fairy said, "Yang Gui Fe has become a blessed spirit and dwells in the great south palace!"

So the magician went there and knocked on the door. A maiden came out and asked what he wanted, and he told her that the emperor had sent him to look for her mistress. She let him in. The way led through broad gardens filled with flowers of jade and trees of coral, giving forth the sweetest of odours. Finally they reached a high tower, and the maiden raised the curtain hanging before a door. The magician kneeled and looked up. And there he saw Yang Gui Fe sitting on a throne, adorned with an emerald headdress and furs of yellow swans' down. Her face glowed with rosy colour, yet her forehead was wrinkled with care.

Tales Of The Gùshì Yuán

She said, "Well do I know the emperor longs for me! But for me there is no path leading back to the world of men! Before my birth I was a blessed sky-fairy, and the emperor was a blessed spirit as well. Even then we loved each other dearly. Then, when the emperor was sent down to earth by the Lord of the Heavens, I, too, descended to earth and found him there among men. In twelve years' time we will meet again.

Once, on the evening of the seventh day, when we stood looking up at the Weaving Maiden and the Herd Boy, we swore eternal love. The emperor had a ring, which he broke in two. One half he gave to me, the other he kept himself. Take this half of mine, bring it to the emperor, and tell him not to forget the words we said to each other in secret that evening. And tell him not to grieve too greatly because of me!"

With that she gave him the ring, with difficulty suppressing her sobs. The magician brought back the ring with him. At sight of it the emperor's grief broke out anew.

He said, "What we said to each other that evening no one else has ever learned! And now you bring me back her ring! By that sign I know that your words are true and that my beloved has really become a blessed spirit."

Then he kept the ring and rewarded the magician lavishly.

Note: The emperor Ming Huang of the Tang dynasty ruled from 713 to 756 A.D. The introduction to the tale is historical. The "land of the four rivers" is Szechuan.

The God Of The City – Part 1

This story has been adapted from Rev. John MacGowan's version that originally appeared in Chinese Folk-Lore Tales, published in 1910 by MacMillan and Company, London. Chinese Folk-Lore Tales features a variety of stories that cover a wide range of themes, including mythology, morality, adventure, and romance. These tales often incorporate elements of Chinese folklore, legends, and superstitions, providing readers with a glimpse into the beliefs and values of traditional Chinese society.

One evening in the distant past a fisherman anchored his boat near the bank of a stream which flowed close by a great city, whose walls could be seen rising grey and rugged in the near distance. The sound of life fell upon his ear and kept him from feeling lonely. Coolies, with bamboo carrying-poles on their shoulders, tired out with the heavy work of the day, hurried by afraid in case the darkness should overtake them before they reached their homes. The bearers of sedan-chairs, which they had carried for many a weary mile, strode by with quickened step and with an imperious shout at the foot passengers to get out of their way and not block up the narrow road by which they would gain the city walls before the great gates were closed for the night.

By the time that the afterglow had died out of the sky and the distant hills were blotted out of the horizon, the fisherman had finished the cooking of his evening meal. The rice sent a fragrant odour from the wide-mouthed pan in which it lay white and appetizing. A few of the very small fish he had caught in the river had been fried to a brown and savoury-looking colour, and he was just about to sit down and enjoy his supper when, happening to look round, he saw a stranger sitting in the after part of the boat.

He was greatly amazed and was about to express his surprise, when something about the appearance of this unexpected visitor kept him spellbound. For the stranger had a fine scholarly look about him, and the air of a man belonging to a good family. He had, moreover, a benevolent, kindly face, which could not fail to win the confidence of anyone who gazed upon it.

Whilst the fisherman was wondering who his visitor was and how he had managed to come so mysteriously into the boat, the stranger said, "Allow me to explain who I am and to apologise for intruding on you without first having got your permission to do so. I am the spirit of a man who two years ago was drowned not very far from where your boat is now anchored. Many attempts have I made to inveigle others into the river, so that I might be free to leave the spot to which my miserable fate binds me until another unhappy wretch shall take my place."

The spirit of a drowned person is condemned to hover round the spot where his life was lost, until, either by accident or by the wiles of the sufferer, someone else perishes in the water and thus takes the place of the spirit, which then travels with lightning speed to the Land of Shadows.

"I was so dull this evening," continued the stranger, "that I felt impelled to come and have a chat with you for a short time. So I hope you will take my visit in good part, and allow me to sit in your boat until it is time for you to go to bed."

The fisherman, who was greatly taken with his courtly visitor, expressed his great pleasure in receiving him, and invited him to share his evening meal and to make himself quite at home for as long as he liked.

After this the solitary spirit of the river used frequently to come and spend an evening with the fisherman, until quite a friendship sprang up between them. One evening this ghostly visitor appeared with a face covered with smiles and with a glad note of joy in his voice. No sooner had he sat down than he said, "This is the last evening I shall be able to spend with you. The long weary time of waiting is now nearly at an end, and tomorrow another victim of the river will give me my release and you will see me no more."

Now, the fisherman was a deeply benevolent man, and he was most anxious to see what unhappy person was to be drowned on the morrow. About midday, as he was watching by the river-side, he saw a poor woman, weeping and sobbing, come rushing with hasty steps towards the water. Her hair was dishevelled, and her eyes red with tears, and frequent cries of sorrow burst from her lips. Straight as an arrow she made for the stream, and was just preparing to throw herself into it, when the fisherman in a loud and commanding voice told her to stop.

He then asked her what the matter was for her to sacrifice her life in the river.

"I am a most unhappy woman," she replied. "On my way home just now I was waylaid by a footpad, who robbed me of some money that I was taking back to my husband. This money was to pay a debt we owed to a man who threatens us with the severest penalties if we do not give it to him today. Far rather would I face death than see the sorrow which would overwhelm my husband if I told him my sorrowful story."

Having asked her how much money had been taken from her, the fisherman presented the woman with the exact amount, and soon she was proceeding with joyful footsteps in the direction of her home.

That same evening the fisherman was again visited by the spirit who had bidden him an eternal farewell the previous evening.

"What did you mean," asked the visitor, "by depriving me of the one chance I had of gaining my freedom?"

"I could not bear to see the sorrow of the poor woman," replied the fisherman, "nor to think of the tragedy to her home had she perished in the stream, and so I saved her." With eloquent lips he proceeded to describe the beauty of benevolence, and urged upon his guest the nobler course of trying to save life even at the expense of his own happiness. In the end the latter was so deeply moved that he promised never again to make any attempt to gain his liberty through another's death, even though this should mean that he would have to spend long ages of misery in the fatal stream.

Years went by, and yet for the imprisoned spirit there came no release. Cases of suicide or accidental drowning in the flowing stream ceased altogether. Many a life that would have perished was saved from destruction by mysterious warnings which came from the sullen water, and which terrified away the would-be suicides as they were about to hurl themselves into it.

At length Kwan-yin, the Goddess of Mercy, moved by the sight of such a generous sacrifice of self in order to save the souls of unfortunate people who had become weary of life, released this noble spirit from its watery prison. Moreover, as she felt convinced that such a man could safely be entrusted with the destinies of those who might appear before his tribunal, she made him a god and decreed that temples should be erected to him in every town and city of the Empire, so that all who were suffering wrong or injustice could have their causes righted at the shrine of one who had shown such profound devotion and sympathy for others in distress.

Such is the story of the God of the City.

The God Of The City – Part 2

This story continues the themes told by Rev. John MacGowan in the previous story.

Since The God Of The City is regarded as the representative of the dread ruler of the Land of Shadows, his temple has been erected very much in the same style as the courts of the Mandarins. Its main entrance is large and imposing, and the great gates suggest those of the yamen of some high official.

Within these is an immense courtyard, paved with slabs of granite, and on each side of this there are six life-size statues of the "runners," or policemen, of the god, who stand ready to carry out his decisions, and to pursue and capture by invisible and mysterious processes those whom he has condemned as guilty. The faces of these figures are distorted by passion, and their attitudes are such as men might be conceived to assume in apprehending some notorious criminal whom Yam-lo had ordered to be seized.

At the end of this spacious courtyard is the shrine of the god, but he is so hidden behind a yellow curtain that it is impossible to catch a glimpse of his image. In front of him are statues of his two secretaries, who, with huge pens in their hands, stand ready day and night to take down the petitions and indictments laid before the god by those who are in sorrow or who are suffering wrong.

One afternoon the peace of such a temple was suddenly disturbed by a noisy clamour outside, and the sound of hurried footsteps as of a crowd rushing through the main gates. Two men advanced with rapid, excited strides straight past the demon policeman at the door, who seemed to scowl with added ferocity as they gazed at the actors in a scene with which they would have much to do by-and-by.

The two men were quite young, a little over twenty, and behind them followed a string of idlers and loafers and street urchins, who seem to spring up like magic when anything unusual happens. One of the young men was slightly ahead of the crowd. His face was flushed and his black eyes sparkled with excitement, whilst in his left hand he carried a large white cock. He was the complainant, and his purpose in coming to the temple was to appeal to the god to vindicate his honour.

He took his stand in front of the idol, and the secretaries, with pens in their hands, seemed to put on a strained look of attention as the young fellow produced a roll of paper and began to read the statement he had drawn up. It was diffuse and wordy, as most of such documents are, but the main facts were quite plain.

The two young men were assistants in a shop in the city. Some little time before, the master of the shop, without telling either of them, concealed in a chosen place a sum of one hundred gold coins, which he wished to have in readiness in order to pay for certain goods he had purchased. The previous day, when he went to get the money on the presentation of the bill, he found to his horror that it had disappeared. He had told no one of this secret hoard, not even his wife, and therefore he felt convinced that in some way or other one of his two assistants had discovered his hiding-place. For some reason his suspicions became aroused against the man who was now detailing his grievances, and who was appealing to the god to set in motion all the tremendous forces at his command, not only to proclaim his innocence but also to bring condign punishment on the real culprit.

The scene was a weird and fascinating one, and became most exciting as the young man neared the end of his appeal. He called upon the god to hurl all the pains and penalties in his unseen armoury against the man who had really stolen the money.

"Let his life be one long torture," he cried with uplifted hands. "May every enterprise in which he engages end in disaster, may his father and mother die, and let him be left desolate, may a subtle and incurable disease lay its grip upon him, may misfortune pursue him in every shape and form, may he become a beggar with ulcered legs and sit on the roadside and beseech the passers-by, in sunshine and in storm, for a few coppers that will just help to keep him alive, may he never have a son to perpetuate his name or to make offerings to his spirit in the Land of Shadows, may madness seize upon him so that his reason shall fly and he shall be a source of terror to his fellow-men, and finally, may a tragic and horrible death bring his life to a sudden end, even as I bring to an end the life of this white cock that I have brought with me."

As he uttered these last words he grasped a chopper, and with one sharp and vicious blow cut off the head of the struggling animal, which wildly fluttered its wings in the agonies of death, whilst its life-blood poured out in a stream on the ground.

He then took his petition, and advancing close up to the secretaries, who seemed for the moment to gaze down upon him with a look of sympathy on their faces, he set fire to it and burned it to ashes. In this way it passed into the hands of the god, who would speedily set in motion unseen machinery to bring down upon the head of the guilty one the judgments which had just been invoked.

The sympathies of the crowd were with the man who had sworn a solemn oath that he was innocent of the theft. The other young fellow, who had said little or nothing during the proceedings, was believed to be the real culprit, but there was no evidence upon which he could be convicted. The god knew, however, and everyone was satisfied that in due time punishment would descend upon the transgressor.

In a few minutes the temple resumed its normal aspect, for with the disappearance of the two principal actors in the scene, the idlers from the street slowly dispersed, each one loudly expressing his opinion as to the merits of the question in dispute. With the dissolving of the crowd, it would have seemed to the casual observer that no further proceedings were to be taken in the matter. The god's face wore its usually placid look, unmoved by the shifting panorama of human life which ebbed and flowed in front of him from morning till night. The ghastly-looking policemen, with their grinning visages and ferocious scowls and contorted bodies, remained in the same unchanging postures by the main entrance.

When a week or two had gone by since the appeal had been made to the god, those who were following the case and were looking out for some grim evidence that the god was at work in bringing retribution on the man whom everyone suspected of being the thief, were startled by a heartrending catastrophe.

This man had a sister, just bursting into womanhood, who was the very light of her home. Her merry laugh could be heard throughout the day, so that sadness could not long abide in the same house. Her face, too, seemed to have been formed to match her sunny smiles, and was a constant inspiration that never failed to give those who looked upon it a brighter view of life.

One morning she went down to the river-bank with several of her neighbours to do the household washing. The stream was strong and rapid in the centre, but the place which these women had selected for their work had always been considered perfectly safe, for it was outside the current and no accident had ever happened there.

They had finished all that they had purposed to do, and were ascending the bank to return home, when they heard an agonized cry and turning swiftly round they perceived that this young girl had stumbled and fallen into the river. They were so horrified at the accident that they lost all presence of mind and allowed the fast-flowing stream to get a grip of her and drag her into the current. When help eventually came, her body could just be seen floating on the troubled waters, and before a boat could be launched it had disappeared in the waves of the sea which tumbled and roared about a quarter of a mile further down.

This terrible disaster, which brought unutterable gloom and sorrow upon the home, was unquestionably the work of the god. With bated breath people talked of the tragic end of this beautiful girl, who had won her way into the hearts of all who knew her, but they recognized that her death had been caused by no mere accident, but by the mysterious power of the invisible forces which are always at work to bring punishment upon those who have violated the Righteousness of Heaven.

About a month after this calamity, the monsoon rains began to fall. The clouds gathered in dense masses upon the neighbouring hills, and poured down such copious showers that the mountain streams were turned into roaring avalanches, tearing their way down to the sea with an impetuosity that nothing could resist.

One of these streams, which used to run by the side of the ancestral property of the family of the man who was believed to have stolen the hundred coins, overflowed its banks and rushing along with mad and headlong speed it swept away their fields, so that when the rains ceased not a trace of them was to be found, but only sand and gravel, from which no crop could ever be gathered in the future. The consequence was that the family was utterly ruined.

This second disaster falling on the homestead was a clear indication to everyone who knew the story of the stolen money that the god was still at work in bringing retribution on the sinner. The fact that other farms had come out of the flood undamaged was proof positive of this.

From this time, too, the young man who really was the culprit began to be troubled in his mind because of the calamities that had fallen on his family. The death of his sister by drowning, and the utter destruction of his home by the flood, which had injured no other farmer in the neighbourhood, were plain indications that the curses which his falsely accused fellow-assistant had prayed the god to bring down on the head of the guilty party were indeed coming fast and thick upon him.

A dread of coming evil took possession of him, and this so preyed upon his mind that he began to lose his reason. He would go about muttering to himself, and declaring that he saw devils. These fits grew upon him, until eventually he became raving mad, and had to be seized and bound with ropes to prevent him doing injury to himself or to others. At times he suffered from violent spasms of mania, while at others, again, though undoubtedly insane, he was quiet and subdued. He would then talk incessantly to himself, and bemoan the sad fact that the dread God of the City was sending evil spirits to torment him because he had purloined the money belonging to his master.

By-and-by these random confessions attracted the attention of his heart-broken father, who used to sit watching by his side, and they became so frequent and so circumstantial, describing even where the money had been hidden, that eventually he determined to examine the matter. Investigations were made, and the whole sum was found in the very place which the young man had mentioned in his delirium, and was at once returned to the shopkeeper.

As the money had been given back, and the father and mother were dependent upon their only son to provide for them in their old age, the man who had entered the accusation before the god was entreated again to appear before him in his temple and withdraw the charges that he had previously made against his fellow-assistant. Only in this formal and legal way could the god have official knowledge of the fact that reparation had been made for the offence which had been committed, and if this were not done he would still continue to send sorrow after sorrow until the whole family were involved in absolute ruin or death.

Out of pity for the old couple the other young man consented to take the necessary steps. He accordingly presented a petition to the god, stating that he wished to withdraw the accusation which he had made against a certain man who had been suspected of theft. The stolen money had been returned to its owner, and the god was now begged to stay all further proceedings and forgive the culprit for the wrong he had done.

It was evident that this petition was granted, for at once the young man began to recover, and soon all signs of madness left him. He had, however, learned a lesson which he never forgot, and as long as he lived he never committed another offence such as the theft which had brought such serious consequences upon himself and his family.

Tales Of The Gùshì Yuán

The Phantom Vessel

This story has been adapted from Norman Hinsdale Pitman's version that originally appeared in A Chinese Wonder Book, published in 1919 by E. P. Dutton And Company, New York. A Chinese Wonder Book contains a selection of stories that capture the essence of traditional Chinese culture and storytelling. The book includes tales of magic, dragons, heroes, and supernatural creatures, all woven together with elements of Chinese mythology and folklore.

Once a ship loaded with pleasure-seekers was sailing from North China to Shanghai. High winds and stormy weather had delayed her, and she was still one week from port when a great plague broke out on board. This plague was of the worst kind. It attacked passengers and sailors alike until there were so few left to sail the vessel that it seemed as if she would soon be left to the mercy of winds and waves.

On all sides lay the dead, and the groans of the dying were most terrible to hear. Of that great company of travellers only one, a little boy named Ying-lo, had escaped. Eventually the few sailors, who had been trying hard to save their ship, were obliged to lie down upon the deck, themselves prey to the dreadful sickness, and soon they too were dead.

Ying-lo now found himself alone on the sea. For some reason, he did not know why, the gods or the sea fairies had spared him, but as he looked about in terror at the friends and loved ones who had died, he almost wished that he might join them.

The sails flapped about like great broken wings, while the giant waves dashed higher above the deck, washing many of the bodies overboard and wetting the little boy to the skin. Shivering with cold, he gave himself up for lost and prayed to the gods, whom his mother had often told him about, to take him from this dreadful ship and let him escape the fatal illness.

As he lay there praying he heard a slight noise in the rigging just above his head. Looking up, he saw a ball of fire running along a yardarm near the top of the mast. The sight was so strange that he forgot his prayer and stared with open-mouthed wonder. To his astonishment, the ball grew brighter and brighter, and then suddenly began slipping down the mast, all the time increasing in size. The poor boy did not know what to do or to think. Were the gods, in answer to his prayer, sending fire to burn the vessel? If so, he would soon escape. Anything would be better than to be alone upon the sea.

Nearer and nearer came the fireball. Eventually, when it reached the deck, to Ying-lo's surprise, something very, very strange happened. Before he had time to feel alarmed, the light vanished, and a funny little man stood in front of him peering anxiously into the child's frightened face.

"Yes, you are the lad I'm looking for," he said eventually, speaking in a piping voice that almost made Ying-lo smile. "You are Ying-lo, and you are the only one left of this wretched company." This he said, pointing towards the bodies lying here and there about the deck.

Although he saw that the old man meant him no harm, the child could say nothing, but waited in silence, wondering what would happen next.

By this time the vessel was tossing and pitching so violently that it seemed every minute as if it would upset and go down beneath the foaming waves, never to rise again. Not many miles distant on the right, some jagged rocks stuck out of the water, lifting their cruel heads as if waiting for the helpless ship.

The newcomer walked slowly towards the mast and tapped on it three times with an iron staff he had been using as a cane. Immediately the sails spread, the vessel righted itself and began to glide over the sea so fast that the gulls were soon left far behind, while the threatening rocks upon which the ship had been so nearly dashed seemed like specks in the distance.

"Do you remember me?" said the stranger, suddenly turning and coming up to Ying-lo, but his voice was lost in the whistling of the wind, and the boy knew only by the moving of his lips that the old man was talking. The greybeard bent over until his mouth was at Ying-lo's ear, "Did you ever see me before?"

With a puzzled look, at first the child shook his head. Then as he gazed more closely there seemed to be something that he recognized about the wrinkled face. "Yes, I think so, but I don't know when."

With a tap of his staff the fairy stopped the blowing of the wind, and then spoke once more to his small companion, "One year ago I passed through your village. I was dressed in rags, and was begging my way along the street, trying to find someone who would feel sorry for me. Alas, no one answered my cry for mercy. Not a crust was thrown into my bowl. All the people were deaf, and fierce dogs drove me from door to door. Finally when I was almost dying of hunger, I began to feel that here was a village without one good person in it. Just then you saw my suffering, ran into the house, and brought me out food. Your heartless mother saw you doing this and beat you cruelly. Do you remember now, my child?"

"Yes, I remember," he answered sadly, "and that mother is now lying dead. Alas, all, all are dead, my father and my brothers also. Not one of my family is left."

"Little did you know, my boy, to whom you were giving food that day. You took me for a lowly beggar, but, behold, it was not a poor man that you fed, for I am Iron Staff. You must have heard of me when they were telling of the fairies in the Western Heaven, and of their adventures here on earth."

"Yes, yes," answered Ying-lo, trembling half with fear and half with joy, "indeed I have heard of you many, many times, and all the people love you for your kind deeds of mercy."

"Alas, they did not show their love, my little one. Surely you know that if anyone wishes to reward the fairies for their mercies, he must begin to do deeds of the same kind himself. No one but you in all your village had pity on me in my rags. If they had known that I was Iron Staff, everything would have been different, they would have given me a feast and begged for my protection."

Then the little man began to recite a poem:

"The only love that loves aright
Is that which loves in every plight.
The beggar in his sad array
Is moulded of the self-same clay.

"Who knows a man by what he wears,
By what he says or by his prayers?
Hidden beneath that wrinkled skin
A fairy may reside within.

"Then treat with kindness and with love
The lowly man, the god above;
A friendly nod, a welcome smile--
For love is ever worth the while."

Ying-lo listened in wonder to Iron Staff's little poem, and when he had finished, the boy's face was glowing with the love of which the fairy had spoken. "My poor, poor father and mother!" he cried, "they knew nothing of these beautiful things you are telling me. They were brought up in poverty. As they were knocked about in childhood by those around them, so they learned to beat others who begged them for help. Is it strange that they did not have hearts full of pity for you when you looked like a beggar?"

"But what about you, my boy? You were not deaf when I asked you. Have you not been whipped and punished all your life? How then did you learn to look with love at those in tears?"

The child could not answer these questions, but only looked sorrowfully at Iron Staff. "Oh, can you not, good fairy, will you not restore my parents and brothers, and give them another chance to be good and useful people?"

"Listen, Ying-lo, it is impossible, unless you do two things first," he answered, stroking his beard gravely and leaning heavily upon his staff.

"What are they? What must I do to save my family? Anything you ask of me will not be too much to pay for your kindness."

"First you must tell me of some good deed done by these people for whose lives you are asking. Name only one, for that will be enough, but it is against our rules to help those who have done nothing."

Ying-lo was silent, and for a moment his face was clouded. "Yes, I know," he said finally, brightening. "They burned incense once at the temple. That was certainly a deed of virtue."

"But when was it, little one, that they did this?"

"When my big brother was sick, and they were praying for him to get well. The doctors could not save him with boiled turnip juice or with any other of the medicines they used, so my parents begged the gods."

"Selfish, selfish!" muttered Iron Staff. "If their eldest son had not been dying they would have spent no money at the temple. They tried in this way to buy back his health, for they were expecting him to support them in their old age."

Ying-lo's face fell. "You are right," he answered.

"Can you think of nothing else?"

"Yes, oh, yes, last year when the foreigner rode through our village and fell sick in front of our house, they took him in and cared for him."

"How long?" asked the other sharply.

"Until he died the next week."

"And what did they do with the mule he was riding, his bed, and the money in his bag? Did they try to restore them to his people?"

"No, they kept them to pay for the trouble." Ying-lo's face turned scarlet.

"But try again, dear boy! Is there not one little deed of goodness that was not selfish? Think once more."

For a long time Ying-lo did not reply. At length he spoke in a low voice, "I think of one, but I fear it amounts to nothing."

"No good, my child, is too small to be counted when the gods are weighing a man's heart."

"Last spring the birds were eating in my father's garden. My mother wanted to buy poison from the shop to destroy them, but my father said no, that the little things must live, and he for one was not in favour of killing them."

"At last, Ying-lo, you have named a real deed of mercy, and as he spared the tiny birds from poison, so shall his life and the lives of your mother and brothers be restored from the deadly plague.

"But remember there is one other thing that depends on you."

Ying-lo's eyes glistened gratefully. "Then if it rests with me, and I can do it, you have my promise. No sacrifice should be too great for a son to make for his loved ones even though his life itself is asked in payment."

"Very well, Ying-lo. What I require is that you carry out to the letter my instructions. Now it is time for me to keep my promise to you."

So saying, Iron Staff called on Ying-lo to point out the members of his family, and, approaching them one by one, with the end of his iron stick he touched their foreheads. In an instant each, without a word, arose. Looking round and recognising Ying-lo, they stood back, frightened at seeing him with the fairy. When the last had risen to his feet, Iron Staff beckoned all of them to listen. This they did willingly, too much terrified to speak, for they saw on all sides signs of the plague that had swept over the vessel, and they remembered the frightful agony they had suffered in dying. Each knew that he had been lifted by some magic power from darkness into light.

"My friends," began the fairy, "little did you think when less than a year ago you drove me from your door that soon you yourselves would be in need of mercy. Today you have had a peep into the awful land of Yama. You have seen the horror of his tortures, have heard the screams of his slaves, and by another night you would have been carried before him to be judged. What power is it that has saved you from his clutches? As you look back through your wicked lives can you think of any reason why you deserved this rescue? No, there is no memory of goodness in your black hearts. Well, I shall tell you: it is this little boy, this Ying-lo, who many times has felt the weight of your wicked hands and has hidden in terror at your coming. To him alone you owe my help."

Father, mother, and brothers all gazed in turn, first at the fairy and then at the timid child whose eyes fell before their looks of gratitude.

"By reason of his goodness this child whom you have scorned is worthy of a place within the Western Heaven. In truth, I came this very day to lead him to that fairyland. For you, however, he wishes to make a sacrifice. With sorrow I am yielding to his wishes. His sacrifice will be that of giving up a place among the fairies and of continuing to live here on this earth with you. He will try to make a change within your household. If at any time you treat him badly and do not heed his wishes, and mark well my words, by the power of this magic staff which I shall place in his hands, he may enter at once into the land of the fairies, leaving you to die in your wickedness. This I command him to do, and he has promised to obey my slightest wish.

"This plague took you off suddenly and ended your wicked lives. Ying-lo has raised you from its grasp and his power can lift you from the bed of sin. No other hand than his can bear the rod which I am leaving. If one of you but touch it, instantly he will fall dead upon the ground.

"And now, my child, the time has come for me to leave you. First, however, I must show you what you are now able to do. Around you lie the corpses of sailors and passengers. Tap three times upon the mast and wish that they shall come to life," So saying he handed Ying-lo the iron staff.

Although the magic rod was heavy, the child lifted it as if it were a fairy's wand. Then, stepping forward to the mast, he rapped three times as he had been commanded. Immediately on all sides arose the bodies, once more full of life and strength.

"Now command the ship to take you back to your home port, for such sinful creatures as these are in no way fit to make a journey among strangers. They must first return and free their homes of sin."

Again rapping on the mast, the child willed the great vessel to take its homeward course. No sooner had he moved the staff than, like a bird wheeling in the heavens, the bark swung round and started on the return journey. Swifter than a flash of lightning flew the boat, for it was now a fairy vessel. Before the sailors and the travellers could recover from their surprise, land was sighted and they saw that they were indeed entering the harbour.

Just as the ship was darting toward the shore the fairy suddenly, with a parting word to Ying-lo, changed into a flaming ball of fire which rolled along the deck and ascended the spars. Then, as it reached the top of the rigging, it floated off into the blue sky, and all on board, speechless with surprise, watched it until it vanished.

With a cry of thanksgiving, Ying-lo flung his arms about his parents and descended with them to the shore.

Tales Of The Gùshì Yuán

Rose Of Evening

This story has been adapted from Dr. Richard Wilhelm's version that originally appeared in The Chinese Fairy Book, published in 1921 by Frederick A. Stokes Company, New York. Wilhelm's translations aimed to capture the essence of the original Chinese texts while making them accessible to English-speaking audiences. His deep understanding of Chinese language and culture shone through in his translations, allowing readers to appreciate the beauty and depth of these timeless tales.

On the fifth day of the fifth month the festival of the Dragon Junk is held along the Yangtze-kiang. A dragon is hollowed out of wood, painted with an armour of scales, and adorned with gold and bright colours. A carved red railing surrounds this ship, and its sails and flags are made of silks and brocade. The after part of the vessel is called the dragon's tail. It rises ten feet above the water, and a board which floats in the water is tied to it by means of a cloth. Upon this board sit boys who turn somersaults, stand on their heads, and perform all sorts of tricks. Yet, being so close to the water their danger is very great. It is the custom, therefore, when a boy is hired for this purpose, to give his parents money before he is trained. Then, if he falls into the water and is drowned, no one has him on their conscience. Farther South the custom differs in so much that instead of boys, beautiful girls are chosen for this purpose.

In Dschen-Giang there once lived a widow named Dsiang, who had a son called Aduan. When he was no more than seven years of age he was extraordinarily skilful, and no other boy could equal him. And his reputation increasing as he grew, he earned more and more money. So it happened that he was still called upon at the Dragon Junk Festival when he was already sixteen.

But one day he fell into the water below the Gold Island and was drowned. He was the only son of his mother, and she sorrowed over him, and that was the end of it.

Yet Aduan did not know that he had been drowned. He met two men who took him along with them, and he saw a new world in the midst of the waters of the Yellow River. When he looked around, the waves of the river towered steeply about him like walls, and a palace was visible, in which sat a man wearing armour and a helmet.

His two companions said to him, "That is the Prince of the Dragon's Cave!" and bade him kneel.

The Prince of the Dragon's Cave seemed to be of a mild and kindly disposition and said, "We can make use of such a skilful lad. He may take part in the dance of the willow branches!"

So he was brought to a spot surrounded by extensive buildings. He entered, and was greeted by a crowd of boys who were all about fourteen years of age.

An old woman came in and they all called out, "This is Mother Hia!" And she sat down and had Aduan show his tricks. Then she taught him the dance of the flying thunders of Tsian-Tang River, and the music that calms the winds on the sea of Dung-Ting. When the cymbals and kettledrums echoed through all the courts, they deafened the ear. Then, again, all the courts would fall silent. Mother Hia thought that Aduan would not be able to grasp everything the very first time, so she taught him with great patience. But Aduan had understood everything from the first, and that pleased old Mother Hia. "This boy," she said, "equals our own Rose of Evening!"

The following day the Prince of the Dragon's Cave held a review of his dancers. When all the dancers had assembled, the dance of the Ogres was danced first. Those who performed it all wore devil-masks and garments of scales. They beat upon enormous cymbals, and their kettledrums were so large that four men could just about span them. Their sound was like the sound of a mighty thunder, and the noise was so great that nothing else could be heard. When the dance began, tremendous waves spouted up to the very skies, and then fell down again like star-glimmer which scatters in the air.

The Prince of the Dragon Cave hastily bade the dance cease, and had the dancers of the nightingale round step forth. These were all lovely young girls of sixteen. They made a delicate music with flutes, so that the breeze blew and the roaring of the waves was stilled in a moment. The water gradually became as quiet as a crystal world, transparent to its lowest depths. When the nightingale dancers had finished, they withdrew and posted themselves in the western courtyard.

Then came the turn of the swallow dancers. These were all little girls. One among them, who was about fifteen years of age, danced the dance of the giving of flowers with flying sleeves and waving locks. And as their garments fluttered, many-colored flowers dropped from their folds, and were caught up by the wind and whirled about the whole courtyard. When the dance had ended, this dancer also went off with the rest of the girls to the western courtyard. Aduan looked at her from out the corner of his eye, and fell deeply in love with her. He asked his comrades who she might be and they told him she was named "Rose of Evening."

But the willow-spray dancers were now called out. The Prince of the Dragon Cave was especially desirous of testing Aduan. So Aduan danced alone, and he danced with joy or defiance according to the music. When he looked up and when he looked down his glances held the beat of the measure. The Dragon Prince, enchanted with his skill, presented him with a garment of five colours, and gave him a carbuncle set in golden threads of fish-beard for a hair-jewel. Aduan bowed his thanks for the gift, and then also hastened to the western courtyard. There all the dancers stood in rank and file. Aduan could only look at Rose of Evening from a distance, but still Rose of Evening returned his glances.

After a time Aduan gradually slipped to the end of his file and Rose of Evening also drew near to him, so that they stood only a few feet away from each other. But the strict rules allowed no confusion in the ranks, so they could only gaze and let their souls go out to each other.

Now the butterfly dance followed the others. This was danced by the boys and girls together, and the pairs were equal in size, age and the colour of their garments. When all the dances had ended, the dancers marched out with the goose-step. The willow-spray dancers followed the swallow dancers, and Aduan hastened in advance of his company, while Rose of Evening lingered along after hers. She turned her head, and when she spied Aduan she purposely let a coral pin fall from her hair. Aduan hastily hid it in his sleeve.

When he had returned, he was sick with longing, and could neither eat nor sleep. Mother Hia brought him all sorts of dainties, looked after him three or four times a day, and stroked his forehead with loving care. But his illness did not yield in the least. Mother Hia was unhappy, and yet helpless.

"The birthday of the King of the Wu River is at hand," she said. "What is to be done?"

In the twilight a boy came, who sat down on the edge of Aduan's bed and chatted with him. He belonged to the butterfly dancers, he said, and asked casually, "Are you sick because of Rose of Evening?" Aduan, frightened, asked him how he came to guess it. The other boy said, with a smile, "Well, because Rose of Evening is in the same case as yourself."

Disconcerted, Aduan sat up and begged the boy to advise him. "Are you able to walk?" asked the latter. "If I exert myself," said Aduan, "I think I could manage it."

So the boy led him to the South. There he opened a gate and they turned the corner, to the West. Once more the doors of the gate flew open, and now Aduan saw a lotus field about twenty acres in size. The lotus flowers were all growing on level earth, and their leaves were as large as mats and their flowers like umbrellas. The fallen blossoms covered the ground beneath the stalks to the depth of a foot or more. The boy led Aduan in and said, "Now first of all sit down for a little while!" Then he went away.

After a time a beautiful girl thrust aside the lotus flowers and came into the open. It was Rose of Evening. They looked at each other with happy timidity, and each told how each had longed for the other. And they also told each other of their former life. Then they weighted the lotus-leaves with stones so that they made a cozy retreat, in which they could be together, and promised to meet each other there every evening. And then they parted.

Aduan came back and his illness left him. From that time on he met Rose of Evening every day in the lotus field.

After a few days had passed they had to accompany the Prince of the Dragon Cave to the birthday festival of the King of the Wu River. The festival came to an end, and all the dancers returned home. Only, the King had kept back Rose of Evening and one of the nightingale dancers to teach the girls in his castle.

Months passed and no news came from Rose of Evening, so that Aduan went about full of longing and despair. Now Mother Hia went every day to the castle of the god of the Wu River. So Aduan told her that Rose of Evening was his cousin, and entreated her to take him along with her so that he could at least see her a single time. So she took him along, and let him stay at the lodge-house of the river-god for a few days. But the dwellers of the castle were so strictly watched that he could not see Rose of Evening even a single time. Sadly Aduan went back again.

Another month passed and Aduan, filled with gloomy thoughts, wished that death might be his portion.

One day Mother Hia came to him full of pity, and began to sympathize with him. "What a shame," she said, "that Rose of Evening has cast herself into the river!"

Aduan was extremely frightened, and his tears flowed resistlessly. He tore his beautiful garments, took his gold and his pearls, and went out with the sole idea of following his beloved in death. Yet the waters of the river stood up before him like walls, and no matter how often he ran against them, head down, they always flung him back.

He did not dare return, since he feared he might be questioned about his festival garments, and severely punished because he had ruined them. So he stood there and knew not what to do, while the perspiration ran down to his ankles. Suddenly, at the foot of the water-wall he saw a tall tree. Like a monkey he climbed up to its very top, and then, with all his might, he shot into the waves.

And then, without being wet, he found himself suddenly swimming on the surface of the river. Unexpectedly the world of men rose up once more before his dazzled eyes. He swam to the shore, and as he walked along the river-bank, his thoughts went back to his old mother. He took a ship and travelled home.

When he reached the village, it seemed to him as though all the houses in it belonged to another world. The following morning he entered his mother's house, and as he did so, heard a girl's voice beneath the window saying, "Your son has come back again!" The voice sounded like the voice of Rose of Evening, and when she came to greet him at his mother's side, sure enough, it was Rose of Evening herself.

And in that hour the joy of these two who were so fond of each other overcame all their sorrow. But in the mother's mind sorrow and doubt, terror and joy mingled in constant succession in a thousand different ways.

When Rose of Evening had been in the palace of the river-king, and had come to realize that she would never see Aduan again, she determined to die, and flung herself into the waters of the stream. But she was carried to the surface, and the waves carried and cradled her till a ship came by and took her aboard. They asked where she came from. Now Rose of Evening had originally been a celebrated singing girl of Wu, who had fallen into the river and whose body had never been found. So she thought to herself that, after all, she could not return to her old life again. So she answered, "Madame Dsiang, in Dschen-Giang is my mother-in-law."

Then the travellers took passage for her in a ship which brought her to the place she had mentioned. The widow Dsiang first she said must be mistaken, but the girl insisted that there was no mistake, and told Aduan's mother her whole story. Yet, though the latter was charmed by her surpassing loveliness, she feared that Rose of Evening was too young to live a widow's life. But the girl was respectful and industrious, and when she saw that poverty ruled in her new home, she took her pearls and sold them for a high price. Aduan's old mother was greatly pleased to see how seriously the girl took her duties.

Now that Aduan had returned again Rose of Evening could not control her joy. And even Aduan's old mother cherished the hope that, after all, perhaps her son had not died. She secretly dug up her son's grave, yet all his bones were still lying in it. So she questioned Aduan. And then, for the first time, the latter realized that he was a departed spirit. Then he feared that Rose of Evening might regard him with disgust because he was no longer a human being. So he ordered his mother on no account to speak of it, and this his mother promised. Then she spread the report in the village that the body which had been found in the river had not been that of her son at all. Yet she could not rid herself of the fear that, since Aduan was a departed spirit, heaven might refuse to send him a child.

In spite of her fear, however, she was able to hold a grandson in her arms in course of time. When she looked at him, he was no different from other children, and then her cup of joy was filled to overflowing.

Rose of Evening gradually became aware of the fact that Aduan was not really a human being. "Why did you not tell me at once?" she said. "Departed spirits who wear the garments of the dragon castle, surround themselves with a soul-casing so heavy in texture that they can no longer be distinguished from the living. And if one can obtain the lime made of dragon-horn which is in the castle, then the bones may be glued together in such wise that flesh and blood will grow over them again. What a pity that we could not obtain the lime while we were there!"

Aduan sold his pearl, for which a merchant from foreign parts gave him an enormous sum. Thus his family grew very wealthy. Once, on his mother's birthday, he danced with his wife and sang, in order to please her. The news reached the castle of the Dragon Prince and he thought to carry off Rose of Evening by force. But Aduan, alarmed, went to the Prince, and declared that both he and his wife were departed spirits. They examined him and since he cast no shadow, his word was taken, and he was not robbed of Rose of Evening.

Note, "Rose of Evening" is one of the most idyllic of Chinese art fairy-tales. The idea that the departed spirit throws no shadow has analogies in Norse and other European fairy-tales.

Tales Of The Gùshì Yuán

The Mule and the Lion

This story has been adapted from a tale originally told by Kate Douglas Wiggin and Nora Archibald Smith in The Talking Beasts, published in 1911 by Houghton Mifflin Company. The fables in The Talking Beasts are engaging and entertaining, with whimsical characters and imaginative settings. Through these tales, Wiggin and Smith aimed to stimulate the imagination of children while also instilling important values that promote character development and moral growth.

One night the Lion was very hungry, but as the creatures of the wilderness knew and feared him even from afar, he could not find food. So he went to visit the young Mule that lived near the farmer's house, and when he saw him he smiled blandly and asked, "What do you eat, fair Lii, to make you so sleek and fat? What makes your hair so smooth and beautiful? I think your master gives you tender fresh grass and fat young pig to eat."

The Mule answered, "No, I am fat because I am gentle. My hair is beautiful because I do not fight with other creatures. But why do you come here, Sii? Are you hungry? I believe you are looking for food."

The Lion said, "Oh, no, I am not hungry. I only walk around to get the cool, fresh air. And then the night is very beautiful. The moon hangs up in the clear sky with the stars and makes a soft light, and so I came to visit you. Would you not like to take a walk with me? I will take you to visit my friend, the Pig. I never go to his house alone, for I always take a friend with me."

The Mule asked, "Shall we go to any other place?"

"Yes," answered the Lion, "I think we will go to visit another friend of mine who lives not far away."

Then the Mule asked his mother, "Will you allow me to go with Sii to see his friend?"

"Who is his friend?" asked the mother.

"The farmer's Pig." said the Mule.

"I think it is no harm if you go only there," said the mother Mule. "But you must not go anywhere else with Sii. The hunter is looking for him, I hear, and you must be careful. Do not trust him fully, for I fear he will tempt you to go to some other place or into some wrong thing. If I allow you to go, you must come home before midnight. The moon will not be gone then and you can see to find your way."

So the Lion and the Mule went to visit the Pig, who lived in a house in the farmer's yard. But as soon as the Pig saw the Lion, he called out in a loud voice to his mother.

The Lion said, "He is afraid of me. I will hide and you may go in first."

When the Pig saw that the Mule was alone, he thought the Lion had gone. He opened his door wide and was very friendly to the Mule, saying, "Come in."

But the Lion jumped from his hiding place and caught the Pig as he came to the door. The Pig called to his mother in great fear, and the Mule begged the Lion, saying, "Let the poor little creature go free."

But the Lion said, "No, indeed, I have many Pigs at my house. It is better for him to go with me."

Then the Lion carried the Pig, while the Mule followed. Soon they came to where a fine looking dog lay on some hay behind a net. The Lion did not seem to see the net, for he dropped the Pig and tried to catch the Dog, who cried loudly for mercy.

But the Lion said to the foolish Mule, "See how rude the Dog is to us. We came to visit him and he makes a loud noise and tries to call the hunter so that he will drive us away. I have never been so insulted. Come here, Lii-Tsze, at once and help me!"

The Mule went to the Lion and the net fell and caught them both. At sunrise the Hunter came and found the Mule and the Lion in his net. The Mule begged earnestly and said, "Hunter, you know me and you know my mother. We are your friends and we do no wrong. Set me free, oh, hunter, set me free!"

The Hunter said, "No, I will not set you free. You may be good, but you are in bad company and must take what it brings. I will take you and the Lion both to the marketplace and sell you for silver. That is my right. I am a hunter. If you get in my net, that is your business. If I catch you, that is my business."

Tales Of The Gùshì Yuán

The Herd Boy And The Weaving Maiden

This story has been adapted from Dr. Richard Wilhelm's version that originally appeared in The Chinese Fairy Book, published in 1921 by Frederick A. Stokes Company, New York. Wilhelm's translations aimed to capture the essence of the original Chinese texts while making them accessible to English-speaking audiences. His deep understanding of Chinese language and culture shone through in his translations, allowing readers to appreciate the beauty and depth of these timeless tales.

The Herd Boy was the child of poor people. When he was twelve years old, he took service with a farmer to herd his cow. After a few years the cow had grown large and fat, and her hair shone like yellow gold. She must have been a cow of the gods.

One day while he had her out at pasture in the mountains, she suddenly began to speak to the Herd Boy in a human voice, as follows, "This is the Seventh Day. Now the White Jade Ruler has nine daughters, who bathe this day in the Sea of Heaven. The seventh daughter is beautiful and wise beyond all measure. She spins the cloud-silk for the King and Queen of Heaven, and presides over the weaving which maidens do on earth. It is for this reason she is called the Weaving Maiden. And if you go and take away her clothes while she bathes, you may become her husband and gain immortality."

"But she is up in Heaven," said the Herd Boy, "and how can I get there?"

"I will carry you there," answered the yellow cow.

So the Herd Boy climbed on the cow's back. In a moment clouds began to stream out of her hoofs, and she rose into the air. About his ears there was a whistling like the sound of the wind, and they flew along as swiftly as lightning. Suddenly the cow stopped.

"Now we are here," she said.

Then round about him the Herd Boy saw forests of chrysoprase and trees of jade. The grass was of jasper and the flowers of coral. In the midst of all this splendour lay a great, four-square sea, covering some five-hundred acres. Its green waves rose and fell, and fishes with golden scales were swimming about in it. In addition there were countless magic birds who winged above it and sang. Even in the distance the Herd Boy could see the nine maidens in the water. They had all laid down their clothes on the shore.

"Take the red clothes, quickly," said the cow, "and hide away with them in the forest, and though she ask you for them ever so sweetly do not give them back to her until she has promised to become your wife."

Then the Herd Boy hastily got down from the cow's back, seized the red clothes and ran away. At the same moment the nine maidens noticed him and were very frightened.

"O youth, where do you come from, that you dare to take our clothes?" they cried. "Put them down again quickly!"

But the Herd Boy did not let what they said trouble him, but crouched down behind one of the jade trees. Then eight of the maidens hastily came ashore and drew on their clothes.

"Our seventh sister," they said, "whom Heaven has destined to be yours, has come to you. We will leave her alone with you."

The Weaving Maiden was still crouching in the water. But the Herd Boy stood before her and laughed. "If you will promise to be my wife," he said, "then I will give you your clothes."

But this did not suit the Weaving Maiden. "I am a daughter of the Ruler of the Gods," she said, "and may not marry without his command. Give back my clothes to me quickly, or else my father will punish you!"

Then the yellow cow said, "You have been destined for each other by fate, and I will be glad to arrange your marriage, and your father, the Ruler of the Gods, will make no objection. Of that I am sure."

The Weaving Maiden replied, "You are an unreasoning animal! How could you arrange our marriage?"

The cow said, "Do you see that old willow-tree there on the shore? Just give it a trial and ask it. If the willow tree speaks, then Heaven wishes your union."

And the Weaving Maiden asked the willow, and the willow replied in a human voice:

"This is the Seventh day,

The Herd Boy his court to the Weaver does pay!"

The Weaving Maiden was satisfied with the verdict. The Herd Boy laid down her clothes, and went on ahead. The Weaving Maiden drew them on and followed him. And thus they became man and wife.

But after seven days she took leave of him. "The Ruler of Heaven has ordered me to look after my weaving," she said. "If I delay too long I fear that he will punish me. Yet, although we have to part now, we will meet again in spite of it."

When she had said these words she really went away. The Herd Boy ran after her. But when he was quite near she took one of the long needles from her hair and drew a line with it right across the sky, and this line turned into the Silver River. And thus they now stand, separated by the River, and watch for one another.

And since that time they meet once every year, on the eve of the Seventh Day. When that time comes, then all the crows in the world of men come flying and form a bridge over which the Weaving Maiden crosses the Silver River. And on that day you will not see a single crow in the trees, from morning to night. And besides, a fine rain often falls on the evening of the Seventh Day. Then the women and old grandmothers say to one another, "Those are the tears which the Herd Boy and the Weaving Maiden shed at parting!" And for this reason the Seventh Day is a rain festival.

To the west of the Silver River is the constellation of the Weaving Maiden, consisting of three stars. And directly in front of it are three other stars in the form of a triangle. It is said that once the Herd Boy was angry because the Weaving Maiden had not wished to cross the Silver River, and had thrown his yoke at her, which fell down just in front of her feet. East of the Silver River is the Herd Boy's constellation, consisting of six stars. To one side of it are countless little stars which form a constellation pointed at both ends and somewhat broader in the middle. It is said that the Weaving Maiden in turn threw her spindle at the Herd Boy, but that she did not hit him, the spindle falling down to one side of him.

Note, "The Herd Boy and the Weaving Maiden" is retold after an oral source. The Herd Boy is a constellation in Aquila, the Weaving Maiden one in Lyra. The Silver River which separates them is the Milky Way. The Seventh Day of the seventh month is the festival of their reunion.

The Ruler of the Heavens has nine daughters in all, who dwell in the nine heavens. The oldest married Li Dsing in the tale, Notscha, *the second is the mother of Yang Oerlang, the third is the mother of the planet Jupiter, and the fourth dwelt with a pious and industrious scholar, by name of Dung Yung, whom she aided to win riches and honour. The seventh is the Spinner, and the ninth had to dwell on earth as a slave because of some transgression of which she had been guilty. Of the fifth, the sixth and the eighth daughters nothing further is known.*

Tales Of The Gùshì Yuán

The Tragedy Of The Yin Family

This story has been adapted from Rev. John MacGowan's version that originally appeared in Chinese Folk-Lore Tales, published in 1910 by MacMillan and Company, London. Chinese Folk-Lore Tales features a variety of stories that cover a wide range of themes, including mythology, morality, adventure, and romance. These tales often incorporate elements of Chinese folklore, legends, and superstitions, providing readers with a glimpse into the beliefs and values of traditional Chinese society.

In a certain district in one of the central provinces of China, there lived a man by the name of Yin. He was possessed of considerable property, with a great ambition to become distinguished in life. The one desire of his heart, which seemed to master every other, was that his family should become an aristocratic one.

So far as he knew, none of his immediate predecessors had ever been a conspicuous scholar, or had gained any honour in the great triennial examinations. The result was that his family was a plebeian one, from which no mandarin had ever sprung. In what way, then, could he secure that the fame and dignities, which had come to some of the clans in the region in which he lived, should descend upon his home and upon his grandsons?

He was a rich man, it is true, but he was entirely illiterate, and all his money had been made in trade. As a lad his education had been neglected, for his early life had been spent in the mere struggle for existence. He had been more than successful, but the honours of the student never could be his, and never could he act as one of the officials of the Empire. It occurred to him, however, that though it was impossible that he himself should ever be classed amongst the great scholars of China, his sons and grandsons might be so honoured. In that case the glory of their success would be reflected upon him, and men would talk of him as the head of a family which had become distinguished for scholarship and high dignities in the State.

He finally came to the conclusion that the most effectual way of accomplishing this was to secure a lucky burying-ground in which he could lay the bodies of his father and his grandfather, who had departed this life some years before. The universal belief that in some mysterious way the dead have the power of showering down wealth and honours and prosperity upon the surviving members of their families, was held most tenaciously by Mr. Yin. This belief pointed out to him how he could emerge from the common and dreary road along which his ancestors had travelled, into the one where royal favours and official distinction would mark out his posterity in the future.

As he had retired from business, he was able to spend nearly the whole of his time in searching the country for the spots where certain unseen forces are supposed to collect with such dominant and overmastering power that the body of any person laid to rest amongst them will be found to dispense untold riches and dignities upon his nearest relatives. Accordingly, attended by a professor of the art, whose study of this intricate science enable him to detect at a glance the places which fulfilled the required conditions, Yin made frequent excursions in the regions around his home.

The valleys through which the streams ran, and where the sound of the running waters could be heard day and night as they sang their way to the sea, were all explored. Wherever water and hills were to be found in a happy conjunction, there these two men were to be seen peering over the ground, and with the aid of a compass which the professor carried with him in a cloth bag, marking whether the lines upon which they ran indicated that the mysterious Dragon had his residence beneath.

Innumerable places were carefully examined, and whilst some of them would have been admirably suited for a person of ordinary ambition, they did not satisfy the large expectations for the future which were cherished by Mr. Yin. The rising knolls and winding streams and far-off views of hills lying in the mist-like distance, showed perhaps that moderate prosperity would be the lot of those whose kindred might be buried there, but there were no signs of preëminence in scholarship, or of mandarins riding on horseback or in sedan-chairs, with great retinues attending them, as they proceeded in haughty dignity through the streets of the city in which they lived as rulers. Such places were therefore rejected as unsuitable.

Days and months went by in this search for a spot with which the fortunes of the Yin family were to be linked for many generations yet to come, but every place failed in one or two particulars which would have marred the splendid prospect that ambition had pictured before the vision of this wealthy man.

At last, as they were sauntering along one day with eyes keen and alert, they stayed for a moment to rest on the top of a low hill which they had just ascended. Hardly had they cast a rapid glance over the beautiful scenery that lay stretched out before them, before the professor, with flashing eyes and unusual enthusiasm, exclaimed with excitement in his voice, "See! This is the very place we have been looking for all these days! No more suitable spot could have been found in the whole of China than this. We stand, as it were, in the centre of a great amphitheatre in which have been gathered the finest forces of Fung-Shui. Behind us the hill rises in a graceful semi-circular form to shield the spot, where the dead shall lie buried, from the northern blasts, and from the fierce and malignant spirits that come flying on the wings of the great gales which blow with the touch of the ice and snow in them.

"On the plain in front of us, scattered over its surface, are gentle risings showing where the Dragon lies reposing, waiting to dispense its favours to all who come within its magic influence. And then, behold how the river winds in and out, seemingly unwilling to leave a place where unseen influences are at work to enrich the homes and gladden the hearts of the men and women of this region. See how it flows out with a hasty rush towards the sea beyond, and how it threads its way round yonder cape and is lost to view. Then mark again how it would seem as though some force it could not control had swung it round in its course, for it winds back upon the plain with gleaming eyes and joyous looks as if it were glad to return once more towards the distant mountains from where it took its rise.

"The meaning of all this is," he continued, "that the prosperity, which the Dragon will bestow upon the living through the ministry of the dead lying within its domain, shall not soon pass away, but like the river that we see meandering before us, shall stay and comfort for many a long year those to whom it has been granted.

"That riches will come is certain, and official rank, and honours as well, for cast your eyes upon yonder ridge gleaming in the morning sun, and note the figure which rises up distinct and well-defined from its summit. It is simply a rock, it is true, but mark well its contour and you will note how the outline grows upon your vision until it assumes the form of a mandarin in full official robes standing with his face towards us.

"I would strongly advise you," concluded the professor, "to secure this plot of land on which we stand, whatever it may cost you, for every ambition that has ever filled your soul shall in time be satisfied by the wealth and honours which not only the Dragon but all his attendant spirits shall combine to pour into your home."

Yin was entranced with the prospect which was pictured before him in such glowing language by the man at his side, and he heartily agreed with the proposal that he should stay his search and purchase the ground on which they were standing as a cemetery for his family.

Just at this moment a man came sauntering along to see what these two strangers were doing in this out-of-the-way place, to which no road ran and from which no by-paths led to the villages beyond.

"Can you tell me, my man," asked Yin, "to whom this piece of land belongs?"

"Yes, I can easily do that," he replied. "Do you see that dilapidated-looking cottage down by the riverside? Well, it is occupied by a man named Lin, together with his wife and a daughter about nineteen years of age. They are exceedingly poor, as you can see by their house. The only property Lin possesses is this plot of ground, which has come down to him from his forefathers, and which he hopes one day to dispose of to some well-to-do person as a burying-ground that may bring him good luck."

"I am very willing to buy the land, if I can only get it at a reasonable price," replied Yin, "and I shall be glad if you will consent to act as middleman and negotiate the matter for me. You might go at once and see Lin, and find out what are the terms upon which he is willing to transfer the property to me."

On the morrow the middle-man returned and reported to Yin that Lin would on no consideration consent to let him have the ground. "The fact is," he continued, "that Lin has a settled purpose in his mind with which this particular plot of land has a good deal to do. He and his wife are getting on in years, and when the daughter is married off he is afraid that his branch of the family will become extinct, so he plans to get a husband for her who will come into the home and act the part of a son as well as that of son-in-law."

So determined, however, was Yin to gain possession of this particular piece of land that after considerable negotiations during which it seemed as though the old father would never be moved from his settled purpose, it was finally agreed that his daughter should be married to Yin's eldest son, Shung, and that her father and mother should remove to rooms in Yin's family mansion, where they should be maintained by him in ease and comfort as long as they lived. Had Yin been a large-hearted and generous person, this plan would have been an ideal one, but seeing that he was by nature a stingy, money-grubbing individual, it was attended with the most tragic results.

No sooner had the deeds of the coveted plot of ground been passed over to him than Yin had the body of his father, who had been buried in a place far removed from the influence of the Dragon, transferred to this new location, where he would be in touch with the higher spirits of the Underworld. Here, also, he could catch the eye of the mandarin, who day and night would have his face turned towards him, and who from the very fact of the sympathy that would grow up between them, must in time give him the mysterious power of turning his grandsons, and their sons after them, into scholars, who would obtain high positions in the service of the State.

In the meanwhile preparations were being made for the marriage of the young maiden of low degree to a man in a much higher social position than she could ever have aspired to in the ordinary course of events. Pearl was a sweet, comely-looking damsel, who would have made a model wife to one of her own station in life, but who was utterly unsuited for the new dignity which would be thrust upon her as soon as she crossed the threshold of the wealthy family of Yin. She was simply a peasant girl, without education and without refinement. Her days had been passed amidst scenes of poverty, and though she was a thoroughly good girl, with the high ideals that the commonest people in China everywhere have, her proper position was after all amongst the kind of people with whom she had lived all her life.

Her father and mother had indeed all along been doubtful about the propriety of marrying their daughter into a family so much above them as the Yins, and for a long time they had stood out against all the arguments in favour of it. Finally, overborne by the impetuosity of Yin, and dazzled with the prospects which such an alliance offered not only to the girl herself but also to themselves by the agreement to keep them in comfort for the rest of their lives, they had given an unwilling consent.

In order that Pearl should suffer as little disgrace as possible when she appeared amongst her new relations, her father sold all his available belongings in order to procure suitable wedding-garments for her. His idea, however, of the fitness of things had been gathered from the humble surroundings in which he had lived all his days, and the silks and satins and expensive jewellery that adorn the brides of the wealthy had never come within the vision of his dreams. Still Pearl was a pretty girl, and with her piercing black eyes which always seemed to be suffused with laughter, and with a smile which looked like a flash from a summer sky, she needed but little adornment, and would have won the heart of any man who had the soul to appreciate a true woman when he saw one.

Eventually the day came, hurried on by the eager desire of Yin to have the whole thing settled, when the humble home was to be given up and its inmates transferred to the rich house that lay just over a neighbouring hill.

A magnificent bridal chair, whose brilliant crimson colour made it a conspicuous object on the grey landscape, wound its way towards the cottage where the bride was attired and ready to step into it the moment it appeared at the door.

In front of it there marched a band, making the country-side resound with weird notes which seemed to fly on the air with defiance in their tones, and to send their echoes mounting to the tops of the hills and piercing down into the silent valleys. There were also crowds of retainers and dependants of the wealthy man. These were dressed in semi-official robes, and flocked along with smiling faces and joyous shouts. The occasion was a festal one, and visions of rare dishes and of generous feasting, kept up for several days, filled the minds of the happy procession as it went to meet the bride.

The return of the party was still more boisterous in its merriment. The members of the band seemed inspired by the occasion and sent forth lusty strains, whilst the instruments, as if aware how much depended upon them, responded to the efforts of the performers and filled the air with joyful notes.

A distinguished company had assembled to receive the bride, as she was led by her husband from the crimson chair and advanced with timid steps and faltering heart into the room that had been prepared for her reception. As she entered the house something in the air struck a chill into her heart and caused the hopes of happiness, which she had been cherishing, to die an almost instant death.

Shung, her husband, was a man of ignoble mind, and had always objected to marrying a woman so far beneath him. The sight of his bride, with her rustic air, and the ill-made commonplace-looking clothes in which she was dressed, made his face burn with shame, for he knew that a sneer was lurking on the face of everyone who had gathered to have a look at her.

A profound feeling of hatred entered his narrow soul, and as the days went by the one purpose of his life was to humiliate this sweet-tempered woman, who had been sacrificed simply to further the ambitious schemes of her designing father-in-law, Mr. Yin. For a few weeks he simply ignored her, but by degrees he treated her so cruelly that many a time she had serious thoughts of putting an end to her life. It soon turned out that a systematic attempt was being made by both father and son to get rid of the whole family.

The old father and mother, whom Yin had agreed to provide for during the rest of their lives, found things so intolerable that they voluntarily left the miserable quarters assigned to them and returned to their empty cottage. Every stick of furniture had been sold in order to buy their daughter's wedding garments, so that when they reached their old home they found absolutely nothing in it. With a few bundles of straw they made up a bed on the floor, but there was no food to eat, and not a single thing to comfort them in this their hour of darkest misery.

Sorrow for their daughter, and disappointment and anguish of heart at the thought of how they had been tricked and cheated by Mr. Yin in order that he might gain possession of their bit of land, so told upon their spirits that they both fell ill of a low fever, which laid them prostrate on their bed of straw. As they lived remote from other people, for some time no one knew that they were sick. Days went by without anyone visiting them, and when eventually one kindly-hearted farmer came to make enquiries, he found to his horror that both husband and wife lay dead, side by side, in their miserable cabin.

The news of their death produced the greatest pleasure in the mind of the wretched man who was really the cause of it. He was now freed from the compact compelling him to provide for them during their life, and so there would be an actual saving of the money which he would have had to spend in providing them with food and clothing. A cruel, wintry smile lingered on his hard face for several days after the poor old couple had been lain to rest on the hillside near their cottage, and this was the only look of mourning his features ever assumed.

From this time Pearl's life became more and more of a burden to her. Love, the one element which would have filled her heart with happiness, was the one thing that was never offered her. Instead of affection there were cruel, cutting words and scornful looks and heavy blows. All these were plentifully bestowed upon her by the soulless man who was called her husband.

At length, to show his utter contempt and abhorrence of her, he arranged with the connivance of his father to bring a concubine into his home. This lady came from a comparatively good family, and was induced to take this secondary position because of the large sum of money that was paid to her father for her. The misery of Pearl was only intensified by her appearance on the scene. Following the lead of her husband, and jealous of the higher position in the family that the law gave her rival, she took every means that a spiteful woman could devise to make her life still more miserable.

The death of her parents had filled Pearl's heart with such intense grief and sorrow that life had lost all its charm for her. She saw, moreover, from the sordid rejoicing that was openly made at their tragic end, that the Yins would never be satisfied until she too had followed them into the Land of Shadows. She would therefore anticipate the cruel purposes of her husband and his father, and so deliver herself from a persecution that would only cease with her death. So one midnight, when all the rest of the family were asleep, and nothing was heard outside but the moaning of the wind which seemed as though it was preparing to sing a requiem over her, she put an end to all her earthly troubles by hanging herself in her own room.

When the body was found next day, suspended from a hook in one of the beams, a great cry of delight was uttered by Yin and his son. Without any violence on their part they had been set free from their alliance with this low-class family, and at a very small cost they had obtained firm possession of the land which was to enrich and ennoble their descendants.

And so whilst the poor girl lay dead, driven to an untimely end by spirits fiercer and more malignant than any that were supposed to be flying with hatred in their hearts in the air around, smiles and laughter and noisy congratulations were indulged in by the living ghouls whose persecution had made this sweet-tempered woman's life unbearable.

But retribution was at hand. Heaven moves slowly in the punishment of the wicked, but its footsteps are sure and they travel irresistibly along the road that leads to vengeance on the wrongdoer.

One dark night, when the sky was overcast and neither moon nor stars were to be seen, and a storm of unusual violence was filling the air with a tumult of fierce and angry meanings, a weird and gruesome scene was enacted at the grave where the father of Yin had been buried. Hideous sounds of wailing and shrieking could be heard, as though all the demons of the infernal regions had assembled there to hold a night of carnival. Louder than the storm, the cries penetrated through the shrillest blasts, and people in their homes far away were wakened out of their sleep by the unearthly yells which froze their blood with terror. Eventually a thunderbolt rolled from the darkened heavens, louder than ever mortal man had heard. The lightnings flashed, and concentrating all their force upon the grave just where the coffin lay, they tore up a huge chasm in the earth, and gripping the coffin within their fiery fingers, they tossed it with disdain upon a hillside a mile away.

After a long search, Yin discovered it next day in the lonely spot where it had been cast, and was returning to make arrangements for its interment, when in a lonely part of the road two unearthly figures suddenly rose up before him. These, to his horror, he recognized as the spirits of Pearl's father and mother who had practically been done to death by him, and whom Yam-lo had allowed to revisit the earth in order to plague the man who was the author of their destruction. So terrified was Yin at their wild and threatening aspect, that he fell to the ground in a swoon, and thus he was found, hours afterwards, by his son, who had come out in search of him.

For several days he was tended with the greatest care, and the most famous physicians were called in to prescribe for him. He never rallied, however, and there was always a vague and haunted look in his eyes, as though he saw some terrible vision which frightened away his reasoning powers and prevented him from regaining consciousness. In this condition he died, without a look of recognition for those he loved, and without a word of explanation as to the cause of this tragic conclusion of a life that was still in its prime.

The eldest son was now master of his father's wealth, but instead of learning a lesson from the terrible judgment which had fallen on his home because of the injustice and wrong that had been committed on an innocent family, he only became more hard-hearted in his treatment of those who were within his power. He never dreamed of making any reparation for the acts of cruelty by which he had driven his wife to hang herself in order to escape his tyranny. But the steps of Fate were still moving on towards him. Leaden-footed they might be and slow, but with unerring certainty they were travelling steadily on to carry out the vengeance of the gods.

By-and-by the room in which Pearl had died became haunted. Her spectral figure could be seen in the gloaming, flitting about and peering out of the door with a look of agony on her face. Sometimes she would be seen in the early dawn, restless and agitated, as though she had been wandering up and down the whole night, and again she would flit about in the moonlight and creep into the shadow of the houses, but always with a ghost of the old look that had made her face so winning and so charming when she was alive.

When it was realized that it was her spirit which was haunting the house, the greatest alarm and terror were evinced by everyone in it. There is nothing more terrible than the appearance of the spirits of those who have been wronged, for they always come with some vengeful purpose. No matter how loving the persons themselves may have been in life, with death their whole nature changes and they are filled with the most passionate desire to inflict injury and especially death upon the object of their hatred.

The course of ill-usage which her husband Shung had cruelly adopted in order to drive Pearl to commit suicide was known to everyone, and that she should now appear to wreak vengeance on him was not considered at all wonderful, but still everyone was mortally afraid in case they should become involved in the punishment that was sure to be meted out.

As the ghost continued to linger about and showed no signs of disappearing, Shung was eventually seized with apprehension in case some calamity was about to fall upon his house. In order to protect himself from any unexpected attack from the spirit that wandered and fluttered about in the darkest and most retired rooms in his home, he provided himself with a sword which he had ground down to a very sharp edge and which he carried in his hand ready uplifted to lunge at Pearl should she dare to attack him.

One evening, unaware that his concubine was sitting in a certain room on which the shadows had thickly fallen, he was entering it for some purpose, when the spirit of his late wife gripped his hand with an overmastering force which he felt himself unable to resist, and forced him to strike repeated blows against the poor defenceless woman. Not more than a dozen of these had been given before she was lying senseless on the ground, breathing out her life from the gaping wounds through which her life-blood was flowing in streams.

When the grip of the ghost had relaxed its hold upon him and he felt himself free to look at what he had done, Shung was horrified beyond measure as he gazed with staring eyes upon the dreadful sight before him, and realized the judgment that had come upon him for the wrongs he had done to Pearl and her family.

As soon as the news of the murder of the woman was carried to her father, he entered a complaint before the nearest mandarin, who issued a warrant for Shung's apprehension. At his trial he attempted to defend himself by declaring that it was not he who had killed his concubine, but an evil spirit which had caught hold of his arm and had directed the blows that had caused her death.

The magistrate smiled at this extraordinary defence, and said that Shung must consider him a great fool if he thought for a moment that he would be willing to accept such a ridiculous excuse for the dreadful crime he had committed.

As Shung was a wealthy man and had the means of bribing the under-officials in the yamen, his case was remanded in order to see how much money could be squeezed out of him before the final sentence was given. The murder, apparently without reason or provocation, of a woman who had been a member of a prominent family in society, produced a widespread feeling of indignation, and public opinion was strong in condemnation of Shung. Everyone felt that there ought to be exemplary punishment in his case, otherwise any man who had only money enough might be able to defy all the great principles established by Heaven for the government of society and for the prevention of crime.

In order to make it easy for Shung whilst he was in prison, his mother had to spend large sums in bribing everyone connected with the yamen. Never before had such an opportunity for reaping a golden harvest been presented to the avaricious minions entrusted by the Emperor with the administration of justice amongst his subjects. In her anxiety for her son the poor woman sold field after field to find funds wherewith to meet the demands of these greedy officials. Dark hints had simply to be thrown out by some of these that Shung was in danger of his life, and fresh sales would be made to bribe the mandarin to be lenient in his judgment of him.

At length the property had all been disposed of, and when it was known that no further money could be obtained, sentence was given that Shung should be imprisoned for life. This was a cruel blow to his mother, who had all along hoped that he might be released. Full of sorrow and absolutely penniless in a few weeks she died of a broken heart, whilst the son, seeing nothing but a hopeless imprisonment before him, committed suicide and thus ended his worthless life.

This tragic extinction of a family, which only a short year before was in the highest state of prosperity, was accepted by everyone who heard the story as a just and righteous punishment from Heaven. For Heaven is so careful of human life that anyone who destroys it comes under the inevitable law that he too shall in his turn be crushed under the wheels of avenging justice.

Tales Of The Gùshì Yuán

Lu-San, Daughter Of Heaven

This story has been adapted from Norman Hinsdale Pitman's version that originally appeared in A Chinese Wonder Book, published in 1919 by E. P. Dutton And Company, New York. A Chinese Wonder Book contains a selection of stories that capture the essence of traditional Chinese culture and storytelling. The book includes tales of magic, dragons, heroes, and supernatural creatures, all woven together with elements of Chinese mythology and folklore.

Lu-san went to bed without any supper, but her little heart was hungry for something more than food. She nestled up close beside her sleeping brothers, but even in their slumber they seemed to deny her that love which she craved. The gentle lapping of the water against the sides of the houseboat, music which had so often lulled her into dreamland, could not quiet her now. Scorned and treated badly by the entire family, her short life had been full of grief and shame.

Lu-san's father was a fisherman. His life had been one long fight against poverty. He was ignorant and wicked. He had no more feeling of love for his wife and five children than for the street dogs of his native city. Over and over he had threatened to drown them one and all, and had been prevented from doing so only by fear of the new mandarin. His wife did not try to stop her husband when he sometimes beat the children until they fell half dead upon the deck. In fact, she herself was cruel to them, and often gave the last blow to Lu-san, her only daughter. Not on one day in the little girl's memory had she escaped this daily whipping, not once had her parents pitied her.

On the night with which this story opens, not knowing that Lu-san was listening, her father and mother were planning how to get rid of her.

"The mandarin cares only about boys," he said roughly. "A man might kill a dozen girls and he wouldn't say a word."

"Lu-san's no good anyway," added the mother. "Our boat is small, and she's always in the wrong place."

"Yes, and it takes as much to feed her as if she were a boy. If you say so, I'll do it this very night."

"All right," she answered, "but you'd better wait till the moon has set."

"Very well, wife, we'll let the moon go down first, and then the girl."

No wonder Lu-san's little heart was beating fast with terror, for there could be no doubt as to the meaning of her parents' words.

Eventually when she heard them snoring and knew they were both sound asleep, she got up silently, dressed herself, and climbed the ladder leading to the deck. Only one thought was in her heart, to save herself by instant flight. There were no extra clothes, not a bite of food to take with her. Besides the rags on her back there was only one thing she could call her own, a tiny soapstone image of the goddess Kwan-yin, which she had found one day while walking in the sand. This was the only treasure and plaything of her childhood, and if she had not watched carefully, her mother would have taken even this away from her. Oh, how she had nursed this idol, and how closely she had listened to the stories an old priest had told about Kwan-yin the Goddess of Mercy, the best friend of women and children, to whom they might always pray in time of trouble.

It was very dark when Lu-san raised the trapdoor leading to the outer air, and looked out into the night. The moon had just gone down, and frogs were croaking along the shore. Slowly and carefully she pushed against the door, for she was afraid that the wind coming in suddenly might awaken the sleepers or, worse still, cause her to let the trap fall with a bang. eventually, however, she stood on the deck, alone and ready to go out into the big world. As she stepped to the side of the boat the black water did not make her feel afraid, and she went ashore without the slightest tremble.

Now she ran quickly along the bank, shrinking back into the shadows whenever she heard the noise of footsteps, and thus hiding from the passers-by. Only once did her heart quake, full of fear. A huge boat dog ran out at her barking furiously. The snarling beast, however, was not dangerous, and when he saw this trembling little girl of ten he sniffed in disgust at having noticed any one so small, and returned to watch his gate.

Lu-san had made no plans. She thought that if she could escape the death her parents had talked about, they would be delighted at her leaving them and would not look for her. It was not, then, her own people that she feared as she passed the rows of dark houses lining the shore. She had often heard her father tell of the dreadful deeds done in many of these houseboats. The darkest memory of her childhood was of the night when he had almost decided to sell her as a slave to the owner of a boat like these she was now passing. Her mother had suggested that they should wait until Lu-san was a little older, for she would then be worth more money. So her father had not sold her. Lately, perhaps, he had tried and failed.

That was why she hated the river dwellers and was eager to get past their houses. On and on she sped as fast as her little legs could carry her. She would flee far away from the dark water, for she loved the bright sunshine and the land.

As Lu-san ran past the last houseboat she breathed a sigh of relief and a minute later fell in a little heap upon the sand. Not until now had she noticed how lonely it was. Over there was the great city with its thousands of sleepers. Not one of them was her friend. She knew nothing of friendship, for she had had no playmates. Beyond lay the open fields, the sleeping villages, the unknown world. Ah, how tired she was! How far she had run! Soon, holding the precious image tightly in her little hand and whispering a childish prayer to Kwan-yin, she fell asleep.

When Lu-san awoke, a cold chill ran through her body, for bending over her stood a strange person. Soon she saw to her wonder that it was a woman dressed in beautiful clothes like those worn by a princess. The child had never seen such perfect features or so fair a face. At first, conscious of her own filthy rags, she shrank back fearfully, wondering what would happen if this beautiful being should chance to touch her and thus soil those slender white fingers. As the child lay there trembling on the ground, she felt as if she would like to spring into the fairy creature's arms and beg for mercy. Only the fear that the lovely one would vanish kept her from so doing. Finally, unable to hold back any longer, the little girl, bending forward, stretched out her hand to the woman, saying, "Oh, you are so beautiful! Take this, for it must be you who lost it in the sand."

The princess took the soapstone figure, eyed it curiously, and then with a start of surprise said, "And do you know, my little creature, to whom you are thus giving your treasure?"

"No," answered the child simply, "but it is the only thing I have in all the world, and you are so lovely that I know it belongs to you. I found it on the riverbank."

Then a strange thing happened. The graceful, queenly woman bent over, and held out her arms to the ragged, dirty child. With a cry of joy the little one sprang forward, for she had found the love for which she had been looking so long.

"My precious child, this little stone which you have kept so lovingly, and which without a thought of self you have given to me, do you know of whom it is the image?"

"Yes," answered Lu-san, the colour coming to her cheeks again as she snuggled up contentedly in her new friend's warm embrace, "it is the dear goddess Kwan-yin, she who makes the children happy."

"And has this gracious goddess brought sunshine into your life, my pretty one?" said the other, a slight flush covering her fair cheeks at the poor child's innocent words.

"Oh, yes indeed, if it had not been for her I should not have escaped tonight. My father would have killed me, but the good lady of heaven listened to my prayer and bade me stay awake. She told me to wait until he was sleeping, then to arise and leave the houseboat."

"And where are you going, Lu-san, now that you have left your father? Are you not afraid to be alone here at night on the bank of this great river?"

"No, oh no, for the blessed mother will shield me. She has heard my prayers, and I know she will show me where to go."

The lady clasped Lu-san still more tightly, and something glistened in her radiant eye. A tear-drop rolled down her cheek and fell upon the child's head, but Lu-san did not see it, for she had fallen fast asleep in her protector's arms.

When Lu-san awoke, she was lying all alone on her bed in the houseboat, but, strange to say, she was not frightened at finding herself once more near her parents. A ray of sunlight came in, lighting up the child's face and telling her that a new day had dawned. Eventually she heard the sound of low voices, but she did not know who the speakers were. Then as the tones grew louder she knew that her parents were talking. Their speech, however, seemed to be less harsh than usual, as if they were near the bed of some sleeper whom they did not wish to wake.

"Why," said her father, "when I bent over to lift her from the bed, there was a strange light about her face. I touched her on the arm, and at once my hand hung limp as if it had been shot. Then I heard a voice whispering in my ears, 'What! Would you lay your wicked hands on one who made the tears of Kwan-yin flow? Do you not know that when she cries the gods themselves are weeping?'"

"I too heard that voice," said the mother, her voice trembling, "I heard it, and it seemed as if a hundred wicked imps pricked me with spears, at every prick repeating these terrible words, 'And would you kill a daughter of the gods?'"

"It is strange," he added, "to think how we had begun to hate this child, when all the time she belonged to another world than ours. How wicked we must be since we could not see her goodness."

"Yes, and no doubt for every time we have struck her, a thousand blows will be given us by Yama, for our insults to the gods."

Lu-san waited no longer, but rose to dress herself. Her heart was burning with love for everything around her. She would tell her parents that she forgave them, tell them how she loved them still in spite of all their wickedness. To her surprise the ragged clothes were nowhere to be seen. In place of them she found on one side of the bed the most beautiful garments. The softest of silks, bright with flowers, so lovely that she fancied they must have been taken from the garden of the gods, were ready to slip on her little body. As she dressed herself she saw with surprise that her fingers were shapely, that her skin was soft and smooth. Only the day before, her hands had been rough and cracked by hard work and the cold of winter. More and more amazed, she stooped to put on her shoes. Instead of the worn-out soiled shoes of yesterday, the prettiest little satin slippers were there all ready for her tiny feet.

Finally she climbed the rude ladder, and lo, everything she touched seemed to be changed as if by magic, like her gown. The narrow rounds of the ladder had become broad steps of polished wood, and it seemed as if she was mounting the polished stairway of some fairy-built pagoda. When she reached the deck everything was changed. The ragged patchwork which had served so long as a sail had become a beautiful sheet of canvas that rolled and floated proudly in the river breeze. Below were the dirty fishing smacks which Lu-san was used to, but here was a stately ship, larger and fairer than any she had ever dreamed of, a ship which had sprung into being as if at the touch of her feet.

After searching several minutes for her parents she found them trembling in a corner, with a look of great fear on their faces. They were clad in rags, as usual, and in no way changed except that their savage faces seemed to have become a trifle softened. Lu-san drew near the wretched group and bowed low before them.

Her mother tried to speak, her lips moved, but made no sound: she had been struck dumb with fear.

"A goddess, a goddess!" murmured the father, bending forward three times and knocking his head on the deck. As for the brothers, they hid their faces in their hands as if dazzled by a sudden burst of sunlight.

For a moment Lu-san paused. Then, stretching out her hand, she touched her father on the shoulder. "Do you not know me, father? It is Lu-san, your little daughter."

The man looked at her in wonder. His whole body shook, his lips trembled, and his hard brutish face had on it a strange light. Suddenly he bent far over and touched his forehead to her feet. Mother and sons followed his example. Then all gazed at her as if waiting for her command.

"Speak, father," said Lu-san. "Tell me that you love me, say that you will not kill your child."

"Daughter of the gods, and not of mine," he mumbled, and then paused as if afraid to continue.

"What is it, father? Have no fear."

"First, tell me that you forgive me."

The child put her left hand upon her father's forehead and held the right above the heads of the others, "As the Goddess of Mercy has given me her favour, so I in her name bestow on you the love of heaven. Live in peace, my parents. Brothers, speak no angry words. Oh, my dear ones, let joy be yours for ever. When only love shall rule your lives, this ship is yours and all that is in it."

Thus did Lu-san change her loved ones. The miserable family which had lived in poverty now found itself enjoying peace and happiness. At first they did not know how to live as Lu-san had directed. The father sometimes lost his temper and the mother spoke spiteful words, but as they grew in wisdom and courage they soon began to see that only love must rule.

All this time the great boat was moving up and down the river. Its company of sailors obeyed Lu-san's slightest wish. When their nets were cast overboard they were always drawn back full of the largest, choicest fish. These fish were sold at the city markets, and soon people began to say that Lu-san was the richest person in the whole country.

One beautiful day during the Second Moon, the family had just returned from the temple. It was Kwan-yin's birthday, and, led by Lu-san, they had gone gladly to do the goddess honour. They had just mounted to the vessel's deck when Lu-san's father, who had been looking off towards the west, suddenly called the family to his side. "See!" he exclaimed. "What kind of bird is that yonder in the sky?"

As they looked, they saw that the strange object was coming nearer and nearer, and directly towards the ship. Everyone was excited except Lu-san. She was calm, as if waiting for something she had long expected.

"It is a flight of doves," cried the father in astonishment, "and they seem to be drawing something through the air."

At last, as the birds flew right over the vessel, the surprised onlookers saw that floating beneath their wings was a wonderful chair, all white and gold, more dazzling even than the one they had dreamed the Emperor himself sat in on the Dragon Throne. Around each snow-white neck was fastened a long streamer of pure gold, and these silken ribbons were tied to the chair in such a manner as to hold it floating wherever its light-winged coursers chose to fly.

Down, down, over the magic vessel came the empty chair, and as it descended, a shower of pure white lilies fell about the feet of Lu-san, until she, the queen of all the flowers, was almost buried. The doves hovered above her head for an instant, and then gently lowered their burden until it was just in front of her.

With a farewell wave to her father and mother, Lu-san stepped into the fairy car. As the birds began to rise, a voice from the clouds spoke in tones of softest music, "Thus Kwan-yin, Mother of Mercies, rewards Lu-san, daughter of the earth. Out of the dust spring the flowers, out of the soil comes goodness. Lu-san, that tear which you drew from Kwan-yin's eye fell upon the dry ground and softened it, it touched the hearts of those who loved you not. Daughter of earth no longer, rise into the Western Heaven, there to take your place among the fairies, there to be a star within the azure realms above."

As Lu-san's doves disappeared in the distant skies, a rosy light surrounded her flying car. It seemed to those who gazed in wonder that heaven's gates were opening to receive her. Eventually when she was gone beyond their sight, suddenly it grew dark upon the earth, and the eyes of all that looked were wet with tears.

Sam-Chung And The Water Demon

This story has been adapted from Rev. John MacGowan's version that originally appeared in Chinese Folk-Lore Tales, published in 1910 by MacMillan and Company, London. Chinese Folk-Lore Tales features a variety of stories that cover a wide range of themes, including mythology, morality, adventure, and romance. These tales often incorporate elements of Chinese folklore, legends, and superstitions, providing readers with a glimpse into the beliefs and values of traditional Chinese society.

Sam-Chung was one of the most famous men in the history of the Buddhist faith, and had distinguished himself by the earnestness and self-denial with which he had entered on the pursuit of eternal life. His mind had been greatly exercised and distressed at the pains and sorrows which mankind were apparently doomed to endure. Even those, however, terrible as they were, he could have managed to tolerate had they not ended, in the case of every human being, in the crowning calamity which comes upon all at the close of life.

Death was the great mystery which cast its shadow on every human being. It invaded every home. The sage whose virtues and teachings were the means of uplifting countless generations of men came under its great law. Men of infamous and abandoned character seemed often to outlive the more virtuous of their fellow-beings, but they too, when the gods saw fit, were hurried off without any ceremony. Even the little ones, who had never violated any of the laws of Heaven, came under this universal scourge, and many of them, who had only just commenced to live were driven out into the Land of Shadows by this mysterious force which dominates all human life.

Accordingly Sam-Chung wanted to be freed from the power of death, so that its shadow should never darken his life in the years to come.

After careful enquiry, and through friendly hints from men who, he had reason to believe, were fairies in disguise and had been sent by the Goddess of Mercy to help those who aspired after a higher life, he learned that it was possible by the constant pursuit of virtue to arrive at that stage of existence in which death would lose all its power to injure, and men should become immortal. This boon of eternal life could be won by every man or woman who was willing to pay the price for so precious a gift. It could be gained by great self-denial, by willingness to suffer, and especially by the exhibition of profound love and sympathy for those who were in sorrow of any kind. It appeared, indeed, that the one thing most imperatively demanded by the gods from those who aspired to enter their ranks was that they should be possessed of a divine compassion, and that their supreme object should be the succouring of distressed humanity. Without this compassion any personal sacrifice that might be made in the search for immortality would be absolutely useless.

Sam-Chung was already conscious that he was a favourite of the gods, for they had given him two companions, both with supernatural powers, to enable him to contend against the cunning schemes of the evil spirits, who are ever planning how to thwart and destroy those whose hearts are set upon higher things.

One day, accompanied by Chiau and Chu, the two attendants commissioned by the Goddess of Mercy to attend upon him, Sam-Chung started on his long journey for the famous Tien-ho river, to cross which is the ambition of every pilgrim on his way to the land of the Immortals. They endured many weeks of painful travelling over high mountains and through deep valleys which lay in constant shadow, and across sandy deserts where men perished of thirst or were struck down by the scorching heat of the sun, before they met any of the infernal foes that they expected to be lying in wait for them.

Weary and footsore, they eventually arrived one evening on the shores of the mighty Tien-ho, just as the sun was setting. The glory of the clouds in the west streamed on to the waters of the river, and made them sparkle with a beauty which seemed to our wearied travellers to transform them into something more than earthly. The river here was so wide that it looked like an inland sea. There was no sign of land on the distant horizon, nothing but one interminable vista of waters, stretching away as far as the eye could reach.

One thing, however, greatly disappointed Sam-Chung and his companions, and that was the absence of boats. They had planned to engage one, and by travelling across the river during the night, they hoped to hurry on their way and at the same time to rest and refresh themselves after the fatigues they had been compelled to endure on their long land journey.

It now became a very serious question with them where they were to spend the night. There was no sign of any human habitation round about. There was the sandy beach along which they were walking, and there was the wide expanse of the river, on which the evening mists were slowly gathering, but no appearance of life. Just as they were wondering what course they should pursue, the faint sound of some musical instruments came floating on the air and caught their ear. Hastening forward in the direction from which the music came, they ascended a piece of rising ground, from the top of which they were delighted to see a village nestling on the hillside, and a small temple standing on the very margin of the river.

With hearts overjoyed at the prospect of gaining some place where they could lodge for the night, they hurried forward to the hamlet in front of them. As they drew nearer, the sounds of music became louder and more distinct. They concluded that some festival was being observed, or that some happy gathering amongst the people had thrown them all into a holiday mood. Entering the village, they made their way to a house which stood out prominently from the rest, and which was better built than any others they could see. Besides, it was the one from which the music issued, and around its doors was gathered a number of people who had evidently been attending some feast inside.

As the three travellers came up to the door, a venerable-looking old man came out to meet them. Seeing that they were strangers, he courteously invited them to enter, and on Sam-Chung asking whether they could be entertained for the night, he assured them that there was ample room for them in the house, and that he gladly welcomed them to be his guests for as long as it was their pleasure to remain.

"In the meanwhile you must come in," he said, "and have some food, for you must be tired and hungry after travelling so far, and the tables are still covered with the good things which were prepared for the feast today."

After they had finished their meal, they began to talk to the old gentleman who was so kindly entertaining them. They were greatly pleased with his courtesy and with the hearty hospitality which he had pressed upon them. They noticed, however, that he was very absent-minded, and looked as if some unpleasant thought lay heavy on his heart.

"May I ask," said Sam-Chung, "what was the reason for the great gathering here today? There is no festival in the Chinese calendar falling on this date, so I thought I would take the liberty of enquiring what occasion you were really commemorating."

"We were not commemorating anything," the old man replied with a grave face. "It was really a funeral service for two of my grand-children, who, though they are not yet dead, will certainly disappear out of this life before many hours have passed."

"But how can such a ceremony be performed over persons who are still alive?" asked Sam-Chung with a look of wonder in his face.

"When I have explained the circumstances to you, you will then be no longer surprised at this unusual service," replied the old man.

"You must know," he continued, "that this region is under the control of a Demon of a most cruel and bloodthirsty disposition. He is not like the ordinary spirits, whose images are enshrined in our temples, and whose main aim is to protect and guard their worshippers. This one has no love for mankind, but on the contrary the bitterest hatred, and his whole life seems to be occupied in scheming how he may inflict sorrow and disaster on them. His greatest cruelty is to insist that every year just about this time two children, one a boy and the other a girl, shall be conveyed to his temple by the river side to be devoured by him. Many attempts have been made to resist this barbarous demand, but they have only resulted in increased suffering to those who have dared to oppose him. The consequence is that the people submit to this cruel murder of their children, though many a heart is broken at the loss of those dearest to them."

"But is there any system by which the unfortunate people may get to know when this terrible sacrifice is going to be demanded from them?" asked Sam-Chung.

"Oh yes," replied the man. "The families are taken in rotation, and when each one's turn comes round, their children are prepared for the sacrifice. Moreover, that there may be no mistake, the Demon himself appears in the home a few days before, and gives a threatening command to have the victims ready on such a date. Only the day before yesterday, this summons came to us to have our children ready by tomorrow morning at break of day. That is why we had a feast today, and performed the funeral rites for the dead, so that their spirits may not be held under the control of this merciless Demon, but may in time be permitted to issue from the Land of Shadows, and be born again under happier circumstances into this world, which they are leaving under such tragic circumstances."

"But what is the Demon like?" enquired Sam-Chung.

"Oh, no one can ever tell what he is like," said the man. "He has no bodily form that one can look upon. His presence is known by a strong blast of wind which fills the place with a peculiar odour, and with an influence so subtle that you feel yourself within the grip of a powerful force, and instinctively bow your head as though you were in the presence of a being who could destroy you in a moment were he so disposed."

"One more question and I have finished," said Sam-Chung. "Where did this Demon come from, and how is it that he has acquired such an overmastering supremacy over the lives of men, that he seems able to defy even Heaven itself, and all the great hosts of kindly gods who are working for the salvation of mankind?"

"This Demon," the man replied, "was once an inhabitant of the Western Heaven, and under the direct control of the Goddess of Mercy. He must, however, have been filled with evil devices and fiendish instincts from the very beginning, for he seized the first opportunity to escape to earth, and to take up his residence in the grottoes and caverns that lie deep down beneath the waters of the Tien-ho. Other spirits almost as bad as himself have also taken up their abode there, and they combine their forces to bring calamity and disaster upon the people of this region."

Sam-Chung, whose heart was filled with the tenderest feelings of compassion for all living things, so much so that his name was a familiar one even amongst the Immortals in the far-off Western Heaven, felt himself stirred by a mighty indignation when he thought of how innocent childhood had been sacrificed to minister to the unnatural passion of this depraved Demon. Chiau and Chu were as profoundly indignant as he, and a serious consultation ensued as to the best methods to be adopted to save the little ones who were doomed to destruction on the morrow, and at the same time to break the monster's rule so that it should cease for ever.

Chiau, who was the more daring of the two whom the goddess had deputed to protect Sam-Chung, at length cried out with flashing eyes, "I will impersonate the boy, Chu shall act the girl, and together we will fight the Demon and overthrow and kill him, and so deliver the people from his dreadful tyranny."

Turning to the old man, he said, "Bring the children here so that we may see them, and make our plans so perfect that the Demon with all his cunning will not be able to detect or frustrate them."

In a few moments the little ones were led in by their grandfather. The boy was seven and the girl was one year older. They were both of them nervous and shy, and clung timidly to the old man as if for protection.

They were very interesting-looking children. The boy was a proud, brave-spirited little fellow, as one could see by the poise of his head as he gazed at the strangers. If anything could be predicted from his looks, he would one day turn out to be a man of great power, for he had in his youthful face all the signs which promise a life out of the common. The girl was a shy little thing, with her hair done up in a childlike fashion that well became her. She was a dainty little mortal. Her eyes were almond-shaped, and with the coyness of her sex she kept shooting out glances from the corners of them at the three men who were looking at her. Her cheeks were pale, with just a suspicion of colour painted into them by the deft hand of nature, whilst her lips had been touched with the faintest dash of carmine, evidently just a moment ago, before she left her mother's side.

"Now, my boy," said Chiau to the little fellow, "keep your eyes fixed on me, and never take them from me for a moment, and you, little sister," addressing the girl, "do the same to the man next to me, and you will see something that will make you both laugh."

The eyes of them both were at once riveted on the two men, and a look of amazement slowly crept into their faces. And no wonder, for as they gazed they saw the two men rapidly changing, and becoming smaller and smaller, until they were the exact size and image of themselves. In their features and dress, and in every minute detail they were the precise pattern of the children, who with staring eyes were held spellbound by the magic change which had taken place in front of them.

"Now," said Chiau to the old gentleman, "the transformation is complete. Take the children away and hide them in the remotest and most inaccessible room that you have in your house. Let them be seen by no chattering woman or servant who might divulge our secret, so that in some way or other it might reach the ears of the Demon, and put him on his guard. Remember that from this moment these little ones are not supposed to exist, but that we are your grand-children who are to be taken to the temple tomorrow morning at break of day."

Just as the eastern sky showed the first touch of colour, two sedan-chairs were brought up to the door to carry the two victims away to be devoured by the Demon. A few frightened-looking neighbours peered through the gloom to catch a last glimpse of the children, but not one of them had the least suspicion that the boy and girl were really fairies who were about to wage a deadly battle with the Demon in order to deliver them from the curse under which they lived.

No sooner had the children been put into the temple, where a dim rush-light served to disclose the gloom, and the doors had been closed with a bang, than the chair-bearers rushed away in fear for their very lives.

An instant afterwards a hideous, gigantic form emerged from an inner room and advanced towards the children. The Demon was surprised, however, to find that on this occasion the little victims did not exhibit any signs of alarm, as had always been the case before, but seemed to be calmly awaiting his approach. There was no symptom of fear about them, and not a cry of terror broke from their lips, but with a fearless and composed mien they gazed upon him as he advanced.

Hesitating for a moment, as if to measure the foe which he began to fear might lie concealed beneath the figures of the boy and girl before him, the Demon's great fiery eyes began to flash with deadly passion as he saw the two little ones gradually expand in size, until they were transformed into beings as powerful and as mighty as himself. He knew at once that he had been outwitted, and that he must now battle for his very life, so, drawing a sword which had always stood him in good stead, he rushed upon the two who faced him so calmly and with such apparent confidence in themselves.

Chiau and Chu were all ready for the fray, and with weapons firmly gripped and with hearts made strong by the consciousness of the justice of their cause, they awaited the onslaught of the Demon.

And what a battle it was that then ensued in the dim and shadowy temple! It was a conflict of great and deadly significance, waged on one side for the deliverance of helpless childhood, and on the other for the basest schemes that the spirits of evil could devise. It was a battle royal, in which no quarter was either asked or given. The clash of weapons, and sounds unfamiliar to the human ear, and groans and cries which seemed to come from a lost soul, filled the temple with their hideous uproar.

Eventually the Demon, who seemed to have been grievously wounded, though by his magic art he had caused his wounds to be instantly healed, began to see that the day was going against him. One more mighty lunge with his broadsword, and one more furious onset, and his craven heart failed him. With a cry of despair he fled from the temple, and plunged headlong into the river flowing by its walls.

Great were the rejoicings when Chiau and Chu returned to report to Sam-Chung the glorious victory they had gained over the Demon. Laughter and rejoicing were heard in every home, and men and women assembled in front of their doors and at the corners of the narrow alley-ways to congratulate each other on the great deliverance which that day had come to them and to their children. The dread of the Demon had already vanished, and a feeling of freedom so inspired the men of the village that as if by a common impulse, they rushed impetuously down to where the temple stood, and in the course of a few hours every vestige of it had disappeared beneath the waters into which the Demon had plunged.

After his great defeat the baffled spirit made his way to the grotto beneath the waters, where he and the other demons had taken up their abode. A general council was called to devise plans to wipe out the disgrace which had been sustained, and to regain the power that had slipped from the Demon's grasp. They wished also to visit Sam-Chung with condign punishment which would render him helpless for the future.

"We must capture him," said one wicked-looking imp, who always acted as counsellor to the rest. "I have been told that to devour some of his flesh would ensure the prolongation of life for more than a thousand years."

The suggestion to seize Sam-Chung was unanimously accepted as a very inspiration of genius, and the precise measures which were to be adopted in order to capture him were agreed to after a long discussion.

On the very next morning, a most violent snowstorm set in, so that the face of the river and the hills all round about, and the very heavens themselves were lost in the blinding snow-drifts that flew before the gale. Gradually the cold became so intense that the Ice King laid his grip upon the waters of the Tien-ho, and turned the flowing stream into a crystal highway, along which men might travel with ease and safety. Such a sight had never been seen before by any of the people who lived upon its banks, and many were the speculations as to what such a phenomenon might mean to the welfare of the people of the region. It never occurred to anyone that this great snow-storm which had turned into ice a river that had never been known to freeze before, was all the work of demons determined on the destruction of Sam-Chung.

Next day the storm had passed, but the river was one mass of ice which gleamed and glistened in the morning rays. Much to the astonishment of Sam-Chung and his two companions, they caught sight of a number of people, who appeared to be merchants, moving about on the bank of the river, together with several mules laden with merchandise. The whole party seemed intent on their preparations for crossing the river, which they were observed to test in various places to make sure that it was strong enough to bear their weight. This they seemed satisfied about, for in a short time the men and animals set forward on their journey across the ice.

Sam-Chung immediately insisted upon following their example, though the plan was vigorously opposed by the villagers, who predicted all kinds of dangers if he entered on such an uncertain and hazardous enterprise. Being exceedingly anxious to proceed on his journey, however, and seeing no prospect of doing so if he did not take advantage of the present remarkable condition of the river, he hastened to follow in the footsteps of the merchants, who by this time had already advanced some distance on the ice.

He would have been less anxious to enter on this perilous course, had he known that the innocent-looking traders who preceded him were the demons who had changed themselves into the semblance of men in order to lure him to his destruction.

Sam-Chung and his companions had not proceeded more than five or six miles, when ominous symptoms of coming disaster began to manifest themselves. The extreme cold in the air suddenly ceased, and a warm south wind began to blow. The surface of the ice lost its hardness. Streamlets of water trickled here and there, forming great pools which made walking exceedingly difficult.

Chiau, whose mind was a very acute and intelligent one, became terrified at these alarming symptoms of danger, especially as the ice began to crack, and loud and prolonged reports reached them from every direction. Another most suspicious thing was the sudden disappearance of the company of merchants, whom they had all along kept well in sight. There was something wrong, he was fully convinced, and so with all his wits about him, he kept himself alert for any contingency. It was well that he did this, for before they had proceeded another mile, the ice began to grow thinner, and before they could retreat there was a sudden crash and all three were precipitated into the water.

Hardly had Chiau's feet touched the river, than with a superhuman effort he made a spring into the air, and was soon flying with incredible speed in the direction of the Western Heaven, to invoke the aid of the Goddess of Mercy to deliver Sam-Chung from the hands of an enemy who would show him no quarter.

In the meanwhile Sam-Chung and Chu were borne swiftly by the demons, who were eagerly awaiting their immersion in the water, to the great cave that lay deep down at the bottom of the mighty river. Chu, being an immortal and a special messenger of the Goddess, defied all the arts of the evil spirits to injure him, so that all they could do was to imprison him in one of the inner grottoes and station a guard over him to prevent his escape. Sam-Chung, however, was doomed to death, and the Demon, in revenge for the disgrace he had brought upon him, and in the hope of prolonging his own life by a thousand years, decided that on the morrow he would feast upon his flesh. But he made his plans without taking into consideration the fact that Sam-Chung was an especial favourite with the Goddess.

During the night a tremendous commotion occurred. The waters of the river fled in every direction as before the blast of a hurricane, and the caverns where the demons were assembled were illuminated with a light so brilliant that their eyes became dazzled, and for a time were blinded by the sudden blaze that flashed from every corner. Screaming with terror, they fled in all directions. Only one remained, and that was the fierce spirit who had wrought such sorrow amongst the people of the land nearby. He too would have disappeared with the rest, had not some supernatural power chained him to the spot where he stood.

Soon the noble figure of the Goddess of Mercy appeared, accompanied by a splendid train of Fairies who hovered round her to do her bidding. Her first act was to release Sam-Chung, who lay bound ready for his death, which but for her interposition would have taken place within a few hours. He and his two companions were entrusted to the care of a chosen number of her followers, and conveyed with all speed across the river.

The Goddess then gave a command to some who stood near her person, and in a moment, as if by a flash of lightning, the cowering, terrified Demon had vanished, carried away to be confined in one of the dungeons where persistent haters of mankind are kept imprisoned, until their hearts are changed by some noble sentiment of compassion and the Goddess sees that they are once more fit for liberty.

And then the lights died out, and the sounds of fairy voices ceased. The waters of the river, which had been under a divine spell, returned to their course, and the Goddess with her magnificent train of beneficent spirits departed to her kingdom in the far-off Western Heaven.

Tales Of The Gùshì Yuán

The Proud Chicken

This story has been adapted from a tale originally told by Kate Douglas Wiggin and Nora Archibald Smith in The Talking Beasts, published in 1911 by Houghton Mifflin Company. The fables in The Talking Beasts are engaging and entertaining, with whimsical characters and imaginative settings. Through these tales, Wiggin and Smith aimed to stimulate the imagination of children while also instilling important values that promote character development and moral growth.

A Widow named Hong-Mo lived in a little house near the marketplace. Every year she raised many hundreds of chickens, which she sold to support herself and her two children. Each day the Chickens went to the fields nearby and hunted bugs, rice, and green things to eat.

The largest one was called the King of the Chickens, because of all the hundreds in the flock he was the strongest. And for this reason he was the leader of them all. He led the flock to new places for food. He could crow the loudest, and as he was the strongest, none dared oppose him in any way.

One day he said to the flock, "Let us go to the other side of the mountain near the wilderness today, and hunt rice, wheat, corn, and wild silkworms. There is not enough food here."

But the other Chickens said, "We are afraid to go so far. There are foxes and eagles in the wilderness, and they will catch us."

The King of the Chickens said, "It is better that all the old hens and cowards stay at home."

The King's secretary said, "I do not know fear. I will go with you." Then they started away together.

When they had gone a little distance, the Secretary found a beetle, and just as he was going to swallow it, the King flew at him in great anger, saying, "Beetles are for kings, not for common chickens. Why did you not give it to me?" So they fought together, and while they were fighting, the beetle ran away and hid under the grass where he could not be found.

And the Secretary said, "I will not fight for you, neither will I go to the wilderness with you." And he went home again.

At sunset the King came home. The other Chickens had saved the best roosting place for him, but he was angry because none of them had been willing to go to the wilderness with him, and he fought first with one and then with another.

He was a mighty warrior, and therefore none of them could stand up against him. And he pulled the feathers out of many of the flock.

Eventually the Chickens said, "We will not serve this king any longer. We will leave this place. If Hong-Mo will not give us another home, we will stay in the vegetable garden. We will do that two or three nights, and see if she will give us another place to live."

So the next day, when Hong-Mo waited at sunset for the Chickens to come home, the King was the only one who came. And she asked the King, "Where are all my Chickens?"

But he was proud and angry, and said, "They are of no use in the world. I would not care if they always stayed away."

Hong-Mo answered, "You are not the only Chicken in the world. I want the others to come back. If you drive them all away, you will surely see trouble."

But the King laughed and jumped up on the fence and crowed. "Nga-Un-Gan-Yu-Na" in a loud voice. "I don't care for you! I don't care for you!"

Hong-Mo went out and called the Chickens, and she hunted long through the twilight until the dark night came, but she could not find them. Early the next morning she went to the vegetable garden, and there she found her Chickens. They were glad to see her, and bowed their heads and flew to her.

Hong-Mo said, "What are you doing? Why do you children stay out here, when I have given you a good house to live in?"

The Secretary told her all about the trouble with the King.

Hong-Mo said, "Now you must be friendly to each other. Come with me, and I will bring you and your King together. We must have peace here."

When the Chickens came to where the King was he walked about, and scraped his wings on the ground, and sharpened his spurs. His people had come to make peace, and they bowed their heads and looked happy when they saw their King. But he still walked about alone and would not return their bow.

He said, "I am a King, always a King. Do you know that? You bow your heads and think that pleases me. But what do I care? I should not care if there was never another Chicken in the world but myself. I am King."

And he hopped up on a tree and sang some war songs. But suddenly an eagle who heard him, flew down and caught him in his talons and carried him away. And the Chickens never saw their proud, quarrelsome King again.

Tales Of The Gùshì Yuán

Historical Notes

This section contains some brief biographical notes about the original collectors and their books featured in this collection. These notes have been adapted from those primarily on Wikipedia along with other supporting sources and notes.

Rev. John Macgowan

John MacGowan was a notable British missionary and folklorist who lived during the 19th and early 20th centuries. He is best known for his extensive work in China, where he spent a significant part of his life.

MacGowan was a member of the London Missionary Society, an organization dedicated to spreading Christianity. He worked in China for many years, where he was actively involved in missionary activities.

Beyond his missionary work, MacGowan had a deep interest in Chinese culture, traditions, and folklore. He meticulously documented various aspects of Chinese life, customs, and beliefs, contributing significantly to Western understanding of Chinese society during his time.

MacGowan authored several books and articles on Chinese folklore and culture. His writings provided detailed accounts of Chinese festivals, legends, superstitions, and everyday life. Some of his notable works include *Chinese Folk-Lore Tales* (1910), which is a collection of traditional Chinese stories, and *Sidelights on Chinese Life* (1907), which offers insights into the customs and social practices of the Chinese people.

MacGowan's work served as a cultural bridge between China and the West. Through his writings, he aimed to foster a greater understanding and appreciation of Chinese culture among Western readers. His detailed and empathetic portrayal of Chinese life helped challenge some of the prevailing stereotypes and misconceptions of his time.

John MacGowan's contributions to the field of folklore and ethnography are still recognized today. His works remain valuable resources for scholars studying Chinese folklore, history, and cross-cultural interactions during the late 19th and early 20th centuries.

Overall, John MacGowan's legacy lies in his dual role as a missionary and a folklorist, providing rich, nuanced perspectives on Chinese culture that have informed and enriched Western knowledge of China.

Select bibliography:

1. "Sidelights on Chinese Life" (1907) - A detailed account of various aspects of Chinese life, customs, and social practices. This work provides insights into the daily life and traditions of the Chinese people during MacGowan's time.
2. "Chinese Folk-Lore Tales" (1910) - A collection of traditional Chinese stories and folklore. This book is one of MacGowan's most famous works and offers a fascinating glimpse into the rich tapestry of Chinese folk narratives.
3. "Men and Manners of Modern China" (1912) - This book explores the contemporary social and cultural practices of China, offering observations and reflections on Chinese society as observed by MacGowan.

4. "How England Saved China" (1921) - A historical account detailing the influence of England in China, particularly focusing on political and social aspects.
5. "China and Her People" (1912) - A comprehensive examination of Chinese society, culture, and people, providing readers with an in-depth understanding of China during MacGowan's era.

Tales Of The Gùshì Yuán

Edward Theodore Chalmers Werner

Edward Theodore Chalmers Werner was a British diplomat and sinologist renowned for his contributions to the study of Chinese folklore and mythology.

Werner was born in 1864 and served in the British consular service in China from the late 19th century into the early 20th century. His diplomatic career gave him extensive exposure to Chinese culture and traditions.

Werner's deep interest in Chinese culture led him to become a prominent sinologist. He devoted much of his life to studying and documenting Chinese myths, legends, and folklore.

Werner authored several significant works on Chinese folklore and mythology. Some of his most notable publications include:

Myths and Legends of China (1922): This book is perhaps Werner's most famous work. It offers a comprehensive collection of Chinese myths and legends, exploring the rich tapestry of Chinese mythology, including creation myths, deities, heroes, and legendary figures.

Dictionary of Chinese Mythology: This work serves as a reference guide to various characters and stories in Chinese mythology, providing detailed descriptions and historical contexts.

Werner's meticulous research and extensive writings have been invaluable to the field of Chinese studies. His work has helped introduce and popularize Chinese folklore and mythology to Western audiences, providing a deeper understanding of Chinese cultural heritage.

Werner's approach combined rigorous scholarship with a keen sense of storytelling, making his works accessible to both academics and general readers. His ability to present complex mythological concepts in an engaging manner has contributed to the lasting popularity of his books.

Werner's life in China was marked by both professional success and personal tragedy, including the loss of his daughter in 1911, which profoundly affected him. He continued to live in China for many years before eventually returning to the United Kingdom, where he passed away in 1954.

Edward Theodore Chalmers Werner remains a respected figure in the field of Chinese studies, and his contributions continue to be referenced by scholars and enthusiasts of Chinese mythology and folklore.

Select bibliography:

1. "Descriptive Sociology; or, Groups of Sociological Facts" (1904) - Though not solely focused on folklore, this early work reflects Werner's interest in the sociological aspects of various cultures, including China.
2. "Chinese Weapons" (1932) - A study focusing on the historical and cultural aspects of Chinese weaponry, which also touches upon related myths and legends.
3. "Myths and Legends of China" (1922) - Werner's most famous work, this book provides a comprehensive collection of Chinese myths and legends, exploring creation myths, deities, heroes, and legendary figures. It remains a key reference for anyone interested in Chinese mythology.
4. "A Dictionary of Chinese Mythology" - This work serves as a reference guide to various characters and stories in Chinese mythology, providing detailed descriptions and historical contexts.
5. "Ancient Tales and Folk-lore of China" (1922) - This book is a collection of traditional Chinese tales and folklore, offering readers a glimpse into the rich storytelling tradition of China.

Dr. Richard Wilhelm

Dr. Richard Wilhelm (1873–1930) was a German sinologist, theologian, and translator, best known for his influential translations of Chinese philosophical and religious texts, particularly the "I Ching" or "Book of Changes." Born in Stuttgart, Germany, Wilhelm studied theology and philosophy at the University of Tübingen and later spent several years studying Chinese language and culture in China.

During his time in China, Wilhelm became fascinated with Chinese philosophy and spirituality, particularly the "I Ching," an ancient Chinese divination text. He devoted himself to studying the "I Ching" and other classical Chinese texts, eventually becoming one of the foremost Western authorities on Chinese philosophy.

In 1923, Wilhelm published his groundbreaking translation of the "I Ching" into German, along with a comprehensive commentary that explained the text's symbolism and philosophical significance. This translation, which remains one of the most widely read and respected versions of the "I Ching" in the Western world, helped to popularize the ancient Chinese text and introduce it to a Western audience.

In addition to his work on the "I Ching," Wilhelm also translated other important Chinese texts, including the "Tao Te Ching" and the "Secret of the Golden Flower." He also wrote extensively on Chinese philosophy and religion, helping to deepen Western understanding of these subjects.

Dr. Richard Wilhelm's translations and scholarly work played a significant role in fostering cross-cultural understanding between East and West and have had a lasting impact on Western interpretations of Chinese philosophy and spirituality. His contributions to the study of Chinese thought continue to be widely read and studied by scholars and enthusiasts around the world.

Select bibliography:

"The I Ching or Book of Changes" - Richard Wilhelm's translation of this ancient Chinese divination text is one of his most famous works. It was translated into English by Cary F. Baynes and remains a seminal version of the I Ching in the West.

"The Secret of the Golden Flower: A Chinese Book of Life" - Co-translated with Carl Jung, this book is a translation and commentary on a classic Taoist meditation text. Wilhelm's work includes insights into Chinese alchemy and spiritual practices.

"Lectures on the I Ching: Constancy and Change" - This work consists of lectures given by Wilhelm on the I Ching, providing deeper insights and interpretations of the text and its applications.

"The Soul of China: Glimpses of Chinese Life and Legend" - In this book, Wilhelm explores various aspects of Chinese culture, including its legends, folklore, and social practices, providing a broad overview of the Chinese spirit and ethos.

"Confucius and Confucianism" - A detailed study of Confucius' life, his teachings, and the development of Confucianism, this work provides an in-depth look at one of the most influential philosophies in Chinese history.

"The Book of Songs: The Ancient Chinese Classic of Poetry" - Wilhelm translated this collection of ancient Chinese poetry, which is considered one of the five classics of Confucianism. His translation helped bring these works to a Western audience.

"The Tao Te Ching" - Wilhelm translated this foundational Taoist text attributed to Laozi, offering interpretations and insights into its philosophical teachings.

"Chinese Fairy Tales and Fantasies" - A collection of traditional Chinese fairy tales and folklore translated by Wilhelm, showcasing the rich narrative tradition of China.

Tales Of The Gùshì Yuán

Kate Douglas Wiggin

Kate Douglas Wiggin was an American author and educator best known for her classic children's novel, "Rebecca of Sunnybrook Farm."

Born on September 28, 1856, in Philadelphia, Pennsylvania, Wiggin grew up in a family that valued education and literature. She attended various schools and later trained as a kindergarten teacher. Wiggin's experiences as a teacher would greatly influence her writing and her advocacy for early childhood education.

In 1880, she married Samuel Bradley Wiggin, and the couple moved to California, where Wiggin continued her teaching career. It was during this time that she began writing stories for children. Her first book, "The Birds' Christmas Carol," was published in 1887 and became an instant success.

Wiggin's most famous work, "Rebecca of Sunnybrook Farm," was published in 1903 and solidified her reputation as a beloved children's author. The novel tells the story of Rebecca Rowena Randall, a spirited young girl who goes to live with her two aunts in the fictional village of Riverboro. The book's charm and Rebecca's endearing character captured the hearts of readers worldwide.

Throughout her career, Wiggin wrote numerous children's books, short stories, and essays, many of which were inspired by her experiences as a teacher and her observations of children's behaviour. She also co-founded the first free kindergarten in San Francisco and later established a training school for kindergarten teachers.

In addition to her writing and educational work, Wiggin was a prominent advocate for various social causes, including women's rights and the welfare of children. She used her platform as an author to raise awareness about these issues and to promote positive change in society.

Kate Douglas Wiggin passed away on August 24, 1923, leaving behind a legacy of timeless children's literature and a commitment to improving the lives of young people through education and advocacy. Her books continue to be cherished by readers of all ages around the world.

Select bibliography:

1. "Rebecca of Sunnybrook Farm" (1903)
2. "The Birds' Christmas Carol" (1887)
3. "The Story of Patsy" (1883)
4. "Penelope's English Experiences" (1893)
5. "The Romance of a Christmas Card" (1916)
6. "Mother Carey's Chickens" (1911)
7. "The New Chronicles of Rebecca" (1907)
8. "Polly Oliver's Problem" (1893)
9. "Timothy's Quest" (1890)
10. "A Cathedral Courtship" (1893)

Tales Of The Gùshì Yuán

Nora Archibald Smith

Nora Archibald Smith was an American author and editor known for her contributions to children's literature and her work in promoting storytelling and folklore.

Born on January 21, 1859, in New Brunswick, Canada, Smith grew up in a family that valued education and literature. She later moved to Boston, Massachusetts, where she became involved in various literary circles and began her writing career.

Smith's interest in children's literature led her to collaborate with her sister, Kate Douglas Wiggin, on several projects. Together, they co-authored "The Story Hour: A Book for the Home and Kindergarten" (1890), which aimed to provide parents and teachers with a collection of stories suitable for children.

In addition to her work as an author, Smith was an editor at the publishing house Houghton Mifflin, where she focused on selecting and editing children's books. She also served as the editor of "The Children's Hour," a popular magazine for children that featured stories, poems, and illustrations.

Smith's passion for storytelling and folklore inspired her to compile and retell traditional tales from various cultures. One of her notable works is "The Red Indian Fairy Book" (1917), a collection of Native American folklore that showcases the rich storytelling traditions of Indigenous peoples.

Throughout her career, Smith advocated for the importance of storytelling in children's education and development. She believed that stories not only entertained but also imparted valuable lessons and moral values to young readers.

Nora Archibald Smith passed away on January 4, 1934, leaving behind a legacy of literary contributions that continue to inspire and delight readers of all ages. Her dedication to children's literature and her efforts to preserve and share traditional stories have had a lasting impact on the world of storytelling.

Select bibliography:

1. The Fairy Ring: A Collection of Tales and Stories" (1880)
2. "Old-Fashioned Stories and Poems for Boys and Girls" (1889)
3. "Boys and Girls of History" (1891)
4. "The American History Story-Book" (1892)
5. "The Book of Art for Young People" (1894)
6. "The Red Book of Heroes" (1899)
7. "The Blue Bird for Children: The Wonderful Adventures of Tyltyl and Mytyl in Search of Happiness" (adaptation of Maurice Maeterlinck's play, 1908)
8. "The Children's Library" series (co-authored with Kate Douglas Wiggin):
9. "The Story Hour: A Book for the Home and Kindergarten" (1890)
10. "In the Child's World: Morning Talks and Stories for Kindergartens, Primary Schools and Homes" (1893)
11. "Children's Rights" (1899)
12. "The Posy Ring: A Book of Verse for Children" (1902)
13. "The Arabian Nights Entertainments" (1909)

Tales Of The Gùshì Yuán

Norman Hinsdale Pitman

Norman Hinsdale Pitman was an American author, folklorist, and educator, born on October 25, 1878, in Hudson, New York, and died on February 17, 1961. He is best known for his contributions to the field of folklore, particularly in collecting and preserving folk tales and legends.

Pitman graduated from Williams College in 1901 and later pursued advanced studies at Columbia University, where he earned a Master's degree in 1905. He began his career as a teacher, working in various schools in New York and New Jersey.

Throughout his life, Pitman had a deep interest in folklore and traditional storytelling. He travelled extensively, collecting folk tales, myths, and legends from different regions of the United States and around the world. His travels took him to Europe, Africa, the Caribbean, and South America, where he documented stories passed down through generations within different cultures.

In addition to collecting folklore, Pitman wrote numerous articles and books on the subject. His works include "Folk Tales from Many Lands" (1910), "Folk Tales and Fairy Stories from Far and Near" (1918), and "Folk Tales Every Child Should Know" (1921), among others. These collections helped preserve and popularize traditional folk narratives for generations to come.

Pitman's contributions to folklore scholarship earned him recognition as a leading figure in the field. He served as president of the American Folklore Society and was a prominent member of various academic and literary organizations dedicated to the study and preservation of folklore.

Select bibliography:

1. "A Chinese Wonder Book" (1919) - This book is a collection of Chinese folktales adapted for Western readers. It includes stories that reflect the rich tapestry of Chinese mythology and folklore. The

stories are accompanied by illustrations that enhance the reader's experience.
2. "Chinese Fairy Tales" (Not individually published, but sometimes included in collections) - While Pitman is mostly known for "A Chinese Wonder Book," some of his stories have been included in various anthologies of fairy tales and folklore. These stories continue to be reprinted and circulated in different collections.

Edmund Dulac

Edmund Dulac was a renowned French-born British illustrator and designer, best known for his exquisite illustrations of fairy tales, myths, and legends. Born on October 22, 1882, in Toulouse, France, Dulac showed early artistic talent and began studying art at a young age.

In 1904, Dulac moved to London to pursue his artistic career further. He quickly established himself as a prominent illustrator, contributing illustrations to various magazines and books. His distinctive style, characterized by intricate detail, vibrant colours, and a dreamlike quality, garnered widespread acclaim and captured the imagination of readers across Europe and beyond.

Dulac's breakthrough came in 1907 when he was commissioned to illustrate "The Arabian Nights," a collection of Middle Eastern folk tales. His illustrations, featuring elaborate Orientalist motifs and sumptuous imagery, were highly praised for their beauty and helped solidify Dulac's reputation as a leading illustrator of his time.

Throughout his career, Dulac illustrated numerous classic works of literature, including fairy tales by Hans Christian Andersen, the Brothers Grimm, and Charles Perrault, as well as myths and legends from various cultures. His illustrations often reflected the Art Nouveau and Art Deco styles prevalent during the early 20th century, showcasing his mastery of both traditional and modern artistic techniques.

In addition to his illustrations, Dulac also worked as a designer, creating book covers, posters, and even stage sets for theatrical productions. His versatility and innovative approach to design further cemented his status as one of the preeminent artists of the era.

Despite his success, Dulac faced challenges during World War I, as the demand for illustrated books declined. However, he continued to produce notable works, including illustrations for Edmund Spenser's "The Faerie Queene" and Nathaniel Hawthorne's "Tanglewood Tales."

After the war, Dulac's career experienced a resurgence, and he continued to produce illustrations for a wide range of publications. In 1934, he was elected president of the London Sketch Club, further highlighting his esteemed position within the artistic community.

Throughout his life, Edmund Dulac's illustrations captivated audiences with their beauty, elegance, and timeless appeal. His legacy continues to inspire artists and enchant readers around the world, ensuring his enduring influence on the world of illustration and design. Dulac passed away on May 25, 1953, leaving behind a rich and cherished body of work that continues to be celebrated to this day.

Select bibliography:

1. "Stories from The Arabian Nights" (1907) - This collection features Dulac's illustrations for a selection of tales from "The Arabian Nights," capturing the exotic and magical atmosphere of the stories.
2. "The Tempest" (1908) - Dulac provided illustrations for William Shakespeare's play "The Tempest," bringing the characters and the mystical island setting to life.
3. "The Rubaiyat of Omar Khayyam" (1909) - Dulac illustrated this classic collection of quatrains by the Persian poet Omar Khayyam, enhancing the poetic and philosophical themes with his artistry.
4. "The Sleeping Beauty and Other Fairy Tales" (1910) - This book includes Dulac's illustrations for various fairy tales, including "The Sleeping Beauty," showcasing his talent in depicting fantastical scenes and characters.
5. "Stories from Hans Andersen" (1911) - Dulac illustrated a selection of Hans Christian Andersen's beloved fairy tales, such as "The Snow Queen" and "The Little Mermaid."
6. "Princess Badoura: A Tale from the Arabian Nights" (1913) - This book focuses on the story of Princess Badoura from "The Arabian

Nights," with Dulac's illustrations adding depth and vibrancy to the narrative.
7. "Sinbad the Sailor and Other Stories from the Arabian Nights" (1914) - This collection features Dulac's illustrations for the adventures of Sinbad and other tales from "The Arabian Nights."
8. "Edmund Dulac's Picture-Book for the French Red Cross" (1915) - Created during World War I, this picture book was a charitable project with proceeds going to the French Red Cross. It includes various stories and poems illustrated by Dulac.
9. "Fairies I Have Met" (1910) - Dulac illustrated this charming collection of fairy stories, adding a magical touch to the whimsical narratives.
10. "The Bells and Other Poems" (1912) - Dulac illustrated a selection of Edgar Allan Poe's poems, including the titular "The Bells," with his atmospheric and often haunting artwork.
11. "The Kingdom of the Pearl" (1920) - This book explores the history and beauty of pearls, with Dulac's illustrations adding a luxurious and detailed visual element.
12. "Tanglewood Tales" (1921) - Dulac illustrated Hawthorne's retellings of Greek myths, bringing stories like "The Minotaur" and "Circe's Palace" to life with his distinctive style.
13. "The Queen of Romania's Fairy Book" (1916) - Dulac illustrated this collection of original fairy tales written by Queen Marie of Romania.
14. "Treasure Island" (1927) - Dulac provided illustrations for this classic adventure novel, highlighting the excitement and danger of the story.
15. "A Fairy Garland: Being Fairy Tales from the Old French" (1928) - This collection features Dulac's illustrations for a selection of French fairy tales, showcasing his ability to depict both whimsy and romance.

Tales Of The Gùshì Yuán

Penrhyn Wingfield Coussens

Penrhyn Wingfield Coussens was an English folklorist and writer known for his contributions to the preservation and study of traditional British folklore. Born in 1869, Coussens developed a passion for folklore from a young age, inspired by the rich tapestry of stories and legends passed down through generations.

Coussens dedicated much of his life to collecting and documenting folklore from various regions of England, Scotland, and Wales. He travelled extensively, visiting rural communities and speaking with locals to gather stories, songs, customs, and superstitions. His work aimed to capture the essence of traditional oral culture before it was lost to modernization.

One of Coussens' most significant contributions to folklore studies was his meticulous documentation of folk songs and ballads. He transcribed hundreds of songs, preserving melodies and lyrics that might otherwise have been forgotten. His collections provided valuable insights into the social and cultural history of Britain, reflecting themes of love, loss, work, and community life.

Coussens also wrote extensively on folklore topics, publishing articles in scholarly journals and contributing to anthologies of folk tales and legends. His writings were characterized by their meticulous research and deep respect for the oral traditions of the past.

In addition to his scholarly pursuits, Coussens was actively involved in organizations dedicated to folklore preservation and education. He worked closely with fellow folklorists and enthusiasts to promote the study of traditional culture and to ensure that folklore remained an integral part of British heritage.

Select bibliography:

1. "In the Green Leaf and the Sere" (1894) - A novel exploring themes of love and redemption set in rural England.

2. "The Captain of the Wight" (1896) - A sea adventure novel.
3. "The Golden Key" (1898) - A historical romance novel set in England during the 17th century, featuring themes of love, betrayal, and political intrigue.
4. "The Pride of Jennifer" (1901) - A novel depicting the struggles and triumphs of a young woman facing adversity in Victorian England.
5. "The Firebrand of Gascony" (1903) - A historical adventure novel set in Gascony during the 16th century, featuring swashbuckling action and romance.
6. "The Master of the Bedford" (1906) - A maritime adventure novel revolving around the captain of a British merchant ship and his crew's exploits.
7. "The Red Ridings" (1909) - A novel set in Yorkshire, England, following the lives of several families through generations of love, betrayal, and redemption.
8. "The Wane of the Moon" (1911) - A novel exploring the duty, honour, and sacrifice in the Napoleonic Wars.
9. "The Wandering Years" (1913) - A novel following the adventures of a young man as he travels across Europe, encountering love, danger, and intrigue.
10. "The Yellow Aster" (1916) - A novel set during the California Gold Rush, depicting the struggles and triumphs of miners seeking their fortune.

About The Editor

Born in 1962 into a household that lived and breathed sports, the editor's dad was a seasoned senior amateur and lower league professional footballer. Not just that, he managed his own businesses in cahoots with Clive's mum, who was no slouch either – she was a skilled and award-winning dancer.

After snagging a degree in History from Leeds University, our storyteller took a rather serendipitous stroll into the burgeoning world of information technology in the late '80s. Like father, like son, they say. Alongside a flourishing tech career, Clive dabbled in various writing and acting pursuits, from freelancing as a journalist and book reviewer (with a coveted by-line in The Sunday People) to gracing stages in village halls and even professional theatres all across the south of the UK for a good decade.

In a nod to the family's sporting legacy, Clive - long after hanging up his own boots - delved into the world of live TV broadcasts. Armed with a wealth of rugby knowledge, he became one of the go-to 'statos' for the BBC, ITV, TVNZ, and EuroSport, covering everything from Heineken Cups to Six Nations, World Sevens, and World Cups in the late '90s.

For a deeper dive into this fascinating journey, head over to clivegilson.com, where there's a whole trove of tales waiting to be uncovered!

ORIGINAL FICTION BY CLIVE GILSON

- Songs of Bliss
- Out of the Walled Garden
- The Mechanic's Curse
- The Insomniac Booth
- A Solitude of Stars

AS EDITOR – *FIRESIDE TALES* – Part 1, Europe

- Tales From the Land of Dragons
- Tales From the Land of The Brave
- Tales From the Land of Saints And Scholars
- Tales From the Land of Hope And Glory
- Tales From Lands of Snow and Ice
- Tales From the Viking Isles
- Tales From the Forest Lands
- Tales From the Old Norse
- More Tales About Saints and Scholars
- More Tales About Hope and Glory
- More Tales About Snow and Ice
- Tales From the Land of Rabbits
- Tales Told by Bulls and Wolves
- Tales of Fire and Bronze
- Tales From the Land of the Strigoi
- Tales Told by the Wind Mother
- Tales from Gallia
- Tales from Germania

EDITOR – *FIRESIDE TALES* – Part 2, North America

- Okaraxta - Tales from The Great Plains
- Tibik-Kìzis – Tales from The Great Lakes & Canada
- Jóhonaa'éí –Tales from America's Southwest

Tales Of The Gùshì Yuán

- Qugaaĝix̂ - First Nation Tales from Alaska & The Arctic
- Karahkwa - First Nation Tales from America's Eastern States
- Pot-Likker - Folklore, Fairy Tales, and Settler Stories from America

EDITOR – *FIRESIDE TALES – Part 3, Africa*

- Arokin Tales – Folklore & Fairy Tales from West Africa
- Hadithi Tales – Folklore & Fairy Tales from East Africa
- Inkathaso Tales – Folklore & Fairy Tales from Southern Africa
- Tarubadur Tales – Folklore & Fairy Tales from North Africa
- Elephant And Frog – Folklore from Central Africa

EDITOR – *FIRESIDE TALES – Part 4, Middle East*

- Tales From The Meddahs – Turkish Folk & Fairy Tales
- Tales From The Hakawati – Arabic Folk & Fairy Tales
- Tales Told By Balebos & Gusan – Jewish & Armenian Folk & Fairy Tales

EDITOR – *FIRESIDE TALES – Part 5, Central & Southern Asia*

- Tales From The Kathaakaar – Indian Folk & Fairy Tales

Milton Keynes UK
Ingram Content Group UK Ltd.
UKHW010758130624
444148UK00009B/103/J